To my not-so-little-anymore dude,

*You are kindness and brilliance
all wrapped into
one of the funniest beings on the planet.*

*Know that you are always loved and
never have to bend yourself
into a pretzel for Dad and me.*

*You are loved exactly as you are
no matter what, no matter if, and even when.*

We are so proud of the man you are becoming.

PRAISE FOR THE SCORPION THIEF

"*The Scorpion Thief* blends Egyptian mythology and Cold War intrigue with a fast-moving tale in which two sisters are drawn to opposite sides of a perilous quest for King Tut's treasures. This atmospheric novel explores the fragile lines between loyalty, love, and betrayal, making for an entertaining and fascinating read."

— MADELINE MARTIN, *NEW YORK TIMES* BESTSELLING AUTHOR, *THE SECRET BOOK SOCIETY*

"Action-packed and dynamic! Set in 1976, the discovery of King Tutankhamun's tomb is the perfect pressure-cooker for international intrigue and family turmoil as Naura Marquette faces off against enemies known and those she can't even imagine. *The Scorpion Thief* will keep you up well past your bedtime, but every page is worth it."

— KATHERINE REAY, AUTHOR OF *THE BERLIN LETTERS* AND *THE ENGLISH MASTERPIECE*

"*The Scorpion Thief* is a deeply researched historical novel exploring the thin veil between love and hate, myth and memory. Perfect for fans of Sarah Penner, and Kate Morton."

— JULIE CANTRELL, *NEW YORK TIMES* BEST-SELLING AUTHOR, *INTO THE FREE*

The Scorpion Thief

© 2025 Janyre Tromp

All rights reserved. No part of this book may be reproduced, stored in a retrieval system, used to train AI, or transmitted in any form or by any means—electronic, mechanical, photocopying, recording, or otherwise—without prior written permission of the publisher, except in the case of brief quotations embodied in critical articles or reviews.

This is a work of fiction. Names, characters, places, and incidents are either the product of the author's imagination or are used fictitiously. Any resemblance to actual persons, living or dead, events, or locales is entirely coincidental—except where noted in historical context.

Published by Grafted Page Press LLC

ISBN (print): 978-1-969773-03-7

ISBN (ebook): 978-1-969773-04-4

Cover design by Janyre Tromp and Rachel Scott McDaniel

Interior design by Janyre Tromp

Library of Congress Control Number: 2025925920

Printed in the United States of America

Threads of the Lost Myth

THE
*S*COR*PIO*N
THIEF

JANYRE TROMP

CRAFTED PAGE

ALSO BY JANYRE TROMP

—Threads of the Lost Myth Series—

History remembers. Myth echoes. The truth lies between.

And every era weaves in another fragment of the thread.

The Scorpion Thief

Guardian of the Red Desert (novella)

Burning the Raven Tree (coming September 2026)

The Oracle of the Silent City (coming March 2027)

—Standalone Titles—

Darkness Calls the Tiger

Shadows in the Mind's Eye

Lovely Life

EGYPTIAN PANTHEON REFERENCED

- <u>Aset</u>: goddess of resurrection and protection, raised her husband from the dead
- <u>Horus</u>: falcon-headed god of order who counters chaos, mother is Aset
- <u>Set</u>: god of chaos, the opposing force to Horus, represented as the blunt-nosed Set beast
- <u>Anubis</u>: the jackal-headed, impartial judge of the afterlife
- <u>Selket</u>: scorpion goddess of protection and healing
- <u>Ma'at</u>: goddess who embodies balance and loans Anubis her feather to weigh souls. Also the concept of ma'at.

1

All the stories start here.
Fire tests us. Truth transforms us.
The shadows never die.
They only change their name.
~From *The Lost Myth*

July 20, 1976

When the woman strolls by the Cairo Museum right in front of Noura Marquette, cool as a cucumber despite the heat, Noura is certain she's mistaken. The last time she saw her younger sister, Estelle was storming out of their father's Tel Aviv apartment, hurling a curse on Noura and her descendants...all sealed with the tiny bloody handprint smeared across Estelle's back.

As the lithe woman passes into a building's shadow, Noura's mind tangles in opposing desires to dart after the woman and to simply walk away as her sister had. And so she stands like some tragic statue, trembling, useless—the same paralysis she's fought her entire life to hide.

The woman so like Estelle emerges to sunlight slashing across her scarred arm, the languid sway of her hip. Petulant laughter lifts from the woman. So familiar she might have crawled from the twisted mire of the past. Noura shakes free of the image.

It's ridiculous. There is no way Estelle happens to be in Cairo at the same moment as her older sister.

Would Estelle want to blow Egypt to smithereens for killing their brother? Perhaps. But walk the streets laughing? Not a chance.

Taking a step away from the apparition is like slogging through quicksand. Yet Noura drags one foot and then another toward the museum steps, the basket on her head tottering with each step so that she has to steady it with a hand. She is nearly free from the blasted biological pull when she realizes what she's just thought.

Noura spins, fingers sparking from the slam of adrenaline. Blow Egypt to smithereens? Knowing Estelle's associates, bombs are indeed a possibility.

"Dr. Marquette?" Dr. Christine Lilyquist's call from the museum archway is muddy with concern. Noura winces. Here she is, dithering about on the street when she would normally be inside the museum already working.

"Coming," Noura answers her mentor, still half-facing the woman curving away.

Noura shades her eyes with a hand. The slope of the woman's nose isn't right. And she has a strand of dark hair escaping her scarf, not blond, right? And so thin. Noura can't help worrying about her sister… the woman…whoever she is.

The apparition disappears around the salmon pink museum building, and everything falls into its proper place—a street full of strangers. Noura steadies the basket and mentally stuffs the messy ache for her sister down with the rest of her childhood memories, and then bricks up that part of her soul. After all, you can't hurt stone.

"Are you all right?" The sun shimmers behind Dr. Lilyquist, turning her hair into a halo of gold. Appropriate since the Met's lead Egyptologist is a near goddess in their field.

"Thought I saw someone I knew." Noura slams down the last mental brick.

"Someone I should know?" Dr. Lilyquist squints into the crowd.

"An old classmate."

The half-truth snaps Dr. Lilyquist from her search. Ferreting out an old classmate, who wouldn't have access to funding or influence, isn't worth the effort.

Noura smiles, exuding all that is harmonious. Her practiced submission is enough to make Dr. Lilyquist nod and then stride through the museum doors. Noura's shoulders relax. Dr. Lilyquist knows little of the festering trouble Noura's siblings caused. If she did, she might never allow Noura near the King Tutankhamun artifacts destined to tour the US. Noura's career would be dead before it came to life.

As the pair ducks under the doorway's keystone sculpture of Aset, Noura can't help but think of how the Egyptian goddess resurrected her slain husband. Powerful, unrepentant, and able to battle death itself. What Noura wouldn't do for such power.

Dr. Lilyquist trots down the few stairs into the sunken display area and strides between the sarcophagi, leaving Noura to scramble along in her mentor's footsteps. They pass one after another of Egyptian royalty laid out in mind-numbing repetition.

But as she passes the statue of the falcon-headed Horus, she shivers, feeling his eyes move with her, spreading his wings in request to help him repeat the miracle his mother, Aset, had made possible. Of course that only set off a rivalry between her son and Set, the god of chaos. Chaos and peace—the *isfet* of Set and the *ma'at* of Horus.

Apparently life thinks Noura needs her peace balanced . Even the thought of her chaotic sister has Noura's attention skittering sideways. Their father would laugh at the preposterous thought of gods or fate.

A pulse of anxiety zings down Noura's arms.

But Father is not here. And as Dr. Lilyquist trots up the back stairs, Noura shoves his accusations in with the walled-off detritus of the past. She braces her basket and scrambles to the second floor. Here, the items from King Tutankhamun's tomb are displayed, or rather, scattered about in horror-filling disarray. Noura itches to reorganize. She knows her place, however, and would never offend her Egyptian counterparts by presuming to know better.

Fortunately for her sanity, the American team's area is more organized. In the front room, Noura slips past precise mountains of foam sheets and various archival packing materials. Behind the piles, one of the British packers lifts his utility knife in greeting and returns to measuring and cutting with focused, if slightly jocular, impunity. If Noura didn't know better, she would think John and his packing coworker were high-performing toddlers bent on world domination. In reality, they've packed Tut's treasures before and are an invaluable resource for the Americans—both for their packing skills and for their knowledge of their Egyptian coworkers.

Noura ducks through an archway into the back alcove. At a table near the far wall, the two conservators bend over a three-thousand-year-old object, painstakingly repairing a crack in the ancient blue paint made from ground glass. Theodore Fabre glances up from his work with a roguish wink, and Noura, who has lifted shy fingers in happy response, snatches her blasted fingers down, praying Dr. Lilyquist didn't notice either the wink or Noura's stupid flushed cheeks.

A quick glance tells Noura her mentor is blessedly ignorant as she strides out the door, frowning over a document.

Noura stomps out the interest flickering in her middle and paces to her tiny desk wedged into the front corner. Theo may be a talented conservationist with a droll sense of humor and a dogged willingness to help her rifle through the souks for the only type of pencil the other conservator, Mr. Frank Caddel, will use. But Noura doesn't have a permanent job in the Egyptology department at the Met. And she will not get sacked for flights of romantic fantasy. Professional women don't have the luxury of appearing weak. And that includes becoming involved with the opposite sex.

Theo's sparkling brown eyes included.

Noura deposits the basket of provisions onto the floor, unwraps the dull brown scarf from her hair, then sets the supplies on a shelf and the bag of food out of the way of the antiquities. The team will nibble at the snacks until they can take a dinner break well after dark.

For now, she unearths her notebook from under the neat stack of fifty-five card files. One file for every artifact Dr. Lilyquist and the Met's director selected for the tour to the US.

When Noura ducks into the alcove to assess where the others are on today's duties, she realizes what the conservators are working on—the necklace with the vulture pendant. Acrid panic explodes through her at how far behind they are.

Noura taps her leg in a semi-useless attempt to scrape away the corrosion eating her muscles. "Still working on the pendant?" She is pleased to hear the complete absence of bite in her tone.

"It needed more repair than we expected." Mr. Caddel doesn't even look up. "And Hoving is on a mission."

Thomas Hoving is the brilliant Metropolitan Museum of Art director with a shifting wish list that sometimes leaves everyone on his team without solid foothold. Noura crosses her ankles and leans a nonchalant hip against the table, but she still has a death grip on the notebook clutched to her chest. "I'm afraid to ask."

"He wants Selket's statue," Theo says.

"Is that all?" Noura laughs. "The Egyptians will never let us have her." They'd consider it a sacrilege to dismantle the chest containing Tutankhamun's organs.

"And yet, Mr. Hoving won't leave without the statue."

Theo is right. The team will be tasked with the impossible.

Feet, Noura thinks, meet the cliff over which your career will plummet.

"It's your fault, you know." Mr. Caddel adjusts his reading glasses so he can glare at her in full 20/20 vision.

"My fault?" If only her notebook could ward off Mr. Caddel's evil eye. That look is one of the many reasons she refuses to call the man Frank like everyone else.

"Ignore him." Theo positions his brush in its holder and rests his forearms on the worktable. "You made a brilliant observation. Frank's peeved because he didn't notice that the goddess was pegged onto the canopic chest rather than carved from one piece."

"It was obvious in the photos from when they discovered the tomb," Noura says. "I've studied those photos a million times."

"Still," Mr. Caddel grumbles into his paint pot, "you're the one who went gaga over the scorpion goddess and convinced Hoving to add her."

"And it'll be a better show because of it." Theo gives his fellow conservator a nudge and picks up his brush again, cutting off the discussion. "We'll be finished soon, and the leopard head won't take long."

Unfortunately, Theo's support doesn't stop Noura's thoughts from tumbling. First, she never convinced the Met director to do anything. And second, she understands both Mr. Caddel's concern and Mr. Hoving's desire. Selket is compelling, as is the scorpion perched on the goddess's linen headscarf. With her long neck curved so she stares over her shoulder, you can practically hear her dare you to take what isn't yours. She is the goddess with a scorpion's power over snakes, who guards the pharaoh, who paralyzes and tightens the throat. She is both the goddess of death and the goddess of healing.

Noura walks the perimeter of the room. Changing the list now, while Mr. Hoving's prerogative, makes the weight of responsibility press heavier. Endless checklists and traipsing through the crowded market aren't what Noura had in mind while capering through art history and museum curating classes. The goal of the actual exhibit—with the clamor of excitement and captivated people—seems a marathon away… and she has never run for anything but danger in her entire life.

She makes a note in her notebook and grimaces as her fingers leave wet marks on the page. Under the stress of the show and heat of construction lights she scrounged from the market, she's now sweating enough to make anyone think she's run that marathon. She flutters the front of her linen shirt, wishing for more than the small reprieve.

"Think New York January cold," Theo says with a sardonic backhand to his voice.

Noura bites her lip to keep in the snort of laughter. She's not certain if he's talking to her or himself or Mr. Caddel, who has yet to stop grumbling under his breath. Though Mr. Caddel's temper is as hot and unpredictable as the stereotypical red-headed Bostonian he is, Theo can rib his friend into better humor.

"Snowmen?" Theo's voice soars louder to trail her across the room. "Skiing? Icicles?"

"New York can keep its January cold." The rejoinder leaves Noura's lips before she remembers her resolve. No relationships. She is stone. She flees through the archway. There will be no sparkling eyes for her.

"How about ice cream?"

Noura hears a scraping of wood upon wood and turns to see Theo standing. He meanders toward her and raises an eyebrow. He is definitely asking her.

His sloppy grin and tapping of his fingers against his leg have her heart screaming *yes!* How do you say no to such reckless adorableness?

"If I remember," he says in a voice low enough only she hears, "you love mango ice."

And she does. Heaven knows she does. What she wants crashes into the reality of her position, and the riptide drags her into a murky pool. "I...that is—"

"We have work to do, gentlemen." John's staid British voice saves Noura from replying.

Turning her back to the conservators, Noura hides her flaming cheeks by peering over the molds John and his coworker are assembling. If she didn't know better, she would believe they're a madman's three-dimensional puzzle tumbled into foam boxes. John numbers a knob of foam, then marks the bit on a schematic of the crate. The two Brits have a method to their madness. Behind her, she hears Theo walking back to his station.

"If those two stop complaining about the temperature long enough to finish," John says, "we will be ready for the piece."

"We'll need photos of the repairs before we pack it."

From John's bored nod at Noura's reminder, he's far less ruffled than she is to be in Egypt, packing ancient burial treasures. She covers her faux pas by checking the stock of packing material and then frowning, making sure to note absolutely nothing on her pad of paper.

Like a novice oaf, she can't quite believe she, or any of the American team, is in Cairo. The tour of King Tut's artifacts is not just archaeological magic. It is a political sleight of hand as well. Until a few months ago, Egypt was on the US's "strained relations" list. And yet, here they are, using the tour to court the country that murdered Noura's brother.

The memory of bombs jars the marrow of her bones. Her muscles ache remembering the strain to keep her body from flying into a million frantic pieces. Estelle's whimper from a needle stick, the slam of the door behind Maman, and Noura's attempt to finish homework under the barrage. And all of that before the final war.

Noura grips the edge of the foam container and sucks in air, inhaling, desperate to extinguish the firestorm erupting in her chest.

"Are you quite all right, Dr. Marquette?" John says from too close behind her.

"Of course."

His bushy gray brows squish together, simultaneously telling Noura that he sees her lie, and he feels obligated to protect her. It's a kind, fatherly gesture that can destroy her career in a smothering, dismissive concern for her suitability.

"Do you need anything?" Noura's words are over-bright as she ushers the bumbling hero away from her carefully constructed walls.

John's attention slides from her to the others, pondering their huddled conversation, and then back in decision. "Provided you've brought a decent goat cheese, I'm right as rain."

Noura wipes the relief from her face and then drops her hand, tranquil, to her side. "I have your favorite."

"You never fail to amaze me," he says. "Though I shouldn't be surprised. You conjured construction lights that didn't cost the entire budget. Of course you found dill-spiked cheese."

From John, a fellow expert in the art of market negotiation, this is high praise, and Noura grins her thanks.

"Hooray for the best vittles this side of the Nile," Mr. Caddel shouts from the other room, as if she's only good for grocery shopping.

Noura bites off the urge to put the pejorative-slinging man in his place and instead smiles at John. "You'll have the crate ready by tonight?"

"Of course."

The waving hand of Mr. Caddel beckons Noura toward his station on the far side of the room. "We're nearly out of polyvinyl acetate." He nods to the bowl of glue-like paint.

Noura flips through her list. "The hotel courier should have brought it this morning."

Mr. Caddel frowns and glances out the door like he wonders if he should report her incompetence.

In a country that moves with the speed of careful respect, it will take time to track down the delivery. And the list of today's tasks is longer than the Mississippi River. Do you have enough for today?"

"Maybe." Mr. Caddel tips the pot toward Theo.

Noura can't read the silent communication flying between the two men, but Theo grinds to his feet. Apparently she and Theo are going to locate the paint now.

"I'm headed to the hotel for a shipment." She tells the disinterested room before grabbing her bag. "Try to get the leopard head's condition report started before the end of the night."

Theo's already holding the door for her, his tie askew under his five o'clock shadow. Noura resists the urge to straighten the silk and instead trundles into the museum proper.

Noura can almost hear her sister grumble about Noura hiding away behind a rambling walk and her meek hesitations. Why can't Noura straighten a handsome man's tie and flirt a little? Loosen up. But then Estelle, who was the American-blond-bombshell type made famous by Marilyn Monroe, never followed the rules and got away with her demands because everyone, including Noura, bent around her.

Until Noura couldn't anymore.

The fact that Noura is in Cairo is proof she isn't who she used to be. So maybe Noura can flirt a little. Especially with the one coworker who seems to view her as both a desirable woman and a talented curator.

As Theo opens the door to the street, Noura does her best to sashay up the steps, where she slips her hand into his elbow. Her fingers tingle at the strength in his biceps, and her knees shake at her audacity. To her delight, he rewards Noura's boldness with a golden grin—the sun god, Ra, waking for the morning—and no one could miss Theo's little hop-skip as they stroll from the building. His tailored suit and square jaw scream that he's far too mature for his goofy nature and the wild crook in his nose. There's a story behind the dichotomy that tempts her curiosity enough to distract from her normal catastrophizing.

The Nile Hilton, where the paint should be, is across the street and down a smidgen. Noura forces herself to match Theo's unhurried steps, even when he stops to pluck a tiny rose from a bush in the front garden. Somehow, despite how warm she is already, her neck flushes further.

"Do you mind diverting a bit?" Theo twirls the delicate pink blossom in his fingers as he plucks the thorns from the slender stem. His lashes bow, penitent, across his cheek.

"Oh, I don't mind." Noura's voice is as soft as she imagines the petals are. It's the answer the world expects of her. She truly doesn't mind the momentary reprieve from the stifling room and harried preparations... as long as this side trip isn't held against her.

"Good." He toys with the flower until she tears her attention from the safety of the rose to the man standing a breath away.

"Noura." Her name sounds long and round in his mouth. Theo waits, seeking permission, something few have ever done for her.

She swallows, vainly searching for her professionalism.

At some unbidden signal from her, his knuckles coax back the edge of Noura's headscarf, and he slips the rose behind her ear. Her entire soul is now nestled obediently in the man's palm.

"A beautiful flower for a beautiful woman," he says, and she stiffens as the words circle, a writhing snake of memories plucking her from her comfortable nest and plunging her back two decades.

Noura's father, talking to Maman. When they'd been happy. Before a pale-faced Maman almost evaporated, and Grandmere swept her away. Noura shakes her head, dragging herself from the labyrinthine memory. It's a common enough sentiment.

"Thank you." She touches the edges of the fragile flower, reminding herself that she, like a rose, is not without protection.

Theo's brows curve in quizzical confusion.

"Sorry," Noura says, scrambling for explanation. "Got pricked."

His expression clouds.

"From a thorn?" Her voice lifts stupidly, like she's asking his permission to lie.

He doesn't seem to catch the odd tone and holds his elbow out for her. His lips slide into a hopeful quirk, and she's stunned to realize that this hardworking, cheeky man is nervous. She makes him nervous. The idea unbends her, and she shakes off the tentacles of the past and the relentless crush of the onrushing future.

By the time Theo purchases a mango ice for her and they wander toward the hotel, the sun reclines below the roofline. Though Noura is exhausted, Theo's puppy enthusiasm makes her forget herself for the first time in years. As they arrive at the hotel steps, she bats her eyelashes as Grandmere demanded she do for Charles. In contrast to her ex-fiancé's laughing response to the one time she tried, Theo's crooked smile blooms in response.

Theo opens the door for her, and they whisk into the hotel reception, full of expected success.

"I am sorry, miss." The desk clerk twists his hands. "The delivery was sent this morning. Perhaps you misplaced it?"

"I didn't misplace it." She grits her teeth as the entire charade crumbles under the earthquake of understanding. It's one thing to use unfortunate events to court her or even to contrive for time alone, but quite another to lie and make her look like an incompetent fool who can't keep a delivery schedule straight.

Noura bows to the clerk, then spins on her heel, striding through the lobby and out the doors before launching into Theo. "Why did you let me ask for the paint when you knew it was already at the museum?" The nerve of the scheming man. Charles was right. She's a romantic fool.

"I didn't...that is..." Theo extends his hands in entreaty, brows pinched together.

She backs out of his reach, hating the impotent shake in her arms and the churning sound of tears and anger in her voice, and despising her confounded heart for hoping that her mind is wrong.

"I didn't..." Theo sucks in a breath, considering.

Again. Noura let herself be fooled again. "But you guessed."

At the inclination of his head, Noura stalks across the street. Perhaps she was wrong about Maman's selfishness. Maybe she abandoned them because Father belittled Maman's intelligence one too many times. Theo dogs her footsteps, but Noura's determined to arrive first, to control the narrative.

As she rounds the corner onto the narrow sidewalk of Nile Corniche, the same woman she'd glimpsed earlier materializes from the shadow of a palm tree. This time, she stops square on the pavement. A challenge tied to Noura's very blood. Then the woman's attention flicks to Theo, who is bustling to catch up. The woman tenses before she spins, lifting the edge of her scarf to hide her face as she flees.

Noura chases in a horrific sprint. Her lungs, ravaged with too many emotions, reject the air.

The woman dashes between cars. Lights catch her face for the barest of moments. Despite the shadow floating across her, Noura is sure now.

Estelle is in Egypt.

2

From across the street, Estelle hears her sister call, "Estelle! Estelle!" Her words crumble like dust in the afternoon heat.

Estelle ignores Noura and darts between people—not quite enough of a crowd to conceal her—and then scrambles down the stairs to the Nile walk and leans against the cool cement wall. She'd waited for hours, only to have Noura pop around the corner, flirting with *him*.

Noura, Estelle thinks, may be one of the smartest people she knows...and also the stupidest, most blind creature on the planet.

Yes, the man Noura's with wears respectable clothes and sports a respectable haircut now. But the last time she saw him, he was fencing stolen artwork and asking about some of the most dangerous people of Estelle's acquaintance.

Estelle extricates a packet of Camels from her bag and lights one with a shaking match. The irony of the American brand taking advantage of something distinctly non-American isn't lost on Estelle. She's traveled the world and doesn't much like what she's seen of her countrymen.

Estelle drags in the warmth, calm careening through her. A cloud of smoke escapes and billows to the endless blue sky where a white falcon perches atop a dark lamppost. The bird cocks his head, studying Estelle in accusation.

"It's not my fault," she whispers to the winged predator.

She didn't set out to steal some of the most famous artifacts in the world. She took the job to pay off Mehedi's debt. Once she realized Noura was in Cairo, Estelle hoped to gain better access. Noura would have keys and knowledge of the schedules. But now? Estelle will have to try for the artifacts again on her own. Ducking her head, Estelle resumes her walk, conforming to a dutiful posture—barely seen and never heard—escaping the vigilant watch of her sister's handler as well as her own. There's a reason she dyed her hair black. It isn't safe to stand out when you do what Estelle does.

Above her, the falcon squawks his displeasure and swoops over the older sister to roost on the museum roof, watching for his next opportunity.

TRAFFIC SHIFTS, and a piece of paper flutters to the ground at the older sister's feet, where Noura stomps on it. Bending over, Noura retrieves the page and straightens. It's a list of items—items she recognizes intimately.

"Good heavens. Where's the fire?" Theo gasps behind her.

"I thought..." Noura stops, realizing how absurd the explanation sounds. What is she supposed to say? *I thought I saw my sister, who disappeared six years ago? Or I saw my sister, who hates Egypt?* Or was the woman a mirage? An image conjured by a desperate woman—one who'd sworn to protect her sister and failed. "I..."

"I honestly didn't know the paint had already been delivered." Theo's apology floats disconnected in Noura's mind, not quite bridging the marshy places Estelle left behind. "Frank means well. He's a romantic at heart and...well..."

When Noura doesn't move, Theo leans over her shoulder. The smell of cedar and cinnamon, distractingly close, makes her think of Christmas in Ann Arbor, curled next to a fire with Professor Anderson's family. Her last real home.

"What's that?" he says.

She glances at the crumpled sheet. Somehow, she'd expected a letter from Estelle. An "I'm sorry for disappearing, but I'm in danger" missive.

She flips the page and frowns at the inventory of Tut artifacts. What is Estelle doing with the list of antiquities Noura's team is packing?

Not sure what to do with Theo or the war of pros and cons rising in her, Noura spins and thrusts the note between them. Maybe he'll understand it.

"It's a list of King Tutankhamun's artifacts." Theo snatches the paper, and Noura stiffens.

"I do have a brain." She plucks the paper back.

"I didn't mean to say you were stupid," he says gently. "I'm saying it's odd."

Noura plants her fists on her hips in mimic of every woman on the planet dealing with blatant stupidity.

"Of course." His face mottles, and he has the decency to appear apologetic. "That's why you picked it up."

"Probably harmless, though," she says, praying it's true. "Maybe a tourist excited to see the exhibit in the States. Or someone from the museum staff double-checking we don't pilfer something on our way out." She shoots Theo what she hopes is a dazzling smile as she folds the paper and stuffs it in her pocket to examine later. Maybe her disinterest will be enough to distract him from her bizarre plunge into the street. And maybe Estelle is innocent.

And maybe tonight, King Tut will rise from his wrappings to enjoy a game of the chess-like senet.

"Why would the Egyptians check up on us?" Theo says, seemingly unruffled by Noura's pushback. "They're right there as we do our work. We aren't Howard Carter without supervision and heaped with so much debt we're drowning."

She cringes at the reference to the British man who uncovered Tutankhamun's tomb...and likely retained a few items for himself. "Still, there's always a temptation," she says. "And in the mess, who would know if one disappeared?"

Theo studies his coworker under a lifted eyebrow. An impish grin spreads in teasing question.

Realization drops on Noura. "Not that I would ever take anything." Her mind stumbles over her gaffe. "I meant I understand wanting to hold a piece of history and call it my own." She clenches her jaw to staunch the verbal vomit threatening to prove how witless she is. "Besides, these pieces are too well known to keep or sell. You'd have to be a blithering idiot to try."

Theo frowns, tilting his head like he's sorting her prattle into a sensical picture.

"You know what I mean." Noura shoves her hands into her very sensible pockets and plows toward the museum. She should never have agreed to this. Should never have been lured into such a ridiculous stunt or picked up that list of artifacts. The mango ice churns in her stomach. Unsettled.

A white falcon dives from a palm tree, plunging toward the earth, wings extended, tail flailing as he soars, turns, and dives again into the underbrush. A startled squeak tells Noura the falcon has found his prey, then he shoots back into the sky. Noura squints at the almost entirely white bird. Strange.

Her grandmere would say Estelle's appearance is a warning. Combined with a falcon the color of Egyptian royalty, Grandmere would be arming herself to the teeth. So reactionary. Noura, however, has endured too much, read too many myths to pay mind to boogeyman signs.

Theo catches up to her and gives her a playful nudge. "Relax, I know you would never take anything. And I don't think we need to worry about anyone else, either. It's probably just a coincidence you found that list."

"Probably." Noura pushes out the word through clenched teeth and stalks toward the museum.

Noura knows for certain Estelle would happily exchange what she deems useless for cash to support her newest project. A worthy plan for someone not worried about international repercussions or bending morals for what she believes is right.

But then, who decides what is right and what is wrong?

3

"Noura." Theo swoops in front of Noura, forcing her to shift course around him.

"Please, Noura."

Her toe catches on the cracked walkway, and she flails for balance. Theo snatches her waist, spinning her hard into his chest.

She rebounds, forced to clutch at his arm to prevent an undignified sprawl in front of God and man and the entire gawking cavalcade of police standing at the corner. Theo braces her there, steady, even as her mind scatters and drags itself back together.

Despite the fact that Theo is an academic, he's obviously done far more calisthenics than Noura. And the realization has her choking back a hormonal gush of juvenile appreciation. As she blinks at the chastened twist of his lips, a war takes up residence in her puzzled body.

He's a chauvinist, Noura reminds herself, and she pulls away from his supportive grasp, brushing off the tingle in her arms as if it was a layer of dust. Why Theodore Fabre decided to trick her into a date and dismiss her opinion in the span of an afternoon doesn't matter. Women won the right to vote more than half a century ago, and Cleopatra ruled Egypt thousands of years ago. There's no reason for any man to discount any woman, let alone one who holds a doctorate.

"Noura." Theo starts again, trying to mediate with placating tones that make Noura dig her nails into her palm. "I didn't mean to offend you. The night watchman mentioned strange things happening, and I—"

"Offend me?" Noura snaps. "You mean you didn't mean to *be* offensive...twice. In one day. And for the record, Ghadfa believes in Tut's curse and that the Egyptian deities influence humanity. He's not exactly a paragon of trustworthiness." Noura brushes down her skirt one last time and puts more space between Theo's sparkling eyes and her unreliable self.

"First," Theo says quite reasonably, "it was Frank who set both of us up. And it is offensive...to both of us. Please don't lump me in with him. And second, not only is Ghadfa respected, but Sir Arthur Conan Doyle believed in the curse too."

An unladylike scoff escapes her lips at his adorable misunderstanding of history. "It was Doyle's job to create boogeymen for Sherlock to hunt down. Trust me. There's nothing to Tut's curse, and Horus isn't flying around as a falcon fighting the Set animal."

At his sharp blanch, Noura pinches the tender skin under her arm, banishing the aggravating impulse to apologize. When that fails to quiet the emotions battering her, she whirls and marches up the sidewalk toward the museum gate. *Running away as usual.* She can hear Grandmere's disdain for Noura's inability to stand up for herself, and her shameful tendency to either run or freeze when someone uses her people-pleasing tendencies to haul her into line. From her father, when he commanded her to refuse her appointment to Egypt. To Charles Berry, who demanded Noura button up and become the perfectly trimmed housewife, ornamenting his arm as he scaled the political ladder. To Estelle, who required Noura's immediate agreement to her every whim.

Theo calls her name, but Noura doesn't turn, doesn't slow.

Maman was the one who clawed her way out of her own mental anguish to convince Noura not to surrender her dreams. Maman, who reminded Noura how spectacularly suited she was for Egyptology. Maman, who informed Grandmere, Charles, and Father that Noura was gone after she packed her daughter's bags and hired a driver to take Noura to the airport, where part of Noura prayed for another hurricane to roll in and submerge Moisant Field. A hurricane would have been an act of God big enough to convince Noura to stay, to avoid the personal Category Five storm spinning out from her abandonment of house and home.

Maman was right though. Noura would never have made Charles happy, nor he her. All those people judging her, requiring her to bend into their opposing shapes. She would have become a pieced-together monster slogging through the muck of New Orleans society.

Noura yanks the rose from behind her ear, clutching it, not letting go even when a thorn pierces her skin. A reminder not to give up. Even in the gentle face of Theo.

She will not abandon her opportunity to dig into history, point to the fascinating people of the past, and maybe, just maybe, wipe away the debris enough for people to see one another clearly.

See? Sometimes retreating and regrouping is the best option. Sometimes it brings people exactly where they're meant to be.

She shoulders through the crowd, more determined than ever. She has not survived a hurricane to allow a scorpion sting to kill her now. If Mr. Caddel thinks her career is a joke, she will simply banish anything suggesting otherwise.

Noura darts across the street toward the museum gate, intent on returning to the workroom straightaway. Perhaps the others won't realize she's been duped.

Shrill car horns and the sound of splintering metal fracture the murmur of the city, summoning a surge of bumping and jostling people to bar her way. A situation rife with the threat of pickpockets and ne'er-do-wells, and that is if you are a man. For a woman, the streets are never quite safe—a fact Father had drilled into his daughters and one of the many things that drove Maman home to Louisiana.

Pauvre bête, Estelle's voice whispers, mocking, in Noura's ear, pitying the poor, scared little beast Noura has become. Noura stops, and there is Theo. Before she has a moment to analyze her movements, she snatches the impervious crook of his arm. He swoops her out of the street, down the bristling walkway, through the doors of the museum, then stalls.

Unfortunately, Noura's feet haven't gotten the message, and his momentum shift spins her to face him, one hand slamming into his heaving chest, the other still cradled in his elbow. Her pulse sprints right alongside her chaotic thoughts. She should yank free, keep pace with her body's impulse—run—but Maman's etiquette lessons refuse to let her snatch her arm back after she's thrown herself at the man. Why is it so ridiculously difficult to know what one is supposed to do?

Theo's face flickers with hurt, confusion, and she doesn't know what else, then smooths. The calm comes so quickly, Noura is stunned into fascination. She watches Theo reach between their bodies to pry the bruised rose from her fingers splayed across the V of his tawny suit coat lapels. He spreads the flower and smooths the wrinkled mass. His deft fingers minister to the crumpled petals, the muscles in his hand working in bewitching rhythm.

"Sherlock Holmes was a paragon of rationality." Theo stretches his palm toward her, the flower snuggling into his crisscrossed lifelines.

Noura blinks at him until she realizes they've jumped right over their argument, the accident, the burgeoning crowd, and circled around to their previous conversation. She is adrift, and an ache claws into her skull.

"Why do you suppose Doyle chucked his logic to believe in spirits and mummies?" Theo points at the nearest sarcophagus. "Maybe there's something to it."

She shrugs noncommittally. "I read Doyle's 'Lot No. 249' when I was a child." That night, she awoke, screaming with a nightmare. The next day, her father gave her a nonfiction tome about mummies. She's been hooked ever since. "You know as well as I do that a real mummy is more like dried leather shrunken over bones than Doyle's description of a lurid black creature who has enough vitality to climb from the grave at any moment."

Theo's flinch tells her she is hard and cold as ice.

"I'll check in with Ghadfa," Noura concedes, lifting the flower from his palm in an absurd attempt to blunt any offense. She doesn't believe in the night guard's boogeyman, but the list doesn't sit right either.

"Don't worry about Ghadfa. I didn't..." Theo runs a hand over the curve of his mouth.

Noura falters, her sweating palms pressing against the sides of her thighs. "It's my job to ensure the safety of the collection while in our possession. If that means running down Ghadfa's nighttime fantasies, I will."

"That's not what I mean." His contrite tone calls her to divert, but she channels Grandmere, the thorns of the rose, and hardens herself against his charm. Even if he doesn't hold this afternoon against her, the others will. And she is far from irreplaceable.

"Noura." Theo reaches across the divide, but Noura slides away, bumping into a marble pillar.

His hand lingers extended, a friendly dog that's unsure which cruel person kicked him in the gut.

"I'll talk to Frank." Theo thrusts his rejected hand in his pocket. "As for Ghadfa, someone probably misplaced an artifact after photographs."

Not knowing what else to do with the barrage of information, Noura nods, begins walking with him, only to branch off on the pretense of using the facilities. Let Frank Caddel chortle and rib Theo outside her presence. While they collect themselves, she will do the same.

THE RESTROOM DOOR SWINGS CLOSED, and Theo hesitates. What should he do?

Ultimately, he leaves Noura to herself and trudges through the museum. At the base of the stairs, he pauses again, listening. Something, some sound, some smell, some niggle has ruffled him. His hand flattens over the silver falcon feather pendant nestled under his shirt. His mother gave him the medallion when he graduated. A reminder of where she'd been and which paths lead toward honor and justice and truth. He's let her down so many times.

Safely out of the sight of his official coworkers, he shakes the tension from his body and breathes. With this stunt, Frank has made Theo's life incredibly difficult. Frank doesn't realize what he's done, so Theo can't be too angry. He'll have to act like the professional he is and do his job. All of them. No matter what that means for the woman trying to hold herself together while she hides from the world...or perhaps she is hiding something *from* the world.

Theo isn't sure which yet. Either way, he doesn't relish the turn the afternoon has taken.

He would like to have the list Noura found. But he has no good reason to ask for it. While she doesn't seem to recognize the stylized mark on the bottom of the page, Theo does. The T supporting tall square ears. A forked tail wrapping around it. The stylized Typhonian Beast accompanying that list makes one thing very clear: Typhon is hunting. Theo has hoped for this moment and dreaded it in equal measure. Theo doesn't know who the vicious man is, but Typhon took on the Greek interpretation of Set for good reason.

Leaving Noura downstairs, Theo trudges upstairs, intent on doing as much damage control as possible.

When the restroom door swings closed on Noura, she melts onto the bench of the tiny sitting room. The Middle Eastern tradition is something she missed in the States.

Leaning her head against the gilded wallpaper, she plucks at the front of her dress. On the wall in front of her, a painting of a falcon hovers, too big for the wall. Noura frowns at the reminder of Horus, the sun god, the god who's supposed to balance out chaos. Aset should have disposed of the chaos-inducing Set rather than raising her useless husband, Osiris, from the dead. Now everything's a mess. "Where is the balance? Huh?" Noura's voice echoes dull in the empty room, and she shifts away from the self-pity she hears bouncing back.

The paper in her pocket crinkles, a reminder of all the snarls in the last few hours. She drags out the page and spreads it across her lap.

The writing is nothing like Estelle's impatient hen scratch. Tension releases from Noura's gut.

But if her sister didn't write the note, who did? Words scroll down the page:

Selket

Mask

Tut on leopard

Vulture collar

The words list the artifacts in brief, unprofessional terminology until it terminates with a red scrawl across the bottom. Noura turns the page and squints, but she can't make much out of the odd smudges. A T perhaps? And a Y? Or is it a dog? Giving up, Noura returns to the list itself. Not an inventory a museum curator would write. More like a grocery list.

Who writes a grocery list of priceless artifacts?

And then to circle a handful like Estelle used to circle Christmas toys in the Sears catalog? It smacks of childish, self-focused desire.

I want this and this and...

Noura's heart drops into a sinkhole.

A thief.

Theo had chalked Ghadfa's concerns up to misplaced artifacts. But the Met team is meticulous. A thief, however, would scribble out a list and then circle the items a buyer wants. A Christmas list for a collector.

And the first item on the list is Selket. Since the team just learned about her inclusion themselves, that means someone has intimate access. But who? Just because it isn't in Estelle's handwriting doesn't mean she isn't the thief. It wouldn't be the first time Estelle has stolen something.

Maybe the night guard stumbled over more than the ghost of a long-dead Egyptian king, and he's caught Estelle or her cronies in preparation. A warning indeed.

Noura charges from the restroom, scuttles up the stairs, and bursts into the workroom, catching the door a hair's breadth before it slams against the wall. Not a soul witnessed her blundering entrance. Still she nods demurely and closes the door. Dr. Lilyquist bends over a Styrofoam box, inspecting the forms inside. The full jar of paint is open, and Theo is dabbing at the statuette on his table.

Well, he mixed that paint double-quick. Or had he flat-out lied?

As if he senses her attention, Theo stills his clotted brush and glances up. His smile melts, dragging his brows down. *OK?* he mouths.

Noura's teeth clench against her murderous words. Redemption will come with the prevention of a theft. "Dr. Lilyquist?" Noura's voice breaks through the easy quiet.

Instead of lifting her head, Noura's mentor points to a spot deep in the crate. "Here."

Next to her, John's bushy brows push together until he sees the issue, nods, and marks the spot with a marker.

"Dr. Lilyquist?" Noura repeats, her voice raised.

Every member of the team pauses—paintbrushes, pens, and instruments aloft. Noura's fragment of paper crinkles, voicing a concern. She has no actual proof of a planned theft.

A man can be excused his earnest mistake, but the same will label a woman an unreliable, flighty wild card. Too unstable to be trusted. Even the eminent Dr. Lilyquist wouldn't be able to save Noura from her fate.

But the paper combines with what the night guard saw and mixes with both the poverty of the area and the general lack of security. All that leaves theft too big a possibility to ignore. Noura will not let Dr. Lilyquist down.

"Ma'am." Noura presses the page onto the crate lid. Her sweat makes the ink smear, the paper as flimsy as she is beginning to feel.

Dr. Lilyquist stirs, giving her assistant half attention.

"I found this outside, and with what Ghadfa saw last—"

"Ghadfa?" Dr. Lilyquist shifts, gamely searching for the picture behind Noura's rambling.

"The night watchman," Noura says. "He—"

"Theo told me he was drunk." Dr. Lilyquist turns her shoulders away, dismissing Noura. "What about the list?"

"I'm afraid...that is—"

"I trust you to take care of everything."

And then she is gone. Noura stares at the offending page, blank of real threat, and blinks back a humiliating burn in her throat.

Theo didn't tell Noura that Ghadfa was drunk. In fact, he argued that the man was lucid in his drivel. Furthermore, the night guard is a practicing Muslim with three hungry children. He wouldn't drink or do anything to threaten his job.

She folds the paper along the old lines and secures it in her pocket.

Whatever game Theo is playing, she will find him out.

4

That evening, as the rest of the team leaves, Noura declares the need to fix a conveniently ruined set of condition cards. While technically the job of conservators, Noura has the experience and the know-how, thanks to her sister's three-month obsession with art restoration. While Estelle flounced off to the next hobby, Noura acquired a taste for the meticulous work.

"I'll save you a plate of dinner, if you'd like," Theo says.

She ignores his overture and lets him stand, breathing for a moment...then two, while she stacks papers, taps them into alignment. She is stone.

Frank says he'll bring mango ice, and someone laughs—Mostafa, the Egyptian curator, she thinks. She wedges her body into indifferent lines, immobilized until the door clicks shut. Then Noura releases her rigid shoulders, slumps in her chair, and kicks the table leg.

Ignoring the offensive banter is far more effective than fighting it. But whoever said sticks and stones are the only things to hurt you has never had their heart stabbed with a well-placed verbal attack.

The sound of her teammates' laughter dims, stretching into history itself.

Noura lifts Selket's tea-soaked condition card and blots it with a towel. She always stores food and liquid far from the objects, so Selket was never in danger...just Noura's desk and notes. But this kind of eventuality is why Noura duplicated all the notes, and this is a third set she has for Selket.

Noura lays out the backup cards of Mr. Hoving's beloved scorpion goddess. Saying Mr. Hoving adores her is an understatement. He'd come in cradling her like a baby, chortling about how he won a bet with the Egyptians to bring her with them. If she's honest, she agrees with Hoving. There is something about the goddess of healing and protection that calls to her too.

She slides a crisp card from her bag and frowns at the two-dimensional photographs. They somehow lack the charm and personhood of the original. Perhaps because of the flatness of Selket's ever-keen eyes or the reversal of her features in the negatives. Perhaps.

Apprehension trails Noura's spine, as if Selket, the wielder of magic, has not recognized Noura and turned away, rejecting her.

Snatching her pen, she recreates the precise notations, then tucks the photos and cards in the file as carefully as Maman had packed the china she shipped to the States.

Noura's watch says that Ghadfa should arrive presently, give or take a quarter hour. In the meantime, Noura creeps into the museum proper.

Security here is abysmal...not that American art museums are much better. Still, Noura hefts the heavy flashlight from the storeroom and clicks it on. It won't stop a gun or a knife, but Noura's father ensured that she is semi-capable of defending herself. Something Maman vehemently resisted. *If a place isn't safe enough to walk the streets, one shouldn't live there.* As if the world's population can up and leave like she had.

Besides, Noura's quite sure there isn't anywhere that's truly safe. Which is why her heart's pounding and she's tiptoeing into the main hall like some kind of spy. Early evening light sneaks grudgingly through dirt-encrusted skylights running the length of the building. From the far side of the room, the two-story statues of King Amenhotep III and Queen Tiy stare down at the mere mortal crossing in front of them, daring her to bear the gravity of their stories, their country.

"I'm trying," she whispers.

Although Noura has worked in Egyptology for years, the little girl in her is terrified of being locked in with the sighing wraiths, who may very well groan to their feet and exact revenge on the invading foreigners. Why their resurrection is possible only in the dark is a silly holdover from her brother's ghost stories. Still, she's unspeakably grateful that Mr. Hoving convinced the director of lighting at the Great Pyramids to hot-splice an electrical cable into a streetlight for them. If only the construction lights she procured still flooded from the upstairs rooms.

Her weak flashlight beam catches a flash of metal, and she shuffles cautiously to the display case. A tiny silver pendant with an all-seeing Eye of Horus is caught in the door hinge. The irony of the symbol of order being out of order isn't lost on Noura. She swallows hard and reaches for the delicate chain.

A rattling sounds from the front entrance. Noura sucks in air and spits it out in rapid succession. Must be Ghadfa checking the security of the front doors. Or so she tells herself.

When the rattling doesn't continue, Noura thinks she's right and forces herself to slow her breath until her lungs stop clogging with the tumbling scramble for oxygen.

While she waits for the guard, Noura tucks the pendant safely back into the display. No one would likely know if she took it, but that isn't the point, is it? She aims the flashlight beam around the main hall, searching. For what? She doesn't know. She's read enough Agatha Christie to know a good detective has instincts about danger and clues and such. When Noura has completed a circuit of the room, she's reviewed the menagerie of Egyptian artifacts, left her fingerprints on the dusty, mildewing surfaces, and found exactly nothing.

Some Detective Poirot she is.

She lets the flashlight bang a restless rhythm against her leg. Turning, she dissects the now familiar shadows and frowns. On the floor, a feather flutters in a nonexistent breeze. Strange. She bends to pluck it from the ground and holds the incredibly soft fluff to the light, spinning the white and gray marvel. It looks almost like Ma'at's ostrich feather, only smaller than the enormous one Anubis used to weigh a human's heart. Where did it come from? A grinding behind her makes Noura spin. It sounded like the very stones under her feet were moving. But the main hall is still as a tomb.

A flapping streaks from the ceiling straight for her, and Noura screeches, ducking behind a sarcophagus, knocking into the standard holding the description notecard. The base teeters in ear-numbing clanks that echo loud enough to wake the dead.

Between thuds, a deep chuckle lifts from the far side of the room. Noura spins, pointing the flashlight like a gun.

"You've met our pigeon." Ghadfa appears under the entry from the back rooms. He bows. And when he straightens, Noura realizes his long face is disturbingly stripped of emotion. Too calm, too studious—a crocodile lying in wait or a gentle heron?

Noura clenches the edge of her shirt and forces a returning bow. Ghadfa was educated in a British school and speaks English as well as any prep school student. It's why the museum hired him to be the main night guard while the Americans are here. But with his education, couldn't he have gotten a better job than the temporary night watchman of a run-down, if famous, museum?

"He enters there." Ghadfa points to the ceiling.

Noura squints up, making out a lighter square where shattered panes let in more dying sunlight.

"It has been broken for months." He shrugs. "I informed maintenance, but they are busy elsewhere."

Noura wants to shout that someone needs to take this seriously. A teacup of rain or a standard dust storm could ruin the entire museum. Not to mention that the hole is a perfect opening for a thief. Instead, Noura scuffs her foot against the dirt collected at the base of a display. Most Americans chafe at the seeming lapses in the Egyptian processes. But this history belongs to Egypt. They are entitled and privileged to protect their collection in whatever way they deem appropriate. Still, part of her wants to scale the roof and at least secure boards over the hole. Wouldn't that set the men to vapors?

Climbing this building couldn't be worse than adjusting the TV's rabbit ears perched on the six-story apartment roof in time to hear Israeli Defense Minister Moshe Dayan admit the Sinai was overrun. She's still not sure if electricity truly snapped through the metal antennae, or if her body knew, even then, that her brother, Harry, was gone, and Saira and little Miriam too, the familial connection between them forever severed.

"The pigeon made a nest in a storage room." Ghadfa's voice snaps her attention from the red bleeding through the broken window.

The guard is eerily still, military straight, and Noura can't help picturing him across the Suez Canal, manning a missile launcher aimed at Saira.

Quick as lightning, uncertainty flickers through his expression, chased by the thunder of temper and the howling winds of indignation. Something in her expression made him forget his customary bland mask.

Noura wrestles with her instinct to apologize. She's done nothing offensive, said nothing wrong. Perhaps he's upset by her mere presence in his museum. Or maybe he's angry his concerns were dismissed.

But then his face clears, and what remains is a slightly foolish guard. Calculated or real? She doesn't have time to decide as he beckons her.

He leads her to a wooden bench sprawling outside the restrooms, and he perches on the far edge. "How may I help you?"

She gapes at him. "How did you know I was looking for you?"

"The gods talk. If you listen, they will tell you what you wish…for a price."

Noura blanches, and he lets his mouth move into a semblance of a self-deprecating crocodile smile. The hint of humor.

"You never stay behind alone." He cups his calloused palms loosely over his knees.

It's a deliberate move. To make her think he has nothing to hide? The edges of his black felt uniform blend into the darkness.

Noura's mouth goes dry, and she resists the urge to cross her arms and instead sits, easy, in control. "We don't have much opportunity to sleep. I rest when I can."

"You don't wander the museum. But in the souks, you know your way and go where you will. Which means there is something here you need. And since I am the only one here, I assume you require something from me."

Ghadfa's gaze hasn't left her face. Her grip tightens on the scrolling arm of the bench, preparing to launch herself. The feather trembles slightly under her palm.

"Perhaps Mr. Theo sent you?" Ghadfa smooths his mustache, his hands covering his mouth like he's protecting the words.

"Mr. Theo?" Noura's voice squeaks, reminiscent of a scurrying mouse.

"I was mistaken." Ghadfa stands with an awkward bow.

"No!" She shoots to her feet.

The edges of his sleeves billow behind him. The only movement in his impassive stance, and there is no breeze to speak of. She's read about spirit mediums in the '20s rigging miraculous levitating tables and assistants moaning from beneath the floorboards. But there's nothing like that here. No guidewires or hidden trapdoors.

The bird flutters above them and jerks Noura from her bizarre examination of the floor and bench.

"That is…I mean." Meaning to disarm him, she switches to Arabic and stuffs the feather into her satchel. "Please tell me what you saw two nights ago."

Ghadfa lifts a single black eyebrow. He shifts, the equivalent of a stagger to this rock-like man. The Arabic was a mistake. No doubt he detected the Israeli tinge to her accent.

"Did Mr. Theo send you?" Ghadfa's voice crests in an odd mix of threat and fear, still in English.

Peculiar. Unfortunately, Noura doesn't know what answer is right. Maman would tell her to lie, to weasel and pretend…to hide. Noura's fingers tangle in the folds of her skirt. But Maman had opened a deep marsh that swallowed them all. Truth is always the right path, isn't it?

"No."

Ghadfa nods and spins on his heels.

"He told me though. I believe you saw something." The words tumble out in a torrent, crashing against the far wall and slamming back against Ghadfa enough that he hesitates.

"Dr. Lilyquist doesn't know the real story," she says into the sliver of opening he's given her. "Please, tell me."

Ghadfa cocks his head, and Noura can almost hear the whispers of the relics surrounding them. The tensions between people groups here stretch to Abrahamic times, but Noura has never understood why, on every continent, in every city, people hate one another. Is there anything, any place, that can heal? In her father's embassy library, she read how her own country regularly stuck its nose into events, claiming to help. The reasoning was often thin and led to disastrous results. No doubt Nixon and Kissinger even now plan to dangle the possibility of peace to distract from the Watergate fiasco, Vietnam, and the whole—

Wait. Reading. The library.

"My father was a librarian." Noura opens her arms wide in a self-deprecating shrug.

He half-turns, listening now.

"He's a brilliant man. Knows all the legends and myths from every country he was ever stationed in. I grew up listening to tales of Egypt and Persia. I wanted to be Cleopatra when I grew up, even though she was Greek and not Egyptian, and I am neither. I wanted to be either her or Amelia Earhart."

Ghadfa snorts.

"I know." Noura's shoulders relax. Books and self-deprecation rarely fail to crack another person's defenses. "My brother often reminded me I didn't have the courage to be either...especially after I refused to jump from a tree to see if I could fly."

Humor lifts in the man's brows.

"But I don't need courage to sense something isn't right," Noura says. "I want to protect King Tutankhamun's artifacts."

"And why"—Ghadfa leans against the doorway, half in and half out —"why do you care about our antiquities?"

Noura swallows at another crossroads—to tell the truth and nothing but the truth? Or hold back something that might hurt everyone? "I don't want anything stolen if we can prevent it by fixing a glass pane or monitoring more closely."

Ghadfa studies her, mumbling to himself. Noura wills herself to remain still. Though her entire family says her head is so buried in history she's no good to the here and now, Noura knows knowledge is the first step. And right now, history and common sense tell her she cannot allow Ghadfa to know her entire family is dead set against

Nixon's political maneuvering and would rather witness Egypt swallowed by the Nile than become an ally of the United States.

Without a word, Ghadfa pivots, snatching Noura from her thoughts. His enormous stride swallows the length of the building, which leaves Noura scrambling like an undignified squirrel behind him. He swerves into the back stairwell and bounds up the steps on silent feet. The waning light hollows and shifts the planes of his body. If she didn't know better, she might think him a ghost or one of the gods himself.

The idea of going further into the lonely building with a strange man sets off a shake in Noura's limbs. Maman's warnings about the vulnerability of a lone woman combine with Noura's failures, creating a catalyst for her fears to explode into everything that has ever held her back.

But she recognizes the faulty formula, straightens her spine, and clatters up the stairs.

At the archway to the second story, Ghadfa looms. When Noura clatters onto the landing, he's shining his flashlight on a tiny hole in the wall. As the light remains focused on the dark spot, Noura bites her lip, stifling the wave of frustration. She may have passed the first test, but she is going to fail this one. What is she missing?

Ghadfa sighs as if she is his dense son-in-law. "Rats carry the spirits of the long dead."

Noura nods in acknowledgment of the Egyptian myth.

"Before you came, I saw one disappear into the walls."

Adrenaline bursts into flames in her vision. She has staked her reputation on Ghadfa's story and then convinced him she will take him seriously, only to discover that a rat is his intruder. "I..." She what? How does one back gracefully from this?

Ghadfa guffaws, slapping his thigh. "Miss, you should see your face. While the rats are a problem for the preservation of our treasures, they are not the troublemakers we are concerned about. Yes?"

Relief cascades through her, and Noura conjures a smile at his prank.

Ghadfa whirls and slips between King Tut's burial artifacts with practiced ease. She traipses behind him, chiding herself for being gullible and promising herself she'll be more vigilant, more careful, less presumptuous, and less downright stupid.

"Here." Ghadfa points to a circle of clean amongst the heavy dust.

"Something was here?"

"A chalice, miss."

"When did it go missing?" Noura squints at the yellowed label, the words lost underneath age, darkness, and dust.

"The night before last. Before then, I heard whispering in the walls, saw footprints in the dust. Other, smaller things have gone missing. It's like someone is testing what we will notice and what we will not."

"Did you see anyone?"

"No."

"But you told Mr. Fabre?"

"Yes." His voice gives away nothing.

"He didn't believe you?"

"I do not know. But nothing has been done except to expect old Ghadfa to protect the building alone."

He's right. Nothing's been done. Why did the man stop at telling Theo? Theo is Dr. Lilyquist's second in command. But others have authority. Mostafa, John, even Noura. She trails her fingers over the dustless circle around and around. Father always told her to trust her instincts, to watch for clusters of behaviors, collections of oddities, and to pay attention to those. Well, Noura's senses are overflowing with not-quite-rightness. The missing objects, the list, her sister, Theo's inaction.

Tapping the empty shelf with decision, Noura turns toward the guard, reverting to Arabic. "I believe you. I'll talk to Mr. Hoving."

The man's grin unveils his particularly long incisors before he gives a curt bow and heads toward the stairs. Noura shakes off the ominous prick of following a crocodile named Ghadfa to the stairwell.

At the last moment, a whisper of footsteps makes Noura spin. A swish of fabric comes from down the steps. She clicks on the flashlight and the beam flickers once, twice, and then collapses on itself. In the darkness, Noura's blood is loud, rushing through her veins, her skin prickling. Something is out there tracking her. A constant flickering at the edge of her vision, and when she turns, it evaporates like the snipers spread over the Sinai Peninsula. Smart, quiet, patient, and hunting.

5

Voices float through the museum, and Estelle freezes. One foot hovers past the thirteenth step—which moans like a dying cow—waiting to haul Estelle onto the quiet fourteenth tread. This is her last chance to slip into the exhibit unencumbered. The last time the way will be clear.

And yet...She cocks her head, listening. A woman? Estelle eases backward, down one stair, and then another. The other woman knows what she's talking about. Yet believes Ghadfa's cockamamie stories. And she has access to the Americans. One of Typhon's agents?

No.

Despite the Arabic, she's American, and...with a slight Israeli accent?

Estelle stumbles, catches herself, and slithers down another step. Noura.

Why is her sister talking with the man who'd bestowed Typhon's orders on Estelle? He's supposed to clear the museum for her, and he's failed again.

Desperate to get out, Estelle sweeps down the remaining steps, absorbing any sound in the flex of her knees and bare toes. She is nothing if not a consummate sneak. It's ironic that Father's insistence on dance classes is what gave her the physical strength and skills to outwit those who thought so little of her. If he only knew.

She flickers past chests and cases, no doubt containing priceless pieces. Regrettably she has no concept of the value of the jars, sculptures, and bits of stone. After the last time she failed to lift the Tut artifacts, she tried nicking a few of the baubles, figuring Typhon couldn't be that picky. She'd been wrong. His agent laughed at her from his booth. Worse, without proof of the validity of the items, even the shadiest traders shooed her from their stalls. She hates how they treated these talismans of the dead.

The whole thing makes her want to abandon her beliefs and bomb the entire world into submission. Fire whips through her, exploding in a headache behind her eyes. How dare the greedy Egyptians raise the rent yet again on Mehedi's widowed mother? How dare the Weathermen suggest he borrow from Typhon of all people? How dare Typhon and his blood-red-marked missives take advantage of the entire situation? Where are the justice and mercy she'd given her life to? And people wonder why so many decide that the ends justify the means.

Estelle pivots around the corner, scrambling for the back entrance before her sister realizes someone else is here.

Of course Estelle had called her contacts with the Weather Underground, and they assured her that Typhon supported the cause. Then shrugged their shoulders in response to her pleas for them to help Mehedi. Estelle suspects Typhon wants more than money. From all appearances, the "loyal" socialist has more of a personal stake in this heist than he's let on. Or maybe it's the Weathermen who want to interrupt Nixon's chummy overtures. Regardless, Estelle has few options. The people who once promised to protect her have chained her to the fourth circle of hell and blindfolded her for good measure. And she's no real idea why.

If she can't steal the artifacts, she needs another plan.

Estelle bends around the corner, striding to the exit.

If she can get to Chicago, she can force the Weather Underground to protect their own. Can't she? She knows far too much for them to ignore her. But she has to be in the Windy City for any threats to carry weight or for the Weathermen's protection to extend over her and Mehedi's heads.

So she needs the help of someone with contacts in the government to get her a passport and with access to wealthy donors to bribe the right people. Estelle hesitates. Someone who would do anything for Mehedi. Someone who can read what people want and then deliver it.

Someone like Noura.

Estelle has seen her sister in the souks. Noura is never the same person twice. It makes her a remarkable negotiator, a terrible sister, and exactly what Estelle needs to get out of this mess. Why hadn't she thought of this before? Why steal anything when there's another, easier way?

Knowing both Estelle's life and Mehedi's are in danger, Noura will at least try to get her sister a passport, if not the funds to help Estelle get Mehedi out of his predicament.

But if Noura catches her sister plotting to steal the precious bits of stone and wood, Noura will slam the door in Estelle's face. And then Estelle will have no option other than to break down the doors, throw the pieces in a bag, and hope she can run faster than the guards.

As she abandons the rejected pieces on a random table, she whispers an apology to the dead, then slips out the receiving door, more hopeful than she has been in weeks.

Concealed by long shadows, she pauses behind the fence, watching for a distraction, and lets her mind travel the well-worn path of frustration. Why does Noura care if Egyptian artifacts are missing? Are they worth more than a homeless child? Than her own sister?

The last time Estelle was in the same room with her sister, Noura stood, twisting the edges of her skirt as Estelle told her what had happened to their brother's family. Alone, Estelle had hauled the still pregnant body of their friend, their sister-in-law, Saira, to the mass burial site. And then little Miriam's. Her niece was the same age Estelle had been when she'd been dumped in a Tel Aviv hospital to survive her disease…or not. At least the doctors saved Estelle. Miriam hadn't been so lucky.

At a slight jostling on the sidewalk, the crowd turns away to monitor the situation. Estelle clambers over the fence and drops to the sidewalk with ease.

Except something in her mind taps her shoulder. The urge is ridiculous, but Estelle risks a glance back to be sure.

Noura's man stands at the corner, a picture of alert stillness in the swirling crowd. She faces forward, walking with purpose while her heart screams against her ribcage.

FABRIC FLUTTERING at the top of the gate had yanked Theo from his lazy conversation with the guard. As Theo watched, dumbfounded, the bundle landed, quiet as a cat, mere yards in front of him, then morphed into a woman striding from the museum. The guard hadn't even noticed, and Theo was too stunned to react with anything approaching speed.

But then the woman turned. The security light haloed her from behind, eclipsing the moon of her face. Her attention slammed into his long enough for his brain to catch up. The infamous Star in the flesh? She flinched and then tucked herself into the crowd as neat as a magician.

Theo blinks, the world returning to normal speed, snapping him into action. Star is a contact he cannot afford to lose again. He makes a bungling excuse to the guard and launches after his inroad to Typhon's organization. Her red headscarf sparks his attention, and he elbows through the crowd, swooping in when the woman hefts a child to her hip.

Theo stops. Not her.

Stationing himself at the front corner of the museum, he squints into the shifting landscape of humanity. In the waning light, individuals are as ubiquitous as shifting sand in the desert. He closes his eyes to picture the woman's form, to memorize it before hunting in the blowing expanse of humanity once more. Nothing.

Her movements were familiar though. Sleek. Like a jackal. Has he met her before? In the bazaar?

The consciousness of Theo's alter ego, Randall Sykes, rears his shaggy head. In the stall for his not-so-legal oddities? Or the museum?

Theo knows Typhon gave or perhaps forced the museum assignment onto the mysterious vigilante.

The front door of the museum groans open, and Theo darts into hiding. Noura skitters from the gaping maw, gives a hesitant half-wave to the dark rectangle, and then trots toward the hotel.

Easing forward, Theo swivels his attention from her to the doorway. Ghadfa.

Garish streetlights etch a frown into his long face. From the twist of his lips and the tap of his thumb against his side, Ghadfa is calculating, plotting his next move. What is he playing at? The man acts innocent as a lamb but has more shady connections than Kissinger himself. Theo wouldn't be surprised if Ghadfa is the source of the missing artifacts.

Theo's attention diverts to Noura, who startles sideways, recovers, then squats down to hand a girl something. Noura's laughter trickles across the open expanse, and Theo leans against the wall with a helpless smile. In the market, Noura did something similar with a little boy. Down on one knee, she made a coin appear from his ear, then her nose, then she turned the penny into a mango for the boy to share with the little sister who hid behind him. Theo added the bread he'd bought, and the two kids scampered off to share their bounty.

A doctorate in the esoteric subject of Egyptology, yet the woman sees people. Really sees them.

The idea seems idiotic now, but with Noura's skills in the market, knowledge of artifacts, and mastery of languages, Theo had thought *she* might be Star. But her desire to hide comes from something other than outright deceit. Noura is delightfully guileless, and her very real outrage at being used nearly made Theo quit his hidden job on the spot and beg her to forgive him...for everything.

Of course that particular subterfuge was not his. Frank had watched Theo study Noura's movements and assumed Theo's interest was of a relational nature. Frank put two and two together and got forty-five.

Noura is beautiful and interesting beneath the bland persona. But like his childhood hero, US Marshal Matt Dillon, Theo cannot risk any real relationships. "I'm the first man they look for and the last they want to meet," he whispers to the crowded street. "It's a chancy job, and it makes a man watchful—and a little lonely." It's the first time the

Gunsmoke line feels less than heroic. Not that he sees himself as a hero. He has good reason to take Typhon down, but revenge is hardly valorous, and he does far too many things most people find unforgivable.

The museum door eases shut, and Theo takes one last visual sweep of the street before darting after Noura. His employer will not be pleased Star slipped away. But the fact that she's here and skulking about means Theo's on the right track.

From behind a palm, Estelle watches the man scan for her. Typhon had warned of competition. She will have to be careful.

Estelle adjusts the headscarf, tugging the fabric over her mouth to cut the exhaust fumes. If only it were this easy to remove even half of the world's metaphorical stench.

Here they are, two years after the Yom Kippur War, a year since Vietnam, and the nations are still sniping at one another while children starve. And once again, Mehedi's life depends on Noura.

To be fair, Noura would do almost anything for him. But in the wake of the war, when Mehedi was missing, Noura chose to pack Father's books before tracking down the kid.

And yes, Noura found Mehedi and got him out of Israel. But then she dumped him, helpless, in the States with strangers. What else was Estelle supposed to do but introduce him to people who would protect him from small-minded despots?

Estelle shakes the burgeoning anger from her fingertips.

Mehedi is forever telling Estelle she lets things get under her skin too easily. He's safe, living with good people, and training to be an electrician. In Mehedi's mind, at least, Noura's list of virtues is endless. But the bottom line is always the same: Noura does as little as possible to assuage her conscience. Small. Cautious. Always following the rules. Never wanting to offend...when an absolute overhaul is what the world needs.

As if to illustrate her point, Estelle's stomach growls loudly. She hasn't eaten since breakfast...yesterday. She can't take food from the children at the mission. And yet, if she doesn't eat, she will die. And where does that leave the mission and Mehedi? Fortunately she still has a supply of insulin Maman sent. So Estelle slinks into the market. Slick as a lie coming from Nixon's mouth, she snatches a bun, turns the corner, and resumes her walk to the bus.

Noura would be horrified. Estelle smirks. The one time Noura ever did anything contrary to their father's rules was when she chucked everything and flew to Egypt. Dumping Charles was smart, but helping this farce of innocence? Both sisters know the cultural exchange treaty and tour is anything but a cute curiosity. Egyptian President Sadat is angling for absolution, and Nixon is desperate to claim anything resembling a win. Wouldn't ill-gotten peace be a lovely way to whitewash his crimes?

So there Noura is, and here Estelle is. The older sister working against everything the younger is working for.

Estelle will simply have to remind her sister that she owes her.

6

July 21, 1976

At the ring of her hotel phone, Noura wakes, bleary-eyed and ready to smack whoever is calling. "Yes?" She croaks into the receiver.

"Wake-up call, miss."

"Thank you." She manages the polite words but not the kind attitude, and she drops the phone on the hook.

Flopping onto her pillow, she shuts her eyes against the newborn sun. Last night her thoughts circled endlessly—a rat carrying the broken spirit of Saira, wailing in lament for her people, her tears carving pale trails on her cheeks as Harry's disembodied voice pronounced warranted judgment for his sister's failures. Just as Noura banished her sister-in-law's specter, the boy Tutankhamun stumbled in, bearing a falcon on his fist. He cried great black tears, confused and searching for his stolen afterlife. Behind him, a cluster of Selket's scorpions swarmed the floor, curse-bound to bestow a revenging sting.

Noura knows the weird dreams are a figment of her overstressed imagination, but once she's imagined the scorpions, she can't unhear their claws clicking on the tile floor.

Even in the bright light of day, Noura's only half sure creatures aren't hiding under her bed waiting to scrabble at her ankles like Harry used to do. She never did figure out what made her brother shift from rescuing hero to tormentor and back again.

Noura lies on her bed until the laughter of Theo, Mr. Caddel, and John rises from the street, telegraphing that she is going to be irretrievably late. Flinging off the sheet, she slams her feet onto the scorpion-free floor, throws on a dress, and wrangles her hair into a chignon. As she stumbles down the stairs, she tells herself she will survive on the blackest of teas and determination, and no one will suspect her lapse.

In the lobby, two British women giggle in the corner, obviously lost and in need of assistance. Noura skirts behind a drooping palm tree, pops out the other side, and is caught by the younger one *yoo-hooing*. Even diverting to talk with Ahmed, the doorman, doesn't deter the bouncing blond. She slips her go-go boots between Noura and the Egyptian.

"Would you be an absolute dear and help Elizabeth and me?"

Completely ignoring Noura's shaking head, the woman grasps her elbow and manhandles her out the doors and to the queue of various taxis, Ahmed and the other woman trailing behind.

"These men"—the woman gesticulates to the line—"don't understand a simple question. We're in town for a few weeks and have been quite abandoned by our husbands. We're stuck inside, and we'd like to go to the real shops. But none of them will take us."

Poor Ahmed has gone white—caught between the demands of these wealthy foreign women and the culture which they've invaded. While much of Cairo is patterned after Paris, the outer reaches of the city are a warren of a much older and more conservative world. Noura can't imagine this woman bartering in the souks without causing pandemonium.

How to explain? "Ma'am."

"Oh heavens." The woman stops. "We've not been introduced, have we? I'm Lizzy Cahill. Isn't it simply ghastly that we both have the same name?"

At the questioning flick of Noura's gaze, the other woman releases a controlled sigh. "We're both Elizabeth. She goes by Lizzy."

"Because it's so less...well, Elizabethan!" Lizzy titters. "Anyhoo. You march out every day as if you know exactly what you're about, and we figure you might find someone to take us to the shops or even..." She gasps as if she's thought of the most wonderful idea. Noura's survival instinct screams to bolt. But before Noura can execute a retreat, Lizzy whirls to her friend, garnering backup. "She simply must come with us."

Too late.

"I..." How does one extract oneself from quicksand?

"Lizzy," Elizabeth says with the immense patience of a long friendship, "she's a busy woman. We can't ask her to—"

"Not right now, silly." Lizzy thrums in anticipation.

Experts say not to struggle against a quagmire of muck, but—

"In the next week or so," Lizzy says, like she's solved world peace. "You must want some girl time. Not that some of the men you're with aren't positively scrumptious, mind. But, well, you are adorable underneath that get-up, and I do so need a project." Lizzy lifts a perfectly manicured brow in assessment, and Noura fights the urge to cover herself with a protective arm. "Let me dress you up a bit," Lizzy says. "My George won't realize his account is missing a few pounds. I would have so much fun. And that Robert Redford look-alike won't forget you any time soon."

Noura's mind spins, snatching at pieces of sense and reassembling them in an abstract picture of what the Tasmanian Devil of a woman is saying.

"What is it you do that this"—Lizzy waves dismissively at Noura's dress—"is what you wear?"

"Lizzy!" The one word from Elizabeth curtails the out-of-control twittering friend.

But Lizzy isn't wrong. Noura had hoped her drab wardrobe would help everyone see her as an equal. Obviously her wretched clothing choices haven't helped. "I suppose I could—"

"Oh!" Lizzy claps.

"But I can't today." Noura rushes into the pause. "I'm expected at the museum."

"You're working on the King Tutankhamun exhibit." Elizabeth's voice lifts, impressed.

"You know about that?"

"Indeed." Elizabeth taps her thigh with a manicured finger, calculating.

Noura's sure the refined woman will find her wanting and, for whatever reason, Noura wishes it weren't so.

"Lizzy is right," Elizabeth says. "You should never hide a brain like yours underneath poor fashion. We shall await your call in the next few days. And now, I daresay, you should be off."

Noura opens her mouth to object to the assigned itinerary. But oh heavens. Elizabeth is right about the time. By the time Noura swings around the hotel drive, sweat pools under the cotton of her bodice. She knows she's not a fashion plate, but Elizabeth's words make her squirm. Has she been hiding? After Charles's degradation, the last thing she wants is someone's interest because she has, as Maman said, "Audrey Hepburn's poise, Sophia Loren's cheekbones, and the wisdom to keep your mouth shut." Noura wants someone to fall in love with who she is underneath the contorted self she has become.

THOUGH THE OTHERS don't react when Noura enters the workroom, Theo releases the breath he's been holding. He knows he will only hurt her, and yet he cannot resist the reassuring idea that if he lets her, she can weigh his heart and know exactly who he is and what he needs. But there are too many lives at risk for him to let down his guard.

He needs to find Typhon, destroy his network, and get out before anyone suspects anything. Pushing from the table, he turns his back on her. Even as he digs in the supply bin for an unneeded tool, he knows he won't be able to walk away. He will forever want to earn the quirk of her smile, the steady wisdom that has a habit of catching him off guard.

ACROSS THE ROOM, Noura forces herself to focus on the reports. Slowly, the mundanity of lists and reports drowns her nightmares. At noon, the team filters out, leaving Theo shifting foot to foot behind her chair. Noura forces herself to continue working until he trudges away. She will not allow anyone to call her lazy. As Noura sips on lukewarm tea, she sweeps away her own whispered accusations—unworthy, unliked—and ignores the grumble of her stomach, which makes her think of the gaunt woman her sister has become. Is Estelle safe? Does she have insulin?

Noura knows it's pointless to search for her sister. Estelle will be found if and when she wants to be found, and not a moment before. The press of her bladder forces Noura to abandon her station, and when she returns, the team is back on task. Of course they returned at the single moment Noura isn't hard at work.

Nodding to no one in particular, Noura lurks around the perimeter until the smell of cumin registers and lures her to her station. She lifts the lid and enters heaven itself.

Lamb shawarma slathered in the spices of her childhood. And cucumber, hummus, and pickled turnips. Noura's gut growls. Bittersweet. No one can mix spices like Saira. Her cooking is what finally won Noura over.

Noura banishes the loneliness and takes a bite, letting the sweet cinnamon and sharp cayenne bite the edges of her tongue, the hummus soothing over the top. The shawarma isn't Saira's, but it's close...and certainly not from the hotel restaurant, which caters to European palates. Noura shovels in a few more mouthfuls and sighs in delight. Saira never once reacted to Noura's early incivility. Saira understood being an outsider. Understood protecting her family. Understood abandonment.

Noura didn't know what to do with the young woman's understanding. Still doesn't.

Noura clutches the flatbread and sucks in a breath.

Saira had been a scared thirteen-year-old Bedouin who'd long been responsible for caring for Noura's family.

Noura pokes at the lamb and doodles on her to-do list. Behind her, John trades joking barbs with Mr. Caddel. The pair sounds more than a little like Gomez Addams and Uncle Fester, plotting how to use dynamite caps in the basement of the creepy Addams Family mansion. Being friends seems so easy for them.

She misses knowing where she belongs. Ever since the marshes of

New Orleans sucked Maman to her family home, there was a bomb crater between Noura and the rest of the world.

Saira couldn't possibly have cured Noura's scorched desert of abandonment, but she tried to douse the thirsty longings. Like most grieving children, Noura interpreted Saira's care as interference. Then, before Noura could adjust, Mehedi appeared. One more person for Noura to worry over. One more sibling for her to fall in love with...and make no mistake, Noura fell hard in love with the grinning mayhem of a child. In the end, Noura let both Mehedi and Saira in, only to have them disappear and take her siblings with them.

No. Noura taps her pencil on the tablet. That isn't true. Harry took them and left Noura behind because she'd wavered in understanding his increasingly vitriolic rantings.

Still, it ended with Noura alone, on the outside.

"Good?"

Noura catapults to her feet, slamming her knee against the underside of the table in the process.

Theo stands frozen. The rest of the room holds its breath, then it slowly pulses with contained laughter. The heat of their stares sets fire to Noura's lungs. Planting a hand on her desk, she pastes on a smile. Though Mr. Caddel makes her the butt of all his jokes, she's eminently qualified to be here, no matter what anyone says.

"The shawarma is delicious." Noura's words are a cracked patina over the memories.

"Did I get it right?"

"Right?" She parrots ridiculously back.

"The shawarma. It's how you like it, isn't it?"

She touches the fork still stabbed into a tender piece of lamb. How did he know lamb shawarma is her favorite? "Thank you," she manages, but she sounds like a bad recording. She'll replay this moment in her head all night, searching for how she should have responded.

You've done your best, Saira's words whisper from a grave Noura never saw. Saira's blood, her child's blood, staining her sister's body. The tiny handprint on Estelle's back. The memory marks Noura even now.

"It's an apology offering," Theo says, a hair above a whisper. He means the words for Noura alone.

Behind him, the others return to work, but they angle their bodies to have the best chance at eavesdropping. Well, Noura won't give them any more logs to throw on the fire of her smoldering career.

"Apology for what?" She smooths a lock of hair behind her ear and takes care in settling on her hard wooden chair before nibbling on the lamb...which tastes like cardboard now. Setting the fork on the desk, she ignores Theo lingering next to her desk and busies herself with perfunctory work. Rather like cardboard herself.

"I didn't know Frank set us up. He—"

"You said that." There's a dismissive snap in her voice.

When Theo doesn't move, she glances at him over her shoulder. "Is there something else?" Perhaps if she acts confused, they can go back to the way they'd been before: Noura bemused at his antics; him scarcely noticing her in the corner. Except that isn't what she wants, is it? She wants the rose-toting, Detroit-grit, Robert Redford look-alike who is meticulous in his work and discreetly gives bread to hungry kids.

Noura sorts through photos she's already sorted, feeling his presence at her side.

When she doesn't turn, he shoves his fingers through his enticing mass of dark curls. "You're smart, Noura. You know that, right? Smarter than everyone here. Me especially. Do you know how I got on the team?"

Noura drops the photos into their file and lifts her chin in permission.

"Frank was my roommate in college." Theo nods in Mr. Caddel's direction. "He was a disaster outside the confines of our room. We'd be out, he'd say something stupid, and he'd get walloped. Every single time. Got so bad we developed a signal for him to shut his trap. I'd wink at him and pray the man-child would shut up. Didn't always work, but now, anytime somebody winks at him, he ducks first and asks questions later."

This she can picture. Mr. Caddel, at a bar, with big goofy glasses, mouthing off about the history of seduction using alcohol.

"Anyway." Theo's finger traces the whorl of wood grain on Noura's chair. "Frank landed a girlfriend way out of our league. I'm still convinced she dated him on a lark. So when she publicly humiliated him, I helped him break into her room and nick her school bag. She was a first-class prig and one hundred percent deserved payback for how she treated him. But we got caught, I took the fall, and he owed me one or ten."

"And if I believe you, I'm a monkey's uncle. Yes?" Noura shakes her head and chuckles, but Theo doesn't look up from his study of her excessively boring chair.

"Are you serious?" Noura whispers, whirling to him now, her knees bumping the side of his leg.

"As a priest." He snatches a chair and drags it screeching across the room, oblivious to the attention he draws. He deposits the chair at Noura's feet and drops into it. "I really am sorry. I know I'm a bit of a Hawkeye."

"Hawkeye?"

"You know, the jokester from M*A*S*H?"

"With those curls, you're more of a McIntyre," John mutters.

"That makes her Houlihan," Mr. Caddel hoots from the other side of the room.

Noura forces a benevolent chuckle through her clenched teeth. Better to pretend not to care than to act like the priggish Houlihan, who only got along with those she could manipulate.

"I'm not a straightlaced academic." Theo ignores the clamor and positions himself in the chair so his shoulders block his joking compatriots. He is so close, the crisp pleat in his pant legs canoodles the edges of her skirt. With the wall behind Noura, they're tucked into their own private nook. Theo's long hands splay across the curve of his knee, and Noura studies the length of his pinky, exploring the slim distance between them.

"But," he says, letting his pinky scale the distance and land upon her knee. "But that doesn't mean I'm not good at my job."

"I never said you weren't." Noura is unable to drag her attention away from his fingers smoothing over the weave of his trouser leg. How does he keep the pleat so crisp in this humidity? Does he iron them every morning? Again at lunch? And the thought of him bent over an ironing board in his undershirt sends Noura's pulse ratcheting to unseemly heights.

"You know the whole paint thing wasn't me. And if you know I'm good at my job, you must wonder why I told Dr. Lilyquist something different from what I told you."

Noura's entire body goes rigid, not quite yanking back, but probing to define the undercurrent that's sneaked into the conversation. She concentrates on remaining primly perched in her chair, waiting for him to commit to a direction.

"Mr. Hoving already knows."

A pin pricks Noura's rigid composure, and she deflates in relief. "Already knows?"

"It isn't just random pieces that have gone missing," Theo says.

Noura fights the urge to laugh at how much he sounds like a middle school girl spreading hot gossip.

Theo leans closer. "Yesterday, Lilyquist discovered that the gems in some of the artifacts are glass."

This flambés Noura's laughter, leaving a horror of ash behind. "How?" is the only word she can conjure. Never mind a hole in the roof, a pigeon, and an ostrich feather. The police will drag the Americans away, throw them in the abyss of an Egyptian prison, and never look back.

"Lilyquist is studying the settings with Mostafa. No one wants the thieves to get spooked and shift tactics." Theo leans on his elbows, letting his clasped fists hover over Noura's thigh.

"I talked to Ghadfa last night," she says.

"I know." A tease lilts in his voice, and Noura recoils from the implied ridicule.

"Why didn't you—"

"I promise it isn't a habit...to follow you, I mean." Theo's exhale stirs the errant wisp of hair on her cheek. "Ghadfa thought you might be the thief, and I wanted to be sure he didn't handle things himself. I should have told you, but I wasn't sure you'd believe me."

"You're probably right," Noura concedes.

"And I guess it's a habit to watch after people I care about."

"Care about?" Noura's voice contains a hitch of...she doesn't know what. One part of her screams, *Think about your job, you idiot*, but the other melts in the flickering gold flecks of his blasted twinkling brown eyes.

"I've been watching out for my sisters since forever," he says.

His sister. Cold water dumps over Noura's melted bits. Platonic. Friendly. "Oh." Noura lifts shaking fingers to cover the vulnerable triangle at the base of her neck.

The motion snaps Theo's attention to the curve of her collarbone before it drags back to her eyes. "Noura, I…" He lets his fingertips drift to her knee, where they thrum so merrily that Noura has inadequate brain space to process his words. "I know what your job means to you. And I'm aware of all the ways that this…that *I* could be a problem for you."

Noura swallows her neurotic chagrin. As much as she'd like to fling herself across the infinitesimally small distance between her body and his, he's right. Curling her hands into one another, Noura holds on to logic for dear life—strangling it right there in her lap. "And so?"

Noura swallows as Theo contemplates the motion of Noura's lips, the dip in her throat, and traces the path of her disappointment, seeming to undress her reaction.

Noura doesn't move. Can hardly snatch a breath. He is fire. Warm and inviting. Scorching.

"What have we here?" Mr. Caddel smacks Theo on the back and reaches over them both to snatch a cucumber from Noura's plate. He contemplates it a moment, then pops it into his mouth. "Delicious, I'm sure." He leans back, smacking his lips.

What? How dare he?

Theo nudges Mr. Caddel with an elbow, even as Noura's fingers close around her pencil. She's more than tempted to slam the tip of her pencil into Mr. Caddel's leg, which leans possessively against her desk. The obnoxious man deserves it, but the other man? The driven, protective, thoughtful Theo? Noura's mind spins into full-fledged confused paralysis.

"That'll be enough." Dr. Lilyquist stands in the doorway, reminding Noura that revenge would be short-lived.

With one strike, it wouldn't matter what outfit Lizzy selects for Noura. She would forever be relegated as unhinged.

"I will not have you run off the most qualified person in the room." She stares pointedly at Mr. Caddel.

"Most practical too." Theo nods agreeably, stretching himself to his feet. He pats Noura's shoulder before striding to his workstation like a conquering big-brother hero.

Noura hunches over her desk before Dr. Lilyquist or anyone else can distribute any more pity on the poor Marquette girl. Dealing with that man is like the breath before a horrific khamsin hits. One minute you think you're in a glorious, sunny place, and the next, a wall of sand decimates your entire world.

7

July 27, 1976

Estelle slips behind the crumbling wall. The girl in her arms whimpers, and Estelle murmurs in Arabic, soothing the child back to sleep. She didn't plan for this rescue. She was walking to the mission after failing to contact her sister, again, when an enormous black dog popped from a doorway and forced Estelle down an alley, where she stumbled upon the child. The girl was bleeding, trying to clean herself outside a known brothel, and Estelle just…snapped. She didn't care she was being followed. She helped the girl wash, talked to her for a bit, and convinced her to escape. And here they are running.

A clatter of stones behind her sends Estelle scampering. She slams her bare toe into a loose brick she didn't and almost drops the girl, even as Estelle stifles a scream of frustration and pain. Angry male voices clash. She recognizes the pimp's but not the other accusatory one. She uses the distraction to dive across a bright intersection and into a bus, which has blessedly pulled to the curb. She's no idea where it's headed other than away.

Tipping her head against the grimy window, Estelle breathes, humming a leftover bit of song. "Amazing Grace," she thinks. The one Noura used to sing when Estelle was small and frightened. She desperately needs her sister now. Over the last few days, Estelle hasn't been able to get close enough to the hotel or Noura to communicate. With the clock ticking down, Estelle is running out of options. She'll have to find a way to bring her sister to her.

Almost a week has passed with Mr. Hoving suspiciously absent and Theo often gone on what Dr. Lilyquist calls "errands." Rumors fly as to why. Noura's convinced they're smoothing over relations with the Egyptian muckety-mucks. For several days, Dr. Lilyquist, Mr. Caddel, and the Egyptian team studied the fake lapis lazuli and some other gems, which were meticulously created glass.

Noura's sure the foundations of the museum shook with relief in response to the team's conclusion: due to the great age of the glass and the old mounting techniques, the fakes are ancient—likely used as substitutes when trade routes were interrupted in Tutankhamun's time.

That discovery was chased by Theo's exuberant whooping when he uncovered the missing chalice and a few other pieces on a table downstairs. Plainly, there is no pillaging anarchist. Estelle or otherwise. The weird encounter on the street was coincidence, and Estelle was as flabbergasted as her older sister to come face-to-face with a ghost.

There is no need for anyone to panic. Or at least that's what Noura tells herself as the cheering dies down. She retrieves the list, intent on throwing it away. But she can't quite banish the voice of the FBI agent who told her graduate class that several of the communist groups stole museum pieces to buy bomb material.

But bombing isn't Estelle's style, and she isn't likely to be party to anything that could harm innocent people.

Then again, Noura doesn't know her sister anymore. Noura stuffs the confounding list into her bag next to the feather. What she wouldn't give to be able to weigh hearts like Ma'at. But she can't. So she'll just have to live with her misgivings about too many coincidences in one time and place.

She doesn't have time for solving quandaries or celebrating...not with a miles-long list of chores. So for the next three days, Noura chases details and people and deliveries and collapses on her bed every night, taking a sip of sleep before she's dragged out the next morning and the next, never a spare moment to breathe, let alone recover from her anxiety-fueled nightmares.

No wonder she's jumping at shadows.

And she's not the only one. This morning, Theo fell asleep at his station, head resting across his arms. When Noura whispered his name, he jerked upright, and Noura easily imagined him as a boy using the slow blink he'd given her to weasel his mother into granting his every wish.

He disappeared for a bit and now reappears with a samovar full of the blackest tea she's ever seen and a basket of snacks.

Grateful, Noura refills her mug and snatches bread and cheese—the only thing she's eaten all day. Noura glances at the calendar and recounts the days until August 2. She clambers over the panic and returns to work, shuttling and organizing and pitching in.

By the time her body is vehemently pleading for dinner—all lightheadedness and snarling belly—the team has finished most of the repair work, constructed the twenty-sixth of the twenty-nine cases, and has a handful of pieces left to pack into foam puzzles.

As Noura checks the supply of packing material on the loading dock, the delivery door latch grinds open. She frowns and shouts to the harried team, "Do we have another scheduled delivery today?"

Theo drops the hammer next to the frame he's building, grinning. "Yep!" He bounds to the door and heaves it open. On the other side stands Ghadfa, surrounded by three crates.

"I asked Ghadfa to build the last of the crates we'd need so we could finish early." Theo claps Ghadfa on the back like a proud papa.

"They're not supposed to be delivered until the end of the week." Noura drags her finger along the checklist.

"I've taken care of things." Ghadfa bows, showing Noura the deference Theo hadn't.

Theo shrugs. "I have Selket ready to be packed and nowhere safe to put her."

She can't argue with that.

Using a hand truck, Ghadfa wheels each crate to the base of the stairs, where he and Theo wrestle the boxes to the top and plop them, one by one, onto another truck. Mr. Caddel wheels the crates into the room and cracks open the lids. The smell of freshly hewn wood makes Noura think of Maman's hastily packed steamer trunks. Abandonment.

She plummets into her chair. No one is deserting her. They are a team. Aren't they? But what happens when they leave Cairo? Noura doesn't have a job, which means traveling to whatever museum will have her. It means leaving Theo.

Theo leans over a wooden case, his full bottom lip caught in concentration as he and John lift the foam container from the worktable.

"We're going to make it." Theo grins at her as he passes.

"Don't jinx us." John shifts his side of the foam box.

Noura wants to throw herself into Theo's arms and tell him to slow down. But if they miss their shipping date, they may lose their jobs, not to mention the international repercussions. She and Theo will have to work things out as best they can.

Ghadfa stands in the corner, scrutinizing Noura and stroking his beard. Noura's skin crawls as she thinks about him standing in the dark, the sleeves of his uniform ruffling in the nonexistent breeze, the flash of crocodile teeth in the darkness. Was he the one to misplace the artifacts, only to return them? It's ridiculous...unless he did it on purpose to make them shrug off the possibility of theft.

Noura grips the edges of the condition report, scrunching it in a desperate attempt to strangle the thought. Though she's loath to admit it, she has felt a hidden, vigilant observation as she's come and gone from the museum. She hoped the skitter of awareness was just Estelle trying to contact her. If it were, maybe her sister had decided to forgive Noura for whatever it is she's done wrong. But if the watcher was the night guard all along, what then? Noura slides deeper into the corner so he can no longer see her. Once the artifacts leave Egypt, they'll be safe from anything that's stalking them here, and she'll breathe again.

The men grunt and heave until the foam-wrapped artifact is buried between the wooden walls. Theo drives in the last nail and skips around the room, pumping his arms like Muhammad Ali, until he reaches Noura's corner. There he stops, stumbling, his toes inches from Noura's no-nonsense shoes. She imagines him lifting her and twirling her around—Fred Astaire and Ginger Rogers, elegant, refined.

Instead, he knocks his knuckles on Noura's desk and spins, open-armed, to the room. "Let's celebrate!"

The team pours from the room, and Noura stands, dizzy with some unnamed emotion. Fear? Excitement? She shakes her head free and snatches her bag, nearly missing the fluttering feather. She bends, plucking it from the ground. Odd. How did the pigeon get in here? She turns the feather in her hand, studying the striped plume. Different than the other she'd found. Smaller, more rigid. Striped. She frowns. Realizing. Pigeons don't have striped feathers. Her fingers smooth the tangled barbs, laying the filaments flat. The ostrich feather could be explained by a duster, but this?

"Are you coming?" Theo bursts through the doorway, and Noura jumps, letting the feather flutter into her bag and banish her questions.

She carefully locks the door and then follows as Theo bounds in front of the Americans in an odd parade down the street to an open-air restaurant. Noura glances at the glowing museum to find Ghadfa frowning at the team, then he turns, the lights flickering a moment before he disappears.

8

As Noura sips her hibiscus tea, she slumps in the chair tucked into the corner of the restaurant, trying to convince herself that Ghadfa hadn't literally evaporated. The last rays of sun sneak through the fabric roof, pressing a wash of color across the table. And as the murmur of the thinning crowd recedes, stress slides off her shoulders, and she laughs at herself. The electricity just disconnected, leaving Ghadfa in the dark. Her wild imagination is proof she needs a break. Fortunately, the team will be finished in time to transport the artifacts, casts, and equipment to the airfield in a few days. All thanks to Theo's foresight in finishing the crates before schedule.

The chatter of laughter rolls through the restaurant, and a cheer rises in rhythm with the grooving bass line of "Play that Funky Music." At the opening, "Hey," Theo shouts, flapping his elbows funky chicken style. Most of the team joins in an electric slide ridiculousness that would have Estelle cackling in their midst, somehow transforming the awkward moves into an elegant dance. But as long ago established, Noura is not her sister, no matter how much she wants to be. The thought makes Noura clench her fist around the glass. She wants to hate her sister. Wants to hate what Noura herself is supposed to be. Instead, she hates that she's stuck in the corner, alone, again, wondering what she's supposed to do, and terrified that she will forever be an outsider, cursed to ruminate on what might go wrong, what has gone wrong, even as a litany of voices enumerates her weaknesses and inabilities. She sees the mythological Set Beast grinning in her mind as he spins chaos like a spider's web.

Noura takes another sip and sets the glass down on the table where it sweats miserably alongside Noura herself. The tea is so sugared it aches.

From the edge of the laughing crowd, Theo signals for Noura to join him. But she can't possibly heave herself from this anxious web, and so she lifts a tiny wave in response and taps a toe to the beat.

WHEN NOURA DOESN'T MOVE, Theo stills. He tells himself that his heart pounds because of exertion, but he knows better. He recognizes anxiety in the stiffness of her shoulders. He thought once the exhibit was well in hand, she would find her footing, but she's spiraled instead.

He cocks his head at the whisper of breeze lifting the edge of her skirt. And before he's fully aware of his decision, he is in front of her, hand extended, the quirk of his mouth forming a supplication that would be the height of impoliteness to ignore. He knows the position he is putting them both in, but he will not regret the flicker of gratitude in her expression, the flutter of her hand as it splays across her breastbone.

DIM ELECTRIC LIGHTS flicker on here and there down the alley and frame his lithe body. To Noura, Theo is glowing—whether demon or angel, she is not sure.

His eyes fixed on hers, he bends and takes hold of her fingers, where his calluses sizzle against her skin. Noura relinquishes her grip on the table, along with her vow to not make waves, and allows him to lift her from her safe corner.

"Everyone's celebrating today," he says. "Even you...maybe especially you. After this, you'll have your pick of assignments."

And the freedom to explore whatever is burgeoning between them... or so she hopes.

Theo secures her in the bracket of his arms and leads her through the hop-jump-slide. Maman wouldn't know whether to cheer for her wallflower or die of embarrassment. Noura is adrift and unable to do anything but float in his wake.

When the song switches to "You Sexy Thing," Theo winks before he spins Noura, ending with her hand against his sturdy chest, his arms around her—a life raft in the sudden ocean waves crashing over her. He's saving her as surely as he saved Mr. Caddel.

"You look lovely tonight." His breath on Noura's neck sends a spark through her limbs.

At her shiver, the edge of his cheek lifts and the stubble of his chin grazes her ear. When Theo leans back enough for Noura to see him fully, she is a breath away, and she forces her perusal away from his gilded eyes.

"My maman always told me to be careful of charming men."

"You find me charming?" He catches the edge of an errant strand of her hair and tucks it into her headscarf.

"Why do you do that?" she says.

"Do what?"

"Deflect with humor."

He blinks. His smile slips, and his arm drops away to slap, dejected, against his side.

"I'm sorry." Noura weaves her fingers through his, desperate to clamber back into the stable moment.

"No." He gathers Noura into the protection of his arm. "You're right. When I'm uncomfortable, I use a humorous sleight of hand to convince people to focus elsewhere." He leads Noura to the table. But instead of stopping, Theo drops cash on the table, snatches her bag, and leads her under an elegantly carved archway into the relative quiet of the street. He meanders to a beautiful mosaic set into the wall and taps on the bright blue in a field of orange. "I'm like these fancy tiles. Flashy, calling attention to myself, but entirely useless without the mortar in between."

"I don't think you're useless." She watches the rise and fall of his broad shoulders. "You single-handedly helped us finish on time by hiring Ghadfa."

"It was John's idea."

"But you executed it. Perhaps you're more like mortar than you think."

Theo turns, leaning a fiercely casual elbow against the wall. "Are you calling me plain?"

"Never." Noura can't help laughing even while noting that he's deflecting again.

"Most people underestimate the value of plain folks," he says. "The world would fall apart without hard-working, heads-down, get-the-job-done people like you."

"Like me?" Noura withdraws, trying not to show the offense.

"That's a compliment, remember? You're Ma'at to the chaos-inducing Isfet." He straightens, like proper posture will convince Noura of the veracity that she is the Egyptian counterbalance, the good, the stable, the right. "We need you, and you've no idea how amazing you are, do you, my lovely Ma'at?" He crosses the width of the street until he's so close she cannot fill her lungs.

This isn't what a big brother does, is it? If she shifts a minuscule amount, she could lay her palm flat against his chest, feel the thrum of his heart beating beneath his shirt.

The thought has Noura wondering what it would be like to do that—tangle her fingers in the neat row of buttons on his chest and let him kiss her senseless. But before Noura's body can oblige, he snaps away, sauntering forward, leaving her scrambling to catch up. As she reaches his side, his voice starts again.

"My family always walks the razor's edge of not enough," he's saying. "Dad works in the Chrysler factory, and Mom stays home. If I grew out of my shoes too fast or needed another class in college, Mom worked her magic. She'd do laundry or babysit or do needlework for the supervisors to earn the extra cash. You know?"

His attention turns to Noura, and she nods. Not that she knows anything about sewing or anything resembling fashion, and Maman has never done her own needlework. That's what the help is for. Noura tightens her jaw. Maman's inability to do simple things is what led Noura's father—and Noura herself—to think Maman was worthless. And yet, Maman challenged Noura not to give up and provided her with a path forward.

Theo stops to admire a relief carved into a nook. His fingers trace the intricate whorls surrounding a sharp-eyed falcon contemplating a red Set Beast. Why did the ancients imagine this mythological creature so similar to Anubis's jackal? The only differences are the Set Beast's strange nose, forked tail, and tall, square ears. And the color, of course —red to Anubis's black. Were chaos and the final reckoning so easy to mistake for one another?

And there, set apart is Ma'at, the goddess commanding Horus to battle for order, loaning her ostrich feather to Anubis to weigh a human's heart. It takes so many to battle the one god of chaos. Perhaps she and Theo could be part of the solution together.

"Mom could make anything on the machine. My sisters always wore off-the-hook clothes. And yes"—he lifts one side of his mouth in self-deprecation—"I did too. My older sister, Judy, was smart as anything, but man, she had horrible taste in guys. I was eight or nine the first time I caught some jerk necking with her under the bleachers after I'd seen him with another girl. I decked him but then got the snot beat out of me after he and his friends cornered me. Dad was proud I took my sister's side but also convinced the Pacific War veteran down the street to teach me karate so I wouldn't get pummeled again."

"And what about your younger sister?" Noura asks as he sets out again.

"Poor Mabel was so quiet she was almost transparent...until you got her talking about her latest animal rescue. She wasn't afraid of anything —birds, dogs, salamanders. She brought home a skunk once. We almost lost Mabel because of diabetes. Mom spent all her tears and waking hours worried about her. It worked though. Mabel turned out to be smarter than all of us. She's a doctor at the University of Michigan."

Noura has barely registered the outcome for the youngest Fabre sibling. "Diabetes?" She knows she sounds like a blathering ignoramus, yet she can't help repeating. "Diabetes?"

Theo frowns. "Yeah. When kids get it, it's—"

"I know. I...my sister almost died from it too."

His face sparks with wonder even as she struggles to keep the horror from her face. Why did she bring up Estelle?

"Then you know how hard it is." He lifts Noura's hand and presses it between his, as if asking her to join him in prayer.

But her sister needs more than prayer, and the last thing Noura needs is—

"I didn't know you had a sister."

That. "I haven't talked to her much since she left home. She's a... humanitarian." Noura's words are breathy and ephemeral at the edges, sparking at the blinding edges of her vision. Everything she said is true...technically. No one in the museum world knows about her sister for good reason. When one is intent on becoming an honored historian specializing in Egyptology, one does not claim a volatile communist as one's sister. "I haven't seen her in years."

"I'm sorry." Theo's brows tuck down. "What happened?"

"She went to college and..." Noura shrugs off the arguments between them. Estelle's accusations. *You never tried to see my side. You accepted Dad's view without even examining reality.* As if Noura missed the reality of Saira's blood. Or didn't ache with the hemorrhaging hole the deaths had created. "She thinks I hate her...or maybe she hates me. I don't know." *You make people believe you support them and then bail when it gets hard. Every single time.*

"Noura." Theo's thumb drifts across the moisture collecting on the dam of her lashes. "Who could hate you?"

At his blissful ignorance, an embarrassingly donkey-like snort escapes Noura. "There's a rather long list." Someday Noura has to return home and face both Charles and Father, all under the glowering visage of Grandmere. It's guaranteed to be a full-fledged blitzkrieg of an argument.

"I don't believe it." Theo leans over her, and she can't risk removing her attention from the open neckline of his shirt, tiny silver feather nestled between the breadth of his shoulders. If she sees his eyes, will she find the lie? The ever-present disappointment? Noura can't fathom what he wants her to be. He's listened, understood why she railed, recognized her fears, and never asked her to be anything.

Laughter erupts in the distance, a reminder of how very alone they are. And yet for the first time in a long, long time, Noura doesn't feel so lost by herself. "Thank you."

His palm cups the roundness of her cheek, a perfect fit. If she could crawl into the feeling and stay there forever, she would, even if he only wanted to be her friend. She could do that.

"Noura." The way he says her name is a magnet, dragging her focus, unbidden, away from the silver symbol of protection to his face—a place that may destroy her. A gentle glow spills across his cheek. His expression is soft and as sweet as the peppermint dancing on his breath.

When did he slip a mint into his mouth?

And why, oh why, can she only think of tasting it? For heaven's sake, they're in an alleyway. Grandmere would slap her silly, and Father would confine her to a convent. She has to finish this job before she can even think about—

"Why do you think people hate you?" he says.

"What?" Noura desperately attempts to recall what's expected of her.

"You're kind, smart, and heaven knows your smile stops any man on the street."

She snorts at the very idea, horrified that she may very well be turning into a mangy donkey. Charles mocked her embarrassment, her flailing attempts to be what he wanted.

"You don't believe me?"

"*Vogue* isn't knocking on my door."

"And who says that rag is the paragon of beauty?" Theo's thumb smooths down her jawline. "Me? I prefer a woman who might have emerged from under Monet's brush or once hid in Degas's bronze, waiting to be released from the mold. Somehow less solid than a photograph, shifting, while still managing to be real and arresting when you take in the whole impression. You, Noura Marquette, are curious and determined and celestial like Monet's lighting, and I love that you know how to make everything work smoothly when I'm all ideas and flashy nothing...and when you do that"—he glides his thumb over where she's bitten the edge of her lip—"you'd make even the most devout man bend his knee in supplication."

There is no trace of his cocky smile, and she suddenly doesn't know what to do with any part of her prickling, overheating body. She certainly can't look at him. Her lungs forget to inhale even as her mind flies. Worse, her hands flutter ridiculously. There seems to be no blood left to make her brain function. What should she say? What would Maman do? Or Estelle? What is she supposed to be in this moment that will make him—

He shifts his weight, closing the minuscule distance between them. She can't breathe. Can't...

"Most folks think hate is the opposite of love." She blurts the words, all the while cursing herself for halting his forward motion.

"It isn't?" His chuckle rumbles against her hand pressed against the buttons of his shirt.

When did she put her hand there?

And then his question registers. *What* isn't? Isn't what? What are they talking about?

Hate. Love. Oh! "The opposite of love is indifference." She cringes at the surprised gape of his mouth, his micro-shift away. Her body misses the press of his.

"This is what I like about you. You think about things. See beauty and pain and insights other people don't. You"—he lifts her hand from his ribs and kisses her blasted, boring knuckles—"are a treasure."

With that, Theodore Fabre turns and leads Noura under another archway, around a corner, and out onto the main thoroughfare.

While her body follows him, she is still stuck in the twisted alley. How she thrust Theo into indifference with her blathering mouth. She tries to convince herself she's better off knowing where she stands—her very essence equals affection, not love, not belonging. She fights to believe she is worthy and still hates herself for her inability to flex enough. To be enough to be loved, or at least not hated.

While it's true that indifference is the opposite of love, hate is still insidious. Not because hate is the opposite of love, but because it's the fruit of fear. You can't be afraid and still love. Love takes risks, and fear lashes out, then runs to protect itself. Fear is the real enemy. It strikes, then ducks down and hides.

And Noura is nothing if not an expert at slipping into the darkness.

9

At the entrance to the hotel, Ahmed opens the gilded door and waves Noura and Theo into the vaulted lobby. The click of her shoes on the tiles combines with the pounding of her skull to cover any sound Theo makes as he leads her to the stairwell.

Only when they reach the door to the stairwell does Theo retake Noura's hand, leaning over their entwined fingers to whisper in her ear. "Regardless of what you may think of yourself, I am neither indifferent to you nor afraid of whatever you've squirreled away. You, Noura, are the Ma'at the world needs. The steady, balancing truth to the chaos. Someday you'll stop running." He presses his minted lips to her palm and sweeps away like a master of ceremonies.

Noura gathers her palm into her chest, cradling it so she doesn't explode into a million tiny pieces. Theo sees through every bit of her, and she has no idea what to do.

THE MOMENT THEO turns the corner, his shoulders slump, letting his persona slip. He's made a mistake. In the past hour, he told Noura more about himself than he's revealed to anyone since before college, since before he had to find a way to pay for his sister's medicine.

He bursts outside, and once out of sight, he slides onto a bench and closes his eyes. He would like to think that showing Noura how he sees her is kind. But if she knew everything, she would despise him. In the tree above him, a falcon shifts, grumbling at him.

"Yeah. Yeah." He fists the silver pendant, feels it heat against his palm. "I know."

What did his mother always say? *If you love something, let it go.* In this situation, his mother would, no doubt, box Theo's ears. *That woman is too sweet for the likes of you.* And she would be right. No matter Theo's intentions, if Anubis were to weigh Theo's heart, the god of the afterlife wouldn't hesitate to feed Theo's dark heart to Ammit, the crocodile beast, devourer of the dead. After all, Theo may pretend to be the hero, but he is nothing he seems to be.

Theo sucks in enough air to deplete the world of oxygen and pushes himself from the bench. He still has work to do. He yanks off his tie and stomps out the door, intent on getting to the locker he keeps at the train station. Sykes wouldn't be caught dead in this getup.

UPSTAIRS, Noura has managed to force her wobbly knees to carry her up the three flights to her room. She stumbles through the door, closes it, then leans against the wood as she crumples to the floor. Saira always told Noura that someone would see through her hiding, and she should not, under any circumstances, let them go. Noura hasn't lost her family. She's let them all go. Too afraid to try. What will she do with Theo?

The thought rumbles in the distance, and she struggles to her feet, locking the door and her what-ifs in the hallway. Leaving her clothes strewn on the floor, Noura climbs into bed and feigns sleep, begging her mind to linger on Theo's sure leading on the dance floor, the snap of fiery mischief in his eyes, his lips on her hand.

Instead, her thoughts stray to the list she's tucked under her pillow, the symbol she's come to think of as a dog's head, and the questions it raises. Even the bizarre feathers.

Noura flops onto her side, trying to make herself believe it's nothing. That Estelle was as surprised to see her older sister as Noura was to see her. The problem is that in her memory, Estelle was surprised only one other time. Noura's breathing hitches at the memory of Estelle as a child, the flicker of fear tightening into a seizure, the moment before Noura swore to save her. And then, time and again, Noura failed.

Estelle didn't care that Noura begged Harry to leave the Sinai, that he refused her pleading over a phone line already crackling with the coming war. If Noura had stopped her sister from going to find their brother herself, would it have prevented their final split? But who can contain a raging fire?

Noura rolls away from the thought, then flips her pillow, trying to find sleep on the other side. Through a gap in the curtains, a sliver of light runs across the room, leaps onto her bed, and cradles itself in her palm. Noura closes her fist over the glow.

When the sisters were born, Maman gave them each a name meaning light, saying they would be the two points of light leading the unsettled diplomat's wife home.

In the end, Noura wasn't enough for Maman or the darkness. As if anyone could be enough under the unrelenting parade of war and anger. The Suez Crisis, the individual bombings—one terrifying, hostile act after another from all sides. At least the hurricanes of Maman's native Louisiana had some predictability and warning. Still, Noura had thought she and her sister would always be tethered. But then came the Six-Day War, and the final eclipsing stroke of the Yom Kippur War.

Estelle slipped between the seams of the world and disappeared, leaving Noura alone. Spilled Marquette blood coursed between Noura and her sister, deep and uncrossable as the River of Night.

So why did Noura choose to help the Egyptian government—the one institution not a single member of the Marquette family trusted?

She knows Egypt's motive for switching allegiances from the Soviet Union to the United States is a self-preserving result of their twice-defeat. And she has zero confidence in slippery men like Nixon and Kissinger. But doesn't understanding a civilization's culture make you less likely to fight against the people who live inside those cultural assumptions and constraints?

Noura has to believe the world can heal the fractures, that her hope isn't displaced, and that peace is findable. If Noura can learn enough, understand enough...

Shoving off the hopelessly tangled sheet, Noura slips out of bed and yanks the curtain closed. With the probing light excised, she sags onto the bed.

Her brain regathers the evidence and stitches it together. Solid and unassailable. With all she has learned and all the understanding she's gathered, peace is still out of reach.

Perhaps Noura is as foolish as a man who flees into the desert without water. Of course a Hebrew did that—fled from Pharaoh into the desert and found a home, then guided his people out of slavery.

He was a hero, at least for a while. Then the people turned on him. Noura can relate. No matter how she twists herself, she is no more than a means to an end. Common as mortar or the packed dirt underneath a traveler's feet. Something to be left behind.

So why has Estelle popped up again?

A musician plucks a guitar somewhere nearby. A woman's voice harmonizes, lifting in a haunting trill. A mourning wail, shrill and broken. Noura clutches the sheet tight against her throat as if the flimsy fabric will protect her from the dog-headed shadow spreading across her bed. But there's nothing in her room that would cast such a distinct shape.

Her arms prick with knowing. Set is in her room, staring at her, laughing, daring her to fight. Noura starts at the ridiculous idea and slams her hands beside her in a defiant show of relaxation. The patch of darkness is only a shadow of something outside her window. She doesn't believe the gods are real, but does she believe in such enormous coincidences? Despite the fact her heart is racing, she certainly doesn't believe the twist in her gut whispering that the god of chaos has crossed the River of Night, intent on the destruction of Ma'at, and not even Selket can save her.

10

July 28, 1976

The next morning dawns with a breeze lifting miraculously from the Nile and shouldering through the open window. Noura luxuriates in the mild air, thankful that the golden light of morning has yet to singe the cool tail of night. It portends a good day. As Saira often reminded the Marquette girls, attitude can make or break a day. And in the bright light of the day, Noura decides she will have a glorious career, her weird premonitions are flights of imagination, and she will figure out what is happening with both her sister and Theo.

Rolling over, Noura stretches like a cat and counts her blessings. First, the mild temperature. Second? Theo's quick thinking saved Noura's career from a premature demise. And finally, today, the team will send the artifacts to the airfield, as they've planned for weeks.

Then tomorrow, Noura can go shopping with Lizzy and Elizabeth. She lets her fingers drift over her cheek where Theo's stubble had sizzled her skin.

Yes. Tomorrow for sure.

She slips a linen dress over her frame, throws her dirty clothes in the hamper, and tucks the strange list into her pocket. She'll deposit it in the street where she found it. Chaos where chaos belongs.

Eschewing her normal drab scarf, Noura drapes her head in the blue- and red-shot silk scarf she threw in her suitcase at the last minute. When Saira gave the scarves to the sisters, she said the shifting red and blue made her think of the two. So different—one more red and the other more blue—yet so much the same and perfect together. Surely Saira's prediction carries weight, doesn't it? Someday the sisters will be together again.

Noura tilts her head at her reflection in the mirror, imagining Theo's appreciation of how the red sets off the deep brown of her eyes. Then, satisfied, she reaches for the bag she always leaves on the vanity. Except the bag isn't there. Gone...along with Noura's museum keys, her passport, her money.

Clutching her positive attitude in a vice grip, Noura turns a slow circle, searching, thinking. The souk, the dancing, walking with Theo... Oh!

Theo carried her satchel home last night. Problem solved. Crisis averted. Career back on track.

Noura skips to the lobby like the naïve fool she is and joins the mass in the dining room for breakfast. She nods at Lizzy and Elizabeth, but Theo isn't there.

No worries, she tells herself. He went to the museum to check on Ghadfa, on the last of the crates, on the last dwindling details. As Noura maintains a veneer of polite chatter, her mind gnaws at the excuses, exposing the rotten levee walls underneath. Why did Theo take her bag?

But then he is there, in the restaurant, dropping into the seat next to Noura, his face ashen. "The Egyptians are refusing to put the artifacts on a plane."

The storm breaks, drenching Noura in panic. "What?" Her voice is pitched low, as if she can contain the swirling whirlpool by not alerting anyone else.

"Lilyquist and Hoving are working on it. But it's worse. Ghadfa is missing."

"Missing?" Noura's anxiety bursts through her hastily built dam.

"He didn't show up last night. His apartment was wiped clean."

Noura thinks of the suspicious dust-free circle, the broken skylight, the skitters of footsteps in the dark, the list still crinkling in her pocket. "The artifacts were returned, right? Why would he quit?"

Theo shrugs—not a dismissal, more of an admission. Of fear? Confusion? Even as Noura scrambles to decode the twist of his mouth, she recognizes the flicker of his eyes. Evasion.

"There was a note at the museum thanking me for the job and saying he was moving." Theo's face smooths even as his forefinger rubs over his broken thumbnail. "He knew everyone was searching for the thief and could have returned the artifacts before being caught."

"Do you think he stole the artifacts?" Noura's pitch skyrockets, her vocal cords closing against the torrent.

"I don't know if it was him or—"

Dr. Lilyquist pushes into the lobby restaurant—spine straight, hawk nose held high—next to Mr. Hoving, whose jovial smile has gone the way of King Tut himself.

"We are working on alternatives"—Mr. Hoving's voice cuts across the background chatter—"but we can no longer ship the artifacts via airplane. Thanks to Theo's connections, we are looking at cargo ships. Dr. Marquette, please work up a plan with Theo to make the necessary changes to the containers and details."

"Yes, sir." Noura is pleased her voice does not betray the fear churning under the surface. Noura's memories of New Orleans are soft at the edges—blurred like an old photo—except for the vibration of jazz in her chest, the buttery taste of pralines...and the strangely sweet smell of a coming hurricane. The sharp tang of lightning and howling wind gathering to drive the ocean through the marshes and up over land, crushing every living thing under the waves.

And that smell. It's here. Now. In the desert.

Run. A cackling voice screams in her head. *Run!*

"Don't worry." Theo leans in so only she can hear his low voice. "We have it under control. Neither the Egyptian nor American governments will let the tour blow up."

Noura sucks in so much oxygen, her lungs might burst, and then she releases the breath. He's right. She doesn't believe in signs, right? Then it is high time she acts like it.

"We'll get to the museum and make a new plan." Theo spreads his arms out in a *ta-da* motion. "Even better, Farid agreed to watch overnight until the museum hires another guard. See, Horus likes you, Ma'at. He's swooping in to set order to the chaos."

"Of course," Noura agrees, as if it's that simple to rewrite the tempest her family has written for her. But she and Theo have work to do. "Thank you again for walking me home last night. I will need my bag though."

Theo's brows dip. "I gave it to you before I left."

Noura mirrors his expression, unsure of herself and her memory.

"Shall I help you search?" He stands and gestures toward the stairwell.

Noura doesn't think she nods, but she must have since he is at her side as she retraces her steps to the third floor, down the hall, and through her door, where she vaguely hovers, distantly grateful she'd made her bed and picked up her discarded clothing. Theo pokes around the side of the dressing table, then leans down to search under the bed.

"Eureka!" Theo leaps from the floor, holding her brown leather satchel.

Noura takes the bag, dumbfounded. It wasn't there earlier, was it? "I—"

"You're welcome." Theo's voice is bright and innocent as he gives a comic bow.

"Thank you." Her words stumble, awkward, jumbled. "I'll wash up and then be down."

"Of course." Theo winks at her, then strides from the room. He is blissfully unconcerned. Isn't he? Or does he know something is coming, and he's given her the signal to duck?

No positive thinking can overcome the pounding signs of fate nipping Noura's heels—her missing bag with passport and keys to the museum miraculously reappearing, a vanished night guard, a wish list of priceless artifacts, and a complete change in shipping plans.

The Egyptian gods aren't real, she reminds herself. Estelle is not Set.

And neither is Noura Horus or Ma'at. No matter what anyone else thinks.

Dutifully, Noura dumps her bag onto the bed and rifles through its contents. There's nothing awry amidst the pens and notebook, the keys and powder. Even the two feathers are still there. She taps the striping. She closes her eyes, rifling through her memory, her studies. A falcon's feather. Horus. And the ostrich feather. Ma'at.

She opens her eyes. Underneath the feather, the strange mark on the list sharpens into clarity. A "T" and the curved forked tail forming a "Y." Typhon...Set.

The smell of a storm wafts from the strewn bits and bobs. Something, someone, hovers just beyond her reach. With shaking hands, she shoves the paraphernalia back into her cavernous bag, slings it over her shoulder, and exits her room, locking it behind her.

In the lobby, Noura is the first American down, and she bounces on her toes, hyper-alert. Lizzy and Elizabeth wave from the restaurant, but she's too unnerved to be polite. There's no way she can go shopping anytime soon. Noura wheels around with purpose and runs ramshackle into the unyielding solidity of a man.

Apologizing, Noura stumbles back, catching a glimpse of his covered face and strange red mark at the edge of his collarbone before he strikes out and latches onto her elbow. "You are meddling in things you know nothing about. You've already sealed the fate of the guard. Do not be so foolhardy as to continue inserting yourself where you do not belong." He yanks her closer and taps her bag. "We can find you wherever you are. The gods are watching." The message is obvious. If they can get to her bag, they can get to her.

Noura bobs her head, a terrified little girl, face averted, obedient, subservient, everything she was taught to be. He shoves a slip of paper into her hands and swings away. When the front door clangs shut, Noura snaps from the past.

She's not a little girl alone in the streets of Tel Aviv. She's a woman in the lobby of a hotel that caters to foreigners. Security is everywhere. Teeth gritted, Noura glares at the paper in her hand. Red slashes upon it form the same symbol as was on the list. Noura tamps down the squall as she plunges toward the exit.

"Did you see a man leave?" She accosts the doorman.

Ahmed steps back, bowing, uncertain.

"He's about this tall." Noura holds her hand above her head. "Has on a black suit." She closes her eyes, fumbling to describe him in a way that distinguishes him in the crowd. He smelled of tea. From the strength of his grip, he was strong but restrained. "He sounded..." Noura scrambles to place the accent. Her eyes snap open, unsure of the soft, elongated vowels. "British?" But not quite.

As Noura opens her mouth to backtrack, she sees a man down the street equal to what she described.

He dodges a bicycle and darts into the alleyway. She half expects to see a forked tail, but she tells herself she's imagining things and clatters down the steps and across the street, hesitating a moment before plunging into the shadows. Around a corner, down a lane, through an alley, bursting out, where she pauses, sucking in searing air. A woman peeks from her loom, her fingers never stilling over the shuttlecock as she estimates Noura's sanity. Noura catches sight of a dark figure and gives chase, weaving through the streets, ignoring cries of consternation. She banks onto another narrow street and stumbles to a stop. A man loiters in the doorway to her right. His hand idles on the leather strap where he was sharpening a knife. His surprise turns into a leer, and Noura staggers backward. While most of Cairo is safe, she doesn't know where she is, and she's outside the normal bounds for foreigners.

The man strides from the arch, gesturing for her not to be afraid, even while he licks his lips. He's close enough that Noura doesn't dare to turn her back. Retreating, she presses a hand on the cool stone wall, searching for any impediments behind her.

She is approaching the freedom of a more populated street when Theo rounds the corner in front of her, whistling. Noura jolts. The knife sharpener gives a shout of victory and snatches her wrist. But the noise alerts Theo, and he glances from the book in his hand. He slams the book shut and launches into sharp Arabic.

The man drops Noura's arm as if she carries the plague, and Theo shoulders past him, wrapping his arm around her waist and forcing her numb legs into motion.

"What were you thinking?" He is speaking through clenched teeth, barely loud enough for Noura to hear. "If I hadn't come along..."

He doesn't need to finish for her to know.

"Someone threatened me."

He glares at Noura from the corner of his eye like she left her sanity behind.

"Not him. There was a man in the hotel. He gave me this." She shoves the slip of paper at him, the Typhonian symbol bleeding at the bottom.

Theo stops cold. "In the hotel?" He swivels around to face Noura, studying her, no doubt appraising for further signs of mental instability. But when he lifts Noura's arms and scrutinizes her cheeks, her neck, she realizes he's checking for injuries. When there are none, Theo glares beyond her.

"Who?" Theo's surveilling the street now, parsing out where the enemy is lurking.

"I—"

Without warning, he slides Noura behind him like one of the Marines or consulate guards.

"What?" Noura peers around him like an eyas hiding behind her falcon parent.

Just inside the threshold of the fabric shop, a woman waits. A black scarf tames most of her dark hair, but it is her eyes that hold Noura's attention. Noura knows what they look like, even if the other woman's face is partially hidden. They are hazel. Green with specks of gold that spark when she's angry. And in case Noura's not sure, in her flame-scarred right hand, she lifts a blue and red shot headscarf—the reverse twin to the one Noura wears on her own head.

Help. The woman mouths over her shoulder like she's the one who's been threatened.

"Estelle."

Noura's cracking voice catches Theo's attention, and he shifts, preventing her from diving through the streets. "We need to get to the museum."

"But—"

"It isn't safe."

Noura is numbed by the threat in his voice...the one that sounds so like the man from the hotel. A different accent, maybe, but the same barking tenor. Noura clutches Theo's bare arms, her fingertips going white.

Father's voice echoes in her head. *Don't create stories and nightmares where there aren't any.*

Shirt sleeves. Theo's in a striped bowling shirt and linen trousers. Not a black suit. And there's no mark on his collarbone. Noura forces herself to relax. He hadn't had time to change. Theo isn't threatening her. He's protecting her. Noura begins to tell him about her sister, to ask him to accompany her. But when Noura points to the fabric store, Estelle is gone, evaporated like a genie's smoke.

Undeterred, Noura drags Theo to the stall. She would think she'd imagined her sister, but there, tied to a rickety metal pole, is Estelle's headscarf.

Theo frowns as Noura unties it.

"This is hers. See?" Noura presses it against her own scarf. The blue silk is shot with shimmers of red, whereas Noura's is red shot with blue. At the ends of each are tiny stitched initials. NEM on one. EAM on the other. "Noura Elana Marquette. Estelle Anne Marquette. It's my sister. Our nanny...my sister-in-law bought us scarves that were mirror images of each other. Said they reminded her of us—fire and water. When Father objected to such bright colors, she replied that the scarves made it easier to track us both in the market. She said we could always use them to find each other too."

Twisting the knob of fabric between her fingers, Noura ducks into the stall. When Noura pushes on the bolted back door, the proprietor shouts, hand on his knife, red-faced in anger.

"No offense, sir." Theo eases her from the shop.

"She was here." Noura hates the break in her voice. The desperation.

"She looks sick, Theo."

The pity in his sigh makes her turn away.

"She knows where you are, right?" he says as he leads her to a main street.

"Yes, but Estelle won't ask for help unless it's really, really bad."

"You can't help if she isn't here."

He's right, and yet, she can't leave.

"Did I ever tell you how I got into art?" Theo's light voice stands in stark contrast to the tightness in his shoulders.

Noura shakes her head, glancing behind them once before refocusing on the man strolling beside her.

"Mom loved art," he says. "She dragged me and my sisters to every art museum she could afford, which means we practically lived at the Detroit Institute of Arts. Her favorite was the Egyptian collection. She told me all the myths. Told me I was Set and Horus all rolled into one. Told me to listen to Horus." With a wry smile, he lifts a silver feather pendant from under his shirt. "I loved her to the core. So I did what any self-respecting mama's boy does: I made myself an expert in what made my mama happy."

Noura's grateful for his purposeful distraction and turns her thoughts from her lost sister. "I can't see you as a mama's boy."

Theo pulls his shoulders back and brushes imaginary lint from his pressed shirt. "Why not?"

She points to the obvious break in his nose.

"That?" Theo laughs. "We had a debate in my senior year government class. One of the entitled football players was sure the world bowed to him and his daddy's money. I disagreed and verbally wiped the floor with him."

"All done with a smile, no doubt."

"Absolutely." Theo flashes his characteristic get-out-of-trouble grin. "After class, he came after me, pretty sure he could beat the snot out of me. He didn't expect this cheeky kid to have a right uppercut that could level a dump truck. Poor guy never had a chance. But he got in one good hit."

Noura imagines a high-school-age Theo—all ungainly limbs and half-studious antics. "So you were a goof off?"

"Yes and no. I hated school. Everyone assumed those of us with blue-collar dads would be blue-collar too. They had my life mapped out for me, and who was I to object? I had no use for math or Mr. Kracowski's beefy gym class. I ducked through high school and spent the next summer in the factory. After two days, I decided not to follow in my father's footsteps. I went to junior college, where my natural charm helped me weasel my way into jobs to pay the bills. I aced the classes though."

"That I can imagine. A grin, a bit of witty repartee, a joke with an edge of light sarcasm. Definitely Set."

"You would have hated me then."

He's right. Noura was intense at the same age. Trying to get through while never upsetting the balance. She hated that everyone wanted something from her, and yet no one cared enough to want her as she was. No, Noura hadn't much liked anyone...including herself.

"Thing is," Theo says. "I got in more trouble for picking fights with the bullies than I ever did for anything else. It's a skill that translated well into—"

Theo stops at the intersection and shakes his head like he's stripping himself of whatever happened in the past. "I bet you never so much as put a toe out of line." He grins at Noura, but the humor evades his eyes.

What has him backpedaling? Noura wads the scarf in her fingers and hears the crackle of paper. Frowning, she untangles a knot in the middle and eases out a page littered in the equivalent of undeciphered hieroglyphics—all random numbers and letters.

"What's that?" Theo's shadow spreads over her, and she fights the urge to tuck her sister's note away.

Noura flattens the message in her palm. Though she recognizes the jumble—Estelle's childhood secret code—Noura lifts a shoulder in feigned ignorance. She saw the expression of distrust her sister gave Theo both times Estelle spotted him. And if Estelle's writing in code, there's a reason she doesn't want anyone to know what she has to say... including, or maybe specifically, Theodore Fabre.

11

Estelle slips undetected through the iron fence and trots to the far side of the alley, where she'll catch a bus south into Old Cairo.

In the last few weeks, she's spotted two men following her. The clunky one, one of Typhon's men. But the other? Estelle caught him by chance, the flash of a silver chain around his neck betraying him in a reflection in a window. He's no lackey. Quiet, careful. Professional. Which means the growing threats are not empty.

Slipping into a throng of people, Estelle takes inventory around her. No one emerges from the alley, but that doesn't mean he, or someone else, isn't there.

She doesn't think Typhon would outright kill her. But he wouldn't hesitate to sell her whereabouts to others who would be delighted to make her pay for rescuing children from their oily grasp. Or even to one of the private citizens scattered across the world who have found themselves one painting or jeweled crown short. And Mehedi? While Typhon hasn't threatened him directly, the "or else" hovers in the air.

Estelle needs to get home and set this fiasco to rights. And soon. Not to mention that the Cairo mission desperately needs funds. It's expensive to care for orphans and create enough noise to wake a sleeping population to their own greed. Which reminds Estelle that the girls will need food, and she has no money. She leans forward, letting her scarf drape across her profile. The sheer fabric gives her a view of the street without alerting any potential marks that they're being watched.

Across the street, a man in an expensive European suit strides between cars as if he commands the world. As he steps onto the curb, Estelle shifts so he brushes against her. In perfectly timed choreography, she reaches into his bulging pocket and transfers the wallet to the inside pouch of her tunic even as she continues shuffling toward the bus stop. The man strides away, oblivious to his lighter weight.

If only stealing the Tut artifacts were so easy. Which brings Estelle back to her sister. Estelle's plan assumes Noura can translate her message. There's a sliver of her childish self that's convinced her big sister won't abandon her. Not again. But the sting of rejection lingers.

If Estelle can't convince her sister, she'll have no choice but to steal as much as she can and pray it will be enough to bribe and beg her way into a passport and plane ticket.

With the wily conservator and the tail watching Noura's every move, Estelle might have no choice. She doesn't know who he works for, but he isn't a conservator as he claims. The wariness in his monitoring gaze and the square of his shoulders has her "near to passing out" as Maman would say.

Estelle trots across the street, smiling at a group of uniformed schoolgirls as she dodges past. She wishes every child had the same opportunities. Unfortunately, even the best political movements are subject to selfishness.

The shadows in the window of the tea shop shift. Not right. Her hand closes around the knife concealed in the folds of her robe-like *gallibaya*.

The bus chugs to a stop, and she clambers on board, settling next to a woman holding a cage stuffed with chickens. Across the way, a tiny girl blinks up at her, and Estelle relaxes the planes of her face. *"Salamo alaikum,"* she greets the girl, granting her the traditional wish for peace to be upon her.

If only Estelle were powerful enough to distribute peace.

A familiar man emerges from the shadows and scowls at the bus as it emits a huge plume of exhaust and grinds away. Yet another problem needing to be dealt with. She lifts her fingers in a rebellious wave and watches him disappear...for now.

THEO ISN'T QUITE sure what has him more concerned—the man in the hotel, the grocery list of artifacts, the coded note, or the feathers in Noura's bag. He may be hazy with exhaustion, but he recognizes the danger and the opportunity. Are the events connected? Was the hotel warning truly for Noura, or was it meant for him? But most importantly, does he need to bolt? Does she? The falcon feather should soothe him —a reminder of his mom, her calm, the order she brought to everything, her belief that he was called to do the same—but it doesn't.

It feels like a warning. *I know what you did.* His fingers find the frigid medallion around his neck.

Who else knows he leaves a falcon's feather to request a meeting? And why would they give it to Noura here and now?

The answers may very well be in her sister's coded message smashed in Noura's palm. He should have waited until tonight to lift her bag. Then he'd have both notes. Alas, it would be too suspicious for him to find it two days in a row. He'd nothing to do with the threat, of course, but someone knew the bag was missing and used the fact it was missing to threaten her. But the fact they even knew it was missing means someone may be watching him too. And to further complicate matters, it's obvious Noura's humanitarian sister doesn't trust him.

Since their brother was not exactly a model US citizen, it's not unreasonable to think Noura's sister is trained to be more than she appears...or maybe Noura is. He didn't get a good enough look at the sister to know if she was the woman he saw leaving the museum. Would Noura look the other way while her sister stole from the museum? Theo can't see his Ma'at allowing anything of the sort. And with the handwriting on the cipher being decidedly different from the list, the sister isn't Typhon. So why the cloak-and-dagger code?

Unfortunately, the woman he leads to the nearest taxi is in no shape to help. Pale. Jumpy. Shocked silent. Every muscle in her body straining to contain the shake. Unnervingly similar to the Vietnam vets he's met on the streets.

The taxi squeals around a corner, horn blaring. Theo braces himself, watching as Noura clutches the window frame, then stuffs the note into her bag. Somehow he'll have to figure out what is on that note and who's requesting a meeting. His life could depend on it.

NOURA DOESN'T REMEMBER WALKING into the museum. But when she regains awareness, she's in the dim sunlight and the tick of the cooling lights in the museum's back room.

Theo deposits her at her desk while he putters around the worktables, muttering with John. With little to do until they find a new way to transport the artifacts, most of the team is off scouring the souks for interesting souvenirs to bring home. Noura can't bring herself to stand, let alone puzzle out how or if she should find the team.

Her sister is on the streets by herself, in trouble. Knowing Estelle, she's living amongst the poor and doing what she can to help. So like Harry.

If we're supposed to be here helping relations between our countries, shouldn't we be helping people? was Estelle's perennial argument.

She isn't wrong. Noura hates when people step around the ragged. But what else is everyone supposed to do? Robin Hood is a hero in storybooks, but his "steal from the rich to give to the poor" mentality is what communists tried and failed to execute.

Noura smooths her hands over her sister's scarf.

Of course Noura often snuck food to the women on the corner or blankets on chilly nights. But that was never enough for Estelle. She'd enlisted Saira's help to organize fundraisers and collections. Maybe that's how the two women became so close.

When she first came, Saira was maybe fifteen. Not much older than Noura. But Noura didn't know how to breach the other girl's fragile quiet. Not that Noura blamed her. When the Israeli government declared Saira's family's land as state-owned property, her desperate parents sent her from the Sinai Peninsula to Tel Aviv in hopes that the young woman would find work. Fortunately Noura found Saira sweeping the halls of the medical clinic where Estelle was receiving yet another checkup and demanded her father bring her home.

Estelle, oblivious to the politics, chattered at the shrinking young woman or complimented Saira's long dark braids or roped her into whatever game Estelle devised.

Noura removes her scarf, carefully folds hers together with her sister's, and then smooths her hand over top. All three women were bound together. But as sure as the tide rises and falls, Noura was edged out. No longer needed to fill the holes Maman left behind. Little bits and pieces of the sisters' relationship washed away, the current eating away the entire bank of their lives, letting the water spread, coagulating until the ground became a marshy mess that seems to have trapped Estelle.

And with Saira gone, Noura will have to step into a sopping morass to save Estelle. Unfortunately, the only way to fix a bog is to wedge rocks along the edge to corral the river. The rocks get mighty banged up in the process, but Noura's made of strong stuff.

Noura spreads the hen-scratched paper on top of her desk, then grabs a pencil and pad of paper. The simple substitution cipher isn't complicated. Just something two bored kids used to inform one another where the cookies were hidden or that Harry was being a jerk.

Historically, they wrote a monthly ciphertext alphabet, which served to tell them which letters replaced the plaintext alphabet. They stashed the cipher in the roots of the tree Harry had named the St. Louis Cathedral after their grandmother's favorite building in the world. But Noura has no key.

She taps the pencil to her lips. Noura flips over the page, and there it is. Twenty-six tiny letters flipped upside down. Noura scribbles the key at the top of her page.

"Figure it out?" Theo asks from the other side of the room.

Ignoring him, Noura decodes the message. And then frowns at the absolute nonsense, flips the paper, then frowns again. She chucks her pencil, sending it skittering across the desk and ricocheting onto the floor.

Why does Noura even try? Why not a simple phone call? Why does Estelle insist on toying with her?

Noura drops her cheek to the desk, staring sidelong at the offensive page. That's when Noura sees the tiny dot above the third letter. Estelle's added a skip. Noura snatches the pencil and acts the dutiful scribe, taking down every third letter.

When she's done, there's the word Mehedi and perhaps the name Mark. But the rest is gibberish.

THE TIGHT LINES of Noura's shoulders tug Theo toward her desk. He hovers in the archway, pulse thundering as if Typhon has never threatened his life before. But this time, Noura is in the man's sights too, and Theo is beginning to think Typhon is more than just a single man. His mother would cross herself and say the devil was at work. Then tell him to keep his pendant close—an odd conflation of Catholicism and Egyptian myth. Theo isn't sure exactly what supernatural forces are out there, but ever since he arrived in Cairo, he's heard whispers like the city is one of Mom's thin places. And he can't deny the connection he has with Noura—her Ma'at to his Horus. He needs her and she him. If he's going to make headway, he has to get a look at her notes, and so he slides by, asking if she needs anything.

She waves him off, arm over her paper like she's preventing him from cheating on a test. For sure, he's failing right now, and he slinks to his table to reform his crumbling plans. He's far too proud and cunning to let everything tangle into a mess.

Picking up the phone, he dials a familiar number. Mr. Hoving has tasked him with finding another way to transport the artifacts, and he will. But he has another call to make first. He needs a different passport and an exit plan. His various bosses won't be happy, but he may not have a choice. He's played too many sides too many times and has learned too much to be caught in anyone's full frontal assault. As the phone chatters in connection to the operator, he turns from John and watches the woman in the other room. His one regret will be leaving Noura in danger…if she is who she says she is.

. . .

Noura squints at the page. What is she missing?

After Noura left for college, every communication she had with her sister was laced with a bewildering maze of frustrations. But Noura kept at it until Harry traveled to Tel Aviv, intent on opening a clinic with his newly minted medical degree.

Like moths, Saira and Estelle drifted toward his zealous fire, and he swept them along with him. Father temporarily subverted Estelle's involvement by sending the youngest Marquette to America for school. But Harry, an adult and able to make his own choices, stayed, married Saira, and used her contacts to open his clinic barely inside Israel's border.

Estelle swore that when she graduated, she'd join them. Estelle always had more courage than Noura, and she's always been better at languages than her sister too. She could travel and actually help because she—

Noura sits up. *Languages.* Estelle was a whiz with languages. Noura squints at the words, willing them to take the form of a transliteration of Hebrew or, failing that, Arabic.

She pinches the bridge of her nose and stifles a scream. Still nothing.

Across the shadowed room, Theo mutters into a phone, occasionally glancing over his shoulder.

Behind Noura, Theo scribbles on a sheet of paper as he crafts a request to the US Navy. Theo knows the names and ranks of the men, as well as their personalities. It's a strange knowledge set for a middle-class boy from nowhere.

Noura swallows against the unbidden thought that maybe Theo isn't what he seems. It's a wild idea, fueled Estelle's penchant for conspiracy theories.

Squinting at the page, Noura wills herself to conjure meaning. What other language or code would Estelle use?

In Tel Aviv, the sisters learned English, Arabic, Latin, and Hebrew. And after that, Noura has no idea where her sister went. She probably studied some language in college, but Estelle couldn't count on Noura knowing whatever that was. But then Estelle always made assumptions about what Noura did and didn't know. Three years ago, Estelle left her sister shocked out of words when she spouted a string of Arabic, English, Creole, and Latin curses because Noura had let Saira take her unborn child into the afterlife without making one more attempt to get her out.

Noura hadn't even known Saira was pregnant.

All three of her siblings disappeared as easily as an entire dynasty is forgotten a millennium in the future.

Wait.

Noura rewinds the memory.

Creole curses?

Estelle definitely used Creole. Would've probably thrown a black chicken at Noura too, if she had one.

Noura bends over the page, and there, in black and white: Louisiana Creole. The main lights flicker and blink out. Theo curses and lights a candle to check all the electrical connections.

Squinting now, Noura parses out the words, rusty with disuse: *Pa di mesye a*, which loosely translates to *Don't tell the man*. Then *I'm at St. Mark's Church. Mehedi needs help. I need help*. St. Mark's? There are a million St. Mark churches in Cairo.

Flipping over her page, Noura translates the end: *Pa Kite moon Joe Ak figi' w*. Literally, *don't let people play with your face*. Noura snorts. Estelle is telling her sister not to let anyone manipulate her. Oh, the irony of Estelle warning against someone else's manipulation. Still, Noura can't ignore her...especially if Mehedi needs help. When Estelle warned of a war before, two days later, Egypt and Jordan attacked Israel and started the Yom Kippur War. She should at least check on Mehedi.

Half the lights flicker to life, and Theo grumbles before picking up the phone again. At the name Hermann Eilts, Noura stiffens. He's the US Ambassador to Egypt. But John is still bumbling about in the room. He will raise the red flag if Theo's doing something underhanded. So Noura scuttles from the room, down the hall, and into the Egyptian curator's office.

Noura gives the operator her graduate professor's number and waits while the line connects.

"Noura?" Surprise echoes down the line, and Noura barely contains her agitation as they drag through small talk. "Everyone is fine." And "I can't wait to see the tour." And all the mundanities that Noura has learned and still hates until she can casually ask to speak to Mehedi.

"Oh, he's not here." The line cracks off the end of Prof. Anderson's voice, but it comes roaring back, "...with friends somewhere."

"Do you know when he'll be back?"

"No. Is it important?"

Noura taps a finger on the desk. "Just thinking about him."

"He's fine. More broody than usual, but exams are coming. He's close to landing a job."

Noura frowns. Maybe Mehedi's trouble is simply the ticking clock of upgrading his student visa to a green card. She thanks Prof. Anderson and hangs up. Perhaps it's worth talking to Estelle...if Noura can figure out which St. Mark's her sister means.

Noura stretches tall. What kind of historian would she be if she can't research where her sister is?

Noura dials the operator and asks for the US Embassy. A second operator answers, and Noura asks for information about a St. Mark's, where foreigners might help the local population.

The operator is unimpressed, noting that most foreigners are oblivious to the local situation and, as a result, are more hindrance than help. He's more than right, but when she presses, the gentleman gives Noura the name of a Coptic church that supplies soup and bread to street beggars. It's in Old Cairo and sounds like a place Estelle would hole up. Noura jots down the information. He asks if she wishes to be connected, but she demurs and hangs up.

However, Noura isn't foolish enough to ignore the mystery man's threat and traipse off alone. But neither is she willing to ignore her sister's plea nor Ghadfa's disappearance. Knowing whoever is involved has power in Cairo, Noura must stretch further afield for assistance. Somewhere Egyptian power doesn't reach.

Noura strides from the room with a determined grin on her face.

She knows two British women married to wealthy businessmen who've begged her to give them a tour. Armed with the address of the Coptic church and a starting place, Noura will execute the first part of her plan—enlisting the protection of the two rather innocent Brits. May God forgive her for using them as human shields.

12

July 30, 1976

It takes Noura forty-eight hours and the lure of the best street food (a garlicky tomato *koshari*), shopping (Noura as the mannequin), and a bit of sightseeing (tour guide included) to convince Elizabeth and Lizzy to accompany her to the church. She's promised them "a real glimpse of Cairo" before taking them the short distance to the Great Pyramids. Because she is who she is, Noura has everything planned. She's hired Farid for his transportation as well as his wisdom and protection. As far as Noura can tell, there isn't a flaw in her strategy.

At the crack of dawn, the two Elizabeths and Noura eat a breakfast of cold boiled eggs, and the British duo tease her for her preference for British tea over American coffee. The moment they step into the lobby, Farid appears as scheduled. He gestures toward the street, grinning from under a thick mustache. He's procured a larger tuk-tuk for them. It's a dinged motorcycle affair rigged to a covered cart that may have been painted green at some point but now leans toward full-on rust.

"Is it safe?" Lizzy's query bursts from behind her hand.

"He works for the British ambassador." Noura opens her eyes wide in the universal don't-be-rude signal before turning to Farid, who is staring anywhere other than at the bare knees poking out from below the Elizabeths' micro miniskirts. Back home, there's nothing unusual about a dress made of approximately three square inches of wild fabric, and most of Cairo is remarkably Western, but in the backwaters, the outfits may border on riot-inducing.

"*Mamnouna Leek.*" Noura nods in thanks, hoping to cover any offense.

Elizabeth curtsies like they're in some aristocratic ballroom, blushing crimson and tugging at her friend as she whispers an acerbic "Lizzy." At least one of them has common sense.

By the time Noura helps the two women into the cart, little room remains for Noura on the opposing side. Farid gives her a commiserating shrug and grants her privacy as she clambers over the other women with a great bumping of bare knees and fumbling of feet.

"There." Noura plops into the seat and rearranges her skirt to cover her ankles. Her clothing may be dull librarian, but there's a reason a white cotton shirt and no-nonsense linen skirt have long been the uniform of choice for Western women in the Middle East. It's cool, non-offensive, easy to work in, and has the added benefit of allowing one to climb over one's companions without exposing one's underthings. Perfectly practical. Noura raises her chin as Farid cranks over the roaring engine and darts into traffic.

UNSEEN BY THE trio of women, Theo steps from the shadows of the portico and frowns at the tuk-tuk leaving the protection of the hotel. Noura figured something out yesterday. But when he asked, she shut down, face impressively blank. "My sister likes to play games. She probably needs more insulin. You know how that goes."

And he does. It's why he's here. It's why he holds multiple passports and can't afford to traipse after the Monet of a woman who's clueless about what she's stepped into. Instead, he'll call to have the tuk-tuk followed and then head to the museum to call in favors for that job and then finally go back to tracking Star and Typhon under everyone else's nose. His to-do list will keep him awake well past dark again. The voice in his head tells him he needs those contacts. That he doesn't have time to play nice. That fighting injustice is sometimes messy. But then there is the memory of his mother telling him stories of Horus and Ma'at. Horus, the god of war, bowing to the steady wisdom of Ma'at.

He stuffs his hands in his pockets and slumps into the hotel restaurant, where he forces himself to eat a depressingly perfect breakfast, which will do nothing to stop him from thinking about Noura, even if he can do nothing to save her.

IN THE TUK-TUK miles down the road, Farid proves to be a boon as he putters south toward their destination. He points out the square towers of Prince Mohamed Ali Palace, the entrance to Al Sayeda Zainab (a market Noura promises to bring them to), and the arches of the ancient Magra El Oyoun aqueduct. Judging from the cheerful prattle and hyperactive pointing, the friends are suitably impressed with the minarets and crowds. Noura blows out a frustrated breath over their exclamations about finding the "real oriental Cairo." The concept is offensive on so many levels. Many Westerners want the city to be what they imagine, not the actual place, which is heavily influenced by Ottoman, French, and British architecture. The onion domes, while beautiful, are remnants of a time when a succession of cruel outsiders ruled Egypt. Not to mention that cultures across Asia are vastly different, and lumping them together under one ubiquitous term smacks of colonial ignorance.

Noura nods at a young woman striding between the masses. An immense bundle perches on her head, and she lifts her chin in recognition before disappearing into the throng—there one moment and gone the next. Quite like Noura's sister.

Estelle has hidden for a decade. Why appear now? Were Noura's arrival, the list, and the odd misplacement of the artifacts merely coincidences? And why drag Mehedi into whatever is happening? Noura is his emergency contact. She's the one who arranged housing with friends and the student visa, along with the schooling he wanted. If Mehedi is in trouble, the Andersons would know, wouldn't they? But why would Estelle lie?

Unfortunately, Noura has spent her life wedged between school and appeasing her always off-kilter parents, while Estelle did whatever she pleased. Which means that, unlike her siblings, Noura is not skilled at either hiding or seeking. Noura leans her head against the cracked plastic seat.

What are you up to, Estelle?

"Where are the pyramids?" Lizzy asks, yanking Noura's consciousness back into the tuk-tuk.

Lizzy peers out the window as if the behemoth structures might sprout from the heart of the crowded city. Of course they rather do, but not near here.

"They're southwest, in Giza," Noura shouts over the strained chugging of the motor as they zig and zag through streets so narrow she could almost reach out and touch both sides at once.

Farid loops another corner, ducks through an opening Noura didn't realize was there, and then brakes in front of a crumbling brick building with crooked plywood covering the window and paint splattered everywhere. The motorcycle gives a moaning snort and then is silent.

"We are here," Farid says.

"And where"—Lizzy turns to Noura in wide-eyed concern—"is here?"

"It's a church." Elizabeth's words are answer and question in one.

Noura squints at the sign, which does, indeed, declare the edifice a Copt church. She hauls herself out of the conveyance and squints at the dubious graffiti slathered next to the church's sign. Above her, a white falcon drops to the roof and eyes the humans below. He shifts, fluffing his lightly striped feathers and chattering at her as if to warn her. There can't be more than a handful of enormous white peregrines in the entire world, can there? Is he following her somehow? She knows very little about falcons outside of their ties to Egyptian mythology. She raises a hand to shade her eyes, and he bobs his head in seeming affirmation as if to say, "Yes, I am talking to you. Beware." Then, message delivered, he lifts his wings, leaping and spinning away. She could use a bit of Horus's insight. Some Ma'at she is. She can't even weigh her own sister's heart.

At least there doesn't seem to be any immediate danger. Perhaps her roiling gut is simply a reminder that the Copts have been persecuted in Egypt for centuries. But Anwar Sadat, the current Egyptian president, named a Copt as his foreign secretary. Noura assumed things had gotten better for them. Perhaps not.

"What does it say?" Elizabeth points at the graffiti. The older woman's earlier tension has slid off, leaving behind a soft kindness, Noura thinks. What does she know of persecution?

"I don't know." Noura's vision flickers. "Academics don't often learn slang."

"You do not wish to know," Farid says. "You will be safe for now, but do not linger."

Lizzy snatches Noura's arm, the tight lines of her face screaming the same thought flitting through Noura's own mind: Is it too late to run?

"Well." Elizabeth taps her thumb against her thigh. "We did ask for the real Egypt. Come along then." She takes hold of Noura's elbow on one side and Lizzy's on the other, and they tramp to the door like teens headed to the first day of school—fear and anticipation twisting together in an indecipherable marsh of emotion.

Noura knocks on the door, firm but hopefully not threatening. They wait a few minutes, and she glances at Farid to confirm they're in the right place. He nods, but unfolds his arms, ready for action.

Noura lifts her fist to knock again when the door jerks before her knuckles bang against the wood. A woman, young, perhaps in her twenties, opens the door. A fairy dust of freckles sprinkles her olive complexion.

"Hello," Noura starts in English and then stumbles, switching to stilted Arabic like she's learned the language moments before. "My name is—"

"I know who you are," the young woman says in perfect English and then opens the door wider. "Please, come in."

"But I...how do you know who I am?"

The woman laughs, a tinkling sound not unlike the animated Tinker Bell. "Farid called us. The church leaders asked me to give you a tour. That is what you wish, yes?"

"Yes." Elizabeth steps forward. "And also to know how we can help."

The girl peers from Noura to the other women, knuckles white against the door.

"Our husbands have business in Egypt." Elizabeth clamps her hands in front of her, almost in supplication. "If they are going to earn money here, we can help. I'm Elizabeth, and this is Lizzy."

A smile lights the girl's face, and she releases the door. "Sameh."

Noura blanches at the similarity to Saira's name but covers it with a bow of acknowledgment and follows the British duo into a dark hall. Noura scrambles to keep up with the others, and then they burst into a moltenly bright courtyard, Ra scorching the earth. They plunge through the tomb-like opening of another hall and into a pantry, then the kitchen.

A cacophony of motion slams into Noura.

Dozens of women scurry in the dim light. Two stir huge vats of curry, while others sort clothing.

At the far side of the counter is Noura's sister, crying over a pile of onions.

13

A hurricane of emotions hits Noura. Happiness, fear, fury. Then it all pauses, swirling in a churning confusion at the dark-headed child nestled her sister's arms. A child?

"Noura!" Estelle's smile encompasses her entire face. Her knife clatters to the table, and she opens her arms as if it's been a matter of weeks since she last talked with her sister. "You came. Sameh, would you bring Farid a meal?" Estelle arranges the child on her feet before marshaling Noura into her chest, then holds her sister at arm's length before towing her in again.

The monster squall inside Noura heaves a breath, only to swirl into an unbearable torrent on the other side. The ground so saturated, the grass disgorges entire rivers of water, pushing out all the buried things. "You left without a word." Noura's words grind out. "Not so much as an 'I'm fine.' I've searched for you for years, Estelle. Years! You have a child and..."

Lizzy lays a hand on Noura's arm.

Instead of confusion on her face, Noura sees compassion, and realization crackles. "You knew."

The woman has the decency to blush, and Noura shrugs her off. Is everyone lying?

"First," Estelle says, calm as a summer breeze, "Heba isn't mine. I rescued her. She's an orphan under the church's protection. Second, I couldn't risk any of your coworkers seeing me. Lizzy has recently helped with my more...shall we say, delicate matters? She's the one who confirmed Mehedi owes a lot of money to some powerful people."

The mention of Saira's little brother stops Noura cold. How did she forget?

"It was Lizzy's idea to bring you here, since I couldn't get you separated from that man."

Noura clenches her fist and sucks in a calming breath. From day one, Estelle had to be baited with the honey of letting her think she's right. Yet right now, all Noura wants to do is smack her sister's queen bee misconception from her petty brain. "You could have dropped a note or called my hotel room."

"You haven't changed a bit. I was trying to be careful." From a plate, Estelle flourishes a perfect slice of baklava, sprinkled with pistachios. Exactly the way Noura likes it. And from the triumphant grin on Estelle's face, she knows Noura can't resist either the honey-coated treat or her peace offering.

Noura snatches the pastry and plops onto the stool across from her sister. Elizabeth places a cup of black coffee in front of Noura as a token apology, and Noura smiles her thanks despite the liquid's sludge-like appearance. But the baklava? Oh heavens. The flaky goodness of butter and almond paste melts in Noura's mouth. Even though she hates that Estelle so easily derails her, Noura can't help but groan with satisfaction.

"It's Saira's recipe," Estelle says.

Noura drops the treat, but Estelle is staring beyond her sister, wistful, not accusing.

"I took her recipe box. I lost it when...Well, I have them all memorized anyway. At least the ones we used to beg her for. I have the one for shawarma too, if you'd like it."

Sitting here like this with her sister in a sparse and ancient kitchen, Noura can almost believe they are still friends. Her mind calculates the sugar in the baklava, the amount of insulin Estelle will need. It was Noura's job for so long, and then... "Why did you leave?"

Estelle reaches out her scarred hand and brushes onion skins into a paper bag, no doubt destined for a compost pile somewhere. Noura forces her bouncing knee to settle. Her sister will answer when she is ready and not a moment before. Behind Noura, women clatter about the kitchen, employing the British duo to help, and still Noura waits. The child toddles across the kitchen, twirling as she gathers the chopped onion, skipping to deposit the white flesh into the vats. Heba's dark hair floats behind her, free. What would have happened to her without Estelle?

Estelle watches the girl with a mix of motherly pride and an odd wariness. The girl is beautiful, maybe three or four. No one would release her without significant payment...or maybe her family was killed. Like Saira and Harry.

"She's about the same age as Miriam was, isn't she?" Noura's voice breaks over the name of her niece.

Estelle's single, stark nod confirms her guess. When Egypt invaded the Sinai, how could Harry have refused to save a child like this? How could he have thought the clinic more important, especially with Saira pregnant again? The family's little garden was within Egyptian gunsights. He could have come to Tel Aviv. It had been Yom Kippur. A time for family. For peace.

Noura grips the table, smashing down the memories of furiously packing her father's bag because he hadn't done it himself, oblivious to where her anger should have been directed, until she felt the vibration of bombs. Too many. Too big to be another market attack. Then the acidic smell of fear as Noura dragged her father to the musty basement shelter. Harry wasn't the only one in danger. The Israeli government had hidden how close the Egyptian army was, that the canal and Harry were already conquered, little Miriam and her mother gone.

"Saira worked her tail off. You know?" Estelle drags her thumbnail across the edge of her other palm like she might dig in and cut out the bad memories.

Noura forces herself to nod, desperate to haul her mind away from the voice screaming for revenge, the mental picture of her friend stuck, burning under a suffocating pile of rubble. And it was true. Saira worked hard. She'd wake before dawn and go to sleep after everyone else. She did her job with a kindness that belied her awful circumstances. Circumstances Noura was too distracted to acknowledge.

"She wasn't given the opportunities we had." Estelle nibbles at her sliver of baklava, then drops it on the table, neglected. Producing a cigarette pack from her shirt, she taps one out—tap, tap, tap—like she's knocking on the edge of memory, asking it to come out. Her hands are pitted, twisted with scars. Most she earned digging through piles of burning rubble, hoping to save their brother's family. And the rest? Who knows?

"Saira was punished for where she was born." Estelle slips the cigarette into her mouth, but then glances at Heba and tucks it behind her ear instead. "Father always viewed her work as having saved her. But did it really? The poor have almost zero opportunity to survive, let alone prosper. If there is a God, his Bible commands his followers to take care of the sick and vulnerable. But Father walked past the beggars. The ones missing a hand or leg. He hated that Harry stooped to help and then married one of them."

"Them?"

Estelle rolls her kohl-rimmed eyes at her sister. "The poor. Or maybe non-American. I think Father believes everyone should earn their place. Or maybe he was selectively blind. He'd react to the smallest flinch of the Egyptians or Syrians or Russians and ignore the swarm of flies around a dying child. Kissinger and his cronies said the US was concerned about the safety of Israel. And maybe the sovereignty of Palestine, but the government cares nothing for individuals. The wealthy want the oil-rich Egyptians and Saudis as allies, but how does your cultural exchange treaty benefit the people?"

Noura flinches like her sister has physically struck her. "It isn't meant to—"

"Would it have benefited Saira? Did it help her to have Bedouin land in a political tug of war between Israel and Egypt?" Estelle's eyes fill with tears, the gold flecks drowning and shimmering all the more for it. "The roof was crushed when I got there. The tattered blue curtain still as death. Dried blood soaked into the dirt floor. The stones were still hot. At the bottom, Saira was wrapped around Miriam. It hadn't mattered. No one could have protected them. I couldn't even find a remnant of Harry's clinic."

A single tear trails Estelle's cheek, bleeding the emotion from her, leaving her stark and carefully blank.

"When the politicians heard rumblings of what the Egyptians planned"—Estelle smacks away the moisture—"Washington forced Israel not to warn anyone or execute a preemptive strike. Do you remember? Father knew there was a threat."

"He hadn't been able to confirm—"

Estelle's acidic snort cuts Noura off. "He knew more than he let on. You must realize that now. He sacrificed his own granddaughter to stand with the politicians."

"Father would have protected them if he could have. He wouldn't have—"

"When did Father ever question American policy?" Estelle brushes at a frail scrap of pastry, sending it crumbling from the table. "If an American is injured, the government demands retribution, but then shuts out the people who really need help. The government bristles with guns and political machinations that don't help their own poor, let alone a refugee."

She's right. Father always believed Americans should protect their own. Noura always saw it as a fatherly desire to protect his family. But if that was the case, wouldn't he have followed Maman to New Orleans? Or done everything he could to protect Harry? Chaos whispers to Noura, threatening to upend her careful world. She clutches her bag with the ostrich feather. Order does bring balance. But who decides whose order is right?

"I guess I had had enough of the hypocrisy." Estelle meets her sister's eye, and there is the little girl she once was. The one who trusted her big sister to take care of her, to read her bedtime stories, and to explain the world. The one Noura was able to balance out for so long.

"You never tried to contact me." Noura's voice sags in childish petulance.

Estelle's laugh is as bitter as the coffee between them. "You made it clear you disagreed with me. You confirmed your position when you blamed me for Father's dismissal. By that point, I was already rescuing orphans, finding refugees temporary housing and food, and organizing funding. There was no home base for me to contact anyone from."

"So why now?"

Estelle drops her hands into her lap, under the table, hiding them even as she faces Noura square on. "I need to get home."

"Home?"

"To the States."

"Okay?" Noura feels as dense as granite.

"I've been blacklisted," Estelle says. "I can't get a passport."

"Have you asked Dad?"

Estelle shoves away from the table. "This is why I haven't called. You take his side."

"I'm not taking his side." Noura sounds remarkably calm despite the flare in her core. "He has more embassy contacts than I do." Noura waits a beat, letting her mind skirt around the bomb crater. Then the evasion hits Noura. "Why were you blacklisted?"

"I was arrested while protesting the draft," Estelle mumbles to the table.

"Estelle!"

"What? Eighty percent of the men drafted to Vietnam were working class or poor. The rich government types wouldn't be so eager to fight if it were their boys being sent to die. I was *doing* something to help."

"Peaceful protesting doesn't get you blacklisted." Noura crosses her arms against the heavy weight of her sister's half-truths.

Estelle taps a fingernail on the table. "A kid from the neighborhood was drafted. He was a little slow, you know? Army didn't care that he'd be cannon fodder. I drove him to Canada. Then I helped another and another. The cops rarely questioned a blond ditz driving the tunnel from Detroit to Ontario. The last time, I was driving this sweet boy and his handicapped mother. He was her sole caregiver. Can you imagine? I still hate that the one time I was caught, it was them. Friends got me out of the country just in time."

Heaven, have mercy. No wonder Father was released. No wonder the FBI called Noura about her sister. And yet, a voice whispers, *What had been the right thing to do? Would Ma'at see Estelle's choice as pressing down her heart or lifting the scale?*

"I didn't want to ruin your career." Estelle reaches across the table and lays her hand on Noura's. It is cool, confident, and just like Estelle.

"Why do you need to get back?"

Estelle slumps, and Noura expects her to say she can't say. Instead, she lifts her chin. "The Egyptians raised the rent on Mehedi's family's land."

"Again?"

"Mehedi borrowed money from the wrong people, Noura."

Noura rubs at the tempest in her skull. "Why didn't he ask us?"

"Pride." Estelle shrugs. "You know him."

"The Andersons said he was with friends."

"He is. For now."

Noura had brought him to Ann Arbor herself. She still doesn't know how he escaped the Sinai. He'd been seventeen. A kid. When she heard he was alive, Noura contacted every person she had ever known until she found him. And then she pulled every string she had to get him to Tel Aviv. Then promised half her life to get him a passport and visa to the States. He'd been safe for so long, she'd forgotten to worry about him. Forgotten his student visa only gave him temporary reprieve. How was she so stupid?

"So we pay the money back," Noura says. "The Andersons will help."

"It's way more than any of us has."

A whirlpool spins in Noura's gut. "Then call the police."

"Because they'll believe a Middle Eastern man whose visa is nearly up."

Noura hates it, but she knows her sister is right. What has the world come to that avarice is the best course?

"How would you help where I can't?" Noura's question is tentative, unwilling to set her sister off.

"I have more contacts than you do, and if that fails, I'm an attorney."

Noura blinks, processing this last piece of information. Her little sister is an attorney.

"Despite her faults," Estelle says, "Maman helped me pay for school, and I worked for the rest."

Maman? Maman paid for Estelle's education? But of course she did. Estelle is Maman's duplicate—same pert nose, same light eyes and hair that attracts so much attention, same desire to make Father pay. Though

Maman's attack is typically a hidden explosive mine, Estelle's is an aerial bomb screaming toward its target. Noura isn't sure which hurts more.

"You didn't know." Estelle blows out a breath.

"How would I know?" Noura's frustration flares. "You never answered the letters I sent. Then, when I last saw you, you were so raging mad, you assumed the absolute worst in me, and then you disappeared. I didn't know if you were dead or alive."

Estelle flinches. "I'm sorry. I—"

Desperate to contain the vermillion emotion, Noura rams a lid over her internal boiling. "It's in the past."

Six years. Maman has been in contact with Estelle for six years. She's punished Noura alongside Father. That fact combines with the creeping heat of the day and threatens to combust.

Sunshine and happiness, Noura thinks.

Lemonade out of lemons. The peaceful calm of Ma'at's presence.

"Good Day, Sunshine." Noura hums the tune to the Beatles song in her head, the interval thirds moving even and harmonious, and she dredges up a smile. It's small, but it is a smile. "There are other attorneys we can hire."

Estelle clenches a fist over the back of the stool, her white knuckles mirroring the anger crackling in the clench of her jaw. She sucks in a breath. "Mehedi, he…" Estelle shakes out her hands once, twice, and then sits, knees turned out like her feet might change their mind and run out the door. "I think he's in real trouble."

The flames and smoke behind the words suffocate Noura, and she clings to her skirt in a desperate attempt to keep herself together. A silent scream builds alongside the desire to claw the eyes out of whoever has done this to her again. As much as she tries to be the steady one, it seems she, like Ma'at, is cursed with a chaos-producing relative.

"I've tried calling," Estelle says. "But I need to be home to track down help."

"I don't have contacts in the embassy. Everyone I knew is either gone or I owe them, not the other way around. I—"

"Mr. Hoving has contacts." Her sister's pleading pumps fear, exploding through Noura. "If someone like him recommends me to the embassy, they'll reissue my passport."

"A recommendation from God himself won't make the government overlook the fact that you're wanted by the FBI."

Estelle gives a conspiratorial lift of her shoulders and leans in. "My friends waited to put me on a plane until the guy testified that I hadn't known he was evading the draft."

"So they don't want to arrest you?"

An impish smirk lifts the right side of Estelle's face. The same irksome expression Estelle gave when, as children, Noura would catch her little sister half a second before she bolted.

"Maybe," Estelle says. "But Mehedi is worth the possibility. Isn't he?"

Noura rubs her sweating palms against her skirt. "I don't know Mr. Hoving well."

"Please, Noura."

Somewhere a dog barks, shadows flicker outside the window, and a pointy-eared dog trots into the middle of the alley. He stops, turns, stares Noura down, challenging her to see him. So much like the blunt-nosed Set-animal. Noura squints, dissecting his long ears, the cock of his head. And that's when she realizes what her sister is doing. Estelle is creating chaos with a classic magic trick—*Look here, so you don't notice that over there.*

"Estelle, what aren't you telling me?"

"Why do you always think I'm lying?"

"Because you almost always are."

Estelle slams away from the table, a whirling dervish.

"And you never beg." Noura tells herself to be stone, impervious to her sister's outburst.

"I have never asked you for anything."

Noura sucks in a breath, refusing to follow the rabbit trail. "I was there for you for every moment of your life until you left. I was a child doing the best I could to watch over you so you wouldn't—You know what?" Noura gathers her bag, her scarf, her scattered emotions. "Never mind."

"No." Estelle launches herself between Noura and the exit. "I won't let you run again. You have to face me this time and tell me why you won't help."

Noura's fingers go numb as the spark of frustration burns her skin, her mind screaming to make it stop. Make *her* stop. But the fuse is lit. "The only reason you contacted me"—she burns faster and faster—"is because you've stirred up trouble again. Over and over, you call me to rescue you. 'Save me from the scary man at the market, the consequences of sneaking ice cream,' or whatever fiasco you throw yourself into. And then, when you're safe, you toss me away. Only to pick me up the next time you're in trouble, wipe me off, and hope I won't notice how many times you've abandoned me." Noura knows she is yelling, that people are watching, yet she cannot stop. Like the myth coming to life—Set roaring from the desert, Horus diving from the sky, and everything in between shattering. Noura's heavy heart outweighs Ma'at's feather in her bag. "Tell me why you really need my help."

Estelle studies her sister, dispassionate, no doubt looking for the right buttons to push, and Noura wishes she could piece her stone wall back together, drink the blasted coffee, choke down the baklava, agree to whatever Estelle wants, then leave her sister in the past where she belongs.

"What happened to family being there for each other?" Estelle is maddeningly calm.

"You and I"—Noura barely restrains herself from slapping the self-righteous smirk off Estelle's face—"we're sisters in blood. Not actuality. Not when you disappear like you do. Not when you—" Noura waves her hand in frustration. "Not when you tell me manipulative half-truths."

Heba slips her fingers around Estelle's leg, her eyes wide in apprehension. To Noura's surprise, Estelle sighs, melting into her chair.

"I'm sorry. I'm used to watching my back. Some powerful people don't like me very much. Mehedi does owe people money. But—" she rubs at her creased forehead, and Noura can't help but think she might have it wrong. Maybe Estelle is more like Anubis than his father Set—stuck in between, but ultimately the quiet authority of justice. "Look, someone is threatening him, and I can't stop it unless I'm home." Estelle shrugs, inviting Noura to fill in the blanks of what might happen.

"Who's threatening Mehedi?" Noura asks.

"It's my fault." Estelle's words stifle her sister's nettled retort. "He came with me to a meeting about helping Vietnam vets. He met some of the more...ardent members of my world. He borrowed money from one of them. I tried fixing it from here, but I made it worse. I don't even know who 'they' are. At this point, it could be the FBI or the mob or someone with a vendetta against immigrants. I have contacts who can help, but I've been out of the country for too long. I have to be there, face-to-face, to unravel whatever's caught Mehedi. Which means I need my passport, and I need money—for tickets, for the mission here, and probably for bribes. I don't know. But I can't...I can't let Mehedi pay for my mistake."

Noura clutches her bag like it's a bulletproof vest. The FBI? They wouldn't be involved unless Mehedi has done something illegal. And the mob? Why would they have a problem with an electrician's apprentice? Noura has seen *The Godfather*. The horse head. The bombs. The strangling. Millions of dollars. All the—

"Noura?" Estelle lays a calming hand on her sister's arm.

"I don't have those kinds of resources!" Noura explodes. "Ask Lizzy."

At her name, the other woman drops the knob of bread dough she's been kneading and lifts her flour-dusted palms in wicked innocence. "I'm helping with the money, but I'm far too well known for my...shall we, say red connections?...to help obtain a passport. And George—he's my husband—is impossible."

"Then Elizabeth." Noura throws a hand out to rope in the more refined woman. Anyone who knows what they're doing.

"I'm afraid," Elizabeth says with regret, "my contacts are not within your government."

"Please, Noura," Estelle says. "You're my best chance. I understand why you bury yourself in the past. But there are times when we have to do something to help the people right in front of us."

Noura is not immune to the fact that her sister is the person in front of her. Estelle, whom Noura pledged to take care of.

"I just need you to get me a passport. I don't have anyone else to ask. Someone's following me in Cairo. He's a pro. They'll find Mehedi if they haven't found him already."

What else can Noura say but "I'll see what I can do"?

Estelle bounds from her seat and wraps her sister in the enthusiastic hug of a toddler, then spins her in a spirited circle, and Noura can't help laughing. Some things never change.

"One more thing." Estelle grasps both her sister's arms and eases her back enough to confirm Noura is paying attention. "Do not tell Theo you've seen me."

"What? I—"

"Please." She turns to Lizzy for confirmation. "He's hiding something. He isn't who you think. And I'm not sure about the rest."

Before Noura catches hold of her wits enough to voice any questions, Farid ducks into the room. "We have to go." He whisks the trio toward the front door while Estelle pulls her headscarf over her unnaturally dark hair and bounds toward the back.

Noura snatches her sister's iconic scarf from her bag and holds it up, but the gathering, hungry crowd has absorbed Estelle. She is gone, and Noura is left behind. Time repeating itself. Worse, she forgot to ask Estelle if she knows anything about the strange list nestled in Noura's bag.

She trudges after Farid's alert stride, wondering if Estelle is right that yet another man in Noura's life isn't as he appears or if she's run smack into another of her sister's schemes.

14

The moment they break into the sunlight outside the church, Elizabeth and Lizzy revert to the ditzy Brits Noura originally met, making Noura feel like she's stepped through the swirling spirals of the *Twilight Zone*. No one would guess the British pair has illegal plots churning beneath their blond bouffants. All Noura wishes to do is forget what her sister asked of her. And so, for the rest of the day, she plays tour guide and mannequin as promised. Lizzy and Elizabeth are the perfect distraction—mostly because Lizzy's carelessly impulsive, but also because Elizabeth's teasing is perfectly timed.

By the time the trio turns toward the hotel, the Brits have coerced Noura into allowing Elizabeth to buy her impossibly white bell-bottom pants, a gorgeous green silk dress with embroidered ostrich feathers, and a black collared casual shirt worthy of Jacqueline Kennedy herself.

As much fun as their excursion was, Noura is done in by the time they arrive at the hotel. Farid helps the other two women out first, giving Noura time to collect the abundance of packages before clambering out.

She distributes the various scarves, silverware, and trinkets between the women, reserving two parcels for herself.

Elizabeth bows to Farid, then nearly drops the box with a porcelain tea set. Lizzy giggles at her friend's uncharacteristically klutzy mistake, and Noura fully releases the breath she's been holding. These women can't possibly be notorious communist activists. They draw far too much attention to themselves. Which means Estelle's predicament cannot possibly be as dire as she portends.

Noura counts Egyptian pounds into Farid's palm and thanks him for his help.

He nods solemnly and passes her a card. "Contact information for your sister."

Forcing herself to smile, Noura accepts the card with a bow and tucks it into her bag. Before she does anything further, she'll call the Andersons again. They'll know where Mehedi is and how to help. He was set to complete his electrician apprenticeship. And with the Andersons's connections, he shouldn't be having trouble obtaining a job and a green card. Maybe Estelle is mistaken. Or maybe she has another reason she's desperate to leave Egypt.

"Do you work with my sister?" Noura asks.

Farid squints into the street. Neither assent nor denial.

"Noura." A voice shouts behind her, and she spins. Theo's strolling toward the hotel, waving and grinning like the proverbial fool.

Farid frowns at Noura, his gentle expression all but screaming, "Be careful."

"I work with the mission," he finally responds. "Nothing more. Nothing less." He tucks his pay into his battered bag and kicks over the engine of the tuk-tuk, chugging around the turnabout as quickly as the contraption allows.

At the corner, Theo and Farid lift a hand in polite recognition. It doesn't appear that Farid has issue with Noura's coworker, nor the other way around.

Still, Estelle said Theo isn't who Noura thinks he is. Whatever that means. Maybe she found out that Theo wasn't as qualified as the rest of the team, and blew things out of proportion.

Theo trots up the walkway, a spring in his step. Sand whips from the drive and stings the tender skin on Noura's face. She doesn't mind though. Wiping her face free of the grit saves her from figuring out how to arrange her expression in greeting—friend or foe?

When she opens her eyes, he's beaming. There's no way this man is anything but what he appears—a goofball turned academic who's found his place in restoration.

"We have the *USS Milwaukee*." Theo hops a jig.

"And that's a good thing?"

"Indeed!" He hooks his arm around hers and hauls her along, laughing, into the lobby. "My friend with the navy says if we transport the artifacts to the port, the sailors will snuggle King Tut's belongings in the refrigerator alongside the hamburgers and give them a ride to Italy, where another group of sailors will transfer everything to the *USS Sylvania*. Then it's a hop, skip, and jump to Norfolk. It'll take longer than a flight, and we'll have to mediate for water exposure, but that's easy enough."

They're sitting in the dining room—white tablecloth draped in front of them, candles flickering—when Theo finally asks the question she's been dreading. "What have you done all day?"

Thankfully, Noura is prepared. "I played secret tour guide."

"Secret?" He leans his chin on his fist.

Noura stifles her triumph. The human psyche is putty in the hands of secrets, and the word has the desired distracting effect, even on Theo.

"Indeed." Noura points him away from anything to do with Estelle. "I'm sworn to confidentiality, but I believe I've made some friends."

"See? People love you."

"People who need free tour guides love me."

"I don't believe it." He slumps in melodramatic shock. "I, for one, know people who are Egyptologists in their own right who rather enjoy your company."

She sips at the wine to disguise the flush rising in her cheeks. "So what do you need from me?"

"Well..." Theo lifts a single, suggestive brow.

"I mean for work."

"Of course." A sly grin creeps across his face, and a laugh bursts from Noura.

"You are incorrigible."

"Encourage away, my brilliant friend," he says with a salute. "I shall go wherever you wish to go."

"Incorrigible. Not encourage—"

The Scorpion Thief

Theo taps his nose in a you-got-it gesture.

"You're worse than Set."

"Ah, my darling Ma'at, unlike the god of mischief and mayhem, I'm not out to kill you or take over your kingdom." Theo smirks and lifts his water goblet in cheers. His fingers against the glass are long, the bed of his nails stained with paint—the hand of a talented conservator. "I'm here to help deliver the greatest museum show ever. We've already commandeered the US Navy. But without Ghadfa to help grease the wheels of his contacts in the city, we need a mastermind to procure supplies and transportation. And you, my dear, are a formidable negotiator. Are you game?"

"Of course." Tension releases from her shoulders. He's far too concerned about his job to be the villain Estelle's made him out to be.

While Theo isn't the stereotypical boring conservator, given his instincts on the streets and his ties to the Navy, he probably funded his college degree through military service. And a military connection would explain Estelle's objection. Estelle is the epitome of the anti-war.

Given the anti-military climate, Noura also can't blame Theo for hiding his background. Furthermore, Estelle's intimation that *no one* at the museum is who they seem makes the idea that Theo is an evil henchman more unlikely.

Across the table, Theo is well into a list of the bits and pieces they'll need to acquire when the waiter delivers their bottled water and takes their order.

Noura rubs the base of her skull and digs for aspirin in her bag while nodding at whatever Theo is saying. Between the additional work, her sister, and Mehedi, Noura doesn't know how she'll accomplish it all and still sleep. She swallows the aspirin and leans against the cushioned chair.

Outside the window, red whispers across the sky, leaching into the haze of dust until the air itself is on fire. Noura frowns at the falcon fluffing itself on the fence outside. He cocks his white head at her, perplexed. As if he's trying to tell her something she is too thick-skulled to understand. Then, seeming to tire of her, he raises his wings and soars into the flaming sky. Whatever information he discovered is gone with him. Horus never was obligated to help mere mortals. Noura starts at the thought.

Theo reaches across the table in giddy excitement, dragging Noura's thoughts back to the present. "We're going to be part of history. Who would have thought that a middle-class jokester and a librarian's daughter would be here?"

It's a good reminder. They have a job to do, and Noura won't let her sister's antics get in the way. Tonight, Noura will call the Andersons again. There has to be a way to protect Mehedi and Estelle too, if she needs it.

Theo's tumble of words continues throughout dinner, and Noura manages to interject grunts of communication between bites of tasteless food. It isn't the cook's fault that her stomach is a crater filled with acid. What if she calls the Andersons and Mehedi really is in trouble? What then? How much does an attorney cost? Maybe Grandmere will loan Noura money if she doesn't know it's for Mehedi. Or maybe Maman. And what about Estelle? She was edgy enough to be in more trouble than she's let on. A woman on the streets of Cairo can disappear without anyone knowing. Maybe she would be safer in New Orleans? Though Father's just a professor now, he must have contacts.

Which means Noura does need to get her sister a passport. But how? Mr. Hoving knows her name, but not much more.

Noura forces yet another bite down her gullet and comes up for air to realize Theo has stopped speaking and is inspecting her like an artifact that has spontaneously combusted.

"Are you okay?"

"Of course." Her automatic response makes his frown deepen. "A lot on my mind."

"What happened?"

Noura stares at the place where his fingers inch closer to her own. *Trust me,* they say. And while Noura doesn't trust Estelle, her sister's rarely wrong. If she took the effort to warn Noura—

"Is it Farid?" Theo's voice has a hidden edge to it, and Noura frowns in confusion.

Then realization spikes. "No!" Even the suggestion of impropriety could cost the tuk-tuk driver his life.

"Then what?" Theo's concern slips into some sort of fear.

"I'm thinking about my sister." The most believable lie is that which contains the most truth.

"You saw her again?" His voice rises.

"I didn't say I saw her again!" Noura squeaks, voice low.

"Ah!" he says, much quieter now. He leans back with infuriating confidence. "So you *did* see her. Did you talk to her this time?"

Noura's mouth gapes. Open. Closed. And absolutely mute.

THEO CURSES HIMSELF FOR MISJUDGING. He already knows the answers to his questions. He hoped his excitement for her would jar her into honesty. The last thing he wants is to manipulate Noura, but Horus doesn't overcome because he's more powerful than his foe. He conquers the unconquerable with cleverness and psychology. And frankly, Theo is running out of time.

"Is she in trouble?" In the time he's tracked Estelle Marquette, the only dangerous thing she's done is rescue a few girls from manipulative scum. Once he had, in fact, happily stepped in to prevent the slavers from tracking Estelle. But Noura is inexplicably torn, almost scared. "What's wrong?" he asks.

"I..." Noura smooths the tablecloth like the answer might appear on the fabric.

He forces himself not to rescue her.

"She got in trouble helping a man and his invalid mother," Noura blurts, the desperate confession pouring out of her. "Estelle needs to go home, but needs a passport." Noura pauses. "Maman is sick," she says.

Theo cringes. He's checked her family. And while the statement is strictly true—Mrs. Marquette has been unstable for two decades—she isn't sick in the most accurate sense of the word. And certainly nothing that would require a lightning-speed passport home.

"They're not on the best terms, Maman and Estelle. Well, none of us are really." Noura continues. "Estelle wants me to talk to Mr. Hoving, but I don't know him nearly that well."

Theo's attention flicks to his lap, considering. It's obvious Noura doesn't quite trust him. But there are also good reasons to help Noura, her humanitarian sister, and their mother, who walks somewhere between her imagination and reality. If Estelle is Star, knowing her passport number and whereabouts would be enormously helpful. And if Estelle is innocent, then Theo hopes one good deed might outweigh a fraction of the bad he's committed, including helping Typhon the first time Theo encountered him.

"I'll talk to Mr. Hoving for you," he says.

"Really?"

"You sound like we're brokering a peace deal."

"Aren't we?" She is mangling the edges of her shirt.

Theo leans on the table and waits for her to look at him. She needs to see his truth if she's to reveal whatever she's hiding. "We're friends, Noura. I don't have to be a genius to know you care about your sister, and from what you've said, your relationship is complicated. If I can make your life easier, I will."

"I owe you."

"You can't repay a miracle worker." Theo huffs on his fingernails and shines them against his shirt.

Noura laughs, and Theo plunges into the space he's made. "Seriously. Helping is what friends do. But I also can't help if I don't know the story."

Noura recoils from the slap of fact. He knows it sounds like a demand for juicy details. Fillet her life and lay it bare for his perusal. But that isn't it.

"If I ask for a favor," Theo says, "I need to know what I'm up against. Mr. Hoving won't be able to argue with the powers that be if he doesn't know what he's arguing against. You can trust me. I've nothing to gain from helping."

"There's a difference between being nice and being trustworthy."

Theo chuckles. So like Mabel, wanting to make everyone happy and not knowing how to make all the pieces fit without cutting off portions of herself to fill the gaps. "But," he says, "you can be both. Nice and trustworthy. Just because some people refuse to help unless they get something in return doesn't mean I do the same thing. In fact, my dad would smack me silly if I didn't offer to go the extra mile."

"Your dad sounds like a good man." She sighs.

"He is a good man," Theo says. And he is, even if he isn't who Noura thinks he is.

"My father was a librarian in the US Embassy in Israel for decades. He was rather..." She stumbles for words to describe her father, but Theo can fill in the blanks from what he's found. Marquette is contentious, stubborn, eccentric, operating in the gray, but brilliant too. Proud of his oldest daughter.

"Father was never amazing with authority," Noura says in her mitigating way. "He's beyond smart but never lets anyone forget it and always thinks he knows best." She rubs down the length of her linen skirt—once, twice. "He doesn't realize how much Estelle's like him. But Estelle's attitude comes with a hefty dose of philanthropy. She once rescued this mangy kitten. Brought it home hidden in her backpack. We all got fleas. When our father dumped the cat in the country, Estelle went on a hunger strike. Every time he disciplined her, she dug in more.

"I'm not surprised she fights for the poor, and against what's happened in the Middle East, then the war in Vietnam, and really against anything that she thinks is unfair. Father, on the other hand, took pains to point out what her pet projects had done or not done to deserve what happened. About the only thing they agree on is that a treaty with Egypt is a mistake."

"And you've dedicated your life to studying Egyptian history?"

He didn't mean the question to be a barb, but she shoves to her feet, anger crashing over her careful boundaries. "I don't do everything my father wants."

Theo laughs, an abrupt cessation of the tempest. "You being here is proof of that. I think it's courageous. Doing what you think is right even when your family is against you."

Noura's eyes flare as if she's seen the warning of a green sky, and he can practically hear her barring herself into the storm shelter.

Theo shifts, giving her space. "My mom used to say, 'If courage is action even when afraid, face your fear, walk into the dark, and watch for miracles.' I've watched, Noura. I've watched you choose to battle chaos, to bring Ma'at."

"I don't think anyone has ever called me courageous before."

"I'm here because my dad told me I'd best make something of myself after all the money I spent on my degree. But you? You have another reason to be here. You don't say half the things you're thinking, let alone defy authority unless there's good reason."

She clutches the top of her chair as if it might shield her. "Sometimes," she says, "peace only happens after you step into the world of the enemy. Weakness isn't being kind or careful. Weakness is refusing to admit you don't understand or refusing to try. Weakness is giving in to fear." She risks a glance up, and he sees the honesty, the fear of poisoning whatever is growing between them.

"If I don't try," she says, "I'll always wonder what I could have done."

"And that"—Theo stands and lifts Noura's hand away from the death grip she has on the chair—"that is why I'm willing to help. You practice integrity rather than simply talk about it. If you're willing to go around the system, it's for a good reason. Just tell me she isn't some kind of terrorist."

"She works in a mission. Takes in street kids. She'd as soon set off a bomb as slit her own throat."

Theo watches for the telltale signs of lying—over-protesting, arm crossing, too much eye contact—but there is none of that. Noura believes she is telling the truth, and that has to be enough for him. The worst Estelle may be is an art thief and exuberant humanitarian.

"Then I'll make sure she gets her passport." Theo mentally curses himself for the promise, but he reaches for the packet of information and photos Noura holds out for him.

"Thank you," she says with a nervous flutter. "I hate being a problem."

"You are not a problem, Noura." She's a colleague, he reminds himself. Look away. But a little sniffle draws his attention to her vulnerable brown eyes, and he has to resist the urge to kiss her knuckles like a white knight. He's a cad for letting his mind wander to a kingdom all their own, for giving her a hint of what he truly wants. But for her, once this is over, he will find a way to throw off all his entanglements. He will bring her the kingdom. For now, the only way to keep her safe is to push her back.

"Well," she says and glances at her watch in a nervous tic.

"Well," he parrots back.

"I promised to call home tonight."

Ever the gentleman, Theo stands and extends his arm like an automaton programmed to polite indifference. Noura slides from the table, and Theo lets her walk sedately away. In the distance, a dog barks in warning, and, as Theo turns to go do his job, he extracts the freezing pendant from under his shirt and tucks it behind his tie instead.

THE FROWN that collapsed the space between Theo's brows makes Noura sprint up the stairs and slam gratefully into her room. She breathes, catching hold of her thoughts, so by the time she picks up the phone, she calmly asks the operator to put a call through to the Andersons. Though it's almost eleven in Cairo, it is late afternoon in Michigan.

"Hello?" The line crackles around Mrs. Anderson's voice, and Noura pictures her in the happily cluttered kitchen, leaning against the chipped Formica.

"Mrs. Anderson? It's Noura. Noura Marquette." Her voice lifts at the end like she's not sure who she is anymore.

"Noura? I thought you were in Egypt." Mrs. Anderson chuckles, bright and unconcerned as her kitchen, and Noura releases her breath.

"I am in Egypt." She lets herself laugh at her earlier fears. Estelle has always had a fantastic imagination.

"Heavens. This is unexpected. What can I do for you, dear?"

"I...I called to check on Mehedi."

"What?" The line snaps angrily.

"Mehedi. May I speak with him?"

"Oh dear. I thought you knew. Mehedi moved out yesterday. Something about a job across state? Or maybe Chicago? I have the number for you."

Noura takes down the number in shaking script and clicks off with a muted "thank you." Mehedi had been terrified of moving away from the Andersons. Why would he move to the west side of the state, or worse, Chicago? Unless something had happened.

Noura reads the number to the operator, then listens to the clicking of the connection, then nothing...nothing. Noura jumps with the screech of three ascending tones followed by the mechanical voice of a woman, "We're sorry, but this number is not in service."

Noura taps the button to disconnect the line and calls the operator again. "Would you try again, please?"

"Of course, ma'am."

But the man's politeness and second effort do not change the result. Mehedi gave the Andersons a false number. Mehedi is in trouble, which means Estelle is too.

The FBI will laugh without any evidence. The Ann Arbor police might listen to Prof. Anderson, but what can they do without any real information?

The fact that Estelle owes someone somewhere something reawakens Noura's fear that her sister's trouble connects to the list of artifacts as well as to the hulking mystery man from the hotel lobby and Ghadfa's disappearance.

And there's little Noura can do except get her sister out of Egypt and hope that will prevent anything from happening to the Tut artifacts. However, it's becoming increasingly clear that whatever Estelle has done is more than a little dangerous. And by asking Theo to help, she has roped him into the trouble as well.

From the look of sanctimonious doubt that crossed Noura's face, Estelle knows she shouldn't have mentioned the man. Lizzy said she hasn't been able to prove Theo is anything other than what he says he is. But as Estelle curls into her blanket on the floor, she can't shake the look of predatory calculation on his face. Worse, though she can't quite place him, she's seen those piercing eyes, that loping walk, more than once. And not at the museum.

Estelle turns, careful not to wake little Heba snuggled into her side. Tomorrow, Estelle will take the girl to friends in the north. It's best for both of them.

If Typhon gets word of Estelle's plans, she'll have mere hours before she's hunted down. Estelle doesn't want anyone in her vicinity then.

While most of Typhon's men are clods, there is the other. She sucks in a breath at the explosion in her chest.

That's where she's seen the conservator, in distorted glimpses in window glass and tiny mirrors. Estelle pictures Theo, hovering in her periphery, with a wig, sunglasses, a striped shirt, dark fedora. She hasn't been close enough to be positive, but both men wear a similar silver pendant dangling from their necks. A falcon's feather. As if that trinket could shield him from Typhon.

But if he works for Typhon, wouldn't Lizzy have caught the scent of that?

Little Heba whimpers in her sleep, and Estelle rubs the girl's back. If Theo isn't linked to the Weathermen or Typhon, then why is he following her? Perhaps Lizzy could set a tail on the conservator.

In the meantime, Estelle will simply have to pray her sister listens and doesn't tell Theo anything. Both their lives may depend on it.

15

August 2, 1976

According to Estelle's contacts, today is when the artifacts leave Cairo. For the last few days, Estelle has watched the increased flurry of activity around the museum. And in that time, she hasn't sensed Theo's alter ego behind her. But neither has she seen Typhon's minion. Estelle knows the missing tail is far from a good sign. Are they watching Noura now instead?

That thought propels Estelle onto the street in the wee hours of the morning. Keeping an eye on the museum, she hunkers down on the corner with her array of hand-decorated scarves and wooden jewelry. In a few scant hours, the artifacts leave the country, and Noura will follow quickly behind. Estelle wants to believe her sister won't abandon her. But how can she know for sure? When the treasure is in transit, it'll be vulnerable. If Noura hasn't gotten Estelle a passport by then, today may be her only chance to save Mehedi and herself. But if Estelle tries to steal the artifacts and fails, she will lose Noura's help.

A cluster of men jostles at the bus stop across the street, and Estelle holds her breath, demanding her body to evaporate into invisibility. The bus groans to a stop, and the mob clatters aboard, smashed into every conceivable crevice, including a handle and scrap of toehold on the outside. But there's a man left abandoned on the curb.

He studies the shadows under the palms where Estelle is camouflaged. Estelle is too disciplined to move, but her heart races. The man runs a hand through his full beard once, twice, and then, when Estelle is gathering herself to run, he turns and swaggers away. A black dog flickers into view and sits under a streetlight. The light flickers on and off, on and off. Lighting the crocodile face of the man who was supposed to have helped her complete Typhon's task.

Ghadfa.

Despite Noura's worry, she managed to find everything the team needed so they could finish packing cases and preparing rigging for a seafaring journey.

The entire time, Dr. Mokhtar flitted in and out of the museum, justifiably concerned about his nation's treasures. But the interruption always came with a delaying observation of hospitality—tea savored, treats procured, discussions about already decided upon steps. The plodding movement stirred a dust storm of anxiety and sent it swirling through Noura's innards. In addition to the general delay, Mokhtar's visits also consumed every extra moment of Dr. Hoving's time, which means Theo hasn't had much time with him, and Noura had only one fleeting opportunity to mention her sister.

Her stammering request for him to help Estelle was met with a distracted "yes, yes. Schedule something, will you?" And what else can Noura do? She can't tackle the man or write a magical Egyptian *heqa* to create her desired outcome. So she's watched time barrel toward when she has to leave the country.

Worse, the frenetic activity has obliterated everyone's concerns regarding the potential theft, Ghadfa's disappearance, the odd displaced artifacts, and then there's that white falcon—which Noura's beginning to think is a hallucination—that keeps showing up outside the museum. All of that and the list too. Noura's worn the paper soft from the number of times she's studied it.

The tie between her sister and the circled words haunts Noura, making it nearly impossible to focus on the inventory pages in front of her. Who cares if they have enough pens or paint or even crates if a thief is stalking the boy king's funerary treasures? And who cares about that if someone is hunting Estelle or Mehedi? Noura lets her head fall to her desk. Between preparations and worry and the fact that it is barely three o'clock in the morning, she doesn't think she's been more tired in her life—Noura tugs at the neck of her dress—and never more uncomfortable. A few hours ago, wearing the green dress Elizabeth had purchased for her seemed like a great way to celebrate. Now she wishes she'd worn gym shorts and a T-shirt.

She desperately wants the crates loaded onto the navy ships and out of harm's way. Which means finishing the inventory, then checking and rechecking the crates and the delivery route. If only the words would stop jumping. She bangs her head lightly against the scarred wood. Pain should make her adrenal glands kick in...hopefully. Noura lifts her head and drops it again. Thud. *Pay attention.* Thud. *Find the way forward.*

"Tea." Theo's quiet voice makes Noura jerk upright.

"What?" Why her adrenaline courses now, she refuses to examine.

He lifts a chirpy half smile—part laughter, part understanding—and salutes Noura with a steamy mug. "It's so dark, it'll give you hair on your chest. But I also added enough sugar for you to start your own sugar plantation."

Noura melts in gratitude as she accepts the mug. It smells like heaven. *See?* she thinks at Estelle's ugly words. He's not a nefarious criminal genius, just a charming conservator who might take advantage of a naïve curator...which Noura may not be opposed to.

"Thank you." She sips at the scalding liquid. Her brain sparks. So happy.

Theo glances over his shoulder. Concern flickers, weighing his brows down. Noura looks too, watching the jump of light and shadows. Is someone there? But his attention returns to Noura, and his face clears.

She sets her mug down and braces herself as he drags a chair in from the neighboring table. He sits, his knees brushing Noura's, and heat snaps through her body. When he leans his elbows across his thighs, he completes the barrier between Noura and the rest of the room.

Private, contained, like the cathedral her brother recreated—complete with candles and a cobbled together cross—under the single tree in their backyard. It was a place for clandestine meetings. A place of reverence. A place of confession. This feeling Noura recognizes—Theo, the priest, and her, the penitent.

"I hate ledgers." Noura grimaces, leaning away, trying to exude dismay over paltry numbers rather than her screaming need to unburden her conscience.

Theo glances behind him like he's about to reveal a state secret before he leans in and says, "We all do" in a droll, overly dramatic stage whisper. "But"—his fingers brush the very edge of Noura's knee, a sifting of air molecules against her quaking skin. "There's good news. Mr. Hoving said we should have Estelle's passport later this morning."

"Oh!" Tea sloshes onto the pages. "Darn." Noura blots at the spill, sopping up the tea along with her spiked pulse. "Thank you, Theo." She manages the words without betraying the crash of emotion—relief, fear, confusion. Soon everything will be different—good or bad.

He spreads his hand over hers, stilling the frantic motion. "When we're done here"—his thumb circles—"we'll sit down and talk. We're close, Noura. Just hold on."

Close? Close to what? To a relationship? To giving someone the perfect opportunity to steal the artifacts? The questions rattle in Noura's mind, dumping more acidic fear behind the stone wall of her heart. Where is the balance?

"Noura?" Theo leans closer, concern bending his brows in on themselves. His breath against her cheek snaps her from her panic. "I don't fail people I care about."

Dr. Lilyquist strides into the room, trailed by a young American cultural attaché deputized to accompany the pieces to the port. Noura has no idea why Tom Homan was chosen to ride with Gamal Mokhtar, the Egyptian antiquities chief. The poor attaché has no experience with priceless antiquities, and, from how he shifts from foot to foot, he's terrified.

So is Noura. Every time she steps onto the sidewalk, her neck prickles. But there is no one there save a large, curious dog, the buzz of normal humanity, and the falcon that must live on the museum roof.

The team loads the pieces onto a single, open flatbed truck with the wood crates tied down with rope. Two ordinary taxis are on their way to retrieve the remaining pieces, as well as Tom, Mokhtar, and a laughably small security team. As the little caravan turns the corner, a shadow breaks free from the buildings, flickers, then blinks out like a light. What in the world? The falcon grumbles above her and then plunges after the truck. It feels like an omen or a call to follow, which is beyond ridiculous. But as she turns for the museum, Noura can't shake the feeling that there is something terribly wrong.

While Noura desperately wants to talk to Theo about her sister, she simply cannot let the artifacts trundle off with so little regard. Especially if a thief has interest in them. Noura snatches her bag, mumbling some excuse about woman troubles, and bolts across the street to the hotel. Blessedly, Farid is milling about, and Noura hires him to follow the taxis leaving the museum.

Noura dives into the tuk-tuk, and they putter off.

This Hollywood chase would be laughable if the consequences weren't so serious. If Mehedi is in trouble, as he seems to be, Estelle will do anything for him, including worming her way into Noura's life to learn where the collection is vulnerable.

Could it be that her sister has been bent on Noura's destruction from the beginning? The conflict of Set and Horus retold in modern times? But she can't quite see Estelle delighting in pure anarchy for the joy of the chaos.

FROM BEHIND THE flow of traffic, Estelle watches the unguarded transport trundle by. The American consulate man sweats profusely as he chatters with the Egyptian official on the other side of the car. There's been no further sign of Ghadfa. All appears well. She leans against the rail in a sigh of relief, then jerks upright.

Why is Noura, who is all nervous fluttering and frantic pointing, following the cars?

Estelle scrambles across the street, scribbles a note for the Elizabeths, and presses it into Ahmed's hands before commandeering a tuk-tuk out from under a cursing British man.

Noura should be celebrating a job well done or, at the very least, tracking down a plane ticket for Estelle. The only reason she would be chasing the artifacts is if Typhon assigned someone else or blackmailed Noura into the task herself.

Either way, her sister and Mehedi are in trouble, and the Nile will run dry before she lets anyone harm her siblings, even if it means stealing the blasted artifacts herself.

16

Noura is drifting off to sleep in Farid's tuk-tuk when the sound of the engine abruptly stops and yanks her into alertness. Jerking upright, she stretches and blinks against the glare of the late afternoon sun.

They're in a small village. Ahead of them, Mokhtar leaps from the taxi, exclaiming to a woman exiting a square limestone house. They're far enough away Noura can't make out what the Egyptian antiquities chief is saying, but Tom's frantic gestures are obvious, pointing to the other taxi driving away. Farid turns in his seat, eyes wide.

"Selket is in that taxi."

Once Noura untangles the meaning behind his words—the statue is driving away unprotected—she shouts, "Go!" But Farid is already cranking over the tuk-tuk, the protest of the engine swallowing her voice as they whiz down the street. The tiny engine of the motorcycle whines with the same urgency grinding in Noura's gut.

Farid winds through the streets, tracking the taxi moving in lazy arcs until it stops in front of a row of apartment buildings. The driver hops from the car and meanders through the door of a random apartment.

What is going on?

When Farid parks in the shade on the far side of the street, Noura taps a fingernail on the window ledge, watching, waiting. She has no authority here, no weapons, no real idea of what to do. Charge through the door? Raid the car? Maybe the driver is having dinner at a friend's home. Is it too much to hope for?

Of course it is. For whatever reason, she scans the sky for the falcon, but the messenger from the gods is absent. Why did she expect it?

A child trots across the dirt track, hesitating in the middle while a strange, auburn-colored dog crosses in front of him. Then, like a predator on alert, the child slides into the shadows. There, a taller shape bends over the boy, whispering into his ear. She—Noura is sure now that it's a woman from the way she pulls a scrap of fabric closer over her face—glances up the street.

Is Noura only imagining her sister in the planes of the woman's face and graceful flick of the wrist?

The woman offers something to the child. He snatches the present and stuffs it into the braided bag tied across his body. Nodding to the woman, the child scampers from the alley directly to the taxi. The boy tries the car door, but it's locked. Undeterred, he digs in his bag and retrieves a bit of wire, which he stuffs through the cracked-open window and neatly pops the lock. With barely a glance back, he opens the door and clambers in.

Farid swings a leg over the cycle. Noura takes this as a signal to burst from the cart. "I'll go after the woman," she says, intending to send him after the boy.

But Noura stops short.

The woman is gone.

A man dressed in a neat Western suit and red tie has taken her place. He is taller than the average Middle Eastern man, and that, combined with his chestnut hair, makes Noura think he's not Egyptian. But aviator glasses cover his eyes, so she isn't... a swish of movement behind him makes her squint. Was that the dog behind him? Or a scarf of some kind? What she sees is a tail, but that can't possibly be right. She steps forward, but a spark of light catches her attention, and then all she sees is the revolver in his hand. The fact that the weapon is pointed at Noura registers just as Farid yanks her behind the cart.

She struggles against his grip. "But Selket!"

"Be still." Farid's voice is harsh in Noura's ear. "We can track Selket, but I can't reverse a bullet wound in you."

"I won't be—"

"That man is not to be trifled with."

"How would you know?" Noura spits.

Farid uncovers a rifle from under the car and crab walks with precision toward the front of the cart, and Noura is transported back to Israel. To watching the embassy Marines train. Who is Farid, who knows and works with her sister and acts like this? Noura studies him as he levels the rifle on the tongue, then peeks around the corner.

That she is trapped between forces she doesn't understand is clear. But the question is: who is her friend and who is her enemy? Is she safer with Farid or on her own?

Noura gathers her feet underneath herself, gauging how far it is to the nearest house. If she were in the States, escaping would be simple. But here, where small towns are once again leaning toward Sharia law, it's unsafe for women to be out alone. Noura grips her bag in sweaty hands. She should have told someone where she was going.

At a gentle touch on her shoulder, Noura swings around, fist clenched. Farid catches her wild punch, engulfing her hand in his. "He is gone," he says and releases her.

"Did he take Selket?" Disbelief coats her words.

"I do not know."

"We have to tell Tom. He can't leave without her."

Farid opens the carriage door for Noura to climb in. A hot khamsin of emotions howls, threatening to bury her, but she shovels herself into the seat and waits.

An eternity later, they return to the first taxi. Tom is pacing under the scant shade of a broad-leafed fig tree. He starts when he sees Noura, his mouth opening and closing in confusion.

Any conversation is cut off when Mokhtar emerges from the house, patting his ample belly. "Are you sure you do not wish tea?" He's entirely unconcerned.

"I..." Tom begins, but he's cut off by the jaunty tooting of another taxi's horn. Tom scrambles to the taxi, demanding the trunk be opened.

The back door of the taxi opens and, to Noura's utter astonishment,

Theo's dark head emerges. Hefted in his arms is the crate marked "SELKET" with carefully stenciled letters.

A bead of sweat slides down Theo's cheek, the only sign that he hadn't been out for a Sunday drive. Theo settles the four-foot crate on the ground, and Tom opens the crate, sighs in relief, and tips it toward Noura. Nestled on her side in her foam puzzle is the golden scorpion goddess.

Theo slumps to the curb, his elbows on his knees, his suit coat as rumpled as he appears to be. A suit bearing a stunning resemblance to the one worn by the man in the shadowy alley. Of course, Noura tells herself, the brown suit is a popular cut—wide lapels, flared pant legs—and the other man was taller, thicker, darker. Or so she thinks. She mostly noticed the gun. And if the man was Theo, he returned with Selket. Maybe he was warning off would-be thieves.

Mokhtar guffaws and pats Theo's shoulder before turning to Tom. "Come, we must go or we will be late."

Theo runs a hand through his hair and stands, relief evident in the posture of his shoulders. Noura has no way to confirm the authenticity of the statue without causing an international incident. Tom glances at her, a question in the lift of an eyebrow. "Check with Dr. Lilyquist," she whispers. She is the only one who might be authorized to delay the shipment to confirm whether the statue is real or forged.

"The seal wasn't broken on the box before I opened it," Tom says, seeming to understand Noura's unasked question.

Relief floods through her. Mokhtar is the only one with the official seal.

Theo reloads the crate into the taxi and pats the trunk, a blessing and send-off to the scorpion goddess. "Can I catch a ride back to Cairo?" He clasps Farid's hand and winks at Noura like they've shared a secret. Perhaps they have. No one needs to know how dangerously close they came to losing part of the exhibit. Now, with the pieces safely on their way again, she's exhausted.

Suddenly and for the first time since Noura arrived in Cairo, all she wants is to be home, in New Orleans, where someone else will straighten out the tangle she's become and tell her what she should think and what she should do and who she should trust.

17

Farid sweeps both Theo and Noura into the tuk-tuk, and adrenaline leaks from her extremities.

"I'm glad you found Selket." Noura murmurs through a jaw-cracking yawn, then leans her head against the window.

"She wasn't exactly missing," Theo says. "The taxi driver had family in the town and stopped to say hello. The burly guy was a neighbor who took exception to people nosing around."

"Seriously?" Noura straightens.

"Seriously. I showed him my museum credentials, and he happily left the crate in my care." His lips lift in a half smile. "I'm glad I wasn't the only paranoid one."

It's Noura's turn to laugh. "More like realistic."

"We make a good team, Noura Marquette. Like Horus and Ma'at." Theo throws an arm around her shoulder and pulls her into what should be a rah-rah-sis-boom-bah, we-helped-evade-an-international-incident, go-team hug. But Theo is far too close, his arm far too reassuring to be merely a teammate.

Heat climbs Noura's neck, and she ducks her head. "I don't know about you, but I'm beyond exhausted." The last thing she wants is for Theo to read her thoughts. She doesn't make friends easily and doesn't want to lose this one because she misread his interest.

"Noura." Theo's voice is deep, rumbling in his chest. Her name, a poem he brings to life.

"Mm-hm?" Noura watches the village pass outside the window, her fingers twisting into the fabric of her bag.

"Noura," he says again. This time, he doesn't wait for her response. One hand covers the anxious twisting, and the other cups her jaw, easing her toward him. "I said we're a good team."

Noura blinks, uncertain how to read the searching of his eyes, the rasping tips of his fingers on her jaw. She's dated one man, and Charles was never interested in Noura for herself. But Theo loves that she's smart, revels in her obsession with history, and makes her forget herself and laugh.

How do you know if someone really—

"My parents would love you." He withdraws his touch, a lopsided grin blooming as he sits back.

To her horror, Noura's body leans in to him, called by the siren's song—love.

"Theo." Her voice cracks.

His golden gaze holds hers, questioning but steady, waiting for her to continue.

Tell him, a voice screams in her head, but she can't possibly obey. "I don't know that anyone could love me."

His mouth quirks—in surety rather than humor. "And why is that?"

"I'm just..." Oh heavens. "Everyone calls when they need me, but I'm not good for other things—to have fun or hang out. I have zero fashion sense, am forever saying the wrong thing. I'm quirky, unsure, stuck in history, and wholly unfit for normal life. I'm a grown woman who plays with dirty antiquities, for goodness' sake."

His smile has grown with each of Noura's exasperated confessions. "It's a good thing my family thinks weird is a compliment then. Nobody who looks or sounds like everyone else ever does anything interesting."

His words trickle into Noura's mind, clearing the debris from every broken channel dammed inside her. She blinks away a tear, but another escapes, and then another. Hope crashing over her walls.

"I'm sorry...I didn't..." Theo wipes the tear from her cheek, the frown on his face real, and possibly even panicked. "My sisters tell me I'm an unconscionable idiot sometimes."

Noura shakes her head. Words washed away by the relief of not having to curl herself into some mold of expectation.

"Noura?" He dips closer, erasing any distance between them. "Please. I'm a jerk. I—"

A bump in the road sends Noura crashing into him, her lips against his—the lightest of brushes, which sends lightning bursting through Noura in equal measures of horror and desire.

Theo clears his throat, his Adam's apple dipping, drawing Noura's focus perilously toward the open neck of his shirt.

"I'm sorry...I..."

Theo merely raises an impish brow. "You are going to be the death of me. But my dear, if you wanted me to duck, you need only have winked."

A blush heats Noura's face, which only makes Theo's grin spread. Before she can beat a hasty retreat, Theo catches the edge of her scarf, worrying the silk between his fingers, watching her face, holding her captive for a breath until the material slips from Noura's hair, drifting into her lap, undone.

"I didn't mean—"

Theo cups her cheekbone, his thumb skimming across her lips. "Noura?"

Her vision sparks, shimmering in the undercurrent. When she cannot bring herself to meet Theo's gaze, he chuckles, tipping her chin. "Noura, I quite enjoyed it." He winks, slow and deliberate, and so gloriously elegant that Noura comes to pieces.

When she does not duck, he slides out of the seat, kneeling in front of her, a lost soul come home. He caresses her hair, his touch drifting down Noura's arms, her elbows. He lifts her hand and turns it, cradling her ink-stained fingers. Dark lashes press against his cheeks as he traces Noura's lifelines with a finger, sending shivers shooting through her bones, crashing into her brain.

"Did you know that our cells have electrical currents?" she blurts.

Theo lifts her palm and brushes it against his lips, and the hum of his affirmative response against her skin snaps through her. Proof of electricity barely contained, seeping from her pores. Blood pulses through every inch of her body. He concentrates his kisses on each of Noura's fingers, each one a question and permission granted. This is nothing like Charles Berry's predatory kisses, the claiming even as he locked Noura out. Theo is nothing like her polished husk of an ex-fiancé. Nothing like her sister, who uses and discards her. Nothing like her father and grandmother, who demand she conform.

As Theo rises higher on his knees, she digs her fingers into the darkness of his hair, guides him to her, the sizzle of his cheek against hers. The taste of vanilla tea on her lips mingles with the mint of his.

This is acceptance, connection. Her Theo. Noura's body thrums with electric adrenaline, and she is desperate for air, for Theo, and she knows. Estelle is not only wrong about Theo, but Noura wants to be more than his teammate. She wants to be his. But...even as she holds on to what she desperately needs, her mind skips. A good teammate doesn't lie. She tries to focus on breathing, on the desert around them, on anything other than the truth. Noura has hidden and lied, and if she can't trust Theo enough to be honest, she will never be free to be his Ma'at.

"Theo?" His name is a breathless plea on Noura's lips.

Theo rocks back on his heels, staring Noura down to the truth of her coiled soul, concern flowing through the cut of his dark brows. His hands are planted guardians on either side of her hips.

"I need to tell you something," Noura says.

THEO HOLDS his thoughts in while Noura tells him about finding her sister at the mission. And he's quiet while she tells him the deeper story of Estelle's reactionary history. But when Noura tells Theo the complete reasons behind her sister's request, he's afraid his face is a neon sign screaming his fear, even as he kicks himself for not doing a thorough background check.

There's nothing truly incriminating in Noura's recitation of her sister's woes and her concern for their brother-in-law, but she has no idea what danger she's put them all in.

"Why didn't you tell me this before?" There's an overly controlled evenness to his tone, but it's better than allowing his unease to explode shrapnel over this woman he's coming to love.

Noura shrugs, and obvious shame compresses her shoulders. "She's my sister."

"Is there anything else?" he asks. His red-hot desire to protect Noura pours over his ice-cold promise of revenge, cracking him down the middle.

Noura's fingers splay over her pocket, and when there's a crinkle of paper, her eyes flick down, widen, and then jerk to Theo's face. Guilty.

"What is it?" Theo holds out his hand.

"The list?" she says with a thin veneer of innocence.

He breathes deeply, watching her face flicker through emotions, then settle into indignation as she hauls a paper out and slaps it into his lap with a triumphant "the one you said was nothing."

Theo's jaw tightens so suddenly, he's surprised his teeth don't shatter.

"This was your sister's?" He is positively growling now.

"I..." Noura stares at the page, as does Theo.

The words there would give him more answers if they were hieroglyphs. Where is his mother's promised wisdom now? The only mark that makes sense is Typhon's. The seal hasn't changed in the two decades since he first saw it on a missive addressed to him. Then, he had no idea who Typhon was. No idea what he was capable of. No idea what it meant to transport a package, no questions asked.

"She didn't write it," Noura says with certainty she shouldn't hold.

"That doesn't mean it isn't hers." Theo watches emotions surge across her face, hardening. "Do not prevaricate with me, Noura. Those artifacts are under our care."

"I am not prevaricating. All I know is Estelle didn't write it. I told you when I found it, I thought someone was trying to steal the artifacts, and you made me look like a fool. At this point, I don't know what you're playing at, trying to blame me." Noura snatches the page and hides it in her pocket.

Yes, she did tell him. But, looking back, he'd been blinded by one of the most obvious facts in this whole stinking mess. "If someone is trying to steal the artifacts, they could easily have done so with the information you know. You're the one in charge of setting the routes. Are you working with her?"

Sucking air through her teeth, Noura knocks on the panel between them and Farid. "Mr. Fabre will be getting out here."

Farid jerks a glance over his shoulder, frowning. But he eases to the side of the road without question. Noura is missing the point, and Theo cannot allow Farid to access the rifle and force him out of the tuk-tuk in the sparsely populated desert. They'll all end up dead.

"Noura, stop and think." Theo leans his elbows on his knees, the feather pendant swinging out and back, beating against his chest, reminding him of his promise to his mom to follow the right path, to be the protector of Ma'at. And he desperately wants to. He's been in worse scrapes before, but never one where he cares so much for the person who might be his adversary. What if Noura isn't Ma'at as he thought? What if his mother was wrong about everything?

When Noura doesn't answer and continues staring down the endless desert on her side of the tuk-tuk, Theo shifts, his knee smashing into hers, demanding attention. "You remember I said that the taxi driver's neighbor didn't like all the people sniffing about?" He pauses, and the hesitation lures Noura's focus.

"There was a woman," Theo says. "He says he caught her with Selket."

She'd seen the woman. She'd been nowhere near the taxi. But it wouldn't matter, would it? The man's word against a woman's. Noura's fingers clamp onto his thigh, pinning him to the seat. "Is it her?"

"I don't know. She could have been the woman we saw in the bazaar. I—"

"Where is she?" Noura's assumption that the woman is her sister is condemning indeed. "Even if I could stomach leaving my sister behind, Estelle is Mehedi's best hope. And she'll do anything for him."

While Noura doesn't say it, Theo knows Noura will too.

Theo drums a thumb against his thigh, his brain whirring to find a solution. Any solution. "The neighbor, he's a police officer."

"Farid," she shouts. "Turn around. We're going back."

"I don't think—" Theo is cut off by the revving of the engine.

Theo's trailed Estelle enough to know she's been practically adopted by Farid's family. He's as invested as Noura, which is good, because they're going to need more help than Theo alone can provide. He already called in favors to obtain Estelle's passport. He would sell his soul to be Noura's hero, but there isn't much of it left to give. If she'd only told him sooner. If he'd only told her.

They speed into a town where Farid slows down to navigate the traffic. But Noura leans forward, trying to urge the motorcycle engine faster. The deluge is coming.

Beside Noura, Theo has gone still. She can feel him watching her, and she can't stand to stay quiet. "She wouldn't risk this if she wasn't in real trouble."

"You do realize Weather Underground steals art and artifacts to fund their bombings, right? Typhon is one of the most wanted criminals in the world, and he's one of theirs."

Noura's glare does nothing to wipe the confidence from Theo's posture. "My sister isn't whoever this Typhon person is." Estelle is smart, but not like that.

Theo reaches for Noura's hand, and she snatches it away, curling it against her chest.

"And," she says, "just because Estelle belonged to Students for a Democratic Society in college doesn't mean she'd steal or bomb anything. She may not even be part of what became Weather Underground. Most of those kids had no idea the leadership was off its rockers. They wanted the war to end and for the US to get out of Vietnam. We all know they were right."

"She told the police her name is Star Rouge." Theo stares at Noura, eyebrows raised, willing her to put together something just out of grasp. "I know for a fact," he says, "that Star works for Typhon."

Star...Estelle means star. Estelle Red. If Noura's sister is this woman, she has planted herself firmly in dangerous territory.

"What if—" Theo sucks in a breath, whether to fortify himself or her, Noura doesn't know. "What if Estelle tried to steel Selket to help buy more bombs?"

Noura's ears rush with the sound of an apocalyptic flood, and she crosses her arms against his baseless attack. "Mehedi is truly missing." The desert skids past again, blurring as the tuk-tuk speeds back the way they came. Theo shifts to the seat opposite Noura. She refuses to see the predatory cut of his cheekbones, the relentless perfection of his argument.

"The war is over." Theo's voice is calm, edged with self-righteous omniscience. "The Weathermen are still only interested in violent revolution."

"Estelle isn't the Weathermen."

"What if she's using you, Noura?"

In Noura's peripheral vision, she watches him jam his hands through his hair much like she did a few minutes ago. The memory searing, pleading. But she cannot abandon her rebellious sister for a man she barely knows. No matter how capable and kind he is.

"You said it yourself." He leans close enough, his breath feathers across her cheek. "She uses people."

Noura is spared answering by the skidding stop of the tuk-tuk in front of a white-washed building. Farid opens the door, and Noura allows him to deliver her from the cart with the grace of an American princess, completely ignoring her hangers-on. Noura fiddles with the scarf around her neck, pondering the best way to force whoever is inside to release Estelle. Subterfuge is her father's bailiwick, but Grandmere always got her way in a more direct assault. Within two days, she'd convinced half their Tel Aviv neighborhood she was some kind of empress.

Noura runs her thumb over the embroidered threads, the tiny flair of ostrich feathers, and grins. Ma'at stands for truth and justice. She is regal and wise. It is her feather that weighs against humanity's heart. And now, Noura knows exactly what to do, and she whispers blessings to the Elizabeths for making her wear this ridiculous dress. Of course if she tells Theo her plans, he'll tell her that she's silly or incapable. So, in the distinct Arabic of the Bedouin tribes, Noura tells Farid her plan and asks him to act as the interpreter for the Empress of the Mississippi Delta. "No need to let them know I speak Arabic. Yes?"

Farid gives one flickering glance at Theo and motions Noura through the door, a wicked grin growing on his face. "No need to release any advantage. Diplomacy at its finest."

Noura sweeps through the doors, channels Grandmere, and strides to the counter. When the bored police officer behind the desk doesn't even look up from the newspaper, Noura turns, preparing to launch into a tirade for Farid to translate, but Theo steps around both of them. He leans over the desk and murmurs something. The man jerks from his seat, his red-rimmed eyes flick to Noura, then he salutes Theo and spins on his heels.

With a great clanging of keys, the officer disappears behind a door, and Theo rounds on Noura. "Do you have a death wish? You can't bully the Egyptian police. They'll throw you in prison, along with whoever is back there."

"How dare—"

"And you"—he shoves a finger at Farid's aquiline nose—"should know better."

Farid shrugs. "I think you underestimate her."

Noura blinks between the two men, emotions veering between frustration and awe, anger and gratitude.

"What did you tell him?" Farid asks. "We have to know how to behave when he returns."

Leave it to Farid to think of logistics. No wonder Theo thinks Noura's a ninny.

Theo tilts his chin as if the conclusion is obvious. "She's the Empress of the Mississippi Delta."

"How did you...?" Noura looks from Farid to Theo, mouth flapping like that ninny, like somehow one of them will flourish a white rabbit as the end of their magic trick.

"I might be a semi-hack in the art world," Theo says, "but the museum chose me for more than one reason. There's a large Arab and Bedouin population in Detroit. My best friend taught me Levantine Bedawi Arabic so we could talk in school without anyone understanding. And it wasn't hard to learn modern Arabic after that. For the record, the whole empress thing wasn't a bad idea, just lacking in execution. I told them you believe they've arrested your lady's maid. If they don't retrieve the woman arrested while assisting with the transport of antiquities, the full might of the United States will be upon his head."

"And he believed you?"

"The fact that you're wearing Ma'at's feathers didn't hurt. But honestly, one look at you and anyone would believe me. You have to trust me for this to work, Noura."

A blush crawls up Noura's cheeks, but the door crashing open saves her from any further blubbering. The police officer drags a disheveled woman into the reception area and shoves her in front of Noura. "Is this her?" He pulls back the woman's hair, and Noura nearly cries.

"No." Her voice cracks under the swell of confusion and frustration.

The officer is triumphant as he yanks the poor, cowering woman against his chest. "You Americans barge in here and tell us what to do. You are infants. All of you."

A drop of spittle lands on Noura's cheek, and she straightens, anger crashing. "Farid, take this officer's name and report him to Hermann. And take that woman with us."

Farid rapid-fire translates, but Theo clamps onto Noura's arm, even as she prays she's not overstepped. US Ambassador Hermann Eilts may remember the precocious twenty-year-old who pestered him about Arab history while she visited her father. But he wouldn't take kindly to any disruption to his work...especially over some woman.

Theo inserts that the woman might know something of Noura's servant, and they would like to speak with her. When the man hesitates, Theo extracts his wallet, withdraws a layer of Egyptian pounds, and holds it out to the officer. The officer snatches the bills, then shoves the woman at Noura. The woman is bird-thin and filthy. Bruises cover her cheek and neck.

They all back out of the building, bowing, hoping their profuse thanks will cover their disrespect.

Outside, the woman squints into the glaring afternoon. "You are looking for a woman?" She directs this to the ground.

"Yes." Noura answers in Arabic, which surprises the woman enough that she risks looking fully into Noura's face.

Shock ripples through Noura. The woman can't be more than fifteen.

"She was kind to me, protected me," the girl says with a thread of pleading. "She said only she could choose my death. They do not like her."

She glances at Farid and Theo, then Noura. "She looks like you."

Who knew your entire world could shatter with four words?

18

The world sparks. Flashes of frantic Arabic penetrate the cotton fluff of Noura's thoughts. The barking laugh of a dog. A man's voice in the distance demanding clean water.

"Madam?" The girl's voice jars Noura from the tornado of realization.

"Madam, we have to get her out."

That officer lied to their faces, took Theo's money, and Noura cannot leave Estelle, no matter what she's done.

"Do not worry, Madam. I have the keys." The girl grins wickedly and lifts her fingers, where a set of keys dangles innocently.

The keys to hades. If Noura takes these, if she breaks her sister out of jail, what does that make her? What does it make the child standing in front of her? She runs a sweaty hand down her dress. Justice is above mere law. Is it not? Ma'at looks for the lightness of heart. Even Father's Jesus says humanity must obey goodness above man-made rules.

"What's your name?" Noura asks her.

The girl stares at her fingers. "Everyone calls me Yasmine."

"But what's your name?"

"I don't remember." The girl's chin lifts in defiance, and Noura erases the wince from her face.

"Well, Yasmine." Noura catches the girl's fingers in hers. "You and I will retrieve my sister, and then we will help you too. Yes?"

The girl taps a nail on her thigh once and then twice before nodding and flickering a hesitant smile.

"Farid?" Noura calls.

He steps around the doorframe. "Mr. Theo has gone for water."

What will happen to Estelle while they wait? She will just have to make do. "We need a distraction."

Farid strokes his beard, then strides toward a group of young boys playing in the dirt. Before Noura quite knows what's happening, the boys are setting off fireworks in a cascade of running feet.

The officer bursts from the police station and careens after the boys.

Yasmine and Noura scurry toward the building, and the girl unlocks the first door and the second in a way that confirms Noura's suspicions. She is a thief. Noura ignores Theo's chastising voice in her head and scrambles behind Yasmine.

The girl unlocks a third door and throws it open. On the floor is a lump of bloodied clothing. No, a woman. Stooping down, Yasmine croons to the woman who is poured across the cement. The woman lifts her head, and Noura forces herself not to blanch at the bruise on her neck or the bloody gap in her mouth where a tooth is missing. Fear and anger spill through Noura. "Estelle. Estelle."

"Help." Yasmine beckons. *Help!*

Noura drops to her knees, throwing her arm around her sister, lifting Estelle to her feet.

Noura's sandals skid on the grimy floor. She's loath to think about what substance is inordinately slippery and also causes a disgusting slurping with every step.

In the main room, the shouts of the officer rumble above the laughter of the boys. Coming closer.

Farid bursts through the door, panic etched in his frantic beckoning. Yasmine flips Estelle's arm over Farid's shoulder, and he scoops Estelle into his capable arms so they can sprint out the door, into the blistering sun, and down the road. Noura dives into the cart, then accepts her sister across her lap, Yasmine climbing in after. Farid slams the door. In one swift motion, he leaps onto the motorcycle and starts the engine.

"Where's Theo?" Noura asks, but Farid shakes his head.

They cannot wait for him. Her stomach drops. Theo is stuck in a village where he'll be blamed for Noura's recklessness.

Estelle stirs, and Noura leverages her upright.

Tears fill Estelle's big eyes, a single drop winding its way through the blood and dirt.

"I have precious few siblings left." Noura shrugs, a twin tear to her sister's bursting the dam. "And I promised I would always protect you." Still, her heart is anything but light.

"Thank you." Estelle curls against the window frame.

Noura spreads her strong, sure hand over her sister's shaking one.

A LITTLE MORE THAN a quarter hour later, Farid slides the tuk-tuk into the shade of a crumbling sandstone wall outside the next village. He hesitates, ear cocked, listening. Yasmine is frowning out the window.

The air, already stifling, presses heavy on Noura's shoulders. "Is something wrong?"

Noura watches Yasmine's face as it flickers from fear to concentration, and finally, she gives a tiny shake of her head.

As if in agreement, Farid swings a leg over the motorcycle and strides to the cart. The only sign of continued concern is how he repeatedly flicks his hands. It's what Noura does to shake both water and stress off.

Farid opens the door and leans in. "I will go for water to clean her wounds. If anything happens, use this." He passes an ancient-looking revolver to Yasmine, who takes it with a stoic nod like she's practiced for this her entire life.

The possibility tightens Noura's lungs around what little air she can take in. "Do you think that's necessary?" Who knows why Yasmine was in prison, let alone what she might do with the opportunity to kidnap two American women.

"We must trust someone," Farid says.

"I refused to pay my father's debts by becoming the concubine of a rich old man," Yasmine says, her voice so detached, so blunt that Noura is bludgeoned into silence.

"Your sister would have escaped if she hadn't stopped to help me." Yasmine shrugs an elegant shoulder, and Noura realizes how pretty the young woman is. "I owe you both a debt."

Estelle reaches across the seat and takes hold of the girl's hand. "I only did what all of humanity *should* do."

"I will hurry." Farid pats the wall of the cart and scurries toward town.

"He's afraid news of our escape has reached here, isn't he?" Noura asks.

Estelle nods, tears gathering on her lashes. "I'm sorry, Noura. I keep trying to do the right thing, and then..." She sniffs, trailing off.

Noura's glad she helped her sister, glad she helped Yasmine. But at what cost? The idea of leaving Theo in that place... Noura forces herself to breathe the scorching air. In. Out. How will she save him? She'll have to tell Mr. Hoving what she's done. It will cost her career, but what is her job in the face of Theo's life? She clutches the falcon feather in her pocket, willing Theo to be safe.

By the time Farid returns with a skin of water and clean rags, Noura is clutching the edges of the bench seat and the frenzied tail of her fear.

He pokes his head in the door with a lopsided grin. "It appears the jinn have seen fit to bless me today with a cart full of women as beautiful as goddesses."

Estelle's head lolls to face him. "I have no words to thank you enough, my friend."

"You can thank me by eating a few of these"—he drops a packet of flat bread onto her lap—"and allowing your sister to minister to your wounds so I can drive with haste."

"I didn't try to steal anything," Estelle says. "But they don't care. You can't hide me anymore, Farid. It isn't safe."

"Then I'll get you out," Noura says with a surety she doesn't own. But as sure as the sun is a ball of gas and not Ra driving a fiery chariot across the sky, Noura won't allow her sister to come to more harm. She will fulfill her promise this time.

Farid squeezes Estelle's hand and releases it to her lap.

"I have sent friends to assist Mr. Theo. We will do what we can."

But Noura knows it will not be enough. Somehow, she must save Theo and her sister. How she will do both is beyond her, but she will try. With everything in her, she will try.

BY THE TIME they reach Cairo, the lights of the motorcycle struggle to cut through the pressing darkness. Above them, the first star of the night flickers, and Noura watches its steady glow. If only a star could make wishes come true. But Noura's begun to think home and family and peace are as unreal as the goddess Ma'at, or at least not possible for someone like her. And she is exhausted from trying. Noura digs out the two feathers, intent on letting them fly out the window. But she can't quite release the reminder of Theo. So she tucks the falcon feather into her bag and the ostrich feather into her sister's pouch. Maybe it will serve Estelle better than Noura.

At the hotel, Farid parks out of the reach of the lights. Noura opens the door and then attempts to untangle the trap her dress has become. Farid reaches in, and he hauls her upright, which allows the wrinkled dress space to shake itself out. He taps Yasmine awake, and the girl climbs out, immediately clamping onto Noura's arm and using the older woman's body to shield her. It's obvious she's never seen anything so grand as the hotel, with all its marble and gold filigree, nor the men in matching black and gold livery.

Farid kneels in the cart, gathers Estelle to him, eases her from the cart, and sets her on her wavering legs. He cannot carry her into the hotel without causing an unwelcome scene that might very well lead to his arrest.

"Elizabeth," Estelle whispers. "Get Elizabeth."

Reinforcements. Yes. They need reinforcements.

Noura gathers her skirts to bound into the hotel, but Estelle snatches her arm. "Slowly. Nothing is amiss."

Of course. Noura straightens, donning the empress persona once more. She is beyond disheveled at the moment. Still, she breezes through the door and up the stairs. When she arrives at Elizabeth's door, she's shaking and out of breath.

Noura lifts her fist to knock, the momentary silence nearly shattering her brittle courage. For her sister, Noura knocks and falls into Elizabeth's arms the moment the door cracks open.

"Help. We need your help."

Elizabeth listens to the story with the aplomb of a real empress, nodding at appropriate moments and not expressing an iota of dismay at Noura's description of Estelle's state or that Noura broke two women from jail and somehow left Theo behind.

"Right-o," Elizabeth says with a practiced nod. "You clean yourself up, find Mr. Hoving, and explain that Theo has likely been jailed. I will take care of your sister and Yasmine. Your Theo already delivered a new passport for Estelle. I shall secret her away. And Yasmine and Farid will be right as rain with me."

"But..." Noura sits gaping at her. How did this pampered woman have such confidence in manipulating a foreign government on so many levels?

Elizabeth raises a disapproving brow at Noura's hesitation, and, though Noura has never had a stern British tutor, she jumps to her feet as if she has had her knuckles cracked more than once by such a person.

"I'll go change then." Noura resists the urge to bow.

"What the devil did you do to yourself?" Lizzy's indignant voice lifts from behind Noura.

"Lizzy." Elizabeth pushes against Noura's back, driving Noura nose-to-nose with her friend. "There's no time."

"There is always time for fashion...especially when things seem most dire." Lizzy stands her ground. "I've heard bits and snippets. Come, darling. I have the perfect outfit to convince your Mr. Hoving you're a person of consequence and not a lily-headed nitwit. Impressions are everything." She grasps Noura's elbow and neatly spins her out one door and into the next, all the way through to a bursting wardrobe. "Here." Lizzy lifts a gorgeous terracotta silk pantsuit. "I bought this for you." She holds up a hand, forestalling Noura's objection. "A thank you will suffice."

Noura steps behind the screen and sheds the bedraggled dress, hanging it carefully before slipping into the pantsuit. She cannot bear the thought of Theo in that place as she primps. If they beat Estelle, what will they do to him?

"Now." Lizzy pats the overstuffed stool in front of the vanity.

Noura will not win the argument, and so she sits like an obedient child, clutching the falcon feather that is the soft twin to the one Theo wears.

In mere moments, Lizzy fixes Noura's hair and sprinkles makeup across her face. When the Brit spins Noura toward the mirror, she is who she is, but not. At least Noura looks the part of a sophisticated woman, someone who can be trusted. Noura calls the operator and asks to speak with Mr. Hoving. The man says that Mr. Hoving is in the lobby, and Noura should look for him there.

"Thank you," Noura says. Her voice sounds calm, but her hands shake so much, Lizzy has to take the receiver and settle it in the cradle. How does one act confident when one is anything but?

"I will pray he looks on you with favor." Lizzy leads Noura to the door. "You are doing what you must to protect the people you care about."

Noura knows she is right. But is this the way? She demanded and manipulated to secure Estelle's release, and look how that turned out. Despite herself, she wonders what Ma'at would do. *Find the balance.*

"Be careful." Lizzy's words prick, and Noura wants to shove them away.

Noura's desire to evade must show on her face because Lizzy turns Noura to face her. "Why do you assume your sister is guilty of trying to steal that statue?"

"The neighbor saw her."

"He saw her take Selket from the car?"

Noura thinks back to what Theo said. "No," she says. "Theo is the one who said someone tried to steal her."

"If one were going to steal a priceless object, wouldn't one employ an expert in repair and reconstruction to create a forgery?"

Noura blanches. "I wouldn't even know how to do that."

"No." The sorrow in Lizzy's voice confuses Noura, and she stands, waiting for the clarification the other woman is so obviously hesitant to give.

"Curators don't reconstruct artifacts." Lizzy's gaze flicks to Noura and away. "That's the conservator's job."

Understanding floods Noura.

Theo. She means Theo. "Why would he—?"

"And he's also the one who brought Selket back. Isn't he?"

"But he's the one who told me about Estelle being in prison. And he's probably in prison as a result."

"Shoulders back, head high." Elizabeth's words snatch Noura from the spin in her brain, recalling Maman as she clung to what little dignity she had left. "Hurry now, Mr. Hoving is waiting. I've sent my manservant down to protect your sister. I'll join her momentarily. Have no fear."

Habitual obedience propels Noura to stride down the stairs and across the lobby into the restaurant, where she finds a frowning Mr. Hoving and a road-worn, furious Theo. The falcon feather drifts from Noura's fingers and lands, forgotten, on the intricate carpet.

19

"Theo." The name escapes Noura's lips in a combination of confusion and relief. "You're okay. How did you...?"

Mr. Hoving stands, towering over Noura, gesturing to the seat across from the two men. Mr. Hoving has a reputation for being a shark, but she's never seen the comparison until now. There's no outfit perfect enough or words diplomatic enough to disarm whatever threat has the hairs on her arms standing to attention.

Noura sinks to the chair, the arms closing her in, the back too straight. She feels like the little girl caught at her mother's table while wearing old lipstick smeared outside the lines.

"Well?" Mr. Hoving says.

To her horror, tears prick. Noura digs her broken nails into her thigh —thinks of her sister's black eye, her broken lip—and scrapes together her wits. "It seems Mr. Fabre has extricated himself from trouble. Since things are in order, I'll retire. I'm sorry to have disturbed you." She rises from the seat.

"Sit." Mr. Hoving's voice allows no room for retreat.

Noura sucks air through her nose and resettles. *Don't fail me now, Grandmere.*

"Mr. Fabre has regaled me with quite the tale."

Theo is watching Noura steadily, like a falcon, circling, studying her weaknesses. How had she mistaken his watchfulness for kind regard? There is no softness in him now.

"Yes?" Noura straightens her fingers across her lap, forcing herself not to fidget.

"Did you provide a way for your sister to steal Selket?"

Noura relaxes a fraction. "No, sir." She answers with the force of truth.

"Did you know she might attempt it?"

"No, sir. And as far as I know, she never attempted it. Has anyone come forward saying she did?"

Theo stirs and slides the list Noura had found across the table.

Sweat pricks her armpits. "I found the list on the street. I notified both Theo and Dr. Lilyquist. Theo said—"

"The authorities knew about the list." Theo's eyes flash like the falcon-headed Horus. God of order and protection, yes. But also the god of war. "But you didn't tell any of us you thought the list belonged to your sister."

"I never said it belonged to Estelle. In fact I said the opposite," she spits at Theo. "That isn't her handwriting, Mr. Hoving."

"Perhaps. But you did break her out of prison after you asked for my help in getting her into the States. Yes?"

The stranglehold of Noura's mistakes tightens around her throat, leaving her barely able to speak. "Yes, but—"

"But nothing." Mr. Hoving is disturbingly absent of emotion. "You abused my good graces."

Noura wants to tell him of the work her sister does with the poor and abused, but he is unlikely to hear anything from Noura if Theo has told him otherwise. Theo, the wunderkind who rescued the mission. Why is he doing this?

"Where is she now?" Mr. Hoving's voice softens.

Noura shakes her head, not trusting her voice.

"Noura..." Theo starts but clears his throat and begins again. "Miss Marquette."

"*Doctor* Marquette." Anger sharpens Noura's words. "I do not know where she is, Mr. Fabre." Noura stands, knees locked against the trembling.

"Dr. Marquette, I am only trying to help." Theo is placating now, treating her like a child as he spreads his hands in a gesture of good faith, all while he holds a metaphorical knife ready to stab her in the back again. "Don't sacrifice yourself for someone who's using you. The Egyptian police are rightly upset. If we can't help them, we'll have no choice but to—"

Mr. Hoving stops Theo with an impatient gesture. "You are one of the finest young curators I have met. Dr. Lilyquist is thrilled with your assistance. Unfortunately, the Egyptians have made my choices clear: surrender those who attempted to steal Selket, or you are no longer welcome in their country. If I have to send you home, I have to fire you. Dr. Marquette...Noura."

But Noura will not betray her sister even if Estelle is Star Rouge, and even if Noura knew where Lizzy and Elizabeth had spirited her sister.

"Excuse me, gentlemen. I need to pack."

The walk to her room feels like the march to the death chamber. She expected Estelle's behavior. But Theo? He'd promised to protect her.

Her throat closes over the scream pushing against her ribs. She understands now why Set hated Horus and his pompous, presumptuous form of justice. Noura hates her sister. Hates Theo. But even more, Noura hates the anger that proves she still cares.

By morning, Noura is packed. Lizzy stands in Noura's doorway, weeping, promising to help. But a British aristocrat can't salvage Noura's career. What will Noura do with the rest of her life? The triumphant cackle of the Set Beast accompanies her footsteps down the stairs.

Theo is in the lobby. He's stony-eyed, dark shadows bruising his face like he's been waiting there all night to be sure Noura didn't slip away.

Noura ignores him and strides to the doors, her heeled sandals clacking on the tiles, emphasizing the finality of her wayward steps.

"Noura," Theo calls. "Ma'at."

But she slams through the doors, not waiting for the doorman to open them.

Theo could have called last night to explain how he managed to avoid the police and return to Cairo. But he didn't. And now Noura is more convinced than ever that he had something to do with the theft. He could have forged Selket and prepared a duplicate crate for her. He could have colluded with Ghadfa to swap it and then scare Noura off. Even easier still to bribe a random small village police officer to look the other way.

The powerlessness of the situation is maddening. But Noura has no recourse, no way out. Why did she ever trust this man? Why did she ever allow herself to hope? She was ridiculous to let herself think she might possibly be able to balance out the world just a little. She can't possibly be Ma'at when everything inside her is chaos.

Of course the taxi has not arrived yet. She's cursed to be on time and organized for every event but the one unfolding in front of her.

"Noura." Theo touches her elbow, and she jerks away, resisting the urge to slap him.

"I know you don't want to hear this," he says with a glance over his shoulder. "Your sister is in trouble."

When Noura pretends to dig in her purse, Theo steps in front of her. "Noura, please."

Blessedly the taxi driver toots the jaunty horn and eases to the curb.

"Thank you for your concern." She snaps her purse closed. "But I don't know where Estelle is."

"I'm trying to help."

"Help?" Noura's voice is slightly unhinged. "Is that what you did? You make me think my sister may be in trouble, so I turn around. Then you disappear in the village long enough for me to rescue her. I was terrified for you. Ready to risk my life to save you. But here you are. Not a hair out of place, tattling to Mr. Hoving for no reason whatsoever… unless you have something to hide and needed to deflect attention before someone could shine the spotlight on you."

Theo opens his mouth, but Noura flips a palm up to stop him and steps closer. "You used me from the beginning. You set me up as a flighty female, one who couldn't be trusted. Meanwhile, you're the only person in the position to not only make a passable forgery of the artifact, its case, and seal, but you are also one of the few who knew the route to the docks ahead of time. Maybe you even arranged for the taxi driver to stop in that village. So no, Mr. Fabre, I will not help you because the only person you are trying to help is yourself."

Noura slides into the blazing hot taxi and rolls up the window as the driver starts the car.

"Why was she there?" Theo's muffled voice worms through the glass. "What brought Estelle to the middle of nowhere, exactly where we were? They were off route. I begged Mr. Hoving to talk to you because I knew you weren't involved."

Theo's attention flicks around the empty drive until it lands on the falcon perched on a tree limb and frowning down at them.

Theo growls at the bird, then leans in to plead with Noura. "Why are you protecting her?"

If she didn't know better, Noura would think he's taking direction from the bird and that they're both scared for her. But that's as absurd as thinking he's interested in her.

As the taxi eases into the street, she closes her eyes against the man and the city she once thought she might be able to love, and slams a lid over the voice calling her to Ma'at's peace.

20

Somewhere south of Chicago, Illinois
August 30, 1977

Sharp-edged clouds lower over the horizon, cutting the busload of people off from the Chicago lights. Almost a year ago, Elizabeth transported Estelle to the United States, where she's tried to keep to herself. Estelle doesn't know where Yasmine or Farid are. She doesn't know what price they paid for her freedom. But her sister? Estelle knows how much she owes Noura. And yet Estelle is on her way to ask yet another favor as if nothing happened.

She leans her head against the appallingly dirty headrest and tries not to think about whether the feds are still trailing her. If they are, she may very well be walking into a trap. At least the man across the aisle isn't FBI. He overflows everything—his suit coat, dress shirt, even his seat. In fact he splays his legs so far, his running shoes touch her pinky toe tucked under the seat in front of her.

Estelle nudges the man's foot, and he grunts at her. She touches the Ka Bar knife in the small of her back, tempted to remove his big, hairy toe.

Not that she would. But a growling voice in her mind tempts her to throw off caution.

Instead, she lifts her leg as if to stretch, points her toe in a perfect, seated grand battement. She catches him staring at her calf, then slams her stiletto heel into the top of his shoe.

He leaps to his feet, slamming his head on the ceiling in a concussive wave of swearing. The men surrounding them pivot, encircling Estelle in a protective barrier. Though it's 1977, Southern men still pack their women in cotton batting, and there isn't one of them who will allow a chauvinist to swear a blue streak at a dewy-eyed ingenue. They don't have to know Estelle's no innocent or that she resents their own brand of chauvinism. She simply relaxes with a mental sigh of thanks to her mother's insistence on dance lessons and a grudging acknowledgment that dear old Dad did something right by teaching his daughters defensive techniques.

One of the men switches places with Big Hairy Toe, saying the jerk is lucky he's not being dumped on the side of I-57. Estelle smiles her gratitude.

Not sure how real her passport and other documents are, Estelle keeps her head down. Worse, both Lizzy and her sister are increasingly curious about Mehedi—where Saira's brother lives now, what his job is, if they can see him. Estelle can't exactly tell anyone that Mehedi is in jail for a theft he didn't commit.

Estelle rubs at the throbbing in her forehead.

Her rescuer offers Estelle a chocolate, but she demurs with an "I couldn't." Estelle has enough insulin left to get to New Orleans… maybe…if she constrains herself to two meals a day. Then she'll have to throw herself on the mercy of her family. Estelle hates being controlled by her disease, forced to either die or endure needle after needle—one expensive vial of medicine after another. Still, she's lucky her family is able to afford testing and medicine.

When the man leans over, asking if she's sure about the sweet, Estelle bats her lashes against her cheek and digs for her cigarettes as an excuse to unearth a book from the bottom of her satchel.

Estelle sits upright with book and Camels in hand.

When the savior, lighter in hand, leans across the aisle close enough that Estelle can count the copious hairs in his nostrils, she opens her book and makes sure the man sees the bold black title—Karl Marx's

Communist Manifesto. He scrambles backward so quickly, one might think Estelle threatened the man's life. Though given his three-piece suit, superior ways, and wedding ring, she might very well have.

Opening the window a crack, Estelle flicks a match and lets the flare touch the cigarette. She inhales, the warmth spreading, before she blows the smoke in the general direction of her would-be savior.

His indignation has earned Estelle silence, and after the first stop, an empty row for the rest of the nine-hundred-mile trip. The reprieve gives her time to think and plan. She's spent the last six months alternating between waitressing at Don's—a ramshackle diner off Michigan Street —working at the Greater Chicago Food Depository, and quietly maneuvering to keep Mehedi safe. Each week she visited, and he sat across the table, his dark curls hanging over his smiling face, dexterous fingers loosely clasped on the table in front of him. But the last time she went to see Mehedi, he was gone. She got a message a few hours later and flew to the prison where he, once again, sat across a table, relaxed as ever. But Estelle knows there will be no grace for a foreigner. No one cares how hard he worked to get to the land of the free, only to find every door slammed in his face.

It doesn't help that his public defender is worthless and probably complicit. He is, after all, the one who gave her the sealed envelope with her new orders. Despite Weather Underground's claims to want to assist the underdog, they've abandoned Mehedi to his fate. Estelle can't help but wonder if their refusal to help is tied to her subverting Typhon's first request. Where there is money, there is power. And vice versa. But more probably, they won't help because the leadership is avoiding J. Edgar Hoover's crusade by bolting to Cuba.

No matter the reasons, Estelle is on her own. If only her license to practice law hadn't been revoked when her passport was.

"Give me your tired, your poor, Your huddled masses yearning to breathe free"...and then I shall throw them to the wolves.

Estelle closes her eyes against the twisting of the famous poem gracing Lady Liberty.

Estelle eases the ostrich feather from between the pages of her book. She still doesn't understand why Noura left it for her. Elizabeth said that

Egyptians believed that the feather belonged to the goddess Ma'at. She was the keeper of justice and truth, and it was this feather that judged whether a human's heart was heavy with evil. But Estelle has very little idea of where the line between good and evil is anymore. She tucks the feather back into the book and stuffs everything back into her bag.

Every option Estelle thinks of has the same problem—she needs money and alternatives. In the meantime, she's headed home, where she's not sure whether it's good or bad that Noura will be there too. Estelle is thrilled that Noura's in a place she loves. But from the little bits Estelle's heard about the tour stop in Chicago, the King Tut exhibit is struggling with its security system. And that is bad news for both sisters.

The security lapses led Typhon to reissue his demand. Steal the artifacts...or else. Estelle wants to save Mehedi, but how is she supposed to steal one of the most famous pieces of the tour and arrange for transport? In Egypt, at least she had a network with questionable ethics. Typhon said to contact the conservator, but the last thing Estelle wants is to work with Theodore Fabre.

She doesn't trust Typhon or Fabre to tie her shoes, let alone fulfill their promise to get Mehedi out of trouble. But Typhon needs to believe Estelle's obeying commands, which is why Estelle is on the blasted bus, enduring a seat spring jammed into her thigh.

Why is Typhon so interested in these specific artifacts anyway? Has he promised them to someone powerful? Is he trying to disrupt the alliance with Egypt? And why is he so determined to make Estelle the thief? Why not someone who wants the job?

Perhaps she'd be better off raising money for a lawyer for Mehedi and a PI to track down Typhon. Revenge would taste oh so sweet. But that would cost more than she can scrape together in a hundred years of waitressing.

Estelle's brain works the problem the entire ride south, and no god steps forward with an answer.

When the bus finally arrives in New Orleans, Estelle is the last to drag herself off, but it is more strategy than exhaustion. By the time she hails a taxi, she's lifted enough cash from Would-Be Savior, Big Hairy Toe, and a few others to catch a taxi to Grandmere's villa.

Perhaps New Orleans will roll out its voodoo curses and play nasty with the boy king. Then Estelle will be saved from the choices she is, even now, making.

But history has taught her that the powerful win and the weak pay the price.

21

New Orleans, Louisiana

The wrought-iron gates of La Villa Poitiers arc across the drive, opposing the taxi's entry.

"Miss?" The cabby peers through his shaggy mane at Estelle.

"This will do. Thank you." She hands him cash far exceeding the fare. Cabbies hole up in the most abominable places, and Estelle knows how much it costs to buy your way into driving a cab in the city.

She won't need the extra twenty dollars...provided Maman is home to stand up to her mother on Estelle's behalf. Saying there's tension between Grandmere and her youngest granddaughter is like saying that the Mississippi is a nice little river. Whether Grandmere's prejudice is on account of Estelle's humanitarian friends or her choice not to hoard every dime she makes, Estelle long ago decided Grandmere's demands will not dictate her actions.

Estelle steps out of the cab, then presses the doorbell hanging on the gate. As she waves the cabby off, she dabs uselessly at the sweat pooling at her hairline and flaps her long skirts around her ankles. She cocks her head, listening.

No one answers the buzz. She doesn't expect them to. Today is

Tuesday—Maman and Grandmere will be at a Mystick Krewe of Comus meeting, planning the group's secret Mardi Gras parade and ball... because they've apparently nothing better to do.

When the cabby disappears around the waxy-leafed magnolia on the corner, Estelle lights another cigarette and sweeps down the length of the archaic stone wall. Concealed in the shadow of a spreading oak, she stands for a moment flexing and pointing her toes, watching, waiting for a distraction. Her stomach growls, and she frowns, fighting the temptation to rush. She hates being here, hates begging, hates having no other option and no control. When an enormous black dog prowls around the corner, she decides not to find out if it's a descendant of the vicious dog that used to chase her and Noura. She chucks her bag over the wall, tucks her skirt into her waistband, and uses chipped bricks and the sturdy spines of ivy to clamber to the top of the wall. There she pauses to scan the garden before hauling herself to a sitting position and dropping lightly onto the soft moss.

It's been years since Estelle's snuck into Maman's home, but the door to the porch still jiggles. She takes a draw of her cigarette and blows it out before she lifts the handle and pops the door open with a stiff shove of her shoulder.

Inside the open-air enclosure, arborvitaes stand like evergreen soldiers protecting the inner sanctum.

Estelle pads across the white marble tiles and up the back stairs to the home built in the 1800s. Maman's people weren't there then. Like most of the neighbors, they were carpetbaggers who came to "help out" destitute plantation owners after the Civil War.

Estelle clambers onto the head of the seated lion, then pushes to her tiptoes. Thrusting her arm through the ornate ironwork of the second-floor balcony, she pats around until she bumps into the iron key. Exactly where she and Noura hid it years ago when they were forced to visit their dour grandmere for yet another summer.

Grandpa was alive then and told the sisters about Grandmere's hoydenish tendencies while gallivanting in Europe after the First World War. At some ball for traveling Americans, Grandmere was raising money for the destitute of Europe and those afflicted by the revolution in Russia. She'd mercilessly flirted with everyone but Grandpa until he couldn't stand it any longer and asked her to dance. She promptly snubbed him until he pleaded with her to marry him...which had been her aim all along.

The only highlight to Estelle's trips to New Orleans was Grandpa's pure joy at helping the sisters circumvent Grandmere's control. Palming the key, Estelle leaps from the jungle cat to the ground. She inserts the key, jiggles the door, and shoves it open...breaking in like Grandmere's ancestors had. She takes one last pull on the cigarette, drops it to the cement floor, then stomps out the embers.

Of course Estelle has no sympathy for the plantation owners who'd been run out of town by their slaves. Natural consequences if you ask her. Someday, the wealthy will trip over their own inflated heads and—

"I see you found your way in." Father's voice booms through the kitchen, and Estelle nearly drops the key.

He slathers another layer of Creole mustard on a po'boy sandwich and drops the knife in the sink. In the years since she's seen him, his hair has become mostly gray, and time has carved his face with lines and hollows.

When he waves an enormous paw at the stool across from him, Estelle sinks onto it, acutely aware of the travel smell lingering in her tangled hair.

"The women of the house are out." He bites into the sandwich, and Estelle's mouth waters with the memory of sitting here while Noura made her dinner, enticing her to play nice.

Is that what Father is doing? Manipulating her?

He studies Estelle for a moment, no doubt looking for weakness. Then he seems to decide something and leans back, lifting the bread knife from the counter. "Noura said she talked to you a few weeks back." The knife bites into the bread with a satisfying crunch as Father saws off half the sandwich.

He offers Estelle half the roast beef sandwich. Her pride screams "no," but her stomach chooses this moment to complain about her neglect. Father's lips lift in a knowing half-smile, and he lays dinner on a crisp, white linen napkin. Estelle cringes at the thought of whoever will scrub out the spreading stains, but it's done now. She barely constrains herself to a dainty bite. Father may believe Estelle is an unruly monster, but she knows etiquette. She just chooses not to follow arbitrary rules created by men intent on domination...unless it serves her interest. At the moment, it behooves Estelle to avoid as many questions as she can.

"There's cola in the refrigerator." He gestures to the monstrosity in the corner.

She stands and opens the door. The novelty of cool air freezes her into blissful stillness until Father clears his throat.

Turning with two icy bottles of Coke, she forces a quizzical smile—benign and placating. Estelle can't possibly drink the soda. She sets down the soda and fills a glass with water instead. Estelle has barely enough insulin to eat the sandwich. She hopes. He scrutinizes Estelle like he knows how low her supply is and how badly she controls the bane of her existence.

"Why are you here, Estelle?"

She feigns ignorance with a slight tilt of her head. Even as he wipes his fingers on the napkin, his knowing gaze does not leave his daughter, does not lower to the reddish brown spreading across the white fabric like blood.

Estelle chokes on the breadcrumbs, suddenly regretting stuffing her face.

She has seen too much blood, too much suffering.

Part of her wants to curl into her father, tell him about Mehedi, trust him to do the right thing, to some way, somehow stop the pain. But here they sit in a safe Garden District mansion when St. Thomas Development is a few blocks away. She knows about white flight and the subsequent heroin flood into the projects. And heroin isn't the only thing flooding the poor neighborhoods. Every year, water gobbles huge swathes of land—and along with it, houses, fields, and businesses. It feels so hopeless. And this is only one city in the vast array of cities.

Estelle sips the water, washing down the bread, along with the clogging frustration.

A king of the ruling elite will never understand the desperation, and so Estelle does not even attempt to explain to her father. "I'm here to see Noura."

"Does she know you're here?"

"I know how to use a telephone." Which isn't a lie, but it doesn't answer his question.

In a single fluid movement, Father grabs one of the Coke bottles and taps the cap on the edge of the counter, flinging the metal across the kitchen. Estelle cringes at the damage he's done but says nothing. When he lifts the second bottle, she shakes her head.

He frowns at her and sets the sweating bottle on the counter. "The only reason you decline soda is if you don't have enough insulin."

"Something like that." Estelle shrugs, not willing to beg.

A frown crinkles her father's forehead, and he stands. "Give me a moment."

Despite Estelle and her father rarely seeing eye-to-eye, she knows he would take her diabetes from her if he could. But God stubbornly refuses her father's authority in the matter. It's a reminder of the fallibility of an earthbound man, or perhaps the incomprehensibility of his unseen God.

Estelle nibbles at the sandwich, avoiding the broken teeth still tender from her beating in an Egyptian prison. She hates that she must hide if she wants to help Mehedi without landing in a CIA black site. She knows better than most that the world will keep burning even if she sacrifices herself or Mehedi. There must be a way to save them all, even with the heavy chains that came with Mehedi's temporary freedom.

In the other room, her father confirms pick-up times and murmurs to some friend or other.

It must be nice to have friends to call for help.

Too bad Fabre's on the wrong side of this. He's slippery as a fish, and Estelle has never more needed someone with street smarts to help her figure out what to do. But even if Lizzy trusted him and Typhon didn't, Fabre is in New York, working in the basement of the Met, safely away from Estelle, her sister, and King Tut.

22

Father worked his magic and, by late afternoon, Estelle is in the kitchen, alone, injecting insulin into her arm. Father still cannot watch. It's as if he thinks that if he doesn't see it, her pain cannot exist.

Thirty minutes have passed, and Estelle is sipping her soda when Maman strolls through the door with a flutter of color and excitement as if the Mardi Gras parade is marching through the living room. "Estelle, darling!" She drops her packages in a pile of frippery, then folds her daughter into a European air kiss. *Mwah! Mwah!*

Maman likes to pretend she hails directly from France or descends from a Creole princess, depending on the day and the audience. She's always quick to remind Estelle they are descendants of Prince Bohemond VI of Antioch from the thirteenth century. Though the scant tie is eleven generations back, Maman is absolutely an aristocrat of a disappearing land, at least in her own mind. The whole idea is something Grandmere sneers at except when it's convenient for her. The fact is, she's the one who initiated the fabrication when she flounced across France in the '20s. But the personality of her artifice is more akin to a Russian czar's iron fist than Maman's fluttering aristocracy.

Holding her daughter's shoulders, Maman studies Estelle a moment before releasing her into the stony examination of Grandmere. When Estelle refuses to cower beneath her grandmother's dark-eyed contempt, the matriarch snorts and stalks up the stairs as quickly as her aging body will take her. Her tantrum has made her position clear. Estelle is as unwanted as the lip stain drifting into the creases around her mouth. Unfortunately for Grandmere, Grandfather left his fortune to his daughter, not his wife. A situation from which Estelle derives a certain amount of sadistic pleasure.

Her parents drift from the room in opposite directions. Maman, to the front porch to wave like a float princess to all the neighbors. And Father to his study, where he does heaven knows what amongst his books and papers—the small kingdom of a small university professor.

Estelle wanders to the sitting room, fingers traipsing over the dusty chairs, the dark brocade davenport nearly a century old. Solid and unmoving. On a side table sits a photograph trapped behind glass. A family—seemingly happy, if not smiling—stands in front of this very house. Estelle's rebellious brother, as a dapper five-year-old, is dressed in a brown tweed suit and pageboy hat. Her sister, a baby, is swaddled in lace-edged blankets. Only Estelle is missing.

Was it Tel Aviv or Estelle herself who broke everything?

She wanders into the kitchen, unsure what to do to earn her place... if there is any place for her, and if the cost is worth the entry.

Moments later, Noura stumbles through the door, pale-faced and drenched in sweat.

Estelle grins at the dishevelment of her normally proper sister. "Your blood thickened up north," she ribs, even as she offers her sister a chilled bottle of soda.

Noura hesitates in the archway, no doubt stuck between personas—the protective older sister and the loyal daughter who bows to the wishes of others. Dropping her leather satchel on the floor, Noura hesitantly takes the bottle from Estelle and presses it to her swan-like neck. Noura has found a middle road as she always does, tucking herself in so tightly she can navigate between two immovable forces. But fitting in is not the belonging all of humanity wishes for.

"How are you?" Noura asks, slumping onto a stool.

"Hanging in there." If only Estelle could confide in her sister and they could figure a way out of the choking chaos Estelle's created. "How's your new job?" she asks.

"I love being in a museum again." Noura smiles, and Estelle wants to hug the woman peeking from underneath the false bravery.

Noura has always been beautiful, smart, and had everything going for her. Yet she manages to let all that potential sit stagnant and useless as marshland hidden behind a phalanx of cypress. If she'd redirect the tiniest bit—

"How was the trip?" Noura's gaze doesn't leave the floor as she shucks off her sensible brown heels. Definitely hiding behind a wall of practicality. "How is Mehedi?"

At Estelle's pause, Noura's head jerks up, and Estelle flicks her head to point out to the patio.

Noura pads across the kitchen and slides out the back door, Estelle following. How easily they've reverted to their younger selves, stealing out to tell secrets or to play soccer with the neighborhood kids. Noura would pack insulin, snacks, and her ever-present notebook. And when their neighbor elbowed Estelle in the nose, Noura decked him. Didn't matter he was twice her size. She always had her little sister's back.

And now? Is Estelle willing to bargain her innocent sister for Mehedi's life? There has to be a way to outsmart the devil.

Noura ducks behind the massive trunk of an ancient oak and crouches on the rotting roots of their secret meeting place. A strand of dark hair escapes Noura's chignon, and she tucks it behind her ear in a furtive flick of her wrist. She is, every inch, a hesitant trickle of a woman.

Estelle takes a massive quantity of time to arrange herself across from her older sister—pulling out a cigarette, lighting it, then sipping her cola. Noura doesn't push her, but Estelle feels impatience wafting off her. She's tired, hot, and no doubt hungry.

"What's the museum like?" Estelle asks, breathing out a nonchalant breath of smoke.

Noura picks off a piece of porous root and fiddles with it. "I've been working the front rooms and upstairs," she says carefully, not committing to any emotion. "They're completely unprepared, and the security system is abysmal. The only reason they hired me was because they were desperate, and Maman convinced Grandmere to twist some arms. The pay is terrible—a whopping four dollars an hour. But I'm in a museum."

Estelle nods, trying to find her way into what she has to do, what she can possibly say.

"Why are you here, Estelle?" Noura tears a chunk from the wood and drops it. "Not that I don't want you here, but..."

But it's obvious she doesn't want her sister here. And can anyone blame her? Still. "I...I need money, Noura." Estelle rubs at the bridge of her nose.

"Again?" Noura's uncharacteristically caustic tone makes Estelle blanch.

"Sorry." Noura sighs. "It can't be easy having to lie low. But with the exhibit opening soon, there are all kinds of jobs."

"No, I—" Estelle had been about to say she doesn't need a job, but then she realizes what Noura said and backtracks. "The museum is hiring?"

Estelle sets down the Coke bottle so her sister can't detect the shake in her hands. Securing a job at the museum might give her the access and insight she needs in order to fulfill Typhon's demand.

"I don't know if we can get you anything at the museum." Noura smiles even as Estelle's heart sinks. "But as long as you try to get along with everyone, we can work together. Maybe we can even convince Grandmere to help." She winks, and Estelle responds with a weak nod.

And just like that, Estelle has sold her sister for ancient gold plating. She straightens and takes another swig of Coke, forcing down the knot building in her throat. For Mehedi.

DINNER IS WRETCHED. Grandmere presides at the head of the table, facing Maman at the opposite end. Estelle sits beside her sister on one side, with Father relegated to a place opposite the sisters—the place of a child.

With little forewarning of Estelle's arrival, the cook, Mrs. Villiers, has outdone herself—cold salads followed by what looks like the most delicious bouillabaisse Estelle's ever seen. And as tradition demands, Mrs. Villiers chops the precooked fresh fish in front of the family before distributing it on plates for them to add to the broth. Job finished, she curtsies to Grandmere and disappears through the swinging doors like a French Creole grand chef. The woman is a wonder.

"So," Father says as he adds monkfish and a bit of lobster to the spider crab already swimming in the deep orange broth. "You never did tell me. What brings you to New Orleans?"

Estelle's fork hesitates over the plates of fish. "The truth?"

"Of course." His sarcasm is as biting as the peppery rouille sauce.

Noura drops a gentle hand on her sister's leg as a reminder of her promise to get along.

"I'm here to help a friend." Estelle squeezes her sister's fingers hard enough that Noura winces, but not hard enough to draw her ire.

"What kind of trouble is this *friend* in?" Father's emphasis on the word friend suggests all of Estelle's friends are of one stock—troublemaking ne'er-do-wells. If he only knew she was the one to lead Mehedi astray, to introduce him to what she thought was a group that would do good things. What would Father think of that?

"He's a friend from Israel," Estelle says. "A good man with a good family who is stuck in a bad circumstance."

"From Israel?" This frowning remark from Grandmere draws an answering frown from Maman. Estelle silently curses herself for drawing all three to the same side. Anything related to the Middle East returns Father to his failures and Maman to the harrowing tribulation that was her time in the foreign service. And Estelle has dropped the reminder onto their dinner table.

"Is Mehedi okay?" Noura means this to help, Estelle is sure. But it produces drawn brows from Maman like she's trying to place the name, which is downright tame compared to the volcanic color of Grandmere's face.

"Mehedi? Saira's Mehedi?" Grandmere's voice is the picture of calm, but Noura and Estelle both stiffen. There is the merest sliver of stone between them and the blistering lava of her temper.

"Yes." Estelle mirrors the calm voice, yet folds her napkin, preparing to battle her grandmother's explosion.

"Why you insist on walking in the muck of the past is beyond me." Grandmere turns from Estelle to Father. "You have done nothing but bring trouble to this house."

Father leans away from the table, his focus flicking from Estelle to Noura. Since when does he gather his words?

"As opposed to you?" Estelle snaps.

Noura's grip is a vise on Estelle's leg, but the older sister is not Moses, and the younger is not the Red Sea meekly obeying her request to desist the flow.

"Maybe the present is the best place to redeem the past," Estelle says. "It's a place where you can make a mark, and it'll stay long enough for someone else to notice. Maybe you should try it."

Grandmere's face turns positively volcanic red. But before she can erupt with her self-justification, Estelle slams her hand on the table. "But you can't possibly do anything worthwhile. You prance around in the past, which you know nothing about, and sling the mud at your family, all while asking us for favors. Everything in New Orleans is sludge, Grandmere. Every bit of dirt was dragged here either by the Mississippi or the ocean and dumped on the shoreline, little by little, until there was enough here for us to scratch out a living. Whether you like it or not, Mehedi is family, and if we don't work together, I don't know how we'll survive. We're the leftovers no one else wanted...including you." Estelle stands, scraping together her frayed breath.

Noura's face is blanched white as death. And while Estelle knows she's absolutely right, her stomach rebels against the idea that she's ruined any chance at helping Mehedi. With a shaking hand, she lays her napkin on her chair to signal she's finished her meal. "I'll see myself out."

"Wait." Father stands. Maman wavers on her feet now too.

"I can't say I'm thrilled to know you're"—he waves his hand about as he searches for a word—"involved with helping this man. But no daughter of mine will sleep on the streets."

"I will not lose another child." Maman directs this at Grandmere before turning to her youngest. "You may stay with Noura...for a few days...until you find something else."

Estelle nods, acknowledging Maman's words, but remains standing, rigidly straight, fighting ridiculous tears of relief.

"Now sit and finish your meal." Maman's command isn't optional, and Estelle cannot risk being kicked out. The Poitier family has enormous influence in Louisiana, and she needs Maman's help to get that museum job.

NOURA PICKS at Mrs. Villiers's soup. No doubt Estelle thinks it's for her. But the cook made it for Noura. A celebration of sorts.

When the security system went haywire in Chicago, Noura thought for sure the Egyptians would shut down the tour. But they hadn't.

And mitigating the issues has made the New Orleans Museum of Art desperate for knowledgeable help. Enter Noura—an experienced, if disgraced, curator specializing in Egyptology. She originally took the desk job as a way to be near the exhibit. But today, the museum asked Noura to assist Dr. Virginia Lee Davis, the resident Egyptologist. Even better, the head curator, William Fagaly, has taken a shine to Noura, calling her an "indefatigable and creative woman who has the perfect insight into Tut and impeccable connections to New Orleans." Noura adores his flamboyant joy. And under his tutelage, if she plays her cards right, she may be able to salvage her career. Just as she began to hope again, Estelle materialized. Noura's little victory short-circuited by her sister's homecoming and Estelle being...well, herself.

Estelle is the only person Noura knows who can walk into a room, throw a verbal grenade, and then act like the explosion is someone else's fault.

Noura drops her spoon, the clanking drawing the ire of Grandmere. But Noura ignores the clearing of the older woman's throat.

Theo's last question forces itself to the surface: Why was Estelle in the village? What brought her to the middle of nowhere, exactly where the artifacts were? Had she been at fault and then looked to blame someone else? It's a question Noura hasn't dared ask her sister. Knowing the answer won't change what happened. But now? If Noura was the sacrificial lamb for Theo, she likely was for Estelle as well.

Which makes Noura wonder why her sister is here at the precise moment the Tut exhibit is arriving.

Noura wouldn't put it past her sister to try to steal the artifacts. Estelle is bent on mayhem. If she attempts to steal King Tut's artifacts, she could, quite literally, start another world war. Set, indeed.

Across the table, Estelle sips at her soup. Where is Horus or Anubis to help a girl out?

Noura hears the whisper of Ma'at. *Find the truth. Weigh the human heart.* Noura swallows. She'd thought she left the strange whispers in Egypt. But it seems Estelle dragged them with her. Set stirring up trouble again.

Well, if Estelle is Set, Noura will just have to be the avenging woman who protects herself from a duplicitous sibling and sets the world to order. No. She will be the measure of good and evil. Ma'at. It feels right until she hears the nickname in Theo's voice. She shoves him away to focus on the immediate problem.

What does Estelle plan to do to help Mehedi, and how illegal is it?

Noura takes a mindless sip of the soup. It might be the stupidest thing she ever does, but if Noura gets her sister a job at the museum, she'll be able to monitor Estelle while keeping her busy. And make no mistake, Noura is not as dull as Estelle thinks she is.

Noura dabs a bit of bread into the bottom of her bowl, soaking up the last bit of broth.

Keep your friends close and your enemies closer.

23

After dinner, Estelle slips into the sweltering heat radiating from the fabled Garden District streets. Ancient oaks spread arthritic arms, *à la quatrième devant*, over the street. Estelle mimics the trees, stretching her arms out wide into second position and pushing one foot forward in rigid attention. If she drapes herself in ivy, can she disappear into an oak? But no. She rubs a palm over the gnarled scar of her arm. To be static is to be complicit.

She ambles two more aimless blocks when she registers footsteps stalking her and turns, expecting Noura.

Instead, it's him. The man from Cairo.

Estelle reaches for the knife she carries tucked into her fabric belt. But it isn't there. She'd let down her guard, foolishly thinking she was safe.

"I will scream." Estelle balls her fists, even though she'd never overpower the man towering over her.

The man Noura knows as Ghadfa is a mere two steps from Estelle. He lifts his hands to show innocence. As if she'll believe that. Estelle trusted him once. She doesn't know his real name and can only guess at the connections spiderwebbing from him to who he works for, to Typhon, to the Weathermen, to herself...

"Just a reminder. We're watching." Ghadfa lifts his greasy bowler hat in a leering bow. He smooths his wild dark hair, then runs his tongue against his crocodile teeth as if the idea of stalking her tastes sweet. While she was in Egypt, she read about the creature waiting to devour human souls. Looking at this man, she could easily believe the myth.

"I'm interviewing for a job at the museum." Estelle catches herself before she informs him that her sister works at the museum. His boss already knows Noura's connection to the exhibit. But they don't know how innocent she is, how she'll do anything to protect those she loves. In Egypt, Estelle let him get close to Noura, making it easy for him to come and go from the museum. He promised to help, then disappeared. Probably because he'd alerted the local police about a female thief and then used the distraction to attempt to steal Selket himself.

"Does Typhon know you tried to double-cross him?"

In answer, Ghadfa thrusts a falcon feather at her, and she groans, knowing what it means. A meeting with the second-to-last person she wants to see.

"I hope you don't do your job. I will enjoy the consequences." Ghadfa blows her a kiss and then disappears toward the French Quarter. Perhaps he'll find himself face down in a drain with a knife in his back. A girl can dream.

"Who was that?"

Estelle spins at the nearness of her sister's voice, her heart pounding at the reminder of its own fragile mortality. She unclenches her fists and refuses to look behind her. "He was looking for the French Quarter."

"Well." Noura watches the man long enough that Estelle wonders if her sister recognizes the Egyptian night guard. But then Noura slips her arm through Estelle's, apparently discarding the image of a complete stranger. "He has a long walk ahead of him."

"Indeed." Estelle palms the feather and walks with Noura past the eclectic Garden District homes. A Greek Revival with serious Corinthian columns contrasts with the relaxed Italianate, which boasts dome-like cupolas, and then the block finishes out with an eccentric Queen Anne. Estelle's mind conjures the mournful tones of *Swan Lake*'s deadly theme and the staccato beats of the ballerina's tiny steps across the stage in her death throes. A cluster of blackbirds startles as if the group smells death and swirls upward, screeching at a soaring white falcon. Estelle frowns at the bird, the reminder of her obligations—bow to the troublemaker in hopes he'll save you from destruction.

"I'm glad you're doing well." Noura saves Estelle's sanity by nudging her shoulder as if they're guileless sisters enjoying a walk.

"You too," Estelle says with a churning politeness that she despises. What wouldn't she give to go back to being the child who traipsed after her sister? Noura tried to protect her, but there is no levee strong enough to contain surging pain forever. Estelle rubs her eyes, pushing back the irony. The levee system—the one built to protect people from the water—is what's responsible for all the truly horrific floods. At some point, confining the water only makes matters worse.

The sisters turn onto Euterpe Street.

"New Orleanians have always had a flair for the dramatic." Estelle nods to the street sign, and Noura lifts her chin, blinking like a sleepwalker waking in another universe.

"What?" Noura asks.

"You know. The muse streets. The Greek goddess of tragedy."

Noura smiles weakly and, under some unseen pressure, plunks down on a bench facing the Coliseum Square fountain. Estelle eases next to her.

"You okay?"

"Of course." Noura bites her lip in opposition to her chipper voice. She's a horrible liar.

"Is work not going well?" Estelle's question sounds perfunctory—what she should say to her upset sister rather than what she wants to say. But she is trying.

In response, Noura lifts a self-deprecating smile. "Either the Tut curse or voodoo magic is at work on the security system. And with my history, if anything happens, I'll be blamed."

Estelle holds her breath. If the security system really is failing, she stands a good chance of fulfilling her part of the deal. Somehow, the thought fills her with dread.

"New Orleans wasn't even supposed to get the tour. Did you know that?" Noura kicks at a discarded Dixie beer can, sending it rolling away. "An engineer from New Orleans magically removed the wreckage from the Suez Canal after the Yom Kippur War, and President Sadat asked him what he wanted as a thank you. The guy asked for the tour to come here. Ironic, isn't it?"

Estelle wipes the horror from her face, then lifts a single shoulder. It isn't just ironic, it's unfathomable. As if a few artifacts could raise Saira from the wreckage of her home. As if gilded funeral pieces could soothe the horror. Anger resurrects and propels Estelle to her feet.

She paces toward their parents' home, trying to shake off the frustration. Anger causes mistakes. Noura's confirmed the easy part—defeating the security system, which can be tricked with a couple of tennis balls, a package of chewing gum, a saw, and a ladder. Estelle pushes away thoughts of the crocodile-toothed guard tracking her steps.

Noura and Estelle slip into the house unnoticed and scurry to their room before anyone can quiz them about where they've been.

NOURA FLOPS onto her bed and stares at the tiny cracks in the ceiling. Just thirty and she already resembles the old plaster.

"You feel it too?" Estelle asks, testing the bed springs.

It's probably the nicest room Estelle has had in years. Honestly, it's better than anything Noura has been able to afford too. But Noura doesn't think it's the bed Estelle's referencing.

"It's hard to be back with them." Noura shucks off her shoes, letting them clunk to the floor. "They're cold as the Antarctic to one another. It's hard to resist being who I was then—never questioning, you know?" Noura lies back and shuts her eyes. She's still trying to decide what to say to her sister and how. Not that Noura has found any attack that works against her sister.

Estelle's bed protests as she sits on the edge and tucks her hands under her thighs. With a snap of clarity, Noura realizes she's making her sister uncomfortable. Estelle never hides behind stillness.

"I know why I'm subjecting myself to their stifling judgment"—Noura tiptoes into the shimmering quiet—"career advancement and all that. But you can get a job anywhere. What aren't you telling me?"

"Mehedi's in jail."

Noura sucks in a breath at Estelle's brutal bluntness. But unlike when she was younger, Noura refuses to turn away from finding the whole truth.

Estelle shifts. "I know people here who will help raise the money to get him out."

"I can imagine what kinds of people they are." Noura doesn't even try to keep the sting from her voice as she swings her legs over the edge of the bed and leans her elbows on her knees. "Your friends in the old Students for Democratic Society are considered terrorists. They've planted thousands of domestic bombs in the last few years."

"I know that."

"Tell me the friends you're consulting aren't them."

"My friends aren't the Students for Democratic Society."

Noura doesn't miss the specificity of her sister's response. They've called themselves Weather Underground for years. Noura doesn't respond, waiting for her sister to tell her the rest.

"I'm trying to help him, Noura. If they deport him, they'll kill him. You know they will."

"I thought his green card was in order."

"Someone stole tools from a job site and, in lieu of a real suspect, the police arrested Mehedi about a week ago."

"So we prove he didn't do it."

"Good luck with that. He's a Middle Eastern man." Estelle's voice screams contempt, and she holds her sister's gaze long enough that Noura breaks away, pushes from the bed, and plops in front of her dressing table mirror.

Noura can still see her sister, but a pane of glass now sits between them. Such flimsy protection. Noura rubs her thumb across the edge of the table dulled from the touch of generations of women. Had any sat here contemplating how to prevent their sister from starting a world war? Grandmere would tell Noura to stop being dramatic. But she has yet to banish Theo's concerns about Estelle. And there's Mehedi to consider. Perhaps another way around? *Find common ground.*

"Look," Noura says. "I'm not thrilled to be supervising people painting the street a psychedelic mix of colors because someone thought it was a groovy fusion of Egypt and New Orleans. And if I'm not doing that, I'm rummaging through Mardi Gras Krewe's costumes to outfit a fake Nefertiti for another fundraiser, or worse, acting like a glorified janitor following the crowds with a broom and dustbin."

"Then why stay?" Estelle unties her shoes and lets them clatter to the floor.

"We're all doing it—from Mr. Fagaly down. And this job...it's the only way back to what I love."

"You're too willing to do what anyone asks you to do."

Noura bristles at their long-rehashed argument. "Doing what someone has to do, you mean. It's called adapting."

"Sometimes you adapt so much I don't recognize you."

"Again, Estelle. Someone has to do those things. You talk about helping others, then traipse off to be the hero while stepping on anyone who gets in your way and neglecting the people right in front of you."

"Maybe the people in front of me should step up. Maybe the things others ask you to do aren't necessary. When are you going to accept that we don't belong to the status quo?"

"Of course we do." Noura spreads cold cream on her cheeks. "We're Marquettes, not Poitiers."

"What does that even mean? You can play amnesiac about what happened in the Sinai, in Vietnam, even in the US to everyone not born with privilege, but I will not."

"And what do you propose differently?" Noura clutches the leash on her temper. "Do you know what your blessed communist Russia did during World War II? Let me see if I can get Trotsky's quote right: 'Dictatorship is rule based directly upon force and unrestricted by any laws.' *Unrestricted* force. Do you truly believe that?"

"Trotsky wasn't the only communist thinker." Estelle's voice slashes, low and vicious.

"You're right." Noura parries. "Stalin, Trotsky, and Lenin constantly fought amongst themselves...which means there is no perfect world. You simply have to accept what is and do your best inside it."

"You always were a fatalist." Estelle rips off her stockings and drops them in a wild pile.

"A realist, Estelle. I am a realist." Noura's grip is slipping, but she is so tired of catering, of bowing down.

"A namby-pamby flip-flopper, you mean. All talk and no action.

There's a difference between keeping peace and making peace. And I will not settle for peace kept."

"You have no idea what you're talking about."

"I don't." Estelle's voice drops in a sarcastic barb.

"I do what I can, when I can. But you!" Noura releases the tether of her anger. "You suck the air out of every room you walk into. You're a parasite, strangling the joy out of everyone around you in the name of whatever you think is right. Well, maybe you're wrong."

Estelle sits back, finally speechless, finally listening, finally taking a sip of her own medicine.

"Do you realize"—Noura glares at the wavery form of her sister in the mirror—"that when you were born, our parents shut me out? I was three, and they literally shut the door on me. I sat on the cracked tile listening to you cry. I tried helping with the bottle but dropped it. The glass shattered in a sticky pool. Maman was livid. I promised to do better, be better. And I did. Every day of my miserable life, I molded myself for you.

"I let you trail me down the streets, under the palm trees, toddling after me everywhere. The entire population was enamored with your blond frizz, and I was terrified someone would snatch you. So I tucked every strand of your hair under a scarf and made a game of it. You were red and shimmering. But I wasn't jealous. Not then. You were mine." Noura plucks a tiny picture of the sisters from the corner of the mirror and flings it at her sister.

THE PHOTO FLUTTERS to the floor, and Estelle leans over, plucking it from the floor, even as she flips back in time. "I remember you splitting open mangos for me and playing my stupid games." She reaches for Noura. "I thought—"

Noura yanks away. "I found a way to serve you and make it all okay... Until you got sick."

"I can't help that!"

"No. You can't, but after that, you shut me out too. Physically and emotionally. There were needles and charts and tears. So many tears. It was summer. So hot."

"I remember the heat," Estelle says, trying to find her way in, but Noura bulldozes on, forcing her sister to see the truth.

"I couldn't even feel my sweat because of how fast the air dried the moisture. Fans couldn't coax the air to move. And you, my vibrant, silly sister, were laid out, evaporating too. And no one did anything." Noura's voice hiccups.

"Stop." Estelle clamps her hands over her ears, trying to slam the door of memory shut. But it's too late.

Noura had sneaked Estelle out of the apartment, down three flights of stairs, Estelle's head bobbing against her sister's neck, and into the courtyard. The neighbor woman who watched them always said fresh air was an underused cure—that and candied ginger.

"But the ginger." Noura's voice burrows beneath her sister's frail barrier. The buzz of Noura's fingers across the fabric of her dress drags Estelle back to the same sound that had ambushed Estelle's head.

"I nearly killed you," Noura says. "I set you in the grass where you sucked on that stupid sugared root. And I left you to find the blasted cat."

Noura had scampered to the scraggly bushes surrounding the sandstone wall. It was the orange cat's favorite hiding spot. Estelle remembers the world sparking, flickering like a flame...opening her mouth to call her big sister back.

"Your eyes rolled into your head, the whites showing, and you flopped to the ground, slamming your head over and over and over. White foam puffing from your lips. I screamed and screamed, terrified to leave you and terrified not to go for help. Dad thundered from the apartment, shoving me out of the way as he scooped you up. I still remember the frown carved into his mouth. Your frozen, contorted face. The flapping of Dad's unbuttoned shirt. The tail, waving like a superhero cape. And I lay there, knee bleeding, in the courtyard as he dove into a taxi with you."

Estelle doesn't remember any of that. Just the fuzz—static in her ears, spots in her vision. Even her fear was spongy on the sides.

"I knew I would pay penance for the rest of my life. If I hadn't taken you outside, hadn't given you the candy, you wouldn't have seized. Dad didn't have to say a word." Noura lifts her gaze to her sister's, steady despite the churning in the air. A dare, Estelle decides.

"From then on," Noura says, "I didn't take a step out of line. I followed it toe-to-heel, watching you blossom and take on the world, knowing I would only ruin things if I tried too. I did whatever was necessary, all the jobs no one else wanted to do. Stuffed down my thoughts, my desires, my dreams. Dammed it all up for you."

"Noura, I—"

"And then you left."

"I left?" The injustice propels Estelle from the bed. "How can you—"

"After Saira." Noura runs right over Estelle's objection. "Your health wasn't the issue. You chose to leave me behind to clean up from the implosion of our family. And I did. I mopped up the mess you left behind. You pretend to be the strong one, but you shut people out and leave them behind every single time."

Estelle is stunned silent, her well-worn objections barricaded behind shock. Noura is the one who left for school only to return and treat Saira like a servant and Estelle like an errant child.

"And now?" Noura's face is brilliant red. "You come waltzing back here, lying to me, expecting me to believe you're innocent and trustworthy, all the while plotting behind my back. I don't know why you were in Cairo or why you're here now. You've never explained how you were in a remote village at the exact moment we stopped. But I swear if you even breathe over the line, I will turn you in. I am done being the careful one. Done being peaceful. I put my reputation, my career, my love life on the line for you. And this is how you repay me." Noura slaps a worn paper in her sister's dumbfounded open hand, then stomps from the room, flinging an "I'll sleep on the couch" over her shoulder.

When Estelle finally gathers the wits to look down, she realizes the epicenter of her sister's anger—the list Ghadfa had given Estelle. The list of artifacts she's been asked to steal. The horrid mark of Typhon, blood red on the bottom.

The worst part is that even though Noura and Estelle haven't always gotten along, Noura would do anything to rescue her little sister from dire straits.

Estelle crumples the paper and chucks it across the room. It lands in a pitiful heap under her sister's bed.

Estelle has no way forward and no way back. Yes, Mehedi was accused of stealing stupid tools. She can prove he hadn't done that. But there is little doubt that he was part of the Weather Underground. He was the one to suggest he work off his debt instead of Estelle. She should have known the Weathermen's errands weren't runs to the grocery store. And now Typhon holds proof of Mehedi's side job—building bombs for the Weathermen to use on banks and government buildings.

How is she supposed to choose between Noura's career and Mehedi's life? The song of the treacherous Odile echoes, and the ballerina spins and spins and spins. Thirty-two *fouettés* whipping out, deceiving everyone, killing the faithful swan princess, Odette.

Estelle knows, deep down, there is no choice. If only she can someday convince Noura of the same.

24

August 31, 1977

By the time Noura is in her car on the way to the museum, daylight barely breathes across the sky. She's exhausted and stiff and annoyed with her life. She'd waited for Mother to go to sleep before she curled onto the stiff, ornate couch. Noura would rather sleep with Estelle than explain the rift between them. Still, Noura woke early enough that her sister couldn't ask for a ride. If Noura can't be in a room with Estelle, she doesn't know how she'll deal with her plan to keep Estelle close enough to sniff out her plans. That is, of course, if her sister will still apply to the museum. Stupid. Stupid. Stupid.

She hears Theo's voice in her head telling her she's smart and worthy. But the baritone voice only stabs now. He was lying. Telling her what she wanted to hear.

In Agatha Christie's books, Poirot is always ten steps ahead of the reader. Why can't it be that way in real life? Why is Noura always ten steps behind?

With virtually no traffic, she has nothing to distract her from her churning fears. With her sister's reaction last night, Noura is almost certain Estelle's here to steal one or more of the King Tut artifacts. How that helps Mehedi, Noura doesn't know yet.

Not yet anyway.

There's very little Noura can do against someone who's never been afraid of consequences. But Noura has things her sister doesn't have: patience, persistence, and the ability to listen unobserved. She will stop Estelle from ruining them all, even if it's the last thing she does.

Noura parallel parks on the street and shoves her keys back into her bag. There, nestled next to her pocketbook, is a tattered ostrich feather. If Estelle thinks the reminder of Ma'at will stop Noura from fighting for what's right... Well, Noura snaps her bag shut over her sister's obvious attempt to manipulate her into moderating herself. Clutching her bag, she stalks the few blocks to the museum. A man sprawls under an oak near the pond, and she frowns as she steps onto the brightly painted street, trading the darker side of New Orleans for the cheery, devil-may-care one. Perhaps Ra has woken and wiped everything clean in the rebirth of day. Noura is confident she has it all under control. She will find the truth.

And then she swings around the building and slams into the chest of Theodore Fabre.

Of all the rotten luck, her world is positively teeming with the stinking stuff.

"Noura." Something like relief settles on his features.

Noura steps back. He's supposed to be in New York, at the Met.

Theo glances behind her, and she looks too. But there's a whole parade of nothing. When Noura turns back, he is studying her.

She resists the urge to smooth down her semi-styled hair. "Why are you here?" she snaps.

"I work here." Theo gives her a weak smile and opens the steel door to the employee entrance. He waits for her, eyeing her like a bird of prey. She's forgotten how deadly falcons are.

Noura plasters on a smile, which she's sure does little to cover the horror churning in her chest. All she wants to do is run. Run and run and run from the shambles her life has become. Instead, she ducks into the jaundiced light and paces down the hallway as if her executioner isn't dogging her steps. What will he do when he finds out her mother left a message for the hiring manager last night recommending her sister for a job? What will he do when he finds out Noura was the one who asked Mother to do it?

Noura swallows past the noose around her throat and drops her lunch sack in the break room refrigerator.

"Noura, about Cairo. I—"

"Theo...Mr. Fabre." Noura closes the door of the refrigerator. "My sister was beaten unconscious. Did you know that? And they withheld her insulin. You have sisters. Would you have allowed either of them to remain in those conditions?"

He has the good grace to drop his gaze to the floor. "I didn't know. I didn't—"

"No. The answer is no. You wouldn't have left either June or Mabel to die, and you didn't give me a chance to explain. So you're right, you didn't know. And yet you ruined me. Because you didn't trust me and went behind my back, I couldn't find a way to both save my sister and find out what really happened with her or with you or even figure out if the Selket in that crate was real or not. So do not stand there and act like you merely called me a nasty name or didn't invite me to a party. You are a lying, manipulative jerk who used me, then threw me out."

"Noura, I'm—"

Mentally shoving away his lame apology and overly concerned brows, Noura snatches her badge, punches her time card, and stalks down the hallway. The sound of her angry footsteps pursues her like she stupidly wishes Theo would. Despite herself, she wants him to explain, to have some rational reason why he'd played her for a fool. More, she wishes he'd been wrong about Estelle. But Noura is as certain of her sister's innocence as the possibility of alien life forms. No matter that her sister seems blameless or that traveling to the moon is no longer just a dream, Noura can't know for sure one way or the other what the truth is.

She bursts into a storage room and, along with the broom, leans against the cement wall. If only she could be as implacable and stoic as the building. Noura swipes at the blasted tears leaking from her eyes.

She is tired of bending herself into a pretzel for everyone. The problem is, the last time she remembers being herself is when she was standing on that wall holding that stupid cat for Estelle. Proud she'd solved the problem…except she hadn't. And then, just as Noura began to feel the echo of her old self in Cairo with Theo, life came swooping in and made her its breakfast. How can Noura learn to be herself when every decision she makes creates another disaster?

Sucking in a breath, Noura pushes through the door and bustles to her station on the upper floor. She arranges her face, her limbs, like she is assured and confident, but it's the stillness of prey hoping the predator will miss.

THEO BENDS to retrieve the ostrich feather that fluttered to the floor in Noura's wake and twists it in his fingers as he watches her stumble up the stairs. He's been told to deliver a message to meet her sister, but he hates that he's here. Hates that he cannot destroy every single one of his personas. Hates that Noura no longer believes she can be Ma'at to his Horus. The pendant around his neck burns against his skin, screaming to pay attention. And Sykes mutters in his mind, *Don't give up your life for a dame.* But he's already gutted. Already committed. He's helping his sister. Doing the best he can. Somehow, some way, that will have to be enough.

He jams the feather into his pocket and turns to find his new desk. He has a job to do.

25

Estelle forces herself out of bed before seven and into the only decent pair of bell-bottoms she owns, which she combines with a white peasant top that brushes her belt buckle. Standing in front of the full-length mirror, she ties her red scarf around her head to cover the startling blond roots. Not the most professional outfit, but the best she has unless she raids Noura's closet. And Estelle has taken enough from her without borrowing her stiff clothes too. There is nothing she can do about the darkness under her eyes. She spent the night writing about the plight of the incarcerated men and women she met in Chicago.

The piece is both scathing and far too emotional for anything but her own mind cleansing. But she will desensitize it, add the legal ramifications, and send it over to *Harper's Magazine*.

The irony of Estelle's attempts to help those who shouldn't be in prison isn't lost on her.

Estelle has kept her known communist self away from Mehedi. If the prosecutor so much as senses Mehedi's involvement with communist organizations, there's not a lawyer on the planet who can protect him. He'll be deported. And there is no justice in that.

Of course Estelle cannot condone the bombs, but Mehedi's bombs hadn't hurt anyone. Further, the bombs he built were an attempt to get someone...anyone...to listen to the plight of those dying in the slums. Do the ends justify the means?

A voice growls, "Is bombing an empty building wrong if it saves people?"

Estelle sucks in a breath and carefully turns, confirming that the beast hasn't crawled from last night's nightmares into reality. "You're not real," Estelle's unsteady voice bounces back at her, twining with the rough laughter.

She snatches a slice of toast from the kitchen and slams the door before hoofing it to Jackson Street to catch the bus to the museum.

The bus motors past the outskirts of the French Quarter, still tucked in for the night, then bends away from the mighty Mississippi toward Lake Pontchartrain. The warm temperature and restless night have Estelle fighting sleep and motion sickness the entire hour drive. Noura has a car, but Estelle is loath to ask her for a ride. There are personal reasons of course. But there's also the jolt of otherworldly electricity snapping underneath her skin whenever Noura is close. The demand to destroy, to *make* people listen, to...

Estelle leaps to her feet, tugging the rope to signal she wants off, and then clutches her fringed bag to her side while the bus lumbers to a stop near Esplanade. After shuffling down the aisle, she slips onto the brightly painted Lelong Drive. With two huge columns bracketing the grassy neutral ground between lanes of traffic, there can be no doubt where the King Tut exhibit will be.

Plumes of exhaust envelop Estelle, spitting her back to her own dirty reality—no outside evil is responsible for where she put herself. She trudges the last half mile in the shade of the oaks marching up the drive. If anyone harbors any remaining doubt that King Tut is in residence, it's obliterated by the obelisk standing guard over the entrance. With the forewarning of the swamped Chicago and DC museums, the New Orleans Museum of Art is anticipating floods of people in a few weeks. They've already built bleachers to hold the line and information booths for lost souls and coordinated a host of other preparations.

Of course there are some things the team can't plan for, and meteorologists are watching a tropical storm brewing to the south. Wouldn't it be ironic for a hurricane's arrival to celebrate the opening of the exhibit? Nature's perfect stamp of dissatisfaction with the arrangement.

At the front entrance, Estelle steps around a burbling of activity and wanders to the ticket counter. "Noura Marquette arranged an interview for me?"

The harried woman gives Estelle disjointed directions even as she funnels other women in the same basic direction.

Outside the Stern auditorium classroom, women sign in to become Tut aides during the exhibit. But Estelle slips past the snaking line and into the mostly empty exhibit space.

Eventually the gleaming room will mimic the tomb as Howard Carter discovered it. For now, workers hang enormous images of ancient antechambers and debris-strewn hallways. From one image, a steely-eyed falcon glares from a jumble on the floor of the photographed tomb. Egypt's boy king immortalized on the museum walls.

If it weren't for the politics, the show's arrival in New Orleans would be fitting. For one thing, both New Orleans and Cairo each hunker on a bank of one of the world's largest rivers. And for another, the cities aren't just places where land imperceptibly slides into water. New Orleans, like Cairo, is a place where the lines of life and death blur in a world of mysticism and remembrance of ancestors hovering on the other side. Mostly, though, eternity is ever-present in the cities of the dead. Here, entire blocks of mausoleums make the dead part of neighborhoods. And Cairo's pyramids celebrate their long-dead while ignoring entire fields of white crosses to the east.

With the breath of the underworld on her shoulders, Estelle almost believes the curse of Tutankhamun and the battle of Set and Horus brought to an end with the scales of the god of the dead. Anubis—stoic, just, and loyal. Everything she wishes she was. Estelle peers into a long acrylic case destined to hold jewelry. She has no idea how she can possibly break into the pressure-controlled cases. She's not a cat thief. Her thefts were always a matter of chance. She touches her reflection on the case that will house the mask, her eyes staring, echoing the darkness of the mask—

A blaring alarm sends Estelle scurrying backward, heart pounding. A man in a blue jumpsuit on the far side of the room lets out an impressive series of invectives, including one particularly imaginative one about what kind of voodoo curse his Creole grandmother will place on Tut if he doesn't stop meddling. Estelle can't help but grin at the mix of southern and New York City in the man's New Orleanian accent.

Hand still covering her chest, Estelle steps further into the room, watching the man clamber up a ladder and dismantle a box on the ceiling. It's obvious he's done this more than once. Is this the faulty security system?

The sound abruptly stops, leaving Estelle's ears echoing. He'd shut off the alarm in a few minutes. And this fact has her analytical mind humming. How often does the security fail? And how long will it be before they restarted it? Estelle shuffles into the alcove between displays to watch as she mentally ticks off the seconds.

"What are you doing here?"

The male voice next to Estelle causes her to stiffen, but she tamps down the reaction and spreads on an innocent smile. A smile that wavers in recognition of Theodore Fabre...or whatever his real name is.

"I didn't know you were working with the museum." Estelle slips her hand into the crook of his flinty elbow and clamps down so he can't extract himself without making a scene. She knows full well a scene is the last thing he wants.

"I asked what you are doing here," he says through gritted teeth.

Theo would be handsome if it weren't for all the glowering. She knows he can be charming. Funny even. She's watched him manipulate her sister.

"You know very well what I'm doing here. We've both a job to do." Estelle flips her hair over her shoulder and stalks across the floor to the jumpsuited man, now threatening his walkie-talkie to cooperate.

"I'm a gonna feed you to a gator," the man growls at the device as Estelle approaches.

"Excuse me, sir?" Estelle flutters her lashes, and the man stumbles all over himself to stand. Where Noura hides in the shadows and sneaks around edges, dance classes and Maman made sure the younger sister learned it's far more effective to use what the good Lord gave her.

"I'll take care of her." Theo yanks her elbow.

Having Theo here complicates her situation. Another watcher to manage. Why can't the powers that be trust her enough to do her job and then hand things off when she is good and ready?

But the jumpsuited man is the glowering one now. Estelle has activated his protective instincts. "Don't know what makes you think you can come in here and—"

"I'm Theodore Fabre. The conservator on loan from the Met. She's looking for my coworker. I'll take—"

"Actually"—Estelle not so delicately removes her arm from his grip—"I don't need a babysitter. I'm sure..." She peers at the man's name tag. "Jim can help. Noura Marquette asked me to stop by the security office for an interview. Would you be a dear and bring me down?"

Jim isn't much older than Theo and puffs his chest in a peacock display of dominance, holding out his hand to indicate Estelle should walk with him. She gives Theo a little wave and barely contains herself from blowing him a kiss. Sending Theo into a full-blown fit will tick Noura off more than Estelle already has.

Shoving herself into character, Estelle stuffs her concerns into her core and swings her hips.

Jim is awkward in the extreme, blushing as he limps next to her. When he opens the door to a tiny room off the main beaten path, Estelle's heart leaps faster. Jim is a big man and a complete stranger, and she doesn't have a weapon. Estelle takes a stutter step, wondering how foolish it is to follow him into the belly of a dark and mostly abandoned building. Jim's smile drops, and she casts around for something to say to extract herself from her complete stupidity.

"I been waitin' for you," he says, obviously confused now. "Noura, she said for me to give you a job. Said you'd work hard, said some hoity-toity wanted you here, and she'd keep a eye on you, so I don't have ta."

"Oh!" Estelle says. "I didn't realize I'd be interviewing with you."

Upstairs, the alarm winds up like a cranky toddler, and Jim growls in frustration. "I'm the only full-time security guard 'round here. The New Orleans PD'll be monitoring the show once the artifacts are up. But we got ourselves a situation in the meantime. Can I count on you to wait for your sister?" At this, he peers down at Estelle like she might, at this very moment, do something foolish...like run out on the job or snoop in the files for one marked "How to Steal King Tut's Mask."

"Of course I'll wait here." Like a good girl. Like Noura would. "Does that mean I have the job?"

"Yep. There's a application right there and some paperwork. Fill that out. Then come by tomorrow, and I'll train you up on what we'll be doing and what is and isn't allowed. Then, provided that hurricane don't roll in, you can help me train the kids who'll come a couple a days before the show."

And with that, Jim gives Estelle a friendly nod and rushes back the way they came. Now what? She sinks behind the man's desk and taps a nail on the wood. Estelle knew Noura would be here. Of course she would. But Theo? She doesn't know how she'll keep it together around him, especially when he's with Noura. He'll convince Noura he's as innocent as a newborn, even while he's working with Typhon. And where does that leave Estelle?

Although working at the museum will provide an opportunity to lift the artifacts, it will also allow Estelle to monitor her sister until she figures out how to extract everyone she cares about from the surging power coming.

She pulls the clipboard onto her lap and fills in the blindingly boring boxes. Her name, her address, her experience, her education. She taps the pen, debating. Estelle records her bachelor's from Northwestern and nothing else. Keeping Jim unapprised of her capabilities seems the best way to enlist his help against Theo's bullying tactics. The less dear Jim knows, the better.

Estelle clicks the pen closed and stands, stretching up on her toes in an *elevé*, then shaking her legs out. If she doesn't find a way to release all the tightness in her body, she might fly to pieces. She sucks in a series of deep breaths and hesitates a moment before re-straightening the pen, then tidying the strewn files on the desk. Despite the stagnant air, a page flutters from the stack and a folder flops open.

And there, in an innocent manila folder, are the specs for Custom Electronic Devices, Inc.'s ultrasonic security system. Estelle glances behind her, expecting the red glowing eyes from her nightmares...which is ridiculous, isn't it?

Her hand flutters over her heart a moment before settling into the chair and flipping the file open, hoping she can make sense of the technical mumbo jumbo noted in the manuals marked "WS-40T-Transmitter" and "WS-40R-Receiver." Isn't it fun how folks slap words like ultrasonic onto things, like that'll make the thingamabob the best thing ever?

But her law degree is useless in the face of servo motors, transducers, and transceivers. She shuts the file and sucks in another breath. She digs through the desk, finds a blank page, and then scribbles nonsensical notes. She'll decode it later. Hopefully.

The blaring alarm hiccups and then stops. Jim will be back soon, and she can't be caught with her notes. Of course if she leaves now, everyone will wonder why she left, but a shuffle in the hallway and a flickering shadow propel her from the office.

She pokes her head into the sterile hallway. There's a big wooden box lurking to her right, and she briefly wonders what's in it. But unless it is a piece that will save Mehedi, she doesn't care what it is. Estelle shifts a bit further to peer around the case. The art museum basement is decidedly boring and blessedly deserted.

Estelle scuttles into the hallway, out the loading dock door, and into the street. Holding the door open with her fingertips, she lifts her face to the sun, letting the light spot against her lids. If she leaves, she is committed to the theft, to betraying Noura. Isn't communism supposed to be about the greater good? There is nothing good or right about her choices, and yet here she is. She can't help but wonder what the black jackal Anubis would do. She pinches the tender skin on the inside of her bicep, focusing on the crack of pain to clear a path through the guilt to make a decision. Staying or leaving? No matter what she does, she is failing someone.

A police officer steps around the corner, and Estelle snaps to innocent attention, giving a little flirtatious wave. He frowns a little, and his suspicion makes Estelle's final decision easy.

There is no way she can sit still, waiting for the inevitable. She lets the door close and taps a cigarette out of the pack before striding down the boulevard past the bus stop. Once free of the museum's shadow, Estelle breathes deeply of ancient oaks and the river, letting the bubbling laughter in the distance seep into her soul. The last time she let herself feel free was...well, she supposes it was behind the apartment in Tel Aviv, pretending to be conquering princesses with Noura. The princess part coming from Noura and the warrior coming from Estelle in some strange mashup of Joan of Arc and Galadriel, the powerful Middle-earth elf.

Stopping at an intersection, Estelle glances both ways and stops. Across from her slumps Noura's distinctively dilapidated car, and there's an enormous black dog sniffing something tucked under the wheel.

What in the world? Estelle trots across the street. The dog glances up at her, his canines glaring in the light enough that Estelle hesitates. But the dog's mouth turns into a grin like he knows something Estelle doesn't and then trots off. Bending, Estelle squints until she makes out a beak among black feathers. She jerks upright and backpedals. A black chicken.

She's not lived long in New Orleans, but the dog hasn't left behind lunch. This is evidence of a voodoo curse. Electricity sparks through her as she spins a slow circle. The sisters may not get along, but their blood weaves them tight together.

Estelle will burn whoever's done this to the ground.

26

By the time Noura navigates the car onto the cracked driveway that evening, she's a jittering mess. On her way out the museum door, Jim thanked her for bringing her sister in, and then said that Noura had ushered Estelle out so quickly, he plumb didn't have a chance to give her a uniform. Would Noura bring it home? But Noura hadn't even seen her sister, let alone ushered her out.

With his head buried in the guts of the security system receiver, Jim missed the confused cock of Noura's head. But Theo, who'd been conveniently parked in Noura's way every second of the day, surely didn't miss Noura's reaction.

Why wasn't he in the basement with the rest of the conservators? But then, he has every right not to trust her. Had Mr. Fagaly or the Met sent Theo to spy on her?

No. Noura yanks the car's parking brake.

If they were concerned, they'd call the police or the FBI. She thinks of the shake in Theo's fingers when he climbed the ladder to hang a sign, the soft curve of his mouth when she caught him watching her. And her confounded skin prickling with memory, with the desire to retreat to the way it was in Cairo, in his arms, part of a team.

Maman waves as she strolls down the street, her blond hair perfectly feathered in a Farrah Fawcett, and her pearls perfectly crowning the top of her perfectly tailored knee-length dress. In comparison, Noura is a crumpled mess. Noura snatches her bag, clomps across the yard, and barges through the door.

In the kitchen, Estelle hunches over the counter, picking apart a ham po'boy. When Noura lets the door slam, Estelle grins at her sister.

"There's one in the fridge for you." She brushes a flake of bread off her shirt with a Cheshire grin. She knows Noura hates ham.

Noura hangs her purse, tucks the keys in the appointed drawer, and leans her hip against the doorway. Estelle is acting as if she didn't ignore security protocol.

"Yours is roast beef, you ninny. Wouldn't be a proper apology if you hated it." Estelle hops from the stool, ducks into the fridge, rummages a moment, then pops out holding a wax paper–wrapped bundle. "Extra Creole mustard and pickles. No mayo."

Noura accepts the offering and sits across from Estelle. Noura can almost imagine her sister, blond hair, chubby cheeks, legs swinging from knobby knees, prattling on about something or another, slipping between English, Hebrew, and Arabic like it's perfectly natural to speak three languages. And for her, it was. Everything is for Estelle.

Noura contemplates the woman sitting across from her. Brutally dark hair with glaring blond roots, creases between her eyes like she was the one constantly worried for the last decade instead of Noura.

"So," Noura says, trying for nonchalance. "Where'd you go after you turned in your application?"

Estelle holds up a finger to finish chewing. "Sorry. I forgot my test kit and insulin."

Unwrapping the sandwich, Noura takes a nibble, giving herself a moment to think. Estelle's explanation is plausible, but her sister is the consummate storyteller. "Maybe you should leave a kit in your locker at work. You won't be able to bolt when you're working."

Estelle sets her sandwich on her plate and laughs lightly. "That's a good idea. I'm entirely unused to a nine-to-five."

Noura clamps down on the zing of irritation. Her sister's not used to a normal job because she's flitted willy-nilly across the globe with no responsibility.

Of course that isn't true. Estelle was working with the poor…probably more hours than nine to five. Perhaps she really is all that is good and right. Noura bites again and shuts her eyes as if enjoying the Sunday cap bread and the sharp Creole mustard. But it's a ruse. Her mind can't afford any reserve energy to parse out taste or sight when she's trying to outflank her sister.

"Why don't you put your kit in your bag now?" Noura says with a smile.

Estelle rolls her eyes with the finesse of a champion. "I'm enjoying my sandwich, Mom."

"I'll grab it for you, then." Before Estelle can object, her sister is rummaging through Estelle's bag and, gosh golly gee, wouldn't you know? Noura tugs the insulin, a needle, and test kits from Estelle's bag and turns like a magician revealing the big surprise.

Estelle sucks in the tiniest of breaths. "I took my small bag to work today." She shrugs. "Packing my entire life for the day will take getting used to."

When Noura doesn't smile, doesn't move, doesn't flinch, Estelle tilts her head and frowns like she's trying to figure out what's wrong. Of all the nerve.

"I'll leave it in here then, shall I?" Noura says. "If you're ready to leave tomorrow by 6:30, I'll drive you. It'll save you a bus ride, and I'll help you remember." Noura sounds like Maman, manipulating and untrusting. For the first time in her life, Noura understands why her mother is the way she is. How many times had Father shaded the truth? Maybe Estelle learned from him. Noura ignores the temptation to point that out. Instead, she tears off another bite of her sandwich. Noura will not let Estelle destroy her life when she's just started to—

"How's Theo?" Estelle asks, innocent as you please.

"How should I know? I've not spoken to him since..." Noura has no words to describe those last moments. "Well, since Cairo."

"He was at the museum." Estelle's brows scrunch together in a fair facsimile of concern.

"Yes."

"Noura." Estelle reaches across the counter and, while Noura eyes her offering like it might be a cobra, Estelle curls her fingers around

Noura's. "Be careful. Please. There are things going on..." Estelle sighs and swings her gaze out the kitchen window. "Just be careful."

"Of whom? Theo isn't the only one hiding something."

It only takes a millisecond for Estelle to rearrange her face into innocence. But Noura saw the flicker confirming what she suspects. "Will you at least tell me before everything blows up?"

Estelle's quick smile doesn't reach her eyes, but she nods, and Noura sees truth there.

"Noura," Estelle says. "About Cairo. About Selket. I was following you. I was worried—"

The hall phone shrieks, and Estelle jumps to her feet, skidding around the corner to answer it.

"Hello." She pauses. "This is." She glances at Noura and turns her back, letting the wall absorb her murmured responses. "Give me thirty minutes," she says and settles the phone into the cradle like it's made of glass.

"Is it about Mehedi?" Noura may have been talking to the wall for all the response her sister gives. "How much money do you need?" Noura asks.

Estelle turns, blinking like she's waking from a nightmare. "Too much." Tears swim under the angry lines of her face, sending protective adrenaline shooting through Noura.

"What is it?"

"Nothing. It's nothing." Estelle yanks on a red beret. "I'm meeting a friend. Make excuses to Maman for me? And don't trust Theo. Promise?"

Noura waits until the door slams before scribbling a note to Maman...like the sisters are ten rather than adult women.

Estelle and I are going out. We'll be late. Don't hold dinner.
Kisses, Noura

Noura knows her sister cares, but Estelle will also mow down anyone or anything in the way of what she thinks is right. And right now, she's intent on getting Mehedi out of jail. Noura sets the note square on the counter and slips out the door. Perhaps it is time to test her mettle against her sister's.

Though Noura is as stealthy as a noisy, furtive little kid, Estelle's sure that her sister believes she's as stealthy as a cat. Estelle knew she would try to follow. But she can't afford for her to.

Estelle ducks into a throughway, over a fence, through a backyard, and over the other side of the fence, all while taking off her red silk jacket and exchanging her beret for an old brown fedora. Fortunately, Noura is also far more innocent than Mehedi ever was, and, in the glass window of the next house, Estelle sees Noura scanning the crowd. While Estelle is grateful her sister never had to learn to be deceptive, her innocence is terrifying.

Dodging a man staggering down the sidewalk, Estelle trots across the street and up another, crossing to St. Charles where she'll catch the streetcar toward the French Quarter and then walk the last ten minutes to the St. Louis Cathedral. She consults her watch and then breaks into a run, sliding into the queue of people as the streetcar comes to a stop.

She's so grateful not to have to wait fifteen minutes for the next ride, she misses the shadow following her to a seat until he bumps her knee as he hovers in the aisle. Estelle reaches behind her back. She didn't forget her knife this time.

"Don't turn." The voice is purely American.

Relief slides through her exhausted body.

Not Ghadfa.

Still, she slips her knife from her belt and coils, ready to unleash herself, but then the man slides a tattered book into view. *The Lion, the Witch and the Wardrobe.* Estelle hesitates, allowing her brain to catch up. The smell of sandalwood. Shaggy blond hair in contrast to the spotlessly clipped nails, and when she registers the peculiar color of his hazel eyes, Estelle barely prevents herself from collapsing into his arms.

Harry. It's her brother Harry.

"Good to see you." Harry sits as Estelle shifts to make room. "It's been a while."

"It's been months." Estelle flips through the pages of the book he read to her when she was eight. "Always winter and never Christmas," Estelle quotes from the book and lets the paperback flop closed. "When we lived in Tel Aviv, I dreamed of playing in the snow, and then I moved to Chicago. I thought I would freeze like the stone statues."

"Do they know?" He's switched to Arabic, but why? The question is bland enough.

"I've kept my promise," she says. The rest of the family doesn't know he's alive, let alone that he's part of the terrorist organization J. Edgar Hoover is systematically hunting. "But we have a problem."

Harry shifts, and Estelle hates how easy it would be to fall apart, throw everything in his lap, and run. But he would muck it up.

"Your patsy is using voodoo curses on our sister," she says.

"Noura?"

Estelle turns fully on him, her voice low, grinding. "Do we have another sister? We wouldn't be in this situation if you'd—"

"If I'd let the Egyptians take me prisoner? What good would that have done?"

"You might have been able to help Mehedi. I was barely twenty-three, trying to figure it out."

"Noura's the one who got him out of the country."

"And then abandoned him." Estelle lifts her chin.

"That doesn't sound like Noura."

"She's not a saint."

"No, she isn't," he says with a dismissive shrug. "But she'd as soon cut off her arm than abandon someone she cares about. She broke you out of an Egyptian prison at great cost to herself."

He obviously doesn't realize that the only reason Estelle followed Noura was to protect *her* from whoever *he* was working for. Of course she can't tell him that. It would risk everything. "Which brings us back to the fact that I found a dead black chicken under her car earlier today. You need to rein in your man."

"Ghadfa isn't my man. But I doubt he had anything to do with voodoo nonsense. His assignment is to monitor. Nothing more. Nothing less."

"I'm the one who vouched for you with the Weathermen, remember?"

"And the only reason I agreed was to get Mehedi out of the mess you got him in. I was fine working behind the scenes."

But if he was fine, why did he find Estelle and let her know he was alive? She's not stupid. Estelle curls her fist around the paperback book, strangling it into submission instead of her brother. "Does your white knight armor make it hard to pat yourself on the back?"

At the rancor in her voice, the woman in front of them shifts, concern etching twin lines between her penciled-on brows.

"Don't worry. He's my brother," she says flatly in English.

The woman shakes her graying head and hugs her bag more tightly to her chest.

"She's afraid of you," Harry whispers, reverting to Arabic.

"Maybe you should be too. Straighten out your shadow man."

"Make no mistake about it; by this mad fury, by this bitterness and spleen—"

"Do not quote Jean-Paul Sartre to me when we're discussing our sister. She is not part of the world needing to be cleansed, and I'm beginning to think the leadership is part of the dirty problem. Maybe Hoover's right to clean them out."

"Estelle, the government killed my wife. Kissinger knew what was coming. Saw the Sinai as a bargaining chip, and no one cared enough about the people there to stop it—not the Americans, not the Egyptians, not the Israelis. I watched them..." Harry sucks in a breath.

The crazy thing is, Estelle feels the sharp bite of memory as well. "I found Saira. Did you know that?"

His nod is nearly imperceptible.

"It's why I've done everything I have." Estelle's voice is tired, frustrated. "But it hasn't made a difference."

The streetcar stops, and the woman in front of them gathers her bright bag and her shopping basket and, with one worried glance at the siblings, hurries through the swinging doors.

With her gone, Estelle leans in closer, her voice low. "How many bombs have the Weathermen set off?"

When Harry doesn't answer, she sits back and answers for him. "Thousands. They set off thousands of bombs in the US, and nothing has changed. They hijacked our movement, Harry. You and I wanted better things for those without a voice. Then those idiots went out and threw bombs at nothing. When are they going to actually *do* something useful?"

"And yet you're planning to do whatever they ask."

"For Mehedi." Estelle sighs. "For Mehedi, yes."

"Then we need to get Noura out of the way, do what they ask, and get Mehedi out."

Anger flares scorching hot, but Estelle snatches tight hold of its tail, yanking it into submission. Yes, she wants Mehedi out of danger. She wants Noura to butt out. She wants to help the girl on the street dressed in rags. She wants everyone to acknowledge what their way of life has done to her, to the girl, to everyone. Estelle wants the villainous establishment to pay for what they've done. But mostly, she wants to grind the pandering leaders of the Weathermen under her heel for promising a solution and squandering her passion and her dedication. That her brother has thrown his lot in with theirs blisters, and Estelle's anger slips from her grip.

"When did you become Typhon's lackey? Tell him I'll get his blasted artifacts. But then I am done, and if I find out he's done anything to Noura or Mehedi, I will personally hunt him down and slit his throat. And then for grins, I'll tell Maman and Father their precious son is alive and well and doing his utmost to destroy them." Estelle pushes herself to her feet and shoves past her brother. "Are we clear?"

Not waiting for his answer, she stomps to the front of the streetcar while the vehicle comes to a full stop. The moment the doors open, she stampedes down the steps and outside. Harry hasn't followed her, and for that, she is relieved.

As she trudges down Royal Street, she curses herself under her breath and digs in her bag for her package of cigarettes.

Empty.

She chucks the carton on the ground.

Why did she let Harry rile her? Despite what he thinks, the Weather Underground is dead. They'd turned into a bunch of yuppies and armchair activists. Worse than idealists like Noura, they actually understood what needed to happen and, when things got difficult, failed to follow through. Noura, at least, is consistent and does a small measure of good.

But Harry? How he justifies using Mehedi to force Estelle to steal for Typhon is beyond her. Estelle suspects Harry is well-connected enough to hire a lawyer, so she wouldn't have to do the dirty work. But of course, he's only been concerned for himself. His neglect only gives Estelle more reason to go behind his back.

Estelle checks her watch, which has been ticking down time without regard for her situation. She's going to be late for her meeting. Slipping out of her heels, she takes off at a trot. At least she's managed to drop her siblings from tailing her.

Ten minutes later, she glimpses her first view of the spires of St. Louis Cathedral, and it's a good thing. The bells toll the quarter hour, and she curses, hastening down the street. She doesn't know why Theo insisted on meeting so far from La Villa Poitiers, but Estelle couldn't exactly argue with Noura listening.

Estelle pauses at the corner of Pirate Alley, wincing at the smell of rotten urine. Estelle pats the cool white stucco wall that stands in solidarity with the minor basilica. The church has been burned, torn down, and rebuilt until she rises over the mighty Mississippi. Such power, and yet she stands silent, her foundations guarding the graveyard hidden under the alley.

Ducking through the doorway, Estelle scans the wide entry. A bank of candles flickers with the breeze she's let in. To her right, a gated stairwell twists up, and to her left, a gift shop shimmers with religious novelties. The iron gate closes over the doorway, but a tiny silver pendant shimmers from the handle. Estelle's skin pricks with warning, but she lifts the chain, frowning at the falcon feather spinning at the end. Games. She is so tired of games. And yet, she appears to be alone.

She clutches the burning hot pendant in her fist and pushes through the white doors. Maybe whoever left the chain for her is taunting her, telling her that she belongs to the wrong side, that they know she belongs to chaos. She'll repay the favor by selling it for bus tickets out of New Orleans.

In the nave, black and white tiles stretch under her feet. Above her, the church creaks, then releases the mismatched peals of bells. Has he left already?

"You're late." Theo's voice behind her makes her spin so fast, she nearly trips on her own feet and barely holds onto the chain.

He catches her elbow, and she shakes him off, shoving the chain into her pocket. Had he left it? If so, why? Just to make her question herself?

The seven bells thunder above them, and he stares at the ceiling, giving Estelle a chance to study this conservator who also plays at Sykes, a notorious art forger and fence. When the ringing peters out, he catches her watching and dips into a half-bow, complete with lopsided grin. If she were Noura, Estelle would blush.

Instead, she stalks down the aisle. She thinks of the pendant she found, his falcon feather calling card. And she makes the connection. Horus. Oh, the irony. He sees himself as Horus, creating order out of chaos, but he works for Typhon. Which means he's evil. Necessary perhaps, but evil. She slides into a pew and plunks down, bag on her lap. Though remarkably comfortable, the wood digs into the back of her legs, and she feels her pulse thrum through her thighs, attesting to her humanity, her fragility. It takes such a small cut to pour out every ounce of blood. She's doing this for Mehedi. For Saira. For everyone still on the street.

Theo slides in next to Estelle and offers her a picture. It's grainy, but clear enough. A dog-eared witch doctor, sliding something under her sister's car. Estelle clenches her fist.

"She's in danger," Theo says.

"I know," Estelle growls, and Theo flinches.

"I didn't have anything to do—"

"It seems no one does."

"What does that mean?" Theo shifts, his knees knocking into Estelle's.

"Nothing." She scrubs a hand over her face, rearranging it to blankness and wishing for a cigarette to burn the rest away. Instead, she passes him the picture. "I'll keep an eye on her."

"The best thing we can do is get this over with quickly." He extricates a cigarette pack from his shirt pocket. "As Typhon requested, I have the replica of Selket and the vulture collar finished. I'll have the mask in another week. We can make the switch then."

He tips the pack of Camels toward Estelle, and she glares at it. She knows instructions are tucked between the paper and foil. Theo tucks the pack into her bag.

"I'll be with you every step of the way." He squeezes Estelle's shoulder. "I'm sorry it's come to this, but you're doing the right thing."

When she doesn't respond, Theo stands and taps the pew in front of them like it might give him a better answer.

"What about my sister?"

Theo's jaw clenches and releases, concerned. "I'm working on it. I know it isn't enough. But I promise you I will die before I let anything happen to her."

Estelle saw how he watched Noura in Cairo, and she believes him. Not that she trusts him. But Noura has done what no one else has been able to do—catch a fingerhold on the elusive Sykes. Estelle pulls the cigarette pack out and taps it on her palm. Perhaps Theo will be more useful than she thought.

She has a week to figure out how to fit the pieces together in a way that saves Mehedi and her sister.

THEO WATCHES Estelle smolder through the door, evaporating like mist. He hates that they're both here, making decisions that will destroy some lives and maybe save others. Rubbing the grit from his eyes, he wishes he'd never tracked Typhon down again, never agreed to this cockamamie scheme. He hasn't slept in weeks as he recreates the boy king's burial pieces. He leans his head against the bench in front of him. He should have kept the past in the past. Except that would free the man who threatened his sister to keep him compliant. And Theo cannot allow that to happen. Not this time.

The pendant around his neck swings free, slapping against his chest, reminding him that Horus is destined to confront Set, and there's nothing Theo, a mere mortal pawn, can do about it. He turns the ostrich feather in his pocket, wishing he had the power to control the sun.

He needs more time.

27

September 1, 1977

It's still dark when the 5:30 a.m. chime of WTIX blares from Noura's clock radio, followed by the deep voice of "Michael in the Morning" announcing "Don't Go Breaking My Heart" coming next. Noura smacks the alarm and rolls, literally rolls, out of bed. The last thing she needs is a reminder of all the folks lying to her.

Last night, she didn't fall asleep until Estelle tiptoed into the room. Noura had lost her sister's trail when Estelle jumped on the streetcar. Sure as the ocean is salty, she'd purposefully ditched Noura. But she had seen the man follow her. She'd seen him sit next to her sister. Blond, tall to the point of being rangy, with a beard that tried to make him look unkempt but was too neatly trimmed. Even his clothes attempted to look like a drunk.

Noura would be worried, but as the car eased forward, recognition sparked in Estelle's face.

Sliding her feet into the glaringly pink slippers Maman gave her, Noura stands. Estelle isn't in the bed opposite. Noura tugs her sheets and quilt over her pillow and then does the same for her sister.

At least she came home. Noura knows better than to ask what Estelle's been doing because she won't answer. Somehow Noura needs to beat her sister at her own game, study her every move until Noura can predict what she's planning to do next.

Noura opens the tiny closet, overflowing now with both her clothes and her sister's. Her fingers float over Estelle's bright blue silken shirt, her white linen pants, and land on the deep green dress the Elizabeths bought Noura in Cairo. One of the few truly beautiful things she owns. Lizzy would be horrified that Noura has reverted to librarian clothes. The Brits had such high hopes. Noura touches her lips where Theo's mouth had bruised hers. Honestly, Noura had such high hopes.

But dreams are just that. Dreams. In the bright light of reality, they wither away.

Noura drops the dress and pulls on her no-nonsense pants and plain white blouse. The outfit is exactly what Noura needs for her job as the museum's Jane of all trades. Just as Noura despairs of her sister ever arriving, Estelle appears in a drab uniform and rides with Noura in drooping silence.

The day passes in a blur of chaos. The security system is still not working properly, and Jim is threatening to turn the "dagblamed thing off." The throbbing at the base of Noura's skull rather agrees, but the team is installing the artifacts. Even though the pieces are behind locked doors guarded by New Orleans Police Officers, every bit of security is necessary. The sliver of light leaking through the crack between the double doors calls to Noura. She once held those objects. To be locked out now only underscores the depth of her descent.

On top of it, she's also dealing with a swarm of new, catastrophically untrained workers. Mr. Fagaly handles it all with gracious aplomb, and Noura tries to adopt the same attitude.

The one bright spot is that she hasn't had to babysit Estelle. The younger sister seems to be dogging Noura's steps rather than the reverse. Which seems a good thing at first. But two hours into her day, Noura's ready to crawl out of her skin. She cannot do a single thing without bumping into her sister—peering over Noura's shoulder as she places directional signage, popping around the corner when Noura restocks the pamphlets by the front door. That alone would have Noura jumping at nothing, but Theo is nearly as bad. He'd have joined her in the ladies' room if he thought he could get away with it. While Estelle and Theo aren't acting as allies exactly, there's something bizarre going on. And the hulking posters of Set and Horus on either side of the main hall aren't helping. She's half convinced the posters are alive and watching her.

At lunch, when Noura swings around the corner, Estelle and Theo cut off whispering in a corner. "That's it." She snatches Estelle's arm, hauling her toward the break room. "You are going to tell me about Mehedi's case and whatever else is going on."

Estelle nods but murmurs that she needs to use the restroom and conveniently escapes. Only to be replaced by Theo, who alternates between poking at his food and adjusting the necklace around his neck.

His quiet presence unnerves Noura most. In the display room, Estelle returns from the restroom and sweeps the same corner for thirty minutes while Theo passes Noura the poster she's just realized she needs, then the fishing line. He climbs the step ladder and patiently moves a placard this way and then that, then back to where it started. Noura's had him up and down the ladder so many times, sweat pools at his hairline. He unbuttons the top two buttons and flaps the front of his shirt, which only makes Noura picture him in the thin white undershirt.

"What is wrong with you?" Noura finally snaps.

Theo hesitates, then climbs down and sits on the bottom rung, his knees ridiculously akimbo. "I'm trying to make it up to you, Noura."

The words are a slap across the face.

"Moving a placard will make amends for ruining my life?" Noura's voice is tight and angry, and she despises how it echoes against the tiled floors. Like the room is noting the addition of a weight against her on Anubis's scales.

Theo takes out a handkerchief and wipes the sweat from his face. When he gathers his long legs underneath him, Noura flinches backward.

But he simply stands with a sigh and rubs his hands down his perfectly pressed khaki pants. "I ruined more than your career, Noura. I broke your heart. Hurting you was one of the biggest regrets of my life. If you let me, I'll spend a lifetime proving that I am sorry. If that means I have to move a placard around for eternity, then so be it. As long as I am with you, I'm okay with that."

He turns, grasps the placard, trudges up the ladder, and waits for Noura's direction.

But she's completely undone and tells him the placement is fine.

Theo ties off the fishing line and lumbers to the ground. "If you want me to change it later, let me know."

Tears burn the back of Noura's throat, and she lifts another placard as an excuse to concentrate elsewhere.

"It's okay to not be okay all the time," Theo says. He's not moved an inch.

"I'm fine." Like New Orleans, Noura's learned to evade, float downriver, and slide past impasses, slowly piling debris until there's enough solid under her feet to live on. It's the only way she knows how to survive.

"Survival isn't fine, Noura."

Noura bristles at how he's able to read her.

"I called Dr. Lilyquist." He steps closer to Noura, his shadow dark and small under his feet. "I explained everything that happened. She said she'd write you a reference if you want."

Noura's head snaps up to meet his gaze. "They'll let me come back?"

"If everything goes well here, she said she'd talk to the director."

Noura opens her mouth and snaps it closed. "Why?"

"I should never have doubted you. And I certainly shouldn't have let fear run away with me. It's understandable that you're angry." He brushes a strand of unruly hair from Noura's cheek and tucks it behind her ear. "You are brilliant, caring, and only trying to do the right thing. And I'm certainly not perfect. When it comes to protecting my loved ones, I've done things that later I wish I could change too."

Loved ones? Noura's hand finds the solidity of his chest, the feather pendant that promises he is exactly what she—

A throat clears, and Theo drops his hand to his side as they both turn.

"All set?" Estelle asks from the archway. The lights are searingly bright, cutting her sister's face into harsh, turbulent planes.

What right does she have to be angry? Noura is so very tired of being afraid.

"Thank you, Theo," Noura says and hefts the rest of the placards.

"Time for us to get back to work." She smiles at him and then shoves the signs at her sister.

AFTER WORK, Noura drives herself and Estelle toward home. But Estelle asks to go to the coffee shop, the fruit stand, the vegetable stand...until at dinner time, when the two return home and collapse into their dining room chairs, barely able to scoop food into their mouths, let alone acknowledge Maman and Father's conversation.

"I'm glad you two are going out together" from Maman.

And "I hope you aren't getting into trouble...ha ha" from Father.

Noura chafes at his assumptions but smiles benignly until Father responds with a lame "I'm trying to protect you."

Maybe he is, but Noura can't find the energy or forgiveness to care as she stumbles to her bed and collapses. Only to wake and do the same for the next two days. This time, Theo joins the sisters for lunch. His shoulder brushing against Noura's as they set up the exhibit nearly sends her into vapors. Estelle seems to notice but refrains from scowling, which leaves Noura wondering what has changed her mind. But Noura has little time to ask as they work and then traipse about the city. It's almost as if Estelle's trying to recreate their escapades in the Tel Aviv market. Despite herself, Noura enjoys her sister's company, her antics.

By Saturday evening, Noura's convinced herself that her sister is simply trying to earn enough money to help Mehedi. But that's when Noura notices the blond man she'd seen on the streetcar. The sisters are at the fruit stand. Noura's digging in the bristly coconuts when she feels a frisson in the air and glances up. A large black dog trots by, the man following in its wake. His chin tips down so his hair covers his face as he slips a tiny square of paper between bananas. Noura sets down the coconut and watches while Estelle surreptitiously lifts the bananas and retrieves the paper.

Noura lifts two pineapples, squeezing each and feigning a tough decision. It's the moment Estelle needs to pop the paper open. Careful not to let her shadow alert Estelle, Noura slides over enough to read the words.

They suspect everything. ~Mehedi

Estelle grasps the edge of the wooden stand, and the paper drifts to the ground, where the dog picks it up and trots off as if he is part of the conspiracy.

"Estelle?" The name slips through Noura's lips even as fear slams through her body.

Estelle's lips lift in a mimic of a smile. "My blood sugar feels low. Would you mind buying one of these for me? I'm going to sit." She waves absently toward the curb.

Noura obliges, buying a few bananas and bringing them to her sister. But now she knows she must find out what is going on with Mehedi immediately. Left on her own, Estelle will only make a hash of things again.

28

Mehedi's note spins in Estelle's mind. If the prosecution suspects what Mehedi's done, Estelle has very little time to appease Typhon.

When the house is asleep, Estelle sneaks down the stairs and dials the number Harry gave her. Despite the fact it's past midnight, a woman answers in a chipper voice. Estelle leaves a message asking to have Harry accelerate all the appointments to next Tuesday.

"The sixth?" Her voice sounds worried. "That's four days from now."

"Exactly," Estelle says with false confidence.

Theo is supposed to have the mask done on Monday, and Estelle will simply have to steal the artifacts that night...before the prosecutor uncovers enough evidence to move from suspicious to charging Mehedi with treason.

As if stealing world-famous artifacts is as easy as tying one's shoes.

Worse, if Estelle's caught, it won't be just Mehedi who suffers. Noura will be destroyed. After the last few months, it's a sacrifice Estelle wishes she doesn't have to make.

IN THE MORNING, Estelle drags herself from bed and cobbles herself together. At the last moment, she slips on the feather pendant she'd found at the cathedral. It's flimsy protection against the cataract of red-eyed nightmares and shifting shadows, but she's grateful for it as she tumbles into the car. Before Noura starts the car, she hesitates, studying Estelle like she has an earth-shattering question. Part of Estelle hopes that the big sister who rescued her from the crazy fishmonger will stop this madness.

Noura sucks in a breath, thinks better of whatever it is, and shakes her head in a never-mind gesture. The grinding of the obnoxious car motor silences whatever conversation they might have had.

Normally Estelle doesn't mind wandering the museum. She's not an uncultured brute, even if she prefers the arts of music and dance. But today, she might as well be deep in a mine. She's already retrofitted a padded bag to protect the artifacts, bought a saw for the vitrines and a tennis ball, and stashed a stepladder in the closet. Now to find the security code for the employee door and lift the keys to the security gates, which will be sealed in front of the locked exhibit doors. She has three days instead of a few weeks to solve every single obstacle.

Mulling the problems, she stands guard over mostly empty halls and wanders the lesser exhibits to ward off any would-be miscreants. Every time she passes the exhibit hall, Jim is sitting outside amidst wires and gizmos.

Jim, with his thick-soled shoes, receding hairline, and quiet voice, has navigated the obnoxious security system, deciding it needs to be returned to the manufacturer. The replacements will arrive in a few days. Estelle prays the delivery will wait until after Monday and that Jim won't decide to attack the problem on his own.

Despite his slow drawl and big-brother smile, the man is smarter than most of the boys Estelle graduated law school with. She's fairly certain the Vietnam veteran could whip together suitable protection with a wire coat hanger and doorbell if given permission. She hates deceiving him almost as much as she hates lying to Noura.

Estelle shoves the thought away. Noura may be the only innocent in the entire Marquette/Poitier family, but the oldest sister should have learned to cope by now.

Meanwhile the alarm blares regularly, sending the team running to the display room and causing the mild-mannered Jim to swear in a colorful combination of English, French, and Creole.

Her wandering opens too much space to think and plot and spiral into fretting. The plan is to have Theo deliver the artifacts to Typhon. But she's jittery with questions. Will Theo double-cross her? Will Typhon follow through? Is he even capable of what he's promised? And then there is Noura's safety to worry about, before and after Estelle finishes this mission.

Amidst all of this, she's not forgotten about Tut's curse...or maybe it's the weight of her heart on Anubis's scales. Maybe God knows what she truly is: weak, vulnerable, and not worth saving. She hopes her maman is right about God being willing to save everyone, but she can't be sure of that either.

Estelle pauses in front of an oil painting of a group of rotund men poring over scattered pages. She squints at the placard. *The Lawyer's Office.* She shifts her attention back to the painting and realizes she'd been wrong. The only well-fed person is the lawyer. The others are gaunt and pleading.

"The rich take advantage, whether it's sixteenth-century Netherlands or twentieth-century United States," she says to the painting. "How did I think I could change anything?"

A breath of movement skitters at the outer reaches of her hearing, and she spins, her braids slapping her cheek. The room stretches behind her. Empty.

Estelle strides past the paintings, the faces and landscapes blurring until she steps into the hall. A dark shadow flutters, caught in the baseboard. Swallowing, Estelle bends, reaching to grab hold, but it slips, *poof*, under the tiny gap. Estelle jerks upright, hand pressed against the freezing pendant around her neck. A man lurks at the head of the back stairwell, and she stifles a scream as recognition registers. Harry.

"What are you doing here?" She grabs hold of his arm and steers him toward the door.

Noura's been assigned to float between the Great Hall and the Stern Auditorium and could appear at any moment. But Harry saunters through the hall, unconcerned even though the rail is open to the first floor.

"Did you know the fastest animal in the world is a peregrine falcon?" he says, nodding to the feather pendant.

"What does that have to do with anything?" Estelle resists hiding the silver under her uniform.

"The falcon isn't fast because of itself," he says, ignoring his sister's question. "It's fast because it works with gravity. It dives headfirst, leaning into its own heaviness as it hurtles toward the ground, making it the fastest animal on earth. Yes, gravity pulls us inexorably toward the earth, anchoring us here. But somehow, someway, we have to leap, trusting our heaviness to give us weight enough to make magic happen. You have to trust the weight of what we're doing, Estelle." He turns now, his stare boring into her.

She forces herself to form something like a smile. To nod. To convince him she believes in the organization that's decided that bombing buildings will save everyone.

"Typhon isn't convinced, little sister."

She doesn't even attempt to stifle her growl of frustration. "I don't know what else he wants me to do. I'm working as fast as I can."

Harry lifts the falcon pendant, letting it swing once, twice. "If you don't come through, Typhon will use one of Mehedi's bombs to remove Noura as a distraction, and neither will see the sky again. The museum might be the perfect—"

"You wouldn't dare." If Estelle thought it would help, she'd slice this pompous traitor herself.

"Try me."

She bats his hand away, an inferno of anger manifesting in her sparking vision. "So help me—"

Footsteps thud up the other stairwell, and Estelle glances behind her. "If that's Noura..." Estelle turns to spirit her brother away, but he's gone as mysteriously as he appeared. She swallows, thinking about the flat look in his eyes, the only emotion a hellish consuming anger. They say anger and unforgiveness gut a person and leave them a shadow of themselves. If Estelle didn't know better, she would think he might already be a ghost.

Jim pops around the corner, grinning, *joie de vivre* exploding around him. "I need someone to celebrate with me. And you're the only other person who seems to care. I figured out part of the system."

With one last glance over her shoulder, Estelle reluctantly clatters down the stairs behind Jim. Her knees threaten to give way under her, the ground rising to swallow her in retribution for the hellfire she's released on her family and this man she's come to respect. He survived a war, gained a limp, and came out smiling. What if Tut's curse hadn't landed on Noura, but Estelle? Typhon ensured Noura and everyone Estelle cared about will be destroyed, no matter what Estelle does. All the bad spewing from Estelle onto them.

"How do you do it?" Estelle's question makes Jim pause, his sparkle dimming an infinitesimal amount.

"Keep smiling, I mean," she clarifies.

"Oh, *cher*, the way I figure it, the good Lord woke me up this morning." He yanks open the door to the empty auditorium and waves her through even as he continues. "He let me have a job I usually enjoy, even if the darn fancy-pants system is giving me fits. Why focus on all I lost or what I wish I had that I don't got? All that does is make a body hate life. And hate? That'll eat you from the inside out. If you ask me, that's where real evil is...in all the hate. Don't matter which side it is. You hate? You destroy? You're evil. Easy as that."

Black and white. Good and bad.

Estelle knows exactly which side she's on and despises herself for it. But where else does she go?

"But," Jim says as he skitters past her to an open area, "if we find ourselves on the wrong side, which we all do at one point or other, we get to switch sides."

If only that were possible.

Jim plunks himself in the midst of the wires, and Estelle squats with him. The wires of a security system are not unlike the wires of a bomb. She can't help but think of Mehedi. Because of the threat to his family, he went from a sweet, scared boy to someone willing to destroy.

At something Jim says, Estelle nods, uncomprehending, and scrolls through her memories, watching as she introduces Mehedi to the Weathermen, skipping through meetings of rhetoric, listening as she pressures the Weather Underground to get Typhon to back off, bouncing through time, until she sees the wires and strange bottles piled neatly on Mehedi's desk and knows. Harry found his sister that afternoon.

She shoots to her feet. Harry found her at the exact moment she realized Mehedi had gone too far. He promised to rein Mehedi in, protect him. Like he's promising to protect her now.

"You okay?" Jim scrambles to his feet. Concern pulls his brows together.

"Fine." Estelle manages the words. "I was supposed to check the basement an hour ago."

Estelle stumbles from the room, leaving poor Jim bewildered. She wants to scream, hating that her sister is kind and gentle and absolutely vulnerable. She hates this stupid exhibit. She hates evil men who twist everything for their own pursuits. Maybe Mehedi is already one of them. Maybe it's too late. But she has to try.

29

September 5, 1977

Monday at noon, Estelle and Theo miraculously slacken their stakeout of Noura enough that she can slip down the street to the payphone. Noura can't call from home. Maman might be sympathetic, but Father and Grandmere would kick her out faster than she can say King Tut.

Noura dials the lawyer she found in Estelle's daybook and shoves a dollar's worth of coins into the slot. She's no idea what to ask the man, but she has to try something.

"Hello?" A harried woman answers the phone on the second ring, not even bothering to give the name of the lawyer's practice.

"Hello." Noura stumbles for words and then remembers Father's advice to smile and introduce herself. She clears her throat and starts again. "My name's Noura Marquette. I'm calling about Mehedi Ibrahim."

"Are you related?"

"Kind of. But I—"

"Are you on his list?"

"List?" Noura stammers.

"Listen, I can't give information if you're not on the list."

"Ma'am." But the line is dead. Noura gapes at the beeping receiver and then sets it into the cradle.

She leans her head against the burning metal phone. She's had nightmares for years about the first time she met Mehedi. Saira, Estelle, and Noura were playing some ruckus game when someone knocked on the door. Thrilled to have an excuse to leave the game, Noura threw open the door, expecting one of her friends. Instead, a child stood moaning like a ghost.

When he fell into her, Noura screamed, backpedaling and trying to extricate herself from his bony limbs. Saira rammed into Noura as she flew around the corner, catching both the ghost-child and Noura.

He was gaunt and so filthy he may have been formed from mud.

When Saira tipped water onto the boy's lips, his eyes fluttered open. Deep and inscrutable eyes like he'd walked through the underworld and survived.

"Thank you." He stared right at Noura. "Thank you."

That night, whatever he'd been through floated straight into Noura's dreams. The bony fingers of red-eyed demons slashed at her mind. While Estelle climbed into bed with Noura, it was Mehedi who told her funny stories of a woman who defeated an evil creature by writing a magic story of his destruction, and a coyote who tricked a camel, only to have the camel trick him back. He became Scheherazade, staving off the executions in Noura's nightmares.

She and Estelle took an oath the next day that they would take care of this boy who had survived.

But how can Noura do that when he willingly walked into the fire?

She flings open the phone booth door...then screams, scrambling away from the twisted mass of dark feathers at her feet and slamming the phone booth door shut. It only occurs to her then to scan the street.

People drift in the tree-dappled sunshine. A man sits on a park bench, eating a sandwich. A woman on roller skates wheels by, her bell-bottoms swishing and hair riding the wind.

No one out of place.

The museum's employee door opens, and Estelle's head pops out. At some point, she bleached her hair back blond, but it's blindingly white in the sun. Estelle has a tendency to overdo everything. Still, Noura beckons her sister.

Estelle squints at Noura, says something over her shoulder, then emerges from the building and trots down the street.

"What's wrong?" she says.

Noura merely points to the carcass.

The moment Estelle rounds the door enough to see the blood, she stiffens, her face going red. She lays a hand on her older sister's arm. Noura's connection with Estelle is the only thing tethering Noura to any semblance of calm.

"Go back to work." Estelle bends and snatches the thing with her bare hands. "I'll take care of this."

And the odd thing is, Noura knows her sister will.

IN THE BASEMENT, Theo nearly jumps through the ceiling when the security alarm blares again. He's struggling to do his job as the time ticks down until the exhibit opens. Ten days. And there are too many people, too many moving pieces, and his assignment is slipping through his fingers. Noura is just starting to speak to him, and yet Estelle is hounding him about finishing sooner rather than later. As if creating a museum-quality reproduction in his spare time is paint-by-number. He's sufficiently completed the face of the mask, curling the Eye of Horus perfectly. But the back? The inscription is delicate and time-consuming. Theo's deadline is tonight, and he—

"I am absolutely done with keeping my sister in the dark." Speak of the devil. Estelle slams into the conservator's office.

Theo drops the illustration of Tut's mask he was studying. "Hello, Estelle."

"Don't hello me. Noura's in danger." Estelle drops a chicken carcass on his desk.

He pokes it with the end of his pencil. "What am I supposed to—"

"It's another black chicken," she says.

"Voodoo?" The word is half statement, half disbelieving question as he struggles to transition from the writing that pleads for Horus to protect the nape of Tut's neck, to witch doctors and black chickens.

"Maman said there was a powerful Catholic bishop who died because he'd been hexed."

"It certainly reeks. I could see it suffocating someone to death."

She growls at his weak humor. "You work for Typhon. Deal with it."

Theo shakes out a clean handkerchief and lifts the offending bird with thumb and forefinger. "Where was it?"

"Outside the phone booth Noura was in." She is nearly stroking out with rage.

Theo whistles low, releasing the tiniest bit of steam that has slammed his lungs. "Who was she calling?"

Estelle crosses her arms like a stubborn toddler who knows far too much.

"How do we"—Theo flaps his hand in a helpless circle—"unhex things?"

Estelle plops into a chair and scoffs. "I suppose I will have to take care of it."

"Then why tell me?" Theo's temper is fraying. If it breaks, they are all done for. He can't think straight if he's blindingly angry.

"She knows I'm trying to steal artifacts. And it's your fault for making her question me as much as it's your fault she doesn't know the whys. It's also your fault that we keep having to prolong this thing. And this"—she pokes the chicken —"is just one of the threats Typhon's issued today." Her voice is loud enough that Tutankhamun can probably hear her in the afterworld.

"I know it isn't easy," he says, "but you know as well as I do we can't tell Noura what we're doing. She'll never agree to keep it quiet. We get it done and then get as far away as we can, so nothing falls on her."

"I'm not leaving her vulnerable. You have one day to—"

The piercing squelch of the walkie-talkie cuts her off. "Theo. Where y'at?" Jim's scratching voice warbles through the speaker, saving Theo.

Estelle throws her hands up in Emmy-worthy exasperation and collapses into the chair.

"Yep." Theo isn't a bad actor either, and his answer to Jim is steady, nonchalant even.

"You got a call on line two," Jim's voice crackles. "The operator's been tryin' to get through, but your line ain't working. Says it's real urgent. Maybe try the curator's office, yeah?"

"Be right there." He shrugs in confused innocence at Estelle.

"Go." She sighs, exasperated.

Theo links his arm in hers and drags her from his office before locking it. "I'll finish the pieces," he says as he nudges her down the hall toward Jim's office. "You figure out how to get into the building, make the switch, and get out."

Theo waits until she's good and gone before he rolls his head between his shoulders. Only one of his personas should be getting calls at NOMA, and almost everyone related to the fun-loving Theo facade is inside this building. Theo ducks into the curator's office and shuts the door with a soft click. If he'd known where it would lead, would he have agreed to transport that first package for Typhon? He'd had little choice, really. The insurance company had refused his sister's meds...again. But here he is juggling all his personas, which has become a full-time job. One he's becoming less and less interested in as he becomes more concerned about Noura...who, fortunately or unfortunately, is finally finding her lovely voice.

"Yes?" Theo says into the receiver. He's not sure who he's supposed to be, and the one word should serve as an opening to whoever's called.

"You have a problem." It's one of Theo's ears inside the FBI. How he found Theo here is disturbing. Theo only calls the other man from pay phones as Sykes.

"Yes," Theo says again, fully aware Estelle may be listening.

"I know you're working on the Tut thing. Things are about to get hot fast."

"Okay." The two syllables are even and unperturbed. "I've already got the necklace and Selket done. My contact and I are working on the rest. We're fine."

NOURA SETS the phone in its cradle. She can't find air. The voice was unmistakably Theo's, but the man on the other side called him Sykes. She sinks into the chair.

"I'm sorry, Noura." Estelle is all saccharine sweet and just as fake.

"Are you?" Noura turns on her sister as a tsunami of emotions crashes in—anger, fear, rejection, determination. "One minute you're promising to protect me and the next—" She brandishes a finger to point at the phone. "You knew what I'd hear. You're the most selfish person I know. If you can't have something, you destroy everyone else's happiness."

"That's not fair."

"Isn't it? You decide what's right and wrong, then punish anyone who doesn't think the same way. Shoving them behind a locked gate, then throwing away the key."

"I've not decided anything," Estelle says. "I told you Theo was lying. He's the one trying to steal the artifacts. I don't understand why you're mad at me."

"Because you wanted to be right. You don't want to love me, but you don't want anyone else to love me either. It's too inconvenient for you. What would happen if someone was looking out for me when you came asking for another handout? Poor Estelle, trying to save the world as she stomps on everyone who ever cared about her. And—"

"I stomp on people?" Estelle fairly grinds her teeth. "The government is the one stealing from its people, pitting us against one another in an unwinnable competition like there's not enough to go around. There is enough, Noura. If we—"

"I'm not saying the government is right. And you know that. I'm saying you're wrong too. How dare you think we're square just because he's in on it?" Noura's throat burns, acid creeping from her stomach.

Noura's been so naive. When Estelle came back, when she didn't make a single move to steal the artifacts, Noura thought she'd been wrong. And she was...sort of. That Noura hadn't thought the list was Theo's was beyond stupid of her. He was with her when she found the list, he made her look foolish when she inquired about the thefts, and then he spiked her career.

But his deceit doesn't change what Estelle is—a self-righteous woman climbing over her sister to get whatever she thinks is important.

"What I don't understand is if you hate him so much," Noura says, "why you're working with him."

"What are you talking about? I'm not—"

"Estelle, he said, 'we.' 'We're working on it.' He has an accomplice."

"What are—"

"I'm not going to play the sap for you. The worst thing is I still love you." Noura slumps in the office chair. "What am I supposed to do when you keep doing the unforgivable?"

Estelle is, for once, quiet.

Noura waves a limp hand, directing her sister to leave. "Don't forget to stock up on insulin before you leave," Noura says as Estelle opens the door.

"I'm not leaving until you're safe." Estelle slams the door behind her.

Apparently forgiving your sister is an acceptance of all the muddy things that slip through your fingers and leave a mess behind.

But forgiving a man for constant duplicity is another thing entirely. Maman has done it her entire life. She hadn't much choice, given that until a few years ago, a woman couldn't open a bank account without a man's permission. Maman had protected Noura the only way she knew how and sent her daughter away from the convenient marriage to Charles Barry...straight into the arms of Theo Fabre, or whoever he is. Still, there has to be an explanation, doesn't there? Why would he lie to her? What could he possibly gain now?

Noura sucks in a breath, compressing the liquid hurt rising in her. Where is her surety when she needs it?

Footsteps echo in the room next door. Theo is pacing, and Noura knows she cannot see him or she will lose her resolve to do something, no matter the cost. But what?

She presses her hands onto the cool wooden desk and sucks in a steadying breath. She has an hour left on her shift. An hour to avoid him. And then she will have the evening to figure out what to do. She could ask for Theo to be recalled to the Met. He is, after all, on loan. NOMA should believe their employee over him. But they might not. A rock settles in her stomach as she realizes he probably lied about contacting Dr. Lilyquist too. Noura is beneath the surface of the water, waiting to drown.

She flips open the Met's full-color King Tutankhamun guidebook and absently drags her fingers over the images of Tut's tomb. No one really knows what happened to the boy king. It was sudden, that much seems clear, and likely violent.

It takes a certain amount of hutzpah to attack a representative of the gods. Of course modern man knows he wasn't a deity. And maybe that's the key. If people know the reality of something, it releases them to act.

Noura forces herself to her feet. Sarai told her often enough that she is stronger than she thinks. Maybe Noura can prove her friend correct. Noura pushes out the door, confident she can push to the surface, defeat the waves…

Right until the moment she ricochets off Theo's chest. He snatches her shoulders to steady her. Even as her mind screams, she knows she cannot let him realize anything is wrong. So she smiles and allows him to step in beside her.

"Where's Estelle?" He glances around like her sister is hiding in Noura's pocket.

He's anxious about something, but what? And then Estelle's calm hits Noura. Estelle had anticipated her sister's reaction, planned for it, maybe even planted the moment.

"She told me everything, Theo, and I put the rest together," Noura says, anger making her foolish, flinging any accusation she can think of to burn him as he's scalded her. "You're not making replicas. You're making forgeries and then will fence the artifacts she steals. You may have the Met fooled, but Jim will believe me, and I bet if he searches your—"

Theo snatches Noura's arm and propels her into the security office. She ricochets off a chair and spins topsy-turvy into the desk. When Theo closes the door with a firm finality, Noura realizes that the one time she let her feelings out may be the last time she sees the light of day.

30

Noura mentally curses Jim for being so unorganized. Where's the cup with a pair of scissors nestled at the edge of the desk? As she backs into the corner of the room, there is nothing here to help her. Not even a paperweight.

No longer the goofy academic, Theo is all hard edges and sinister anger as he leans against the door, massaging the bridge of his nose.

With his eyes briefly closed, Noura scrambles around the desk and wrenches the phone from the cradle.

Theo launches himself. "Oh no, you don't." He wrenches the receiver from her grip and unplugs the phone from the jack. "Listen," Theo starts, but Noura cuts him off with a scream that may very well wake King Tut.

Theo catapults across the room, hauling her into his chest, smothering her mouth with his hand. She bucks and kicks, but the man is used to brawling, and Noura is an out-of-shape academic. Why hadn't she taken a karate class?

She twists and turns, but nothing loosens his grip. Tears well in her eyes, and she can't breathe. Can't breathe. Why has she been so cruel to her sister? Avoided Maman over the last week? Maman doesn't deserve any of this. And of anyone, she will be the one who misses Noura when she's gone. She stills with the thought. *When I am gone.*

She is going to die.

"Noura," Theo mumbles in her ear. "I'm FBI."

She sucks in scant air through Theo's fingers, desperate for her brain to catch up. FBI? Why had he been in Cairo? CIA deals with international crime, doesn't it?

"If you promise not to scream, I'll show you my badge."

Noura shakes her head. Who knows what he'll pull from his pocket if she lets him?

"Fine," he says and shifts so that Noura's still somewhat pinned with one hand. When he reaches with the other hand, she has just enough leeway to pivot, then smash her elbow into his gut and continue her spin, which, according to her defense instructor, should have made her free. Instead, she is wheeled into the wall, one arm pinned behind her with what looks very much like an authentic FBI badge thrust too close to her face. She squints.

Alexander McShane. FBI.

THEO HATES the whimper that leaks from Noura. But when she pushes away, she stands tall and straight. Formidable.

"I'm sorry," he says. "I didn't realize how tangled up Estelle was until recently."

A thick veil of anger curtains Noura's face.

"I would be angry with me too."

She lifts a single regal brow. While Noura was raised to be an elite, Theo barely squeaked through high school and college, dodging bullets and thugs. Pop doing his best to put food on the table. But Theo has years of training and fieldwork. He is the best at what he does in the nation and quite possibly, the world. And yet...

"I need your help," he says.

Noura's face is torn. The flare of her nose, trying not to cry. The clench of her jaw, furious. "Was any of it true?"

What he's supposed to say twists in a hopeless jumble, and he spreads his fingers on the desk to steady himself. "The important parts are true," he says. "My sisters, my mom and dad, even how I finagled a place on the team. The only thing I lied about was my name."

"And why you were there."

Theo concedes her point with a nod so tight his muscles might snap with the movement.

"Does my sister know who you are?"

This is the question Theo's been avoiding, and he reverts to his training to answer. "I don't think so."

"Is my sister trying to steal the artifacts?"

Theo hesitates. If he tells her yes, she'll never let Estelle steal the artifacts. If he tells her no, she'll assume he's lying. "I don't know how to answer that." He's equivocating, and the fist she smacks on her hip proves she's not giving in.

"She's the one who told me to pick up the line. Why would she do that...unless...unless...are you helping her?"

"She's trying to help Mehedi."

"The money." Noura slumps into Jim's chair. "She's in over her head, isn't she?"

The alarm screams through the building, and Theo's spared answering by the rush of personnel.

Noura turns to join them, but Theo steps in front of her and leans in so she can hear him over the wail. "For your sister's sake, you can't tell anyone, even her."

Theo thinks she nods, hopes she nods. But he doesn't follow her into the crowd. Instead, he tunnels to his little workbench and goes back to work on the mask. While his body is busy, his mind skitters. He has to finish this tonight. Any longer and Noura might ferret out the full truth. And then two years' worth of effort will have been wasted.

There is so much of his younger sister in Noura—determined, smart, and refusing to tell anyone when she needs help. Theo slams a fist onto the table. How is he here again? Watching someone he loves dangle in Typhon's clutches. Last time he was forced to let Typhon go for Mabel's sake. Even Horus bowed to chaos in order to protect those he loved. Theo unclips the necklace from his neck and stuffs it in his pocket. This time, Theo will not allow Typhon to escape without paying for what he has done. If he does, Typhon will never stop asking, never stop threatening.

31

By the time Estelle and Jim get the alarm under control again, she is done in. Her conscience grouses that she shouldn't have used Theo's call to distract Noura. But she needed the alarm code for the employee entrance Jim had scribbled on a folder. Not that Theo didn't have it coming, and not that Estelle had much choice. Even if Noura holds a grudge for the rest of her life, she will be alive to do it.

The good news is Estelle only has an hour left of work, and Theo should have the forgeries done. Which means she's almost ready for tonight. She lets her mind drift to the last obstacles to overcome. The security system is continuing to fail. She's figured out how to grab the mask and Selket. The display case surrounding the necklace is strangely harder to access. Estelle walks the halls of the museum as she hunts for weaknesses and a way to lift the security keys.

Then she'll steal the pieces, call the phone number she's memorized, and have Theo deliver the pieces to where she's told. Once Mehedi is free, she'll grab him, fence the one additional piece she'll take, and then get everyone out of the country. South this time. Into South America. She has contacts there. She'll convince Noura to come. Estelle won't let her pay for her little sister's mistakes. Except Estelle has already. It's her fault Theo is involved at all. At least now Noura knows he isn't a golden boy.

Of course after using Theo to throw Noura off her scent, Estelle may very well have to find someone other than Theo to fence the last piece for her. No big deal—sidestep both Theo and Harry *and* sell the piece *and* spring Mehedi from prison before everything falls apart. She can practically feel the hangman's noose. If she could find someone to get Mehedi out, then she could sell the pieces on her own and then bolt. Would that work?

Estelle passes her sister in the hall again. It's almost like Noura has no other duties than to traipse the museum after her little sister. She thinks she's being discreet, carrying a clipboard, which she studiously checks every time Estelle glances up. But Noura's yet to turn a single one of the blank pages.

Near close, Noura enters the exhibit space behind her, and Estelle turns on her sister with a thousand-watt smile. "Could I get a ride home with..." The words die on her tongue. It's Lizzy.

"Hello, darling!" Lizzy opens her arms and, bewildered, Estelle falls into her friend's *bise*—a kiss for each of her cheeks.

"What are you doing here?" Estelle covertly wipes the lipstick from her cheeks.

"My husband fell in love with the boy king and decided to support the tour. I remembered how you and your sweet sister were headed here. He's getting what he wants, and I get to see my favorite sisters. Quite expedient, if I do say so myself."

"Quite." And it is expedient. But not in the way Lizzy thinks. Lizzy's wealthy and connected and sympathetic. And her husband loves Cairo. She may be the buyer Estelle needs.

Lizzy loops her gloved hand through the crook of Estelle's arm and turns her toward the stairwell. "I simply insist on taking you to dinner tonight. On me...or rather on Harold, Jr."

"I don't think—" Estelle starts, as she stutter-steps. Harold, Jr.? Her husband is George. Lizzy lifts a brow, and realization slams into Estelle. Harry?

"You are dressed well enough that I can talk us into Galatoire's." Lizzy tugs Estelle down the stairs, and Estelle stumbles to keep up. "I'm absolutely dying to try real Louisiana jumbo crab."

"But..."

Lizzy's reference to their brother has Estelle all akimbo. Is she in league with Harry? Or just a mouthpiece?

"I'm just supposed to let you know he's okay. I've no idea what that means. These boys, with all their cloak and dagger. It would be so much easier if we just all said what we thought and needed." Lizzy gives her a brilliant smile, then turns to chattering about some hideous trousers someone had foisted on Noura. Lizzy can't possibly be in league with Estelle's heartless brother. She's vetted the woman three ways to Sunday.

Estelle's ugly, non-slip shoes squeak across the floor as she pulls to a stop. "Lizzy," Estelle says. "I need your help."

"Again?" Her laugh is tinkling.

When Estelle's expression doesn't change, Lizzy sobers. Unfortunately, Estelle's lost as to where to begin.

Lizzy steps in front of Estelle. "Just tell me, dear."

"I've gotten myself into a mess."

Lizzy shakes her head like the mother of a naughty yet expansively adorable toddler.

"Typhon wants me to steal some of the artifacts." Estelle didn't mean to blurt it that bluntly, but nothing about this is adorable.

"That would certainly disrupt the peace talks between the United States and Egypt." Lizzy bites her lip. "But you do like your sister, yes?"

Estelle wraps her arms around her waist, trying to hold herself together...or maybe to keep herself from slipping through the floor and dropping straight to hell. "Yes. That's why I have to do it. That and Mehedi."

"I don't understand."

"Typhon promised he'd get Mehedi out of prison if I help. And if I don't..." she can't bring herself to say it.

"He is a nasty one." Lizzy ponders the latticed skylights.

"Please." Estelle hates the pleading in her voice, but she cannot stop now. She can't trust Theo. She can't trust Harry. "I need someone with connections and money to buy the pieces from me and then help me get Mehedi, Noura, and me out of the country."

"And you thought of me?"

"I hadn't until now."

Laughter lifts from the next room, and Estelle loops her arm through Lizzy's in feigned casualness as she guides her friend around the corner and into the gift store, which nine times out of ten is empty. But of course, Noura is there, dusting a replicated amulet—number three on the get list. And poor Jim is counting books into a display of some kind, his keys jangling from his hip. Estelle knows exactly which keys she needs, and they are tantalizingly close.

Lizzy ogles the room for a moment, the display lights sparking red in her appraising eyes. "Yes," she says. "I will."

At Lizzy's voice, Noura spins. "Lizzy!" Noura pops to her feet and scrapes her humidity-frizzed hair out of her face. Somehow, disheveled is appealing on her.

Except Noura's left the cabinet unlocked. Panic and relief crash against Estelle, and she saunters over to ask Jim for the keys to lock up. It's so unlikely to work, it's laughable to even try. But Jim unhooks the keys with a benevolent shake of his head and tosses the wad to Estelle.

Noura is distracted enough with Lizzy—how is George? Elizabeth? Why is she here?—that Estelle's able to remove the keys she needs, lock the cabinet, return the other keys, hustle the other two women away into the hallway, and—

"Are you ladies headed out for the night?" Theo's leaning on the front desk.

Of all the bum luck.

"Well, aren't you a dish?" Lizzy claims Theo with a vice grip around his bicep.

Theo pastes on a smile more fake than Lizzy's blond hair. "Thank you, madam. But I am spoken for."

Lizzy gapes at Estelle. "You didn't tell me you had a gorgeous bloke in New Orleans. No wonder you came home!"

It's a heartbeat before Estelle finds her voice to interject. "He's not...I mean..."

"My eyes are elsewhere." Theo winks at Noura, and she fumbles under the attention.

If only the way he looks at Noura—like he would die for her—was real. But Estelle knows the full truth about Theo. Without him, Typhon couldn't have even known about the extent of the security failures.

Noura deserves someone to take care of her, not sacrifice her the minute things go sideways. Estelle swings out the door, letting it slip from her fingers and swing shut on Theo.

Even before Theo's oxfords hit the marble outside, his skin pricks with the coming storm. He's been trying to avoid this duo of women for months now. Two estranged sisters, each knowing the tiniest portion of who he is. If they put everything together, he's a walking dead man.

All he needs is for Ghadfa to appear. There's no accounting for what he is doing in the States, let alone New Orleans. Ghadfa was beyond useful in Egypt—a local with street connections, likely on the wrong side of the law, but skilled enough to not be obvious and smart enough to be careful. The man was ex-military and had a family. At the time, Theo thought that meant he'd never have to worry about keeping his American-based identities safe from a wily cutthroat. Yet he's lurking around Theo's hole-in-the-wall apartment and following Noura. And then there are the hexes. Surely the man doesn't know a voodoo curse from a game of patty-cake.

If Ghadfa puts her in danger, Theo will have to deal with it. He turns the feather pendant in his pocket, pondering what he can do. Wishing Horus would help him. Despite his efforts to keep his heart unencumbered, Noura sauntered right past his clawing need to succeed and plunked her trusting self in the middle of his deluded heart.

Lizzy weaves her arm through Noura's and drags her into conversation. Listening to the British woman is like chewing cotton candy—completely vacuous and so sweet it hurts. Theo drops behind them. Unfortunately, Estelle has the same idea, and he's stuck trying not to appear like he's avoiding the corrosive dissident.

"We have a problem." Estelle speaks in low tones—not a hissing whisper that would draw attention. She is far too skilled for that rookie mistake. Though talking about their relationship in public, a mere two steps from her sister, might be the biggest blunder anyone could make.

"No thanks to you," Theo says. "The good news is I'm fast on my feet, and we're still good to go...Unless you can't fulfill your part."

"You know I don't have any choice."

"I know." If they'd met under other circumstances, Estelle and Theo might have been fast friends. She's principled, protective, resourceful, straight-talking, and decisive. The same things that make Theo good at his job. But he's threatened her entire world, which means she'll gut him the minute he turns his back.

"I know," Theo repeats. Ancient Egyptian gods went to war with each other to maintain eternal balance and fundamental harmony. And he would love to set her free to form the world into a place of harmony. But there are simply too few good people who are too often at odds over issues that don't matter. And Horus and Anubis have yet to show up, working together to fight the forces of disorder. "I know you don't believe me. But I will do everything I can to protect you both. In the meantime, I'm finished with the mask."

As the pair steps onto the sidewalk, the wind gusts, and the ends of Noura's hair lift, playing in the breeze. She cocks her head, obviously seeing something Theo doesn't thanks to a column blocking his view. Theo's skin prickles.

He's reaching for the pistol at his waist when a black feathered man steps from the shadows. The man's bare torso ripples in tattoos, and the white paint on his face is slick as oil, broken only by the jagged slash of a mouth. In his hands, he wields a wicked sickle-shaped knife. Theo's seen pictures of a witch doctor, but they failed to capture the stench of darkness.

Lizzy skitters back, ramming into Theo, waking him from his strange stupor, and he's catching her, tripping, as the man grins, wide, gaping, swallowing the world.

"We're watching." His deep voice shakes the foundation as Noura steps into his reach.

Theo scrambles to right Lizzy, to fight through the gelatinous air to stop whatever is happening. A white falcon drops from the sky, its laughing call circling, circling, wrenching attention up, away. The man frowns at the powerful bird, lifts his arms, and then, as Theo's pounding feet hit the sidewalk next to Noura, the man disappears. Where had he gone? Theo tucks Noura behind him as he searches the empty shadows. He turns finally to Noura. "Are you okay?" he asks, but she jerks away without explanation.

Theo replays everything in his mind, letting his attention to detail filter everything: the shape of the man's face, the curl of the feathers... that knife he'd been carrying. It had been an Egyptian *khopesh*. Theo closes his eyes. The face paint, he'd been made to look like—

Lizzy loops her arm through Theo's and pats his shoulder. "New Orleans is captivating, isn't it? Strange, no doubt about that. But fascinating. Rather like your Noura, don't you think? She stares down a witch doctor and calls a god to her aid."

Theo gapes down at Lizzy. "A god?"

"Isn't Horus a falcon, and all that? Swooping in to ward off the god of chaos?"

As ridiculous as it sounds, Theo feels the whispers of Tut's curse curling in his gut. Are the problems with the alarm system more than they appear? Set and Horus grappling even still? He studies the space where the man had stood. Theo's read about thin places. Places where other worlds slip in. But he never believed it until he saw a falcon slip through the sky under Noura's gaze and ward off the darkness. Maybe there's a reason New Orleans feels so like Cairo. Both are places where the whispers of the gods grow louder.

"I see you've taken a lesson from us Brits—'stiff upper lip' and all that. But you care more than you let on. Someday you should tell her." Lizzy pats his arm again—her wayward child come home—then sashays to join Noura, who has yet to look at Theo as he trudges behind them.

Theo examines Lizzy's assessment, lets it click into place, and sees the setup. He didn't see a bird gauntlet on the man's arm, but surely it was there. A pretty trick created to frighten him...or perhaps Noura. And there must have been a door he missed. But why?

Ahead, Noura laughs at something Lizzy says and replies, "Are you sure?"

"Of course, darling." Lizzy mimics Zsa Zsa Gabor's French court manners.

Estelle stiffens at the woman's tone and mutters something under her breath Theo doesn't quite catch. Then she turns to him. "Well, someone needs to protect her."

As if Theo didn't try. As if the air didn't solidify and hold him fast. Was that a trick too? Or something more?

Estelle overtakes the other women, leaving him behind with alarm still ringing through him. Noura welcomes Estelle in, even as Noura's attention skips over Theo. And that's when he realizes Noura knows more than she's letting on.

Something about Theo or about the plan for tonight. That's why his alarm is still sounding.

Curse his emotions, his desires, and his fears. He's been blinded to whatever web Estelle has woven. It isn't the witch doctor he should worry about. It's the genuine possibility that Estelle convinced her sister to join her.

Theo strides forward, intending to confront Estelle when Noura gathers Estelle under her arm—a protective charm against anything Theo might have for her.

"Egyptian myth"—Noura's voice slips into a cadence harkening dark caves and smoke—"begins with nothing but dark, swirling, endless water without form or function...After that, all the texts disagree."

"Seriously?" Lizzy stops.

The group watches the grinning storyteller. Grinning? Has Noura let the scare drop? But then he realizes the grin is vicious. A challenge. To him? To the witch doctor? To the world?

"Yep. The ancients believed if they wrote a terrible story down, it would come true. So history was kept in oral traditions. One man told the story to the next man, who embellished the story for his own purpose. After a few thousand years, things change."

"That doesn't make a good storyline. Are all their myths so crazy?"

"To some extent." Noura considers the dipping sun. "We should keep going. The car's just there."

Theo's seen Noura's car before, but he feels the shock radiate off Lizzy. The rusted vehicle is held together with wire, duct tape, and prayer...It's also tiny. Lizzy frowns at Theo and his long legs, then begrudgingly folds into the backseat after Estelle.

He contorts himself into the front seat, securing his feet on either side of the gaping hole in the floorboard. Noura's car roars to life, sputters, and then, with its master feathering the gas pedal, it settles into a rattling hum. Noura jams the car into first, then catapults into traffic. Theo can't help but wonder if she's attempting to sling him from the car.

"Probably the most cohesive story is the conflict between Horus and Set," Noura shouts over the engine, and Lizzy leans between the front two seats.

"One day," Noura continues, "Set, he's the god of disorder, decides he wants to be king. So he kills his brother, Osiris, then takes the crown, cuts Osiris's body into pieces, and scatters them across Egypt. The king's wife is livid. So Aset and her sister turn into birds and hunt down the scraps. They put together the body and resurrect the rightful king."

"As if it's that easy." Lizzy nudges Noura with her elbow, and Noura laughs. It's real and full and entices Estelle into a knowing grin as well.

Noura is a surprisingly entertaining storyteller. She weaves the story of Aset conceiving her son, Horus. Then hiding from Set in the reeds. Aset pleading for help from humans when Horus becomes sick. The desperate mother fashioning healing spells that she also gives to the helpful families.

"When Horus comes of age, he challenges Set and thus begins the age of divine struggle."

"How in the world do gods fight?" Lizzy nudges Theo like he should answer.

"You'd be surprised," Noura says. "From the beginning, the gods took whatever form was necessary to get what they wanted. Ra and Horus were falcons. Aset was an Egyptian kite. But Set? No one knows what he was supposed to be. The Set Beast is simply a vicious animal no one sees clearly."

Estelle sucks in a breath, but the barb isn't for her. It's for Theo. He clenches his teeth against the gutshot. He's bleeding out and can't afford to flinch, let alone bend over the slashing wound.

Noura knows Theo is a character he voluntarily takes on and sets aside. But what Noura doesn't understand is that she's a shapeshifter as well. Unlike Theo, though, she's not able to shake off the act...or maybe she doesn't know what's real anymore.

And as much as Theo wants to tell her the truth about why he's here, it's safer for her, for him, for all of them, if she doesn't know.

Yes, he is neither Theo Fabre, conservator, nor Randall Sykes, stolen art fencer. And yes, he is Alexander McShane, the head FBI Investigator with the Art Squad. But he is not after her sister, nor is he hunting Mehedi Ibrahim or his handler, the shadowy Harold Marquette, Jr., but someone much more dangerous. Someone who uses sick girls to manipulate and destroy. Typhon is here, in the city. And like Typhon's Egyptian counterpart, Set, he will kill them all if Theo doesn't flush him out first.

NOURA SLAMS the car into a parking spot and launches herself from the car. She shakes her hands, flinging anger from her fingertips... Or that's what she hopes. Behind her, the car complains—the door hinges screeching open, the shocks groaning in relief.

Lizzy is blessedly quiet as she saunters into the restaurant and then whispers to the stiff maitre d'. Galatoire's dim lights and plush carpets whisper of wealth and privilege and all the things her sister cannot abide, and it is far too hushed for her screaming thoughts. She can barely move, yet she crashes forward with the rhythm of betrayed, betrayed, betrayed dogging her steps.

Somehow, some way, she has to stuff herself back into the old, putrid persona of benevolent innocence, even as she plots against them. She's already made calls, set plans in motion. She is not without friends or resources.

The hostess seats the group by the window, where they watch the sun fracture over the moody horizon. It is fitting—to watch the sky bleed as a hurricane brews.

Noura watched her sister lift the keys from Jim. Given the furtive conversation she's overheard, Estelle will return tonight and make the switch. Theo will arrest her.

Saira's calm voice lifts from the grave of Noura's memory, tangling with the howl from her nightmares. *You watch over your sister. That is your one job today.*

32

Theo was, surprisingly, the highlight of dinner. His homespun stories about his family strung together with spot-on impressions of Mick Jagger, Walter Cronkite, and even Olivia Newton-John—"Tell me about it, stud"— kept Estelle from coming apart at the seams. Even so, she is beyond grateful when he announces he'll catch a taxi home. That allows the sisters to drop Lizzy at her hotel and wind their way home.

When they arrive home, Noura stumbles upstairs. Estelle yearns to explain, but she can't afford to have her sister try to stop her. Someday, Estelle will make it up to her.

The predicted hurricane will make her job more difficult in some ways—waterproofing for the artifacts. But the storm will also drive people inside and occupy the police. Soon, she reminds herself. Soon it will be over.

While her clothes and tools are stuffed into a knapsack in the hall closet, she needs her insulin and a sandwich or two. She clicks on the kitchen light and stifles a scream at the man's shadow hunched over the counter.

He spins, and she snatches the nearest object—Maman's address book—throwing it at the same moment she recognizes the profile.

Father.

"Estelle." He picks up the book and smooths it out on the counter.

She expects him to lecture about the hour, about avoiding him, about everything and nothing, as he usually does. Instead, he pats the stool next to him. She slides in, hairs prickling.

"I know you and I haven't always..." Father sucks in a breath.

Estelle resists a snort.

Father nods. "I know I've been harsh. I've only ever wanted what's best for you. And"—he holds up a palm to forestall her objection—"I know you think I don't know what's happened or is happening. But there's more to me than you realize."

"Harold?" Maman's voice is pitched in panic from the other room, summoning Estelle's sketchy memories of her mother's instability.

Father sighs and stands. "Please, Estelle. Be careful." He pushes the unopened bottle of Coke toward her and then lets a hand drift over her shoulder before he wanders up the stairs. His deep, soothing voice murmurs from the depths of the house.

Her stark memories painted him as weak and infuriating. But this calmness, this enduring patience with Maman, unlocks the edges of an enigma Estelle had forgotten existed. The voice talking to Maman while Noura scurried to make dinner, to make everything okay. Noura couldn't have been more than twelve when she took the responsibilities of a parent. Maybe Maman was the one who'd sucked everyone dry.

Estelle pops the cap of the Coke and sips, savoring the sweetness. Wherever she ends up, she will have difficulty finding either the treat or the insulin to cover it.

The emptiness roars with the wind as Estelle watches time click away—one hour, two—until she's sure everyone else is asleep. With her shoes in hand, she slips out the door. The static in the air prickles the small hairs on her cheek, and she shivers with the sharp smell of coming rain. Instead of retreating to the shuttered house, she shuts the door and ducks into the carriage house. Her sister's stolen car keys jangle with those of the museum.

Voices rise and fall in the distance—an argument between two women. The teeth of the key bite into Estelle's palm. While both sisters want the same thing, they disagree on how to get there and will only ever cause each other pain.

Estelle opens the car door and releases the parking brake. The car moves more easily than she expected, and she pushes it to the street. As she settles onto the cracked seat, she steels herself.

The engine blessedly cranks over, and she steers toward the museum. Dark clouds spiral in the distance. They're charged with explosions and greedily consume the moon and stars. A single enormous drop of rain splatters against the windshield, and Estelle swipes away its twin on her cheek.

She was wrong to ask Noura for help. She knows that now. She'll finish this job and then disappear. For good this time. Her necklace chain burns frigid against her collarbone in reminder. There will be no more balancing of scales for her after this.

Estelle parks the car in the deserted street next to the museum and climbs out. As she closes the employee door and disarms the security system, the museum is sepulcher quiet. She clicks on her flashlight and stifles a scream.

Noura stands, arms crossed, leaning against the cement wall.

"You're late." Noura relishes the confusion, anger, and fear fighting for dominance in her sister's face.

"You aren't going to—"

"I'm here to help."

"I've promised some very powerful people the artifacts." Estelle squares her feet as the sisters were taught.

Noura doesn't think her sister will actually fight. Then again, Estelle's done a multitude of incomprehensible things. Noura lifts her empty hands in mock surrender. "I'm not here to stop you."

Estelle gapes, and Noura smirks. She's caught her sister off guard. Good. Clicking on her own flashlight, Noura marches to the stairwell.

"We need the replicas," Estelle says, but Noura shrugs her off with an "I have them" and selects a key from the set she lifted from Theo.

"How did you...I mean..." Estelle stammers.

"You're the one who taught me to pickpocket." Noura opens the door and hesitates for her eyes to adjust to the tomblike darkness. "And unlike you, I never got caught...at least by the mark. How do you think I got money for the market when Father refused?"

Estelle slides into the stairwell, wary.

"I hated stealing." Noura eases the door closed. "But I wanted you to have the world. When Saira made me stop picking pockets, I was so angry. But she was right. Two wrongs don't make a right. We've about ten minutes while the guards change shifts."

Noura stalks up the stairs, barely hesitating at the top to confirm the absence of guards before pushing through. If she thinks too much, she will run, and she cannot run now. With shaking fingers, she unlocks the metal exhibit gates and punches in another security code. Estelle scurries in with the step stool and stands behind her sister.

Estelle's flashlight catches the white of the printed hieroglyphic falcon and reflects onto Noura. He's watching. Noura's breath rattles loudly in the darkness, and she sucks it in, holding steady. Estelle nods at her older sister, her image wavering like old, fading film. Outside, wind howls against the building, and Noura shudders with the boarded-over windows. Behind her, Estelle closes the gates and the doors. *Move*, Noura tells herself.

Throwing her shoulders back, Noura stalks past the enormous prints of scarab and falcon, and she dives through the display resembling the tomb as Howard Carter found it in 1922. Harry Burton's black and white photos haunt the walls, shadows of people and gods. They watch her, daring her to end the battle born with Set's betrayal.

Noura pivots at the photos of the Egyptian man standing outside the tomb, then storms into the larger exhibit rooms, past the pieces she cared for in Cairo. While Estelle scampers up the ladder and adheres a halved tennis ball over the receiver on the ceiling, Noura waits in front of the first vitrine, studying her toes. She cannot bear to look through the display's glass into the boy king's betrayed eyes. Once Estelle whispers "done," Noura turns the cabinet lock, pockets the keys, and slips on white cotton gloves. With the receiver blocked, the transmitter under the vitrine is useless.

She sits in the cabinet and beckons to her sister. "I can't cut and hold at the same time."

But Estelle's still. "I don't want you mixed up in this."

"Of course." Noura snorts. "Of course you decide not to help. My whole life, I thought you were Set." Noura lifts the mask out of the bag she'd packed earlier and sets it within reach. "Every time you stole my jewelry or flirted with someone else's boyfriend or picked a fight with a neighbor, I chalked it up to you trying to balance out the good in the world by creating a little chaos. But last night I realized you aren't chaos. Everyone knows what to expect from you—the rebellious thing. But me? I shift and change unexpectedly. *I* am chaos. And since I'm already in this up to my eyeballs, I might as well get what I can out of it." When Estelle merely gapes at her sister, Noura gestures into the cabinet. "For once in your life, stop bellyaching and accept help."

Estelle inspects Noura before wedging in next to her sister. Noura taps a hole with a hand drill and, after ensuring Estelle is prepared, starts cutting. Noura's body is not merely shaking. She's shuddering, turning liquid with the force as she scuttles from the cabinet to help Estelle ease the mask through the hole and then the door.

The pair carefully switches the masks. Then Estelle holds the circle while Noura installs a crisscrossed patch to hold the artifact in place.

When she ducks out of the case, Estelle is holding the bag and staring at her sister in unabashed wonder. "Where did you learn to do all this?"

"Don't you remember all the crazy things I built out of leftover book boxes? Forts, doll houses. I even bought a pulley and used a box and rope to make an elevator for your doll. All to entertain you. I've done what's necessary my entire life." Noura strides through the archway.

As a matter of fact, Estelle remembers the rusty pulley, but not the why behind it. No wonder Saira always insisted Estelle be more gentle. She forgot so much of what Noura had done before Saira. Estelle trails her sister out of the replicated burial chamber and into the first treasury room. The falcon pectoral is nestled in with a solar and lunar pectoral.

"Grab the other one too," Estelle whispers. "We'll need the money to get out of the country."

Noura starts. "We don't have another replica."

"Take something else then." Why must everyone question her?

"I have money, Estelle," Noura says with an eerie calm. "We need time more than money."

To cover her burst of anger, Estelle turns. She knows Noura is right. They can't risk a big deviation from the plan. She needs time to get to Mehedi and get him out before they're discovered. Maybe she can find something of her grandmother's.

"For Mehedi." Noura holds out her pinky, and Estelle grasps hold with her own numb finger. How did it get to this? A wish and a prayer to uphold what's right.

Sweat on Noura's brow belies her calm as she scuttles to make quick work of the falcon pectoral before the sisters slip into the room with Selket. Estelle drops the bag as if it weighs as much as the world.

"Careful." Noura's mothering tone grates on Estelle.

"It's a replica," Estelle whispers.

"One that has to fool everyone long enough for us to escape." Noura's voice is waspish.

Estelle's fingers shake as she crawls into the base with her sister. This is the easy part. The thought of what's still to come exhausts her.

"It's going to be okay," Noura whispers, whether to herself or her sister or the long-dead king, Estelle doesn't know.

As Noura rearranges the artifacts for transport, Estelle shinnies up the ladder and restores the security system to what it was. She scans the rooms one last time. If Estelle hadn't been here, she would never suspect a thing had happened.

A clatter shatters the silence. The sisters freeze.

"He's still upstairs," Noura whispers.

Estelle hefts the bag, leaving the yet unpacked Selket for Noura, and runs, her feet silent. But Noura? Her footsteps are the foot-flailing of a frightened dog.

Standing at the top of the stairs with the door open, Estelle waves Noura forward. *Hurry.* Light flickers in Estelle's peripheral vision. It's bending around the corner, growing in size. Noura ducks through the door, discovery hot on Estelle's neck as they scamper down the steps, through the hall, and burst out the back door. A gale catches the heavy metal security door, and Noura catches it with her foot before it slams against the wall. She stifles a scream of pain as Estelle catches Selket from her arms. Estelle shuts the door, then tucks the statue neatly into a series of towels and stows it all in the bag.

Without a word, Estelle slings Noura's arm over her shoulders and nearly carries her older sister down the street. What the sisters have done flashes through Estelle in the same electrical shocks as those piercing the sky. Somewhere in her mind, Estelle registers that the hurricane is nearly on them. That New Orleans could flood. That all of this could be for naught if they are killed or stuck on the street. Around the corner, Noura's car is tucked under an enormous oak, and Estelle flings open the back door, throwing the bag in first and then unceremoniously dumping her sister in after.

Estelle revs the engine, flooding it. Noura moans in the back, cutting off Estelle's explosion even as an enormous oak leaf smacks against the windshield, skidding across in a macabre dance, much like the two sisters' not-so-stealthy escape from the museum. But they are here. They are safe.

Noura scooches upright and catches her sister's eye in the rearview mirror. Estelle can't help but crack.

"Are you laughing?" Noura's voice skyrockets.

Estelle nods, but even as the tears run down her cheeks, her face crumples until she is truly crying.

"We're going to be okay." Noura rubs her sister's shoulder. Like they are nine and four again, Estelle lost in the market, waiting for her big sister to lead her safely home.

"I thought..." Estelle shakes her head. "I thought for sure I was going to lose you again."

Noura's eyes fill with tears now too.

A blinding flashlight beam pierces the windshield. Estelle blanches and lifts a hand to shield her eyes.

"Don't move, Estelle." It's Theo.

Estelle jerks around, anger tightening her lips. "What have you done?"

"I will always do what I need to do to save you." Tears cascade down her traitorous sister's face. "He's FBI."

Estelle shoves the door open, trying to snag the bag and run at the same time. But the bulky bag refuses to release from the confines of the car. And Theo is there. She is caught, and she knows it. Fire under a glass dome, dying.

He's more gentle than Estelle expected as he turns her toward the car. He pulls a set of handcuffs from his waist, and Estelle exhales.

"What are you going to do with me?"

Theo shakes his head, sad. Like he's the one who's been betrayed. Estelle watches Noura, facing away, and listens to the snick of cuffs as he latches her to the interior door handle of the backseat.

Estelle glares at the darkening clouds, the heaviness of a coming hurricane hanging hot over the pavement. New Orleans, like the sisters, is set to bracing for another storm.

33

Despite Noura's assurance that Estelle would cooperate, Estelle refuses to acknowledge anything Theo says or asks. They couldn't stay on the street, and the only place Theo could think to go was his skeevy apartment in Iberville.

And so that's where they went...where they have been for nearly an hour. Noura is curled on the floor, a thawed bag of frozen peas sitting on the linoleum where she discarded it with a frustrated "I'm fine."

Theo stops pacing and perches on the edge of the only armchair. Literally perching with a fraction of his backside on the grimy fabric. None of his alter egos, including top FBI agent Alexander McShane, can afford more. Even though art is regularly used to launder money for terrorists and the mob, the art theft division is the ugly stepchild of the bureau and has almost no budget. The only reason Theo can trail the exhibit is that Kissinger himself demanded extra protection.

"He's going to help Mehedi," Noura says for the hundredth time.

With her hands cuffed behind her, Estelle leans her head against the couch, looking comfy enough to nap.

Leaning his elbows on his knees, Theo rests his chin on steepled fingers. He needs a different approach and fast. The deal was supposed to run through him. But something spooked her, and she made a left turn. Did her brother get to her somehow? Theo saw him a few times, but he left frustrated, not celebrating. She didn't give in to him entirely. So what—

Theo's phone rings, blaring in the tense silence. He lumbers two steps across the apartment.

"Hello?" he says into the receiver.

"Mehedi is out." It's an immigration officer in Chicago. "He took the bait and skipped bail."

"When?"

"Yesterday morning," the man says through the crackle in the connection. "He grabbed a bus that should arrive this morning, a little after eight."

Theo glances at his watch. Seven thirty. He'll need almost all that time to get to the bus station, even if he can scrounge up a car.

"Tell Roger thank you." He listens to the dial tone a moment before he presses the switch hook, releases it, and dials the police station.

When the desk sergeant answers, Theo rushes over the man's slow, drawling words. "I need to speak with Detective George Lewellyn. Tell him Agent Alexander McShane is calling, and it's urgent."

"I'll see if he's in."

Before Theo can press for urgency, the sergeant is gone. Theo listens to the sound of rain against his flimsy walls and the shuffle of paper.

An interminable time later, George answers, breathless. "Sorry to keep you waiting. This have to do with the Tut thing?"

"Yep. I need an officer at my apartment to watch over a couple of witnesses—one hostile—while I go grab..." Theo catches himself just in time. "An important package." He turns away from the accusations snapping through both sisters. "And I need a car."

"Got it. Someone will be there in five. Less if I can make it happen."

The line disconnects, and Theo sinks against the wall.

This may be the break he needs. He clips Horus's feather back around his neck. He needs every bit of help he can get, even if it means he has to sell his soul to the god of war.

RELIEF BLOSSOMS on Theo's face, which only makes Estelle's stomach curdle.

"You're leaving?" Noura's voice spikes.

Estelle snorts. She should be afraid.

"An officer is coming." Theo's mouth melts into a syrupy smile.

"So what's your name then? Your real one?" Estelle's question crystallizes his face into sharp points.

When he doesn't answer, Noura turns from the leaking window. Sadness etches lines under her lashes and between her brows. It's obvious she believes dooming Estelle to prison and Mehedi to death is the right thing. But in whose eyes?

Arguing now won't do Estelle any good. Not while he's here. Still... "I know about Randall."

Theo leans against the greasy countertop and lifts an unconcerned shoulder. Noura, though, snaps her head around to stare at the supposed FBI agent.

"See," Estelle says to her sister, "how it works is Theo uses museum resources to create forgeries and then throws on a wig, some scruffy clothes, and magically turns into a shady art fence. He's a one-man art theft ring." Estelle starts to settle into the couch, but a puff of mold assaults her nose, and she sneezes. This place is miserable, just like its inhabitant.

Noura blinks from her sister to Theo, anguish rounding her puppy-dog-pleading eyes. Estelle wants to blaze in justifiable anger, but all she feels is the wretched wash of betrayal.

Theo scoffs like a disappointed parent and paces to the window, where he reaches for Noura.

She slides from his touch. "Please don't pretend anymore. You have what you want."

Estelle is proud of the solidity of her sister's frozen words, even if it's too late.

"Noura." The longing in his one word is clear as the air they're breathing. "Yes, I pretend to be multiple people and one of those has worked for Typhon for years, but I'm not—"

"No," her sister says. "Not anymore."

Pain topples his square features. He's either an incredibly good actor or he actually cares. Not that it matters. He is what he is. Someone who pretends to love justice but only fights for what's best for himself. It's there in how he uses the feather as a way to summon his contacts, and yet wears it around his neck like he can summon the god of protection.

As if he's heard her, Theo spreads his fingers over the pendant on his chest like a prayer. Before she can taunt him about his fragile hope of order, a knock sounds at the door. Theo sighs and stalks across the room.

When a uniformed officer steps into the room, Estelle blanches. Is Theo in league with dirty cops? Her mind is fuzzy with lack of sleep and the static of low sugar. Estelle smashes her eyes closed until her vision creases with red slashes and then opens them wide, trying to clear the sparks enough to concentrate.

Theo is murmuring with the scrawny man, but she overhears enough to know they're discussing Mehedi and the bus station, and that's when it clicks. Something has happened.

"Is Mehedi out of jail?" Estelle shouts over the low discussion.

Noura lurches from the wall and hovers behind her sister. They are a unified front once again. Noura is the one who breaks him down, and Estelle has never been more grateful for her older sister.

"In a manner of speaking," Theo says.

Estelle wants to shout for joy. Theo has lost his leverage. She is free. She no longer needs to sell the pieces. She just needs to intercept Mehedi and convince Noura to run.

ESTELLE LOOKS as if she might self-combust right where she sits. She senses something Noura can't quite sus out for herself.

"Mehedi is either free or he isn't. Which is it?" Estelle's voice drops in accusation.

Theo...Alex? Randall? runs a hand through his hair, and it stands on end like he's been shocked. Maybe he has been. Thunder rolls somewhere over the ocean, alerting them to the danger of lightning. Somewhere out there, but surely not here.

"If he's out," Noura says happily as if her voice will smooth over the rumble, "that's wonderful. We can—"

"He skipped bail." Theo's bluntness strikes the room, cold and blinding.

Estelle shoots to her feet, and Noura's sure she misunderstood. "He what?" Her fingers clench against the couch cushion, squishing into the nauseatingly pliable material.

"I will do everything I can to protect him." Theo steps toward the sisters and then stops, repelled by the sibling bond. "I know what he means to you. The only way I can protect him is to pick him up. Typhon won't think twice about snatching Mehedi to keep his leverage over you."

Estelle floats to the couch like cooling ash, lifting her chin. "I circumvented Typhon's plans. I found my own fence. Typhon was threatening to bomb the museum with Noura in it. I couldn't exactly trust him after that."

Theo growls, swinging around with the force of a tornado and cursing under his breath. "Then you're in more hot water than I realized. If he knows you're willing to cut him out, he won't trust you to keep your mouth shut. So if your handler snatches Mehedi before I do, the only thing between you and meeting your maker is that they don't have the artifacts yet. And honestly, they can get cash another way if they need to."

"They want to disrupt the peace talks too," Noura offers, but there's no confidence in her.

"They're more likely to set off that bomb than trust someone who's betrayed them once." Estelle confirms Theo's dire predictions.

"I don't think..." Noura starts, but Estelle cocks her head like a jackal listening for the whispers of the dead, weighing the good and evil. Like Anubis.

Noura sinks next to her sister. And like Anubis, Estelle will fight for justice, no matter what. Anubis may not be his mean-spirited father, Set, but he is no less lethal.

Theo stiffens now too, dark eyes flashing gold with the scent of the hunt. "No one leaves. Clear?"

Noura backs against the wall, and all the courage she started the night with drains through her toes. She thinks of all the times she's heard echoes and strange voices, watched Theo with his feathers and manipulations. Who is this man who operates in the shadows, who restlessly circles, hunting? Is he even a man at all?

Theo bumps the squad car into the bus depot curb as he screeches into a barely serviceable parking job and leaps from the door. The heavens open, emptying themselves onto New Orleans, washing away the ground from under Theo's feet. As long as the levees hold, Theo reminds himself, they are safe enough. He dives into the squat station, hoping he's not too late.

Much to the chagrin of the janitor in the corner, Theo sloshes across the tile floor to the ticket window. "I'm looking for—"

The woman in the box holds up a long fingernail as she uh-huhs into the receiver propped between her overly made-up cheek and her polyester-clad shoulder. She chomps her gum and then blows a bubble, letting it pop before gathering the mass back in.

Theo knocks on the window and smiles. But his politeness is met with a solid rock of dismissal.

"Ma'am." Theo's voice echoes through the empty room.

When she rolls her attention Theo's way, he smacks his badge against the glass. "Hang up the phone now." When she blows another bubble instead of disengaging from the phone, he adds, "It's a terrorist situation."

This makes her bubble deflate along with her defiant expression.

"You're safe," he amends, so she doesn't run screaming from the building. "I simply need to know if bus fourteen has come in yet."

"I gotta go, Sunshine," she says into the phone even as she hangs it up. Squinting at the papers on the table, she runs a manicured finger over the list and then stops. She pulls her lips between her teeth as if holding them there will stem the fear welling in her eyes. "It arrived ten minutes ago, mister. They're...they're gone."

"Did you see this man?" he slaps a photo on the counter.

The woman nods, her mouth working a minute before the words form. "There was a scuffle. Two other men tried to grab him, but Greg over there had just mopped, and—"

"He got away?"

"That's what I'm trying ta tell you. If you'd stop for a dagblamed second and actually—"

"Did he get away?" Theo emphasizes every word.

"I said yes and—"

Theo spins. Noura. He has to get to Noura. A hand smacks Theo's shoulder, continuing his spin until he face-plants into the wall. A gun jams into his rib cage.

"Who are you and what do you want?" The man's voice growls in Theo's ear.

34

Noura's hand in Estelle's is clammy despite the oppressive heat wafting off the bayous. The officer clatters around the kitchen, percolating coffee. He occasionally glances over his shoulder, but it's clear he doesn't view them as a threat. He even unlocked Estelle's cuffs.

The radio murmurs about Hurricane Babe spinning off the coast and bearing down west of the city. Estelle's vision sparks, and she can't tell if it's lightning or her body's warning. Either way, she can't leave Mehedi out there to fend for himself. With her attention on the officer's broad back, Estelle leans into her sister. "We have to get out of here."

"Theo said to stay."

"We have the artifacts." Estelle thinks she's whispering, but her ears are roaring. She can't stay here much longer. "I have another option."

"Typhon will—"

"The Weathermen won't want Mehedi or me in FBI custody. We know too much."

Noura's throat bobs in a hard swallow. She's heard the implication.

"But—"

"Noura," Estelle snaps, and then, when the officer frowns at them, she rubs her head. "I think my sugars are off."

Noura pops to her feet, fear flickering. "She's diabetic." The muscle memory of a protective older sister takes over. "Juice. She needs juice."

Estelle closes her eyes against the clawing darkness, the searing scream of the condemned.

Clattering in the kitchen.

The suck and clang of the refrigerator.

Noura, kneeling in front of Estelle, tipping her head back. Cool glass on her lips.

Swallow. Does Noura say this, or is it memory?

Estelle's breath shudders. The punishing sizzle of her brain leaches away the last of her energy.

She hovers somewhere between worlds as she listens to her sister and a man talk about a dog? Or a child? She's not interested and lets her mind wander. She was fourteen when her sister left—the height of the know-it-all stage, or that's what Mehedi had said. That day, Estelle hid outside the wall. But when Noura couldn't find her and left, Estelle leaned her head against the bricks and sobbed so hard, snot flooded from her nose.

Mehedi convinced Estelle her life wasn't ending. He'd shown up day after day. Even after Harry took Saira and Mehedi to the Sinai, Mehedi had written weekly and visited when he could...even when Estelle's classmates laughed at his poor clothes and even when Father frowned at "that uppity boy" and used the Six-Day War as an excuse to send her to the States.

If Estelle had refused to leave Israel, could she have convinced Mehedi to go to college? Saved them all this grief? She's not sure how she will get out of this. The falcon feather burns against her sternum, a reminder of choices she wishes she could change. She's always thought she could weigh the good and bad and justify her choices. But now? Maybe Theo is right. Maybe she's the problem.

The couch sinks, and a cold cloth presses against Estelle's forehead. Noura leans against her sister's shoulder, her breath brushing the hairs of Estelle's neck.

"I'm tired of being afraid," Noura says.

Estelle's eyes snap open, and she searches her sister's concerned face. "I'm sorry I got you into this." And she is. Estelle wishes she'd never contacted the Weather Underground. That she'd never been so angry, she refused to listen.

Noura nuzzles the side of her head to her sister's like she did when she read at bedtime. Noura joked she was transferring all her knowledge into her little sister's head.

"No," Noura says. "I'm sorry I didn't listen to you. What do we do now?"

"Call Lizzy." Estelle nudges the bag, but Noura twitches her head the smallest amount.

"Now isn't the time to be squeamish." Estelle's raised voice makes the officer lift his head from stirring his coffee.

She has no energy to persuade Noura to take the artifacts and exchange them for money, then find Mehedi and run, but that's the only way forward. Why is Noura always so mulish? Frustration stews in Estelle's gut. She should be able to do this herself, but her blasted body has betrayed her again.

Noura turns the cloth on Estelle's neck and uses that as an excuse to lean closer still. "He won't let either of us leave with it."

Cool logic dribbles into Estelle's gut, freezing her hope solid.

But Noura winks at her sister like she's off to play hide and seek. When Noura stands, the officer jumps to his feet and grabs for his sidearm.

"Good gracious." Noura's hand flutters to her chest like the most practiced of southern belles. Even Estelle believes for a second she might faint.

The officer, duly chastised, rushes forward to assist Estelle's anything-but-helpless sister as she insists she needs to use the necessary. Cupping her elbow, he leads her to the single door in the apartment.

"Thank you, Officer Daley." Noura flutters as she closes the door on the blushing man.

Estelle has no idea what her sister is doing, but she leans back and grumbles at the lumpy couch. Does Theo actually sleep on this thing? No wonder he's so annoying. Anyone would be sleep-deprived and cranky if they slept on this shedding monstrosity.

Theo's too much like Estelle—any spark sets them off. Father always said Estelle would be the death of him...if Harry didn't kill him first. Born to consume.

But Noura? She is water. She bends and flows, persists, finding a way around or underneath when anyone else would just...stop.

NOURA IS SMASHED into a bathroom so small, she can stand in the middle and touch the wall on all sides. There's a drain in the center of the room, and a curtain rod curves around to cut off the toilet and sink from a bare spigot jutting from the wall.

Surprisingly, it's as clean as one can get when one is in a rundown apartment owned by a bachelor.

Unfortunately, the only window is smaller than a sheet of paper. Noura clambers onto the toilet anyway and squints through the frosted pane. She's good and completely stuck.

She steps off the toilet and plops onto the lid, her head in her hands. She feels like Pooh Bear: *think, think, think.* But her brain feels as full of fluff as his was. She needs to rescue Mehedi and get Estelle out of here. Her sister's going to need insulin soon, and Noura's not sure what kind of food—

Insulin. Estelle needs her insulin. Noura pops to her feet and nearly busts through the door before she remembers to complete the ruse. She swings back, flushes the toilet, then turns on the faucet and splashes a bit. There is no towel to dry her hands, and she hesitates, fingers dripping as she stares at her reflection in the mirror. A golden flicker haunts her shoulder, and she flinches. *You can do this,* the voice soothes, and the woman in the mirror squares her shoulders and lifts her chin.

Noura clutches the tattered ostrich feather in her pocket, flings open the bathroom door, and stalks across the apartment. She doesn't even acknowledge the movement of the officer until he scuttles in front of the front door.

"Where are you going?" He towers above Noura, all grim.

"I'm getting my sister's insulin." Noura blinks at him in a stubborn innocence that makes his mouth draw down in befuddled apprehension.

"Insulin?"

"Yes." Noura points toward Estelle, who is flopped over in a semi-believable state of medical emergency. "She's diabetic and will die without it." Which is strictly, if not immediately, true.

"Her bag is in my car, which should be—"

There's a stampeding of footsteps down the hall, and Noura steps away in reaction to the tremor of fear rumbling in her marrow. Officer Daley swings his arm away from the door, catches Noura neatly around the waist, and heaves her to the side as the door shatters inward, bludgeoning her captor and sending him sprawling.

Noura's hip cracks against the sharp Formica corner of the table, and a mew of pain escapes her lips as she spins, scrambling to grasp the knife off the counter.

"Take it easy there, Noura," a man says behind her.

It takes a moment for Noura to register that the enormous, grizzly man standing in the doorway knows her name. His hands are spread wide in placation, but he's holding a gun. Not letting her eyes leave his, Noura sidesteps around the back of the apartment. Intent on retrieving Estelle and scrambling out the fire escape.

"Noura," he says again. "It's me."

She blinks, straightening. Mentally giving the man a shower and shave. And there, underneath, is Father's once golden boy. "Harry?"

The man's face breaks into a grin, and her knife clatters to the floor. Noura bounds across the room and throws herself into his arms. Her big brother is solid as granite and alive. Oh, so very alive. "How?" There are a million questions stuck in the dam, and that's the only one she can get out. "How?"

Harry's chest vibrates in a laugh, and he squeezes her rib cage in the bear hug he reserved for her. Then he releases her, turning Noura toward Estelle, who's pale and struggling to maintain consciousness.

Despite her body fighting against her, Estelle doesn't seem surprised by their resurrected ghost. And she certainly isn't happy.

"What did you do with him, Harry?" She's nearly growling, and Noura doesn't under—

Harry clamps down on Noura's arm, and she winces, instinctively pulling away. But his fingers are locked, his other hand pointing the gun at Estelle.

"Harry?" Noura's voice is weak, dribbling through the explosive holes of fear.

"You two have a habit of tumbling into trouble. You, dear Noura, are maddeningly dense, rolling along and dragging your sister into the hole she's dug for herself. You, I can forgive. But Estelle? Even if I have to kill you, you will *not* pull me in too."

35

"I work for the FBI." Theo's face is smashed against the bus depot wall, and the view of day-old gum and century-old grime isn't exactly enjoyable. Not that he blames Mehedi for being reticent. "Check my pockets."

Mehedi scrabbles through Theo's pockets, unearthing Theo's badge, ID card, the car keys, and, unfortunately, his sidearm.

Mehedi shoves Theo one last time before motioning for Theo to precede him through the bus depot doors. Theo shrugs as if his plan can accommodate the other man's whims and rams through the door into the driving rain.

"Where's your car?" Mehedi hollers over the vengeful storm.

When Theo nods at the squad car parked half on the sidewalk, Mehedi gapes at him like he's lost his mind. Perhaps Theo has. He strolls to the car, slumps into the driver's seat, and waits for the young man to curl into the passenger seat.

Mehedi's everything like the picture Theo has and nothing like it at the same time. The man in the photo seems to be enjoying a rather good joke, whereas this Mehedi has a wariness to him...which includes the gun he still holds and points in Theo's general direction.

"Are you going to kill me?"

Mehedi sucks in a sharp breath and carefully sets the gun on the floor in answer.

"Good. Do you know who's trying to kill you?"

The man doesn't answer. Theo can't quite tell if Mehedi doesn't know or doesn't trust him enough to answer.

"According to Estelle Marquette, it's Typhon." Theo's satisfied to see the flicker of interest, but the other man remains silent.

"I wouldn't believe me either. But if you give me my keys, I'll bring you to where both she and Noura are."

"Noura?" Mehedi says with wonder in his voice.

"She works with me at the museum," Theo says easily.

For whatever reason, the idea of Theo working with Noura unlocks the man's reserve, and he tosses Theo the keys. Not the gun, mind. But it's a start.

IN THE LIGHTNING FLASH, shadows play across Harry, morphing him into a long-eared Typhonian beast. A forked tail flicks behind him, and Noura steps back.

Even when the image fades, her brother's eyes flicker red before fading into dark hazel. An earthquake shudders through Noura, upending everything she once believed. What kind of Faustian bargain has Harry made with the devil? Noura clutches the feather in her hand, willing Ma'at to be as real for her as Set seems to be for Harry.

"Please, be my angel," she mutters.

"Where are they?" He yanks Noura around the chair, superhuman in strength.

"They?" Estelle's voice is tattered.

"You know what I mean."

Noura's siblings are conversing in a code she cannot crack. But even if Harry is no longer the brother she remembers, one thing is clear. "Harry, she's going into shock."

He shoves Noura to the couch, her neck whipping with the force. Stars spark in her vision, and she blinks back surprised tears. Noura drops the feather she's been clutching to rub her sore arm. While Harry often sulked when he didn't get his way, he's risen from the dead as a twisted monster. How ridiculous to think that anyone was listening to her pleas for help. Hasn't she seen evil win over and over?

Estelle slips her hand over Noura's arm. She's grinning. Maniacal like a rabid dog. "You think that FBI agent would leave the artifacts with us?" she says.

Noura smooths the confused frown from her face almost as quickly as it appears, but she's sure Harry caught it. She has no idea what her sister's done with the bag, but it isn't on the floor.

"I don't want to torture my sisters." His voice rumbles with a core of thunder. "But I will. Better yet, I'll wait until Saira's weak little brother gets here."

Estelle stiffens but keeps her mouth shut. She has far more discipline than she used to.

"I don't understand." Noura's trying for conciliatory, but she has no idea how to negotiate with whatever insanity has gripped her brother.

"Do not play stupid," Harry snaps.

"I didn't tell her anything." Estelle's voice is weak. Maybe she actually does need the insulin.

Harry snorts in delighted triumph. "Finally found something to tear you two apart. Who knew it would be me!" He stops, studying Estelle's face. "Or is it Mehedi?" A wicked smile shatters his handsome face. "Poor Noura doesn't know what you did to him, does she?"

Harry plops into the disgusting armchair with a pleased sigh. "You got the kid out of the Sinai. But then Estelle introduced him to the Weathermen. And when he needed money...he's a smart kid who figured out how to put bombs together lickety split. Too bad the Weathermen aren't around to help anymore. Now he's swinging in the wind, and Typhon can't leave him free to flap his mouth."

Noura's nails dig grooves into her thigh. "How dare you?" Her voice is hard, sharp as a knife. "How dare either of you?"

"Spare me your indignation." Harry waves the gun. "You were home cozy and spoiled while I rotted in the Sinai."

"Of all the arrogant, hypocritical things you have ever said, Harold Marquette." Noura shoves to her feet, placing her body between her siblings. "You went to school in the States too. In fact, I wanted to stay in

Tel Aviv, but the Palestinian Liberation Army made Maman apoplectic with fear. She forced Father to send me to school in the US. And when you came back to Israel, you only stayed because you couldn't get Saira out. Worse, when you survived the Yom Kippur attack, you left Mehedi to fend for himself. He was seventeen! Seventeen and an orphan with no family but you."

Estelle's laugh is strangled, whistling and hollow. "Our brother was already working with the communists then. He acted like it was all new to him, but it wasn't. Was it?"

"Harry?" Noura gapes at her brother.

His posture is relaxed, lounging as they talk about the life and death of family as if it makes no difference at all. "It's not my fault you're gullible. Look to our father for that."

Noura drops to the arm of the couch, confusion dousing her righteous indignation.

"This is exactly what I mean," he says. "You still believe he traipsed around as a simple librarian."

"He was spreading goodwill." Noura hears how naive she sounds.

"He trained you to accept what you were told." Harry waves a hand like he's clearing the air of pesky smoke. "And don't be naive about Mehedi either. When I left, he was already working for the Israelis. He could have joined the army officially and been fine. Plenty of Bedouins did. They're great scouts. It's how I got out."

Estelle's eyes blazed. "You used his family to get out?"

Why is Estelle needling him? Drawing attention to herself?

"The great Harold Marquette, Sr. would never sacrifice himself for my wife, my child, or me," Harry says. "The only way to survive was to use whoever was available and convenient."

Noura's jaw drops at his callous dismissal. "What happened to you?" It's the wrong question. She knows it as soon as it leaves her mouth.

Harry shoves to his feet. "Enough!" Anger sparks in the force of his movements. "The artifacts." Her brother thrusts out his palm. It's red, battle-scarred, hardened. Nothing like the careful doctor she remembers.

Perhaps the time has come for him to lie in the bed he has made.

"Where is the bag?" Noura asks Estelle.

Estelle shakes her head, determined.

"Give it to him, Estelle. Or he'll kill us all."

Kill. Kill. Kill. A cackling voice chants, and Harry's face flickers. *Kill the traitor.*

"He'll kill us once he has it," Estelle says with alarming calmness. Can she not hear the voice? "And then he'll use the money for who knows what else."

"No. He won't." Or at least Noura hopes the reality of the myths will hold true. Set cannot kill Ma'at.

"It's not here," Estelle says with a wide-eyed firmness.

Harry shoves the chair with his foot, sending it skittering across the floor. When the chair smashes against the wall, the officer leaps from the floor and snakes his arms around Harry's neck. But Officer Daley is like a fly on the back of a god. The shadows curling and flaring, throwing the image of a forked tail, spreading wings, and collapsing against the force of lightning. Harry's gun wavers as the officer struggles to control the direction of the weapon.

"Help!" The officer shouts through gritted teeth.

Noura is mired, her wits melting under the molten anger of her brother, the bizarre split of worlds. She can't grab hold of what's real and what's the dripping wax of her mangled psyche.

With a roar, Estelle launches herself, punching their brother in the gut. Harry bellows but doesn't go down. The trio skitters across the room and slams into the wall next to the bathroom.

"Grab the bag and go!" Estelle shouts.

Noura spins, frantic. Where is it? She shoves the couch forward, and there, under the edge of the couch, is the black strap. As she lunges for it, the world explodes in a flash, a scream. Her knees bark against the floor, but she is up and stumbling over the couch, crashing to a stop. Estelle is sprawled on the floor, red spreading, cascading over her chest. Noura drops the bag and dives for her sister.

Harry stands over her, the gun still pointed at Estelle, his mouth agape.

"No!" Noura slams her hands against the gaping hole in her sister's chest.

As if waking from a dream, the officer wheels back, yanking his gun, but it is too late. Harry fires again and again.

Noura's body jerks in response to the explosion of shots piercing Officer Daley's body. Horror spikes adrenaline through her, all of it combining, clamoring at her to run, to plead, to do something, anything...but she is stone. She will not leave her sister, will not lift her bloodied support from Estelle's body. She will not abandon her again.

Harry looms over his sisters, shaking his head as if his refusal to acknowledge what he's done can erase it all.

"What do I do?" Noura's whole being shudders. Why hasn't the world shattered from the force of it? "You're a doctor. How do I stop the bleeding?"

"I didn't...I didn't mean..." His Adam's apple dips with the impact of his swallow. His humanity fluttering across his face, sinking underneath a gaping darkness. "She shouldn't have tried to stop me. She is truly Anubis's now." His voice skims cold, the self-justification long ago freezing out the kind, courageous brother who would carry Noura home when she was too tired. "Don't follow me, Noura. I don't want to hurt you. But I have no choice." Harry turns and staggers from the apartment. The god of violence now fully in control. The lights flicker in his wake, and anger sears through Noura, branding desperation deep into her heart.

"Help!" she screams. "Help!"

The world quakes as the wings of the hurricane batter the slim shelter of the building. They need to get away from the lowlands. They'll flood if the hurricane comes close.

"You can't hate him, Noura." Estelle's beautiful face is bleeding color. "Hate is what made Harry and me think we were justified in what we did. We said it was love. But it wasn't."

But Noura does hate him. She hates his lying, his abandonment, his creating all of this. She struggles to keep her mind from splitting right down the middle. She loved him. But what does she do with the awful reality of what he's become?

"You're the best of us, Noura." Estelle sucks in a wincing breath and holds out the ostrich feather coated in her sacrificial blood.

"No," Noura says. "You're the brave one. It takes strength to change direction." Noura smiles down at her even as Estelle musters enough energy to shake her head.

"You loved me when I was...when I was awful." Estelle's breath flutters, a tear trickles down her cheek, and she sips for air around the devastation of her lungs.

Noura twists, desperate to find something, anything to keep pressure on her sister's wound so she can call for help.

"I run and run"—Estelle coughs, blood foaming—"and I'm not running *to* something." Estelle's eyes cloud as if she is searching for something she can't see yet. "I run *away*. But you...You have to stop him. Call...call Lizzy." Estelle's eyes find her sister's, determination flaring until Noura nods.

"And take this." Estelle touches her chest. "You'll need it." She smiles, her cheek muscles relaxing with one long, bubbling exhale.

I'm sorry. The shadows whisper. The lights flicker out. Noura leans over her little sister and tries to catch the last of her breaths, to plead with God to stuff her soul back into her body. But the shadows sag, the pointed ears of a jackal bending low. And then she is alone.

In the distance, Noura hears the front door slam shut. Estelle, beautiful, passionate Estelle, is gone. Noura sits back on her heels, sucking in a sob, and prays her baby sister has found the peace promised on the other side.

But here? Now? She tucks her feather into her sister's hand. "May your heart be light." Then Noura unclasps the necklace from her sister's neck, the force of recognition knocking her to her feet. It's a duplicate of Theo's. In the end, Estelle was trying to find order and goodness. Noura sniffles, wiping a tear from her cheek and then clasping the necklace around her own neck. She will need Horus and Theo to see everything if she's to stop her brother. Hefting the officer's Colt, she feels the power of it. She's never shot at a person before, but everyone in Israel was trained to shoot...even the American librarian's bookish daughter.

Swallowing, she snatches the pair of speed loaders from the officer's patch, but her hands betray her, and she dumps the extra bullets, clanging, onto the uneven floor and watches them skitter under the chair.

There is no bomb, no angry retaliation that can ever bring peace. Still, Harry will shoot anyone coming after him. Noura wants to just let him go, but if he's going after Mehedi, she can't turn the other way. Can she? "Help," she whispers to whoever is there. If Harry has made some sort of bargain with Set, may the powers of righteousness work everything out for good.

Clutching the weapon, Noura throws open the door and surges after her resurrected brother. Revenge can't bring peace. But sometimes love is more fierce than limp acquiescence. Sometimes love is the ferocious fire of justice.

THEO SQUINTS through the rain-soaked windshield as he drives across the city, dodging people and debris stirred by unearthly wind. In less than a quarter of an hour, he eases the squad car into a space by the apartment and waits. Mehedi still holds Theo's gun, and Theo has no wish to die like a fish in a barrel.

"What do we do now?" Mehedi turns from the dilapidated building to Theo.

"The women are upstairs. We could—"

But Mehedi has burst from the car and is sprinting down the street after a disheveled man with a black bag banging against his hip. Theo tilts his head and sucks in a breath before he cranks over the car and tears after the pair. That's the bag with the artifacts.

The tires squeal as he spins around a corner, nearly missing a drenched busker doing who knows what in the middle of a hurricane. Theo should call for backup or something, but he's no idea how to operate the radio, and...where did Mehedi go?

Theo stops and backs up, peering between the buildings and up fire escapes. From behind him, a woman's roar threads through the hammering rain, and Noura hurtles into sight, vaulting over a chain link fence like she might wear wings, sprinting down the sidewalk, running between buildings across the street, and diving into the darkness of another yard.

Half a blink before she disappears, Theo catches the glint of light off a metal surface. Does she have a gun? Where's the officer he left in charge?

Far ahead, two shadows clatter between tight buildings, one catapulting over the stone wall of St. Louis Cemetery No. 1, followed by the other. Theo can't track them in a car, and he's not familiar enough with the city to guess where they're headed. Snatching the keys from the ignition and his backup weapon from his calf, Theo bolts after them. Ahead, Noura wedges a foot into the X of the back gate and scrambles over. Theo launches himself after her. His only hope is that his training will allow him to run longer and faster than any of them. When he lands, no one is in sight. The mausoleum-like ovens brace against the fury. Aisle after aisle of tiny bone houses, plastered in moss and vines. Theo eases around the puddles, listening.

Splashing footsteps to his right send Theo trotting in that direction, carefully avoiding the open grass squares. Who knows who or what's under there or how close it is to the surface? He has no desire to slip through any thin places. A flash of movement convinces Theo to backtrack and sprint down the wider aisle, banking against a grimy brick wall, where two distant shadows dart in front of him. Noura veers from the path of the men. Though she's wriggling between tiny gaps in a rich man's iron fence and the blackened wall of a tiered grave, Theo doesn't hesitate to follow her into the warren.

Even with his blasted dress shoes slipping, Theo gains on Noura as she ducks past a towering edifice of drawer-like graves, a path that should bring them to intercept the men. Theo can hear their voices and grunts, and he tucks his head as he digs for more speed, turns the corner, and slams into a solid form.

Noura squeaks in dismay, but it isn't her arms that descend around Theo's middle. His breath bludgeons out of his deflating lungs.

"Stop!" Noura shouts at the mountainous man.

"Ghadfa, stop." A woman's voice, but not Noura.

Who?

The reptilian man shuffles sideways. Lizzy stands, gripping a semi-automatic Glock.

Theo's arms pop up in surrender even as questions fire through his mind.

36

"Would someone tell me what in the blazes is going on?" Noura's mind whips in a tornado of confusion. Ghadfa. Lizzy. Harry.

"Ghadfa," Lizzy says, keeping the wicked-looking gun trained on Theo. "Go."

With a snaggle-toothed grin, the man Noura thought was the Cairo night guard shoves Theo against a towering marble edifice. He snaps his jaws, then pushes off and melts into swirling shadow, a crocodile god returning to his river.

"Who in the world?" Noura's not sure who she's asking about, let alone who she's directing the question to. "No," she says. "Never mind. I don't want to know." Her head is pounding with too little sleep, and she wants to let super-Ghadfa and weaponized-Lizzy deal with her brother, with the cracks allowing other worlds to slip through.

Noura gives in to her exhaustion, her body crumbling to a narrow ledge. She lifts her face to the growling sky and lets the same rain sluicing down the faces of Mary and baby Jesus wash her own face. There is no hope for her clothes, and her sister's blood will stain her cuticles for weeks. She will never erase what her brother has done, what she allowed to happen.

Lizzy glances at Noura with a frown. Estelle's friend is wavering now, like somehow Noura upset a predesigned plan.

"What happened?" Theo straightens, hands raised but still pinned to the spot.

"My sister said to call Lizzy, but then..." Noura wordlessly pleads for them to understand, for Theo to reach in and extract the words so she doesn't have to say them.

Water flows across the pocked cement, dragging pebbles into the wide metal grate. The darkness hiccups over the white metal lines, twisting through the crevices, jumping with the drops of rain, mixing with the blood from Noura's hands. Her very soul draining away.

"Where's Estelle?" Theo pushes away from the wall, and Noura watches, somehow her brain registering his approach, Lizzy's challenge "stay there," and her gun swinging toward Noura, and yet not quite able to put together any of the connections to make it mean anything. Why is Lizzy here?

"Lizzy," Theo says, trying to draw the woman's scattered attention to him. "I'm FBI and—"

Lizzy's Glock snaps to Theo, her reaction superheated. He didn't expect this. The light at the entrance flickers in the mounting gusts, and he reminds himself that as long as Lizzy's focused on him, Noura is safe. And while the salted rain stings his face, he dares not wipe away the irritation, let alone drift toward Noura, who is shaking in obvious shock.

"ID." The authority in Lizzy's voice has Theo flummoxed, but he slowly digs into his pocket for his badge.

She's careful and professional when she reaches for it and glances down at the name, the face, his badge number. "Why in the name of all that's holy were you in Cairo?" She jams the Glock into a hip holster, then flips open a similar badge. MI6.

As he lives and breathes.

"Ghadfa's your man?" Theo squints into the empty corridor like the reptilian man might reappear.

"We've been working this case for years and—"

"She told me to call you," Noura says. She stands, swaying like a sapling, but her legs are spread in a sure fighter's stance, and the gun Theo'd glimpsed earlier is trained on Lizzy.

"Noura?" Lizzy shifts, gathering herself.

"Don't." Noura sidesteps, distancing herself, but also changing the angle of her shot so Theo's clear.

What is going on? Light catches the silver pendant at Noura's throat, and Theo feels the echoing chill of the feather on his chest. The whisper clear—*be careful.*

"If you're MI6, why would my sister tell me to call you? She was desperate to avoid the police, the FBI, anyone with the law. And you helped smuggle her out of Egypt."

Noura's question is a good one. His attention flicks to Lizzy, just catching the flash of blood red shadow crossing her face. Theo shifts, making his knees pliable, ready to bolt.

When Lizzy laughs, her attempt to be light falls hard as hail. "She's a small fish I kept on my line. And it worked. She called me when she needed a buyer."

"Then you planned to arrest her?" Brain screaming at him through the confusing fog, Theo slides toward cover and wills Noura to do the same. Better safe than sorry. "You can't extradite anyone without permission, and no one informed me of any international operations in my bailiwick."

"My guess is you love protocol as much as I do. And Ghadfa will have Harry soon. Since he answers to me, maybe we can overlook the letter of the law. From one hidden operative to another." Lizzy raises a knowing eyebrow, and Theo isn't quite sure what she's hinting at. "Besides, we need to retrieve those artifacts before they're ruined."

"Why are you here?" Noura jerks the gun to emphasize her question.

"Oh, honey." Lizzy laughs but doesn't take her eyes off Theo, like he's more dangerous than the gun. "I knew Estelle was in New Orleans, and it's my job to—"

"No," Noura snaps. "Not in New Orleans. Here. Right here in this cemetery. I didn't call you. How did you know where to—"

"That's enough!" Lizzy's shout reverberates as she wedges herself into the protection of twin age-blackened structures.

Theo's skin prickles with alert and understanding.

He once found a Van Gogh in a gas station bathroom. The guy hadn't known what to do with the priceless painting he'd stolen. You don't sell a ten-thousand-dollar Rembrandt at the corner store. But art theft investigators? They have both access to the pieces and the connections to sell them.

Lizzy isn't here to help.

She steps back, blending in, edges blurring as her blond hair frizzes into a lion's mane. Theo freezes at the woman's toothy grin. His mother has always insisted the gods are there, like angels, watching. Anat? Set's bloodthirsty concubine?

Noura's eyes have gone wide. She must see something too. He slams a lid over the questions exploding. He can deal with them after he and Noura get out of this alive. As if she's heard his thought, Noura glances at him, and he winks, praying she understands. *Duck and run.*

Noura winces and Lizzy spins to Theo, but he's already yanked his weapon out and is diving behind the nearest oven. Lizzy curses, and Theo pops out enough to squeeze off a round. The shot is off target, but close enough to send Lizzy diving for cover herself, giving Noura time to scramble to the next aisle. It's a wide one and should lead to the exit...as long as Lizzy doesn't follow. Roaring from the sky renders his hearing useless. So Theo shifts to peek down the tiny alley between graves.

A series of shots crack somewhere to the south, and a woman cries out. Theo's training barely prevents him from hurtling toward the sounds. Instead, he pokes his head down the next aisle. A seemingly unhurt Noura scrambles into the scant protection of a moldering oven. Lizzy is, presumably, hit, but it's the hulk of a man bearing down on Noura that concerns Theo.

He squeezes off a shot, and the man veers toward Lizzy's hiding place.

Beneath Theo, the puddles swirl with a toxic sludge. Only heaven knows what's oozing over his shoes. He curls into a small doorway for its scant protection. Theo's fingers tighten as his blood hides from the cold. Leaning his head against the marble wall, he lays a hand over the feather. "Tell me where she is," he breathes to the whispers in the air.

The dank wall stretches until it collides with another heap of debris. They're in a dead standoff. Neither of them able to move without giving the other a clear shot. Theo measures the distance to the exit gate. If anyone is out there, hopefully they heard the shots and called the police. But the buildings' windows looming above them are dark, the top floors cloaked in impenetrable clouds.

His only hope is that Noura calls the police...and that they believe her. And that it all happens before Theo dies of hypothermia or a gunshot.

"Theo?" Lizzy's voice bellows above the thrumming rain. The British accent has washed away, leaving something he can't quite put his finger on. "Ghadfa will have the artifacts by now," she says. "Let's get out of the rain and talk about things."

A shuffling trickles toward him on his right, and Theo strains to separate the sound of the storm from whatever Lizzy is doing. A falcon is nearly powerless in a storm, but a lion?

"Last I checked," Theo says, using his voice to cover his movement as he lifts a broken slab and slides it down in a flimsy shield. "The FBI frowns on negotiating with thieves."

"I have not stolen anything."

"Not yet." He creeps backward, making his way toward the main gate.

"I never will take possession. You know that? We'll be clean."

And that's when Theo hears it, the way all the vowels are trapped in the back of her throat, the slight hardening of the soft consonant sounds. Russian?

"Lizzy, Lizzy, Lizzy. Egypt has no special love for the Soviet Union. You so sure Ghadfa won't betray you? Especially after doing all the hard work...that is, if he makes it against two guerrilla fighters."

"Ghadfa's too afraid of who I work for to fail. Plus, he knows his way around purging the world of little men with little dreams."

"Peace isn't a little dream."

Lizzy's laugh teeters on mania. The gale lifts, redistributing the sound across the city of the dead. "All these fools think peace brings happiness. But what brings peace to you only destroys me." She growls with movement that makes Theo grasp his too-small shield and gather his feet. "The only person who will bring me a shred of happiness is me."

Theo hears the explosion behind him half a breath before he feels the searing pain rip through his biceps. He's spinning.

Blood is sticky against his groping fingers. Where's his gun? Theo falls sideways, awkward, crashing. Light flashes, darkens, flashes again. He blinks at the scorpions crawling across his vision. The scream of an unseen falcon. The urn planter in front of him tumbles, and he is buried.

NOURA'S SHOES skid across the slime as she careens through the narrowest of alleyways, slamming her shoulder against the sopping brick. She cries out, rolling away and forcing her legs forward to find help. How stupid could she have been? Lizzy? How long was that woman seducing Noura into helping her?

And Harry? He's been a terrorist this whole time? No clinic? No mission of peace? Soul sold to Set. She darts through the cemetery gate and across Basin Street, ducking onto St. Louis Street, then stumbling to a stop, torn as to where to go and what to do. Theo is the good guy after all, and he needs help. She didn't miss the sound of gunshots. Will others have heard it? Called the police? She hopes so. But hope is slim protection against reality. Noura pushes her sopping hair from her face. And Mehedi is out there somewhere with a murderer...

Harry is a murderer.

Estelle is dead. That poor officer too.

Noura's vision flickers with the noxious memory, and she sucks in air, clutching a tall wrought iron rail, borrowing its unbending strength. She cannot break now. But the oxygen will not come. She slams her forehead against the bars, once, twice, berating herself for her weakness. The entire world is upside down. Where is the falcon to save them now?

She can do nothing for Estelle, can't change her own choices. But now? Theo and Mehedi need her.

She can do this.

She can do this.

But how?

People. She must find people. Someone with a phone, a CB radio. Noura pivots and scurries with the drowning rats down the street. "Help." She stumbles into a group of laughing people and grasps the arm of the first woman. She balks at Noura's boldness. The group hollers, yanking the woman away and throwing a dollar at Noura's feet like she's a beggar.

"I'm not asking…" But the group scurries away, and everyone else crosses the street, gawking at Noura with unveiled judgment. Noura growls in a helpless rush of frustration.

Under the first awning, Noura pounds on the gate, praying someone is in the apartments, that someone will answer. Water drains from the sullen fabric above her, cascading to the cement and surging to the drowning drain. She closes her fist and pounds again.

As Hurricane Babe wails through the city that never sleeps, New Orleans is sluggish under the barrage. Another couple streams past but ignores her calls, and no one answers her knock at the apartment or the convenience store or the little house next door or the bar beyond.

She leans her head against an ornate door. "Please," she whispers against the unyielding blue wood. How much more can she take? And yet, she may be Theo's only hope.

Dragging energy from her empty well, she trots down two more blocks and stumbles to Bourbon Street.

Headlights bounce down the street. The rain shatters the light into a thousand shards as she steps onto the pavement, both hands raised, eyes clenched shut against the very real possibility that the squealing tires won't stop in time.

Theo could only have been out for a second. And then he's screaming, tangling with another body. Two bodies? His mind is consumed with the fire, ears echoing, life leaking from the blazing hole.

"Stay still, idiot," a man hisses as he ties a ragged piece of fabric around Theo's left arm.

No. No. No. His brain howls, then the plea explodes from Theo's mouth as the other man yanks down a tourniquet. Theo's body arches, and the man catches his shoulder, firm, steadying rather than restraining. Theo's mind scrambles to make sense of his...savior?...captor? The man's hair is graying, and his eyes are dark sockets in the dim light. He's familiar, yet he doesn't fit the catalog of faces in Theo's brain. Not FBI. Not an art contact. None of the people he's been watching with connections to the communist organizations. "Who are you?"

"Good. You're alive." The man releases Theo none too gently, then squats to knot a rope around the arms of the body sprawled out on the ground. "You let her flank you." He grunts, pivoting on the balls of his feet to yank the rope down to what Theo realizes is Lizzy's ankles, trussing her like a cowboy would a calf, and then tying everything to a sturdy-looking fence. His movements are sure and capable. Like he's done this a million times.

Theo scoots up the wall, dragging his arm. Where's his gun?

At Theo's movement, the man wheels around, shoes scraping angrily against the cement, a complete dichotomy to the amusement on his face. "Apparently what they say about the FBI is true."

Theo ignores the jab, continuing to shimmy around the marble oven in a stilted hobble.

"Ain't got the sense to watch their back." He drapes his arms across his knees in a sign of nonaggression.

But Theo's not stupid. The man's anything but harmless. His foot clunks against the metal of his sidearm, and he swipes it up.

The man ignores him as he checks his knots holding Lizzy. "Probably comes from thinking you're in friendly territory. Now CIA? Marines? They're a different bunch. Always in enemy territory. Always a risk of being stabbed in the back." He pauses, staring Theo down so he's forced to contemplate what's being said between the lines.

Is the man CIA? Former Marine?

When Theo pauses, his rescuer nods, which confirms Theo's guess. But as the man says, the other branches are volatile and liable to stab an FBI agent in the back if it brings leverage.

"Getting down's the easy part." He grabs the slippery fence. "It's the getting up that's troublesome. Retirement makes a man rusty." He groans to his feet, giving Theo plenty of room to make an escape. "Suppose an introduction is in order. I'm Harold Marquette, Sr."

Well, smack him with a two-by-four. Noura and Estelle's father.

37

The cat has one hundred percent got Theo's tongue. Wasn't Noura's father a librarian? And what does he want with Theo? Mr. Marquette brushes a bit of mud from his pant leg. "I hear you're interested in my daughter."

Theo hopes the man misses his momentary gaping mouth before he snaps it closed.

"She's far more flexible than her mother." Marquette stands, feet spread in a sturdy stance. "However, I'm not certain I want her involved in this."

"Sir?" is all Theo can manage.

"Noura." Marquette side-eyes Theo like he might sprout tree limbs from his addled brain. "I don't want my daughter with an undercover FBI agent. Especially one who thinks he is the god of justice." Marquette taps the bloodied medallion hanging around Theo's neck.

"Horus is the god of protection, not justice." Theo knows the difference. And the two paths are often in opposition. Theo reaches around the crumbling crypt and bends to retrieve his weapon. "Excuse me, but I have suspects to apprehend. And Noura is out there too."

Unfortunately, Marquette doesn't take the hint and matches Theo's trot toward the French Quarter. "I know where all of my children have been and how much danger Noura is in now."

He doesn't add *thanks to you*, but it's there.

Theo doesn't have time for Marquette's games, so he skirts Marie Laveau's grave and turns toward the entrance.

"How do you plan to find them?" Marquette echoes Theo's own thoughts.

"They went this way." Theo points in a lame suggestion of where to start.

"They'll head to Jackson Square." Marquette is, apparently, as much of a stubborn know-it-all as Estelle. But she's also been right more than Theo cares to admit.

Theo pauses past the ironwork gate, waiting for traffic to clear. "How do you know that?"

"It's where my son always meets ne'er-do-well friends," Marquette says this as if he's reading the synopsis to a predictable play. "And"—he steps into the street—"the cathedral is where I told Mehedi to go if he needed help."

Theo trips into the treelined neutral ground, catching himself on a shaggy palm tree.

"You need my help," Marquette says, "and I need yours. Mehedi was an asset for friends. Did his best to bring Harry back to the straight and narrow. I owe the boy, if nothing else. Can we argue later?"

Assuming Theo's agreement, Marquette traipses across Basin and then breaks into a wolf-like lope, skirting the most trafficked streets. Theo follows, grateful New Orleans is bizarrely absent of alleys that make perfect hiding spots. Instead, each long building is stacked one next to the other, lashed together with wrought iron.

NOURA CRACKS open one eye and then another, surprised to still be standing.

"Are ya out of your ever-loving mind, cher?" A voice hollers at Noura, but she crumples over the pointed yellow taxi hood with relief. He stopped!

"Hey!" The door squeals in protest, and the cabbie looms over her. "If you're gonna be sick, find a gutter."

"I'm not..." Noura drags her body upright.

Looming hardly does the man's presence justice. He's a brick wall, reaching well over Noura's head, and the muscles of his crossed arms strain against his skin.

"Are ya on somethin'?" The man steps back.

"No, please." Noura fruitlessly brushes at her drenched clothes. She'd thought them so smart and roguish at the beginning of the night. Now she feels like a drowned rat. A rat who betrayed her sister. Tears spring to Noura's eyes, and she settles her hands on the warm car hood. All she wants to do is curl up somewhere and pretend this is a dream. A very bad dream. "I—"

"Why're you huggin' my car?"

"Hugging? Oh!" She yanks back. "I didn't...I mean...I need a phone or..." She tucks her dripping hair behind her ears. Why didn't she tie her hair back? She listened to the radio, knew the hurricane was coming. Wait. Radio. "Your radio! Can you call the police? My friend, he's..." Oh heavens. How to explain?

The cabbie grabs hold of Noura's wrist, and she yanks back. While he doesn't release her, his grip is gentle as his dark eyes study Noura's scratched face, stained hands, and torn pants.

"Where's he at, cher?" The cabbie's voice drops into the growl of a dark, avenging angel.

"Oh! He didn't do this. He protected me. And now..." Noura sucks in a hiccupping breath. "Please help."

"You show me the way. I'll call for help while I drive."

She could kiss the man.

"There's a blanket back there," he says and cranks on the heat. "And call me Will."

While Will calls the dispatcher, Noura wraps herself in the heavenly blanket and points the way to the cemetery. The dispatcher tells Will to keep his ugly mug out of trouble. Will grunts but parks outside the cemetery wall.

"You stay behind me, and at the first hint of trouble, you hightail it to that taxi and haul outta here. You hear?"

"I won't leave you."

"I can take care of myself. Uncle Sam made sure of that in Vietnam."

Will lifts the largest handgun Noura's ever seen from the glove box and lumbers out of the taxi. Will skulks down the aisle with Noura following in the lee of his back.

But the first aisle is empty, and the next, and next. Theo is gone. Lizzy is gone. All that remains are a mass of battered weeds and a bloodied bit of marble streaked with rain. By morning, all evidence will be gone.

A gunshot ricochets through the night, and Noura snatches Will's elbow. He cocks his head, listening to the reverberations.

"Maybe half a mile that way." He nods toward where Harry and Mehedi had gone—toward the French Quarter.

Where would Harry go? Noura thinks about his childhood machinations, his stories. He was seven when Father was transferred to Tel Aviv, and Noura three. While she didn't remember much about their mother's city, Harry had regaled her with stories of New Orleans, voodoo, po'boys, jambayla, and—"The cathedral."

Will squints toward the exit. "Lots of places to hide there."

Noura nods, dread swirling at the thought of heading closer to the river and the coming flooding tide.

Even though Noura has no money, Will calls in a fare and warns that there might be trouble. Hopefully the police will make it in time to help.

But Noura's starting to wonder if the ancient Egyptians were right. The gods stand just outside the world, influencing humanity for their own ends. Set for destruction, pulling in gods and humans alike, until they realize what his manipulations lead to. And while Horus and Ma'at and even Anubis guard, protect, and fight, there are casualties. Always casualties. Even Horus's father was murdered. Noura grips the pendant around her neck. Even with the protection of Horus and Ma'at, there is no promise anyone will survive the night.

As Will jams the taxi in gear, Noura prays Maman was right—that the God frozen in the cathedral statue would somehow make everything good. Please let that be true.

A cross dangles in Will's mirror, and it swings in rhythm with the pulsing gale. Maman once told her the story of a man walking on water. Tonight, Noura's afraid rescuing Mehedi and Theo will take a miracle that big. Because as soon as Noura's brother opens the bag Estelle stole from the museum, he'll know the artifacts aren't real.

EVERY SLAMMING step past the drowning world, every ragged breath, sears Theo's arm, and he wonders how long he can go without proper medical care. As he and Marquette veer onto another street, the gloomy businesses loom over them. At the feet of the buildings, people waver in the rain, leaning against one another, stumbling down the brick sidewalk.

Theo doesn't know whether it's more strange that people are out in a hurricane or that the crowd is so small. New Orleans is a world he'll never understand. There isn't a soul in Detroit who would party in the streets with a tornado bearing down.

A crack erupts, and Theo ducks. When the rest of the street carries on unconcerned, Theo straightens. A hanging basket breaks free from its tether, launches itself across the street, and smashes inches from his feet. Theo shies like a startled horse and sprints to catch Marquette. The man has to be in his sixties, and yet, even with all his training, Theo's struggling to keep up.

Marquette pauses at the next intersection, head tilted, listening. All Theo hears is the rain pounding on the deck above them, punctuated by drunken laughter. But then he hears it too.

Another gunshot. The distant blare of a car horn.

WILL'S HORN BELLOWS...AGAIN. Who in their right mind chooses to be out in this insanity? If Noura could, she'd be snuggled in her room, reading Agatha Christie's last Miss Marple book.

Instead, Noura watches water pummel the streets, and she despises every single person flooding Toulouse Street along with the storm surge from the river. The mindless sacrifice of their bodies will never stop the hurricane. They've no idea how quickly, how easily, life is gone.

Will's radio crackles with a report of a tornado. His thumb taps the wheel with a nervous rhythm, and she stares at the solid face of buildings between her and where she must go. Blaring colors pressed, airless, against staid brick.

Will creeps forward, then zips through a tiny opening onto Chartres.

The marching buildings open, revealing the spires of the cathedral, so close she might prick her finger on one of the three tips. Like Sleeping Beauty, doomed to fulfill the curse. But there is no fairytale ending to the story of Set and Horus. If she has somehow stumbled into their story, how does this end?

Will slams on squealing brakes, hurtling Noura forward. As she gathers herself, the throbbing in her head strobes in time to the red flashing lights of a stalled truck.

Will throws the car into reverse, but a small crowd has swarmed around them. Thrusting his head out his window, the cabbie hollers. But no amount of swearing or pleading removes either the truck or the wall of humanity.

Lights flicker through the fogged window, and Noura fists the blanket and drags the slim protection from her shoulders. "Thank you, Will." Her voice sounds calm and impossibly far away as she folds the blanket.

"You can't go alone." He whips around to face her. "There are"—Will's eyes flash from her to the darkness—"there are things out there. Dangerous things. More than just the storm. You understand?"

Noura swallows, forcing herself to acknowledge what she has known and ignored. Yet she can feel the light weight of his soul and will not take this good man into whatever fight is coming. "You can't leave the taxi. They'll fire you...especially if the storm surge comes up. You've done more than enough. More than most would. Thank you. Keep calling the police?"

His massive hand closes over hers. "Of course. Take the blanket and —" He lifts the gun, but Noura shakes her head, not telling him she has the officer's pistol in her waistband.

As she blinks back tears, Noura pops open the door, clinging to the handle so the tempest can't rip it from her. She glances back at Will, who is clutching the cross, his lips moving in a silent plea, and then turns toward what she knows she must do. What she must face.

Without the protection of the cab, the wind bears down on her, the buildings groaning with her. It takes a force of will to shut the door and run, weaving as the gusts off the gulf slam into her. But Estelle was right. In order for life to mean something, Noura has to stand up and race toward what's right.

A FEW MINUTES LATER, Noura clatters onto the flagstone pedestrian path and crashes through the enormous dark wood doors of the cathedral. Inside, it's as if the entire world has been plunged into stone. Noura's breath rattles in the shivering sepulcher-cold entry. Candles flicker, guttering momentarily before settling in their blue glass holders. Water drips from her clothes in noisy splashes, pooling on the marble tile.

She is suddenly conscious of the mess she's making, the destruction she's bringing to this peaceful place. But it cannot be helped, and Noura steps through the second door into the sanctuary.

Rain beats against the stained-glass image of a crowned man holding his hand out to some unseen penitent. As a child, Noura thought he was meant to be Jesus. But he has a sword, and there are no stories of Jesus holding a sword. She steps past the silent confessional.

She wishes Maman were here...wishes anyone were here.

Was she wrong about where Harry would go?

Noura glances back at the statue of Joan of Arc and, rather than gathering strength from the martyred warrior, fear laps at her ankles. Doing what's right doesn't mean she lives. The windows scream from the pressure change, sending battle moans across the empty basilica. Did Joan of Arc ever regret her choices? Did she ever wish she could reverse time and make a different choice? Noura suspects not, and the idea exhausts her. She slumps into a pew. Now what?

A whisper of fabric makes Noura spin in her seat and grab for the officer's gun.

"Cher." Grandmere's voice loosens Noura's sharp tension, and she releases her grip on the weapon.

Grandmere toddles to the aisle, pauses to wrestle off her glove, dips her fingers in the basin of holy water, and then crosses herself. Noura wants to cry *I'm lost* and have the matriarch hold her as other grandparents soothe their progeny. But Grandmere would only sweep Noura aside. Emotions are messy, and Grandmere does not do messy.

She lifts a pointed eyebrow at Noura in question.

But what question?

When Noura cannot contrive an answer, Grandmere sighs with a disappointed shake of her head and settles far enough away that Noura's puddle will not soil her somber skirt. Poitier perfection broke Maman. Ice does not do well under pressure. And make no mistake, the matriarch is pressing Noura now.

Grandmere shimmies her age-sunken hand into her glove. "Where is your sister?"

The reminder slashes Noura's gut with blinding pain. "Estelle... she's..."

"Dead?" Grandmere's word is brutal, stabbing Noura again and again as it echoes in the church.

Noura bends over the pain, but nothing can protect you from savagery, no shield for the agony of a sister gone.

"Now, child." Grandmere waves away Estelle's brutal murder like a pesky fly. "We've time enough later for that."

Noura blanches. "What is wrong with you?"

Grandmere's dark pupils flood with furious red, and Noura flinches, sliding away even as her grandmother growls. "Your fool of a brother has muddled things as usual. But we must keep our wits about us. Yes?"

Too late, Noura realizes she's not the only one with a weapon. Across her grandmother's lap lies a pistol.

38

Theo and Marquette snap around another corner at a full, painful sprint, and the cathedral rises before them, enormous and gloriously close. The sky has opened, and the boundaries of the ocean are obliterated, sending rushing water to tear at Theo, threatening to drag his feet from under him. At least the flood has pressed most people inside the bars, so that the square is eerily devoid of people. A forlorn paper clings to the wrought iron fencing, then skids down the rails, tearing in two, and tumbles, trying to fly, crippled and broken.

Unease ripples through him. Where is the falcon? Theo slips the Glock from his holster, his other hand pressed against the prophetic chill in his chest. The men two clatter under the Cabildo museum's arches. In the distance, the Gulf roars, washing, salty, over their senses. Theo tastes the destruction, the bending levee system. As if he senses it too, Marquette stumbles to a halt. But this is not the time to stop. Theo elbows past Marquette, and the reason for the other man's halt crashes into Theo only as he clears the Cabildo Museum.

A form hovers in the shadows of Pirates Alley, a fluttering reaper's cloak behind him. The gun is unmistakable in the meager, fractured light from the stained glass.

Theo doesn't let his weapon waver in the standoff as he parses out snatches of information. The shape of the jeering face is familiar. Paint the long, straight nose white and...the witch doctor from the museum. The pendant has gone so cold that it burns.

"Harry." Marquette's bland statement fractures the picture before it snaps into place again.

Harry—witch doctor and brother both. And something else.

The apparition glides into full view, weaving as if tugged by the tempest. He was in Cairo too. The clumsy tail he'd seen watching Estelle. The man's eyes flash the red of Set, and Theo's vision blurs, his hands sparking in an ancient and visceral recognition. Set.

"Father."

"Stop right there." Theo blinks against the adrenaline pulsing through him and shifts, using his body to shield the elder Marquette, who has not, as far as Theo can tell, lifted his weapon. There are no falcons in sight. Theo is alone against the impending chaos. "Drop the bag." Theo's voice is calm, habitual, demanding obedience. "You're under arrest for the theft of the King Tut artifacts."

Harry chucks the bag at Theo, and it slams into Theo's unmoving chest before crashing to the ground. Theo winces against the pain battering his body, but in the decade he's worked in the art theft division, Theo made the mistake of dropping his weapon to save a piece of art only once. The old bullet wound in his hip is a permanent reminder. While beyond valuable, art isn't worth dying for.

"If you want to see her alive again"—Harry's gun dips to the bag at Theo's feet—"you'll get me the real ones."

"The real ones?" Theo sounds as dense as the marble pillars and as shocked as if the column had initiated a conversation.

"The artifacts!" Harry shouts with so much force, it knocks him sideways. "I need the real ones. There's plaster showing through the paint chips."

Plaster? "These are replicas?" Theo's question has an edge of wonder. Noura must have traded them out before Estelle arrived. Smart woman.

"Yes, you idiot. If I don't deliver, they're going to kill me."

"But I didn't—"

"I don't care what you did or didn't do! Get the real things and bring them here!" Harry's body weaves drunkenly, fighting against the forces he can neither see nor control. Theo edges closer to the protection of the columns. Clumsy fools are still dangerous, and unlike Horus's, Theo's mother cannot raise anyone from the dead.

"Harry." Marquette lays a quieting hand on Theo's shoulder. "Where are your sisters?"

The question detonates in the sudden stillness, and Theo's thoughts duck from the emotional shrapnel he can't afford to absorb.

"Will you look at that?" Harry's voice is tinged maniacal, lifting with the storm-producing Set. "The great Harold Marquette, Senior, is finally concerned for his children...or at least two of them. The son, though, he was always a disappointment, wasn't he?"

"You weren't a disappointment, Harry." Marquette clears his voice, a great lumbering in his chest. "You just never stood still long enough for me to—"

"You had me hunted down as a traitor!" Harry lunges, and Theo lifts his gun.

The sudden motion sends sparks of pain singeing through Theo's body, piercing holes in his vision. But he holds steady. He must hold steady. "Harry, I get it," Theo says. "He abandoned you and didn't lift a finger to help. Fathers should always protect their families, shouldn't they?"

Harry's attention flicks away from his father.

"Families should help each other, right?" Theo continues.

Harry gives the barest sketch of a nod.

"I'll get you the real artifacts, but I need Noura's help. Where is she?" Theo's voice is light as a feather.

"They're both dead." Harry's arm falters, and a sob breaks through even as Theo gasps for breath. Noura was supposed to be safe. A gunshot slams through the darkness, and Theo crashes to a knee, spinning for the safety of the Cabildo's arches, his training somehow keeping his weapon raised.

Another crack smacks somewhere above Theo and rains marble chips on his shoulders. Marquette slams into the wall a second later.

"Shots are coming from the square." Marquette's voice is a hair louder than the screaming maelstrom and pounding adrenaline in Theo's ears.

Across the way, Harry hides in a tiny alcove created by the jut of the church's hexagonal tower. His cowering proves he wasn't the shooter.

"Where's Noura?" Theo's question is an accusation, lifted high enough for any of the men around him to hear.

"She might as well be dead." Harry's voice is piteous now. "She and Mehedi both."

"Harry!" Desperation catches the name and slings it, tumbling and bloodied across the distance.

"She's in the cathedral with—"

Another shot rings out, and Harry slumps.

Curse words ring through Theo's mind. He's no idea who they're dealing with or where they are. And though Marquette and Theo are two against one, they are pinned down.

He squints into the open square. The trees are too scraggly to provide cover.

"The lampposts?" Theo asks Marquette.

Marquette taps twice on Theo's shoulder and points at the far lamppost guarding the gates to Jackson Square. The lights are out, either from the storm or a bullet. They can't cross thirty yards to the basilica without the gunman cutting them down. But if Typhon wants Theo to retrieve the artifacts, he wouldn't kill him. Unless he and the gunman aren't working together.

"Ghadfa!" Theo shouts. "Harry says these are fakes."

A flash of lightning presses stark shadows into Marquette's face. Pain? Fear? Theo shakes his head free of questions. When Marquette could have done something, he didn't. Men don't change so much that Theo can count on him now.

Theo slides low, blending with the shadows at the foot of the arch, peeking out where the mind doesn't easily place a human face. A shot cracks, and he yanks himself back. He'd forgotten Ghadfa was special forces trained.

Hot dry wind snakes across Theo's face, and he flinches, thinking about Lizzy in Cairo with Noura. She had to be the one manipulating everything, which means Ghadfa is exposed. "Lizzy is trussed like a

Christmas turkey in the police station," Theo says. "You've no one to sell the pieces without either her or me. Right now, she's probably spilling her story and throwing you in to get a deal. If you run, you might get ahead of them. I've no interest in chasing you."

Marquette's sharp "Theo" is a warning Theo understands. He's told a terrorist to run free. It's a calculated risk. His priorities are innocent bystanders and the artifacts. Without Lizzy, Theo hopes Ghadfa will have a harder time escaping. But if he's anywhere close to the intelligent man Theo thinks he is, Ghadfa has a go bag stashed somewhere nearby. Even Theo has two in the city, ready to run at the first sign of trouble.

Theo swallows. He's a born runner. Marquette is right. He's no business thinking about Noura in any way other than as an asset. One he's put in serious danger.

AT THE SOUND OF GUNSHOTS, Grandmere smooths the white wings of hair under her pillbox hat.

Desperate questions ping in Noura's mind—Why does Grandmere have a gun? Where is Mehedi? What does this have to do with Harry? She's not really in danger, is she? But there was that strange flash of red in her grandmother's eyes, and the fact that she swore she'd seen Set's face possess her brother's. Had it all been her imagination? Stress does strange things to people. Noura closes her fingers around the Horus necklace, warm and pulsing.

She fights her lifetime of instincts—all the watching and molding herself into what is expected—and realizes that her weakness is also a strength. If she has a mind to, she also knows where to thrust the knife to cause the most hurt. Remaining silent will ruffle Grandmere more than a mere hurricane.

Though Noura's shivering, she forces herself to be as still as possible. Sucking in air and blowing warmth down her body. Contemplating the altar, the sculptures. The sacrifice. If the church is correct, the God-man depicted voluntarily died for people who hated him. A far cry from her family's penchant for self-focus...except for Estelle, in the end. Noura smooths her finger across the feather barbs on her pendant. Such strength in such small things.

Grandmere shifts in a most undignified way, and Noura stifles a smirk, maintaining the bland, vacuous mien of the fool Grandmere thinks she is.

Noura squeezes rain out of the sodden wool blanket, taking delight in watching the trail wet her grandmother's shoes.

"Oh, for heaven's sake, Noura." Grandmere's frustration batters the marble walls, loud enough that Noura swears even the stone relief of the Virgin Mary glances askance at Grandmere.

"Yes?" Noura turns unconcerned eyes to her.

"We cannot sit here all night."

"Yes, Grandmere." Noura makes no move to stand. She always thought Maman was weak, but perhaps Maman had been wise. If Noura is as pliable and unconcerned as her mother, perhaps she will slip through Grandmere's fingers.

"Do you not wish to know what is happening, or are you too stupid to realize that I will kill you?" The set of Grandmere's jowls confirms she is serious. While the idea that Noura's own grandmother will shoot her leaves Noura hollowed, she's not surprised. She saw what Grandmere did to Maman, met the man she wanted Noura to marry.

The basilica wails, her bells droning in a battle cry against the darkness.

"I have no doubt of your capabilities or your coldness." Noura folds her hands in her lap and faces the altar. If the matriarch wants something from her granddaughter, Noura will not beg or guess.

A painfully human sound groans behind Noura, and she catches herself just before whirling. Grandmere's mouth lifts, sending a cracking blow through Noura's plans.

"You didn't check the confessionals?"

Is someone there? Harry? Mehedi? Noura clutches the feather, reminding herself not to react. Where is Theo? Or even the priests? How she wishes churches were still true sanctuaries.

"I suppose there's a reason you spend your time in drafty museums studying other people's history instead of creating your own. You don't have the capacity to do anything earth-shattering. But I do."

Noura always thought Father's stories of Grandmere were overblown, the histrionics of a storyteller. What happened to make her so vile?

Grandmere huffs at Noura's non-response, fluffing like a disgruntled chicken. "In my day, we made our own way, recovered from our own mistakes. You brought that poor boy to our country and then allowed him to become riffraff. You've all left me to clean up your messes. You. Harry. Estelle. And your father." She shoves to her feet, circling the gun at Noura in an obvious signal to stand.

Grandmere smacks a palm against the top of the pew, and Noura jerks to her feet, muscle memory reacting.

"You will retrieve the artifacts," Grandmere says as if it is an already foregone conclusion. "Then you will bring them to me."

"What do you want with them?" The question slips from Noura's mouth before she can rein in her confusion. Estelle was selling them for Typhon. What could her old-line, staunch grandmother have in common with the unhinged communist?

"Surely your father has told you stories." Grandmere's painted mouth lifts in a scoff, and she steps into the aisle, pivoting and waving for Noura to precede her out of the church.

Stories? Father was always telling stories. About his childhood on a Texas cattle ranch, about wardrobes opening to entire worlds and tornadoes transporting puppies and girls to Oz, and…about a young woman who traveled to Europe for fun and found her voice only to have her husband imprison her for trying to help others when she returned home. Father was sympathetic until he told about the young woman turning into an ogre and imprisoning her daughter. It was the one story Maman hated.

The lights in the church flicker as the pieces click into place— Grandmere's trip to Europe, where she gained communist leanings. Noura hadn't known about Grandfather ratting out his wife to the government though. No wonder she became bitter. But this is overkill. Isn't it?

Noura rubs her forehead and takes the slowest, smallest steps she can. What she wouldn't do for Theo or even Estelle to tell her what to do. Knowing which dynasty a wedjat eye amulet belonged to is useless against a gun.

The confessional shudders with a blow from inside, and Noura shuffles sideways.

"Who…" Noura swallows the shake in her voice and starts again. "Who is in the confessional?"

"That Bedouin boy." Grandmere prods Noura toward the wooden structure. "I'll take care of him while you retrieve my baubles. It's a brilliant plan, you have to admit. Fund my escape to Cuba and destroy the peace talks at the same time. Your father and government boyfriend can do nothing about it."

Father? Noura's feet stumble with her mind, and she collides with the side of the confessional, scrambling for anything to stall. "I need to be sure Mehedi's okay first. You know. Proof of life." Isn't that what they call it on television?

Grandmere kicks the ornate wood, and a man grunts. "See? Alive," she says.

"I'm coming, Mehedi. Just hold on. I'll—"

Grandmere jams the gun in Noura's spine hard enough she yelps, belying her thundering thoughts. Darkness shrouds the tiny square window in each door. If Noura leaves, Grandmere will kill Mehedi. What Noura wouldn't give to transform herself into a vicious hippopotamus like the trickster Set. The doors seem to hum with the thought. *Trickster.* A voice hums in agreement. Horus wasn't above using his wits either.

"The artifacts are at the museum." Noura's words tumble out in a torrential waterfall of obvious desperation.

The truth has Noura's intended effect and makes her grandmother hesitate, her lips pressing in assessment. "You have some spunk in you after all. But your fool brother has them somewhere. He already admitted to trying to swap them on me."

"He doesn't have them," Noura says. "I switched them before Estelle came to the museum."

Grandmere takes the slightest step backward, granting Noura space to breathe, to think, to use whatever wits she has left. "My keys are at

Theo's, and the museum guards will double at six. I'll never make it on foot."

"Then I suggest you run, dear. Because that boy's life depends on it." Grandmere lifts a sculpted brow.

"Why are you doing this?"

"Great leaders deserve great sacrifice."

"Isn't the saying great leaders sacrifice great things?"

Grandmere laughs. The sound is rusted, jagged, far too deep for her feminine vocal cords. "You, my dear, are as naïve as a kitten playing in a war zone." Her eyes flash with an unnatural lightning, and Noura takes an involuntary step back from the cold jaws of Set's lake of fire.

"You skip about thinking if you're good enough, everyone else will be good and kind, and life will be rainbows and butterflies. But you are wrong." Grandmere's spine lends her towering height over Noura. "Life is like the hurricane out there, mindlessly mowing down everything in its way."

Nothing Noura has learned has prepared her to face this brutal, otherworldly Grandmere.

Noura has no choice. She must steal the artifacts...for real this time.

39

Theo stares into the frenzied darkness and sees no sign of Ghadfa fleeing.

Across the alley, Harry shifts. Theo grumbles at him under his breath, like he might hear Theo's admonition to stay still. A police siren whoops maybe three blocks away. Theo's head snaps around, but they'll never make it through the flooded streets before Harry gets antsy and does something stupid.

Theo tucks himself behind the sweating marble and leans his head against the solid surface, borrowing its strength. "Who has Noura?" Theo tilts his head toward Marquette.

The night nearly swallows the older man, but his breath is steady, revealing training or maybe a lack of emotional depth. Theo matches his inhalations to Marquette's, mimicking his bizarre calm.

Theo senses more than sees the shake of his head. He can't know if Ghadfa is working with whoever is inside the church or guess at how to manipulate the kidnappers into releasing Noura.

Theo has to disable Ghadfa before he can charge the basilica. Charge the basilica. Theo looks at the sky, asking forgiveness from both God and his mother, who will never forgive him for breaking into a church with his gun hot and ready. But he has no choice. Following the shadow of the arch, he sidles to where Marquette is plastered against the next column.

Theo points to his chest, then toward the wrought iron fence gate thirty yards away from the cathedral. The dark might hide Theo enough to cross, leap the eight-foot fence, and flank Ghadfa. Theo points to Marquette, brings his first two fingers to his eyes, then points toward the rest of the mayhem and Harry, who is slumped against the church as if his spine has been pulled from his body.

Marquette nods and slides to the forward column. Once Marquette's in place, Theo skims to the darkest point he can find—halfway between the church doors and St. Peter Street. He stuffs his gun into the holster and snaps it into place.

Drawing in a breath, he sprints across the span, plants a foot on the low-slung cement wall and his hands on the top of the fence, then vaults so he has one foot on top of the fence to push himself through the air and tumble to the other side in a relatively noiseless affair. He grimaces at the mud soaking through his clothes. He could double as a walking mud pie at this point. Already moving toward the lampposts, Theo spits out a chunk of dirt, shakes out his screaming arm, and retrieves his gun from the holster.

It's dark as hades by the posts, but the space appears empty. Theo swings a wide arc, sorting the blobbed voids around him as harmless bushes, planters, trash can, bench. No Ghadfa.

There's a clatter muffled by the church door, and Theo spins, weapon at the ready.

The lights inside the cathedral flicker and blink off, dousing the entire square in the slanted red light trickling from braking cars on Chartres. Movement slinks down the front of the church, and Theo squints, praying for his night vision to kick in faster.

The shadow morphs into the form of a person advancing on the upriver door.

Theo's almost certain it's Ghadfa. Theo sidesteps around the dual columns, but his training refuses to allow him to shoot on guesses.

A torrent whips from the Gulf and drives Theo forward, begging him to run, to join in its destruction. Instead, Theo bends, making himself a smaller target, and slinks down the three steps.

A crash erupts from inside, the door flying open, nearly missing the shadowy figure, and expelling another person tumbling in a desperate sprint. Theo would recognize her form anywhere. Noura. Noura has spun into the reach of who Theo's now sure is Ghadfa.

NOURA'S OUT THE DOOR, whipping around, using the heavy wood to shield herself as she yanks the gun from her sodden waistband. She's bringing the weapon around when a vise wraps around her arm and hauls her into a solid chest.

"Stop right there, Mr. FBI." The rumble of the man's threat shudders through Noura's entire body.

Theo? Where?

Salted water slips from her eyes, joining the rain slicking her hair across her face.

"I will shoot."

Noura recognizes the voice. Ghadfa.

The enormous man lifts her off her feet, dragging her away from the door, from Theo. She kicks and connects with nothing. The stench of death lies heavy on him, and Noura cannot breathe, cannot breathe. She waits for the crocodile of a man to open his jaws and swallow her—

"Young man." Grandmere's voice lifts from inside the doorway, and Ghadfa freezes as if he doesn't know what to make of the old lady voice hiding behind the massive church door.

It's apparent from the flick of his attention that Theo is confused by this innocent bystander as well. But Noura knows Grandmere will take great joy in killing an extraneous FBI agent before traipsing off to Cuba.

"No!" Noura twists so her gun points down, and, when she squeezes the trigger, a bullet screams straight into Ghadfa's foot.

Ghadfa's yell is loud in Noura's ear, his arms releasing. She stabs her elbow into his gut, leaping out of his grasp and vaulting to slam the door. But the door snaps wide, cracking against Noura's cheek. Pain explodes along with a gunshot.

She stumbles backward, but she has enough presence to spin and squeeze off another shot, not even bothering to aim. But Ghadfa is already down, a perfect circle oozing from his forehead. Noura doesn't underst—

"Well," says Grandmere in that too-deep voice. Far too close. Eyes glazed a blazing red. "Aren't all of you children a disappointment. I had hopes for Estelle, but she lost her way. Blasted Bedouin boy. He, of all of you, shows intelligence and backbone."

Noura turns toward Theo, who stands similarly cautious but poised on his toes like a raptor, ready to spring.

"Ma'am." The only sign Theo isn't drawing attention to a dusty artifact is the unblinking flick of his eyes toward Noura.

"Do not, ma'am, me, Theodore. Or should I say Alexander?"

Why is Theo hesitating? Noura slides over to peer around the edge of the church door.

"I don't know why your associate is accosting my granddaughter, but you should know I will destroy you."

"You know full well he isn't FBI. I assume I have the pleasure of meeting Typhon."

"Oh dear. You government types are so behind. It's why you will never effect change."

"And you will." Theo's words are half statement and half incredulous question.

Noura eases back. If she can get in the other door, maybe she could—

"Noura. I do not wish to hurt you," Grandmere says. "But your brother is not entirely useless and has, by now, circled the church."

Noura's gaze jerks to Theo, hoping he knows where Harry is, and Theo winks. Duck and run. Noura spins and sprints for the other door, clattering to a stop when Lizzy steps from the darkness.

"I am sorry, princess. As much as I like you, I rather need the artifacts more than ever."

Noura's entire being wants to collapse on the flagstones. She's exhausted, cold, and betrayal threatens to drown her.

"You have to promise not to hurt Mehedi or Theo," Noura says.

"Set your gun on the ground and kick it away." Lizzy is calm, sad, like she'd rather be anywhere else. And despite the fact that she is pale, depleted, there is no give in her.

"You can't trust them!" Theo shouts, his voice far away, the dull sound of reinforcements too distant to arrive in time.

THEO'S FINGERS are numb against his weapon, and his vision flickers. From the loss of blood? Or lightning? A primal, helpless scream rips through his mind. Noura bends, setting her gun on the ground. He cannot let Typhon win. Where are his carefully constructed plans, his logic, now?

"I need Theo in order to get the artifacts." Noura's voice surfaces above the wailing wind and the cry of a saxophone.

"Your little feint won't work." Lizzy presses a hand against the wall in support, like she's had the life force ripped from her.

"She's right." Theo points toward the bag and where the older Marquette had been standing. "The bag is over there."

Lizzy prods Noura toward the open church door. Odd veins of red streak Lizzy's face, but she still moves with the grace of a warrior. Was his mother right all along? Can the gods push and prod people into doing their bidding? He needs to remove her from the equation but has no idea if he can. How did she escape? Her face flickers. Set? It can't be. Can it?

"Well." The old woman's voice is deep and uncaring as her body shrugs, snapping tight like a marionette. "This works better than I could have expected. You"—she gestures to Lizzy—"get the bag. Set still has use for you. My granddaughter and I will take shelter from this." She waves at the raging weather as if it is a disobedient child. "And if Harry doesn't have the real things, you"—she points at Theo, her eyes red and glaring—"will get them for me."

"I..." Theo can't let her—whoever or whatever she is—keep Noura. His mother always pushed him toward order, toward things like Horus and angels and goodness, but he never thought, never truly believed that any of her old stories could possibly be real. But now? What is he to do? What *could* he, a mere mortal, do?

"He doesn't have keys to the building," Noura says. "He's not an employee of NOMA."

Thank heavens for Noura's quick thinking.

"Ah. But you said you'd left the keys at Mr. FBI's apartment. So it seems an easy solution. Yes?"

Noura's shoulders sag with defeat.

Theo will have one shot. If Theo shoots the older woman, Typhon, what will Lizzy do? With the possibility of pay gone, will she let Noura go? Or would Theo be better shooting Lizzy and taking the shot from the grandmother? Would a bullet even stop either of them? Theo shakes his head. It's the only option he has, and he has to try.

Lizzy stoops to retrieve Noura's pistol, giving Theo a shot clear of Noura. Theo swings his Glock and squeezes off a shot. A second shot rings out, and Theo braces himself for the impact. But there is none. Just an inhaled breath from the storm.

Typhon stands, mouth drawn tight in disapproval. Her gun clatters to the ground, and she staggers to her left, falling into the doorframe before dropping to her knees, a blood-red circle blooming at her chest. Behind her, a young man stands, gun trained on the woman. The man nudges her with a foot and kicks her gun. It skitters into a flooded gutter.

The moment he steps from the door, Noura squeals, "Mehedi," and launches herself at her friend, wrapping him in a protective hug.

Theo places a mostly unnecessary finger at Lizzy's still throat, then secures his weapon and Noura's, stuffing hers into his coat pocket. That done, Theo stands, soaked as a fish, outside the church doors.

Noura slips out of Mehedi's arms and turns, and Theo hates the look of fear and mistrust on her face.

He bends to check for a pulse on the frail wrists of Typhon. But she is gone, her face already shrinking away even as the rivulets of blood red streak in her face. Who would believe that he saw Set flicker in her face? Given a few months, will he even believe it?

Theo brushes the woman's eyes closed and turns away from the woman, from the reality of what he just saw. And yet there is still the living to contend with. At the sound of movement behind him, he shifts, smiling softly at the woman clutching her elbows like she might be able to hold herself together. "That might have been the most brilliant stall I've ever encountered."

One of Noura's arms falls to her side, and then the other.

"Are the artifacts—"

"Safe at the museum." Noura releases a breath. "They never left the building."

He groans to his feet, his hand pressing against a worrying stain on his shoulder. "You," he says, "are the most devious, extraordinary woman I've ever—"

A crash from inside the body of the church sends Noura wheeling. In a single motion, Theo yanks her away from the door and shoves her behind him. The door bursts open, and Noura's father stumbles from the nave, weapon raised and looking like something Mom had thrown into the dumpster.

"Stop," Marquette shouts, towing a bedraggled Harry with him.

Theo's laugh is harsh in frustration. "Too late."

Marquette flounders, and Theo nods toward the body slumped near the sputtering bank of candles. "We've got it under control."

"My mother-in-law?" Marquette releases a bound Harry abruptly enough that the younger man stumbles to a seat. With the obvious confusion in Marquette's voice, Theo's sure he hadn't known.

"Typhon," Theo clarifies.

Marquette gapes at Theo, then Noura, who's tucked herself into the lee of Theo's body. A frown droops down the older man's face. Behind Theo, Noura stiffens.

"Your daughter is a brave woman." Theo reaches for her.

She weaves her fingers through his, and Theo's breath catches. Her shaking arm is dangerously cool against him. He needs to get her somewhere warm. Somewhere safe.

"He was prepared to die for me." Her voice doesn't shake, even when it should.

"And that is the problem." Marquette blusters. "He put you in a place where your life needed protecting."

Theo opens his fingers to release her, but her fingers tighten—refusing to let go even though he failed to fully protect her.

"As did you." Noura steps forward, dragging Theo with her. Her face flickers gold, the chain at her neck flashing in dangerous protection, and his answering in warm support. "Only Theo tried to keep me out of it, and then, when he saw what was coming, he gave me a choice. You? My entire life, you lied to me...to us." She gestures to include Mehedi and Harry.

"Your father pretends he's more than he is, and he uses everyone, Noura." Mehedi leans against the sanctuary door like his weight is too much for his own body. "And then he discards them when he's done. He's not even CIA."

"Mehedi?" Noura scuttles next to her friend, acidic concern puckering her brows as she searches for wounds.

The young man yelps when Noura reaches his rib cage. She lifts the stained shirt to reveal a garden of blooming bruises.

"He never intended for me to survive." Mehedi scowls at Marquette. "Did you?"

The rancor makes Theo snap up his weapon and reposition to gain a clear line of sight to both men.

"Have you figured out how he used me?" Mehedi directs the question to Theo and stretches his hands in front of him. His fingers are long and nimble and calloused. A bomb maker's hands.

"I already know who you are," Theo says.

"That's half the story." Mehedi squares his shoulders and propels himself from the doorway, closing the distance between the men with startling speed.

"I didn't use any of you," Marquette says. "What kind of monster do you think I am? He's a good kid who my son failed, and I did my best."

Mehedi sucks in a breath, holding it as anger flares his nostrils. He releases the air and allows the anger to drain from his face. What is left is passionless, cold, and hard, and far more dangerous. "You let my sister die."

Noura stands between the men, directly in the crosshairs of the personal war. Theo shifts, trying to clear his shot lines. No matter what Noura thinks, he will protect her as Horus protects Ma'at. But he's no real idea of who is lying, who is telling the truth.

"No." Marquette huffs in clear condescension. "A week before Yom Kippur, I heard something was coming. I might have been just a poor Texas dirt farmer turned librarian, but I'd been a Marine. I heard things. I knew things. We had satellite pictures of the Egyptians massing on the border and knew it was more than the military exercises of May and

August. The government warned Mossad and Prime Minister Meir, and I warned Harry. I pleaded with him to get out."

Mehedi scoffs. "They only let me cross the border when I agreed to work for them."

Theo frowns at the younger man. "I thought you worked for the Weather Underground."

"He did," Marquette says. "As the eyes and ears for the government. I had a Marine buddy who worked with the agency. Mehedi was perfect for the communist ideals—an orphan who had lost everything and happened to have scouting and explosives skills. Getting him to help was the only way I could get him a visa during the war."

"But Saira didn't come." Mehedi's voice hiccups like the near child he was then, all the fire sliding beneath waves of grief.

"She stayed with Harry." Marquette shrugs.

From the ground, Harry sucks in a sharp breath. "She what?"

"She wouldn't leave, wouldn't even let me get Miriam out."

"Miriam?" Harry's voice drifts, lost, like calling his daughter's name might conjure her from the grave or reverse his wayward decisions.

"I thought Saira would come with Estelle. Maybe I should have gone myself. Made her come. I—"

Noura steps toward her father. But he shakes his head, refusing to take the comfort she's offering.

"It didn't matter," Marquette says. "They were gone, and I was still banished."

"Serves you right," Harry growls. "The entire CIA, headed by Kissinger, was dirty as the Mississippi is out there right now. Even after the attacks, they played fast and loose with supplying the Israelis. I lost everything."

Marquette shifts his weight. "They were doing what they thought was best."

"For who?" Harry shouts, his eyes flickering between green and red. "For you? Maybe. But not for everyone."

"No," Marquette says. "Not for everyone. I wish I could wave a wand and make it right for everyone. But I'm not God, and anyone who thinks they can wield that power without becoming mad with the responsibility or corrupt from the rush is fooling themselves."

"So you tried to get Saira out?" Mehedi's face is a cloud of confusion. "And you refused to leave only to...?" Mehedi spins on Harry. "It was you!"

Noura throws herself in front of Mehedi, grappling with his arms as he weeps on her shoulder. "He left her behind."

"I know." Noura gathers Mehedi to her. "I know."

Clattering feet pound through the two alleyways surrounding the cathedral, shouts floating above the growing voice of the hurricane. God himself approving of the coming justice.

Theo raises his hands, waiting for the police to relieve him of his service weapon, to wrestle the scene into control. Theo's badge is in plain view on his belt, and the officers quickly separate him for his recitation of events.

Noura sits in a pew, her stoic back to the melee behind her. Two officers pelt Theo with questions while a swarm trundles the two other men off to the police station.

As paramedics lift the bodies of the two women—Noura's grandmother and then Lizzy—a female officer slides in next to Noura, unlocking the cuffs from her uncommonly still wrists and spreading a blanket across her shoulders.

Theo's ears ring with the drain of adrenaline and crest of exhaustion, but it isn't until his words stumble together that the officers tell him not to leave the city and then release him. He staggers to unsteady feet and approaches the back of the church. The candles beside him quiver, and he turns in anticipation as the spitting image of an older Estelle flutters into the nave.

Mrs. Marquette swoops past Theo and gathers her daughter to her chest. "It will be okay, darling."

Noura nods, her dark hair curling through her mother's blond. Together, the women are solid as the church's cornerstone.

Balance restored, Theo steps into the night, Marquette's words ringing in his ears. Noura needs someone who will never abandon her... and that someone can never be Theo. Warmth drains from Theo, leaving a hole in his gut. The women slip into the slowly stilling air. The battle between chaos and order has been won. That should be enough to satisfy him...but it isn't.

He clutches the no longer pulsing feather pendant and strides out, following long enough to watch officers tuck the two women safely into a squad car. As the car navigates a corner, Noura turns, her gaze fixing on Theo, sparking gold before yielding to her beautiful brown. He blinks, and she is gone. Ma'at safely away. Horus's mission done.

40

January 1978

Noura perches on the rail of the Spanish Plaza, watching the Mississippi churn and collect bits of soil only to deposit them elsewhere outside the reach of even the tankers. An enormous branch caught in the undertow dips under, then pops to the surface a hundred yards downriver, flipped so that, if Noura wasn't watching, she might think it is an entirely different piece of wood. Rather like her life.

A little more than four months have slid away since Theodore Fabre disappeared with half her family in handcuffs. A few hours later, the police released Noura's father. There wasn't much the police or FBI could hold him on. Noura's still convinced that Theo let the local police haul him in to teach him a lesson on how people should and shouldn't be treated. Influenced by the god of protection to the end.

Perhaps Father's learned a little. Last month, he took Maman to Paris—somewhere she's always wanted to go.

Noura touches the lukewarm pendant around her neck, equally grateful for the man who wore its twin and that the forces on the other side are now blessedly quiet, or that she maybe imagined their presence all along, wanting someone other than her family to blame for the horrors she'd experienced. But she cannot deny the whoosh of wings she heard as the police thudded into the square, or the warmth of Horus's breath. She'd leaned into the feeling of peace, acceptance, even as the future frayed in front of her.

She doesn't want to think that that feeling wasn't real. And she doesn't want to believe she'd imagined Anubis nodding to her over her sister's body. And yet, what does it mean if she didn't imagine it all?

Across the city, she knows that the Olympia Brass Band is belting out a jazzy take on a funeral march as they usher the King Tut exhibit on to the next stop in Seattle. Trumpets are blaring the melody to "Oh When the Saints Go Marching In." Thinking about the juxtaposition of mourning and happy jazz makes Noura smile even while she can nearly hear Estelle grousing—*ain't nothing saintly about the King Tut tour*. She'd be right. There isn't anything saintly about any of them. Not really. And there's no use pretending they're perfect, and there's certainly no use in bending yourself silly to fit in. Isn't that part of what Ma'at represents? The truth?

The world is a better place when you can be yourself, in a place you belong rather than fit, and then let others do the same. Strange how the two often correlate—letting yourself be and letting others be too. Noura wishes she'd figured that out sooner.

Maybe then Estelle would have realized how much a part of her big sister she truly was...is...and Noura would have realized how much she needed her little sister's different shape snuggled against her own. What hope is there for a world where even sisters can't get along?

Still, Noura hopes. She hopes Egyptian President Anwar Sadat's unprecedented visit to Israel means there may finally be peace. She thinks of her sister, choosing to turn toward her in the end, choosing to sacrifice herself to protect her older sister. Noura sucks in a shaking breath.

She hopes the exhibit will bring understanding and, with understanding, people might find grace and a measure of willingness to believe the best of people. Meanwhile, Noura found a group that teaches art in the slums, and she faithfully visits her kids every week. Watching their faces brighten when they see her gives her hope, a way out.

Well, that and her job. Apparently Theo put in a good word for Noura at the museum, and she was encouraged to stay on. Of course no one knows what happened a few days before the opening. The FBI doesn't want to give anyone else ideas about stealing the Tut artifacts.

Precise footsteps sound behind Noura, and she swings off the rail with a false nonchalance. Last thing she needs is a police officer hollering at her.

"Figured you'd be at the museum."

She turns and squints into the bright afternoon light. "Theo!" And then she stops and corrects herself. "Alex." Noura thrusts out her hand in what she hopes is a friendly, nice-to-see-you gesture.

But Alex tilts his head without returning the gesture. The setting sun shadows his face enough she can't tell if there is a spark of amusement or not.

Noura lets her hand drop. Maybe she was just an informant, as Estelle warned. The breeze lifts the edge of his serious black jacket, revealing his service revolver, reminding Noura that Theo, the fun-loving conservator, isn't real.

"Well," Noura says, buying time for her brain to kick in. "I suppose you're here for the trial?"

"Yes, but..." Alex lifts his gaze to the horizon of the river. Together they watch it race under the Greater New Orleans Bridge, running deceptively fast toward them before backing away at the curve. White birds circle above them—gulls, not a falcon.

"But?" Noura leans against the railing and studies the controlled flow of water spritzing from the fountain.

"Noura?" Alex settles next to her, and she bites her lip to stop herself from obediently falling headlong into the arms of a man she doesn't know.

When Noura doesn't answer, he turns, bracketing Noura's body with his confident hands. "Noura Elena Marquette, I know you don't think you know me. Yes, my name is different—"

Noura snaps her chin up, defiant. "And your job." Noura has earned her reticence.

"And my job," he agrees easily, solemnly. But then his lips tip into the playful grin she recognizes. "But everything about who I was in Cairo was real."

"If my sister wasn't...wasn't who she was, would you have told me? Or would you have just disappeared from my life?"

Alex lifts his scarred eyebrow. "You think I can survive walking away from you?"

"I don't know if I can survive knowing what you do, what you risk."

He nods, frowning even as he captures a stray lock of Noura's hair and tucks it behind her ear. "The Noura I know is stronger than she thinks."

"She was naïve and did whatever she thought everyone wanted her to do."

"That's not the woman I see. She's grown, learned. Yes, you sense what people want, but instead of letting the flow of their emotions run you over, you're choosing to bring people together. You are truly Ma'at."

"That's quite a speech."

"It's the truth."

Truth. Noura rubs her thumb over the cold metal rail. "And what is it you want, Alex?"

Alex blanches, his feather pendant swinging free a moment. And she's tempted to ask if he saw it all too. But then he pivots so he's propped next to her, his fingers temptingly close to hers and yet so very far away.

He's letting her go. The freedom bursts, flailing, terrifying. Is this what she wants? Kind indifference?

The fountain bends in the breeze. Lazy tendrils of water curl into the sky, dazzling shards of reflected flame teasing one another until, exhausted from their thrilling climb, they arc and crash with dizzying speed.

"Water has always fascinated me." Alex's voice lifts at the end, almost in question. "Mom used to drive us to Belle Isle once every summer. We couldn't afford to stay at any of the hotels. But we went to the beach, or if it was raining, the aquarium. I loved watching the Detroit River. The waves were constant but never the same, you know?" His thumb taps on the rail once, twice, and then he seems to decide and turns toward Noura. The height of him shades her from the blinding sun. "Just because you're choosing a different course doesn't mean you're completely different or exactly the same."

Where does that leave her?

"I'm not asking you to be something you're not, Noura. Everyone else might, but I'm not. I'm not even asking you to give me a chance... even if I want to."

Noura smirks, laughing softly. But he's steady, waiting until she sobers, until she knows what he's asking, feels what she's avoiding.

"My sister..." Noura's voice fractures against the memory of dried blood cracking along her knuckles. She stretches her clean fingers wide, grasping the crisp January air. "She always told me I needed to stand up for myself. But with everything, I...I realized I don't even know who I am. It's terrifying. You know? What if I make everything worse? I'm not Ma'at, sure of good and bad, right and wrong. I'm not sure I'm able to find myself." Noura sucks in a trembling breath at her sheer audacity and covers her mouth as if she can shove all the words back in. While the Egyptians believed writing down words brought them into reality, doesn't speaking them aloud have much the same result?

"Not able? As in not strong enough?" Alex scrubs his chin, shadowed with a scrabbly beard. "A very wise woman once told me that weakness is when you refuse to look and admit where you're scared or tender or at risk of being hurt."

"Then I want very much to be weak."

"The fact you're searching means that you are strong and good. Exactly like Ma'at."

Noura laughs, all watery with crashing emotion. "Does that make you Horus?"

When he doesn't answer, Noura stiffens, afraid to see if he's taking her seriously or if he isn't.

Alex nudges her with his elbow. "My mom would be glad I've apparently shaken off Set's influence. I'll protect you no matter what. Even if that means walking away. It's okay to not be okay, Noura. And it's okay to be frustrated with what life's dealt you."

His understanding is a soft beach calling Noura to rest. But she knows if she stays, she will be bogged down, swamping them both.

"Give me time?"

"I would love nothing better." He bows, swiveling her toward him, lifting her hand and kissing her knuckles like some English courtier.

Longing crescendos in Noura's heart, crashing against her ribcage, and before she can change her mind, she grabs the lapels of his jacket and tugs Alex closer. She watches his pupils dilate, golden flames shooting through his irises, even while his breath kisses her mouth. "Nothing?" Noura whispers.

Alex's mouth lifts in a delicious grin. "Well..."

Noura's palm rasps over the edge of his jaw, and Alex's smile disappears, his Adam's apple dipping. "Noura?" His voice is anguished in strangling restraint.

"Alex." Noura tastes his name, the playfulness there, the tilt of her lips tipping in permission. Alex's touch slides up her hips in agonizing care, to the spot where wings would sprout if she were the winged bearer of goodness, Ma'at. He holds Noura there, not a captive, but protected. His lips are warm on her forehead, the dip at the intersection of jaw and neck, and Noura pitches forward, arcing into him, their lips meeting, combusting bodies twining, Noura breathless against the rail.

The grating sound of a clearing throat jolts them apart. A uniformed officer stands, brows raised, and heat rushes into Noura's face.

Alex pivots, swiping his jacket back so his badge flashes. "Just got back from a long assignment."

The officer squints at Noura, then nods and meanders away.

Noura lets out a squeak of embarrassed laughter.

"Worse than getting caught by your dad." Alex kisses Noura on the forehead.

Tears gather on Noura's lashes as the world shifts underneath her. What comes next?

"You'll be here for the trial?" Alex drifts his thumb over her lips before stepping back. He will make Noura keep her promise to herself, and for that she is grateful. She thinks.

"I have to testify," Noura says with more solidity than she feels. "But after Mr. Fagaly sent a glowing recommendation, the Met wants me back."

"Will you go?"

"That depends on other factors."

Alex tugs at the collar of his shirt like he's letting out the heat Noura's words have brought.

"And before you ask, you are most definitely one of those factors. You aren't leaving, are you?"

"Care to join my expedition to find the best gumbo in New Orleans?" Alex holds out his hand in invitation, and she tucks her fingers into his.

ABOVE THE TWO HUMANS, a white falcon dips, soaring, monitoring. The woman leans into the man, her heart light as Ma'at's feather. An ally. For now, Set is fettered beneath the crust of the earth while he waits for the final judgment. The persistent struggle is hushed under the whispering strains of the band.

Nodding to the enormous black dog who trots behind the humans, the falcon settles on a lamppost and watches the curse of King Tut wash away on an ordinary January afternoon.

AUTHOR & HISTORICAL NOTE

Warning—If you haven't read the book yet, this note contains spoilers!

The idea for this book dropped into my email inbox without fanfare. The headline declared that the 1970s King Tut tour had a decidedly political purpose. I clicked the link to read more…and dove into a rabbit hole of fascinating history I had never heard of.

When I stumbled on the historical security failures and then Thomas McShane (the real-life historical FBI art sleuth), I was giddy. I imagined a curator destined to protect the artifacts. But then I uncovered the fact that the communist movement in the US often used stolen art to fund their prolific bombings and activities. And I knew I had a compelling conflict: Two sisters propelled by the same event with opposite conclusions and ideologies. One destined to protect the artifacts and the other to steal them.

Much of the story evolved directly from mind-blowing history. There were no lights in the museum, and Thomas Hoving negotiated to have wires run from an electrical pole. While I played with the timeline a hair to suit the story, the Egyptian team, at the last moment, decided they didn't want to send the artifacts via plane. US Navy ships transported the artifacts. Even Selket's last-minute addition, the side trip in an Egyptian village, and hurricane Babe's landing are historical. Though Babe didn't hit New Orleans as directly as I've imagined.

In addition to Kissinger and Nixon, who are widely reported to have made decisions for the reasons portrayed in these pages, characters that were historical people are Dr. Christine Lilyquist, Mostafa, William Fagaly, and several other side characters. For Theo, I borrowed from Thomas McShane, but he wouldn't have been in Cairo. For Noura's character, I cobbled together several real people, including Christel Faltermeier, an independent conservator and restoration specialist, who was the negotiator for the US team in Cairo. The events and dialogue they portray here are invented.

For my research sources or more information about the Egyptian myths or the last myth, check out the book club resources on my website (https://beautifuluglyme.com/the-scorpion-thief-extras/)

I am also indebted to my friend, who's a curator, who answered a million questions as well as the team at the New Orleans Museum of Art who provided me with a mountain of information about the "Treasures of Tutankhamun" tour in general, as well as the exhibit in New Orleans. If you're ever in Louisiana, don't miss their beautiful facility.

Ultimately, *The Scorpion Thief* was a fun, if difficult, topic to tackle. The avalanche of historical and cultural detail was a delight. However, the story's emotional backbone—conflict—is never easy to address.

First, I do not claim to have answers or even meaningful advice regarding discord between nations or family members or ultimately within ourselves. Just an acknowledgment that I often find myself, whether consciously or unconsciously, part of the problem.

Second, I've more than once had people wonder if my books are about specific people or events in my own life. So I want to be clear, should anyone wonder, this book is not about my family. My sister and I get along famously. She's an amazing woman who is kind, gracious, and the type of woman I hope to be. And my kids are, despite *my* personal failings, amazing people too. Not perfect, but all I could desire.

Writing books is a long, harrowing process, and I am indebted to the people who refuse to let me give up or wallow too long.

The list is long enough that it would take an entire book to name everyone. But I am grateful for my writer friends (Rachel, Janine, Susan, Julie, my Tall Poppy Sisters, and all the others), my editors (Linnae & Megan), my family (my hubby, mom, and kids), and to my God, who is kind and patient, loving and faithful, and not much like who I often see in the news. May I be like the one who hangs out with the foreigners, orphans, and widows, who welcomes kids, and who only ever hollers at those who think they know better than everyone else.

In case you missed it, I'm an imperfect nerd who's still learning.

That said, I pray that when we do encounter conflict, we keep trying, keep reaching out, keep believing in the hope of a better way.

If this story kept you up too late or made you feel something new, would you do me a huge favor?

1. Tell the world! Post a review at any bookseller. Even a sentence helps other readers decide what to read next.
2. Don't miss **the free novella that ties all the books in the series together.** Sign up for my *Books & Beauty Journal* (https://beautifuluglyme.com/newsletter-sign-up/), and I'll send you a copy of *Guardian of the Red Desert*.
3. If you have a book club, I would love for you to choose *The Scorpion Thief*. Check out the resources (questions, recipes, etc.) over here: https://beautifuluglyme.com/the-scorpion-thief-extras/
4. Be sure to check out the rest of the Threads of the Lost Myth Series. Where each book finds another thread of the lost myth tangled in history's secrets.

DON'T MISS THE NEXT BOOK IN THE THREADS OF THE LOST MYTH SERIES

Burning the Raven Tree
A 1960s gothic historical thriller in the tradition of *Rebecca*.
COMING SEPTEMBER 2026

A survivor accused of a decade-old grisly murder.
A disgraced lawyer with everything to prove.
And the only witness has stood watch for more than a millennium.

***

Chapter 1

APRIL 6, 1965

There are good reasons Mama always called the wee hours of the morning the witching hour. There are wraiths who wake when the clock strikes two. They tiptoe into your sleep, taunting until you wake with real screams scraping out your throat, chased by the desperate prayer that the navniki ghosts aren't real and that the past won't come crawling into bed with you.

They are the reasons I'm standing at the edge of the cherry orchard again, panting, breath puffing into vapor trails as I try to shake off the memory singed into my closed eyelids. The frigid sting of Michigan's April air burns my lungs, trying to anchor me in the present. But the smell of distant smoke tinges my nostrils and drags me under the dark spell.

It's just the neighbor's wood stove. Just a wood stove.

But the mantra has never worked well.

One hand clutches the Polar Star necklace Mama painted, and the other hand presses against the jagged bark of the oak tree, my confidant. My palm hungers for the strength, the sharpness of the only other memory keeper on the edgelands. With her crown soaring above the field, the tree has seen everything and cradles the memories of generations.

I heave in a breath and hold it, slowing my heart rate. I breathe out. The rush is a cold mimic of billowing smoke. Above me, the spreading branches groan in witness and solidarity with her familiar nightwalker. I clutch the wool blanket to my chest and touch the sole of a trailing shoe bound in her arms. We would change things if we could, the oak and I. But we are powerless.

The tips of the tree stretch, narrow, and there, in the first breath of nothing, is the potential, the thing each branch is becoming. I wonder what is at the end of myself. What is on the other side? How many times have I stood here wishing for a different ending?

A hundred nights?

A thousand?

How many times have I seen their ghosts drift between the moonlit trees and through the discarded scrap of Dad's old mechanic's garage and smithy? I think it goes without saying...being responsible for murder is a heavy burden to bear.

***

Order your copy of Burning the Raven Tree wherever books are sold.

ABOUT THE AUTHOR

Janyre Tromp is an award-winning, best-selling historical suspense novelist who writes fiery myth-laced tales that, at their core, hunt for beauty—even when it isn't pretty.

Her books include *The Scorpion Thief, Darkness Calls the Tiger,* and *Shadows in the Mind's Eye.* But she's also a mom, award-winning editor, and wrangler of all things—including her fantastic teens and crazy fur babies.

You can find her on social media or visit her website, where you can grab a free series novella, *Guardian of the Red Desert.*

www.JanyreTromp.com

instagram.com/janyretromp
facebook.com/janyretromp
tiktok.com/@janyretromp

www.ingramcontent.com/pod-product-compliance
Lightning Source LLC
LaVergne TN
LVHW040040080526
838202LV00045B/3418